Dear Target Reader,

The House Girl began in the spring of 2006 with my newborn daughter sleeping on my left arm and a book held in my right. The book was a biography of Virginia Woolf written by Hermione Lee. It's a great big doorstopper (994 pages) and to this day I still haven't finished it, but I can't really blame Ms. Lee. I stopped reading when I came across two words: *slave doctor.* The term was used to describe a long-gone relation of Woolf's and no more was said about him other than this brief, mysterious description. I closed the book. That day, I started wondering about the circumstances that would cause a person to occupy such a conflicted role: to dedicate your life to healing and yet your patients were destined only for more suffering. Who would do that? And why? From this initial spark of curiosity, I began writing about a slave doctor, Caleb Harper, and two women appeared in his story: Dorothea Rounds, a white woman active on the Underground Railroad, and Josephine Bell, a young artist enslaved on a tobacco farm in 1850s Virginia. They really did *appear* in the story, which sounds a little mystical (I know, I know!), but I can't describe it any other way. They appeared, and I wanted to know more about them.

At this point in time, I was a midlevel associate with a (somewhat) promising legal career and a pesky fiction-writing habit that I considered my dirty little secret. But Josephine, Caleb, and Dorothea kept me awake at night. I couldn't stop thinking about them. And so began a process that lasted roughly five years and spelled the end of my (actually *not*) promising legal career. Over that time, I researched and thought about issues that I hadn't really considered since childhood. My interest in the Underground Railroad and the legacy of slavery dates back to my earliest days: I was born in St. Croix, an island with a brutal history of slavery, and grew up in Stockbridge, Massachusetts, an old New England town with roots in the abolitionist movement. In my research, I was following those childhood interests but looking at them through adult eyes. As I read, a series of questions kept popping into my head: Who wrote this history? Who tells us what and who we should remember? And how do those choices inadvertently shape our own thoughts and feelings about past events? About what we call the *truth*?

These questions became particularly important to me when (after searching long and hard for it because I thought surely there was such a place) I learned that no national monument exists to honor those Americans who lived and died as slaves. No national museum exists to document their experiences of enslavement, to protect the artifacts they created, to record this period of American history from *their* perspective. That to me seemed a profound case of bad memory.

And this is where my modern-day character Lina Sparrow entered the picture. I became interested in how these questions of memory play out individually—when our past is not as neat and pretty as we wish it to be—how do we confront (or hide from) the truth? Lina is a young lawyer struggling to reconcile her memories of a mother she never knew and a father she loves dearly but suspects is lying to her. For Lina, memory is critical to how she sees herself and the kind of person she is striving to become.

Over the course of the five years I spent writing *The House Girl*, the baby girl sleeping on my arm became a wide-awake first grader (with two younger brothers), my pesky writing habit became my new profession, and *The House Girl* became the book you now hold in your hands. I hope that the stories of Josephine and Lina, Caleb and Dorothea entertain you, move you, and keep you up at night, just as they did for me. I am always eager to hear from readers, so please don't hesitate to contact me via my website www.taraconklin.com.

All the best,
Tara

Praise for

The House Girl

"Infused with ominous atmosphere and evocative detail . . . a dramatic montage of narrative and personal testimonies."

—*Washington Post*

"Riveting."

—*Ebony*

"Assured and arresting. . . . You cannot put it down."

—*Chicago Tribune*

"[G]rabs you by the bonnet strings and starts running."

—*Entertainment Weekly*

"[*The House Girl*] is the kind of read that reminds you why holding a good book in your hands is one of the great pleasures of life. . . . Conklin takes us down a curious rabbit hole that drops us before a looking glass of uncomfortable truths about race, power, art, family, law and ethics. . . . *The House Girl* is one of those books in which there's not one, two or three, but about ten good parts you'll want to read and reread to make sure that what you thought just happened did."

—*Essence*

"A sorrowful, engrossing novel in which the pursuit of justice serves as a catalyst to a more personal pursuit for truth. . . . *The House Girl* is also a meditation on motherhood, feminism, loss, and, ultimately, redemption."

—*Pittsburgh Post-Gazette*

"Conklin's research blends subtly into the background while successfully rendering a picture of the complex tensions inherent in 1850s society. . . . A historical novel that succeeds in giving voice to the voiceless."

—*Winnipeg Free Press*

"Luminous . . . the rare novel that seamlessly toggles between centuries and characters and remains consistently gripping throughout. . . . Powerful."

—*BookPage*

"Conklin's sensitive, deft handling of complex racial and cultural issues as well as her creation of a complicated, engaging story make this book destined to be a contender for best of 2013."

—*School Library Journal* (starred review)

"Skillfully executed and packed with surprises, this novel of the ways in which art saves our humanity is an engrossing do-not-miss adventure."

—*Shelf Awareness*

"A seamless juxtaposition of past and present, of the lives of two women, and of the redemptive nature of art and the search for truth and justice. Guaranteed to keep readers up long past their bedtimes."

—*Library Journal* (starred review)

"Conklin . . . is a skilled writer . . . who knows how to craft a thoughtful page-turner. . . . We're glued to the pages."

—*Seattle Times*

"Rich and surprising. . . . Will make hearts ache yet again for those who suffered through slavery as well as cheers for those—Conklin and Lina—who illuminate their stories." —*Plain Dealer* (Cleveland)

"Conklin persuasively intertwines the stories of two women separated by time and circumstances but united by a quest for justice. . . . Stretching back and forth across time and geography, this riveting tale is bolstered by some powerful universal truths." —*Booklist*

"Tara Conklin's wise, stirring, and assured debut tells the story of two extraordinary women, living a century apart, but joined by their ferocity of spirit. From page one, I fell under the spell of *The House Girl*'s sensuous prose and was frantically turning pages until its thrilling conclusion."

—Maria Semple, author of *Where'd You Go, Bernadette*

"There's so much to admire in *The House Girl*—two richly imagined heroines, two fully realized worlds, a deeply satisfying plot—but what made me stand up and cheer was the moral complexity of these characters and the situations they face. I'm grateful for this transporting novel."   —Margot Livesey, *New York Times* bestselling author of *The Flight of Gemma Hardy*

"In this sesquicentennial of the Emancipation Proclamation, *The House Girl* stands as both a literary memorial to the hundreds of thousands of slaves once exploited in the American South and a mellifluous meditation on the mysterious bonds of family, the hopes and sorrows of human existence, and the timeless quest for freedom."   —Corban Addison, author of *A Walk Across the Sun*

"*The House Girl* is a heartbreaking, heartwarming novel, ambitious, beautifully told, and elegantly crafted. Tara Conklin negotiates great vast swaths of time and tribulation, character and place, with grace, insight, and, simply, love."
     —Laurie Frankel, author of *Goodbye for Now* and *The Atlas of Love*

"*The House Girl* is an enthralling story of identity and social justice told through the eyes of two indomitable women, one a slave and the other a modern-day attorney, determined to define themselves on their own terms."
     —Hillary Jordan, author of *Mudbound* and *When She Woke*

"Tara Conklin's powerful debut novel is a literary page-turner filled with history, lost love, and buried family secrets. Conklin masterfully interweaves the stories of two women across time, a runaway slave in 1852 Virginia and a young lawyer in present-day New York, all while asking us to contemplate the nature of truth and justice in America."   —Amy Greene, author of *Bloodroot*

THE
House Girl

TARA CONKLIN

WILLIAM MORROW
An Imprint of HarperCollinsPublishers

P.S.™ is a trademark of HarperCollins Publishers.

THE HOUSE GIRL. Copyright © 2013 by Tara Conklin. All rights reserved. Printed in the United States of America. No part of this book may be used or reproduced in any manner whatsoever without written permission except in the case of brief quotations embodied in critical articles and reviews. For information address HarperCollins Publishers, 10 East 53rd Street, New York, NY 10022.

HarperCollins books may be purchased for educational, business, or sales promotional use. For information please write: Special Markets Department, HarperCollins Publishers, 10 East 53rd Street, New York, NY 10022.

A hardcover edition of this book was published in 2013 by William Morrow, an imprint of HarperCollins Publishers.

FIRST WILLIAM MORROW PAPERBACK EDITION PUBLISHED 2013.

Designed by Joy O'Meara

Map credit to Rutgers Cartography with permission of Lois Horton.

The Library of Congress has cataloged the hardcover edition as follows:

Conklin, Tara.
  The house girl : a novel / Tara Conklin. — 1st ed.
    p. cm.
  ISBN 978-0-06-220739-5 (hardcover) — ISBN 978-0-06-220751-7 (pbk.) — ISBN 978-0-06-220752-4 (ebook) — ISBN 978-0-06-223987-7 (audio) 1. Fugitive slaves—Virginia—Fiction. 2. Corporate lawyers—New York (State)—New York—Fiction. I. Title.
  PS3603.O5346H68 2013
  813'.6—dc23

                                                        2012027370

ISBN 978-0-06-231608-0

13 14 15 16 17 OV/RRD 10 9 8 7 6 5 4 3 2 1

For Freya, Luke, and Rhys

PART ONE

Josephine

Lina

Josephine

Mister hit Josephine with the palm of his hand across her left cheek and it was then she knew she would run. She heard the whistle of the blow, felt the sting of skin against skin, her head spun and she was looking back over her right shoulder, down to the fields where the few men Mister had left were working the tobacco. The leaves hung heavy and low on the stalk, ready for picking. She saw a man's bare back and the new hired man, Nathan, staring up at the house, leaning on a rake. The air tasted sweet, the honeysuckle crawling up the porch railings thick now with flower, and the sweetness mixed with the blood in her mouth.

The blow came without warning, no reason that Josephine could say. She had been sweeping the front porch as she always did first thing, clearing off the dust and leaves blown up by the night wind. A snail had marked a trail across the dew-wet wood of the porch floor and rested its brown shell between the two porch rockers. Josephine had caught that snail with a sharp swoop of the broom, sent it flying out into the yard, and then she heard Mister's voice behind her, coming from inside the house. He said something she could not make out. It was not a question, there was no uplift in tone, nor was it said in anger. His voice was measured, it had seemed to Josephine then, before he hit her, not urgent, not hurried. She stopped her sweeping, turned around, looked to the house, and he walked out the wide front door, a proud front door Missus Lu always liked to say, and that's when his hand rose up. She saw his right arm bend, and his lips part just slightly, not to open but just the barest hint of dark space between them. And then his palm, the force of it against her cheek, and the broom dropping from her fingers, the clatter as it fell.

Something shifted in Josephine then, a gathering of disparate desires that before had been scattered. She could not name them all, there were so many, but most were simple things: to eat a meal when hunger struck her, to smile without thinking, to wear a dress that fit her well, to place upon the wall a picture she had made, to love a person of her choosing. These distilled now, perfectly, here on this September morning, her hunger for breakfast sharp in her belly, the sun pink and resplendent in the sky. Today was the last day, there would be no others.

Afterward, she tried but she could not explain it to Caleb, why this moment marked the course of things to come. The snail she remembered, the curve of its shell, and the hot colors of the dawn. What came later—Dr. Vickers, what Missus Lu had done—did not change what Josephine decided then with Mister on the porch. Even if that day had held nothing more, she told Caleb, still she would have run. Yes, she would run.

As Josephine turned her head back around to face Mister, a warbler called from down toward the river, its *sweet sweet sweet* clear as the brightening day.

Mister said, "Look after your Missus. The doctor coming today, don't you forget."

He stepped off the porch, into the dirt of the front path, and looked up at her, his dark beard dusty from the fields, his eyes shadowed. Last month the curing barn had burned to the ground, and they'd lost some horses too, their screams terrible to hear. The winter before, Mister's father, Papa Bo, had passed on, and the cow stopped giving milk, and Hap the field hand died from a bee sting. He'd got all puffed up and started scrabbling at the ground, Otis said, like he was digging his own grave, save the others the work. Now Missus Lu and her fits. There was an affliction in Mister, he had cause for sorrow. But Josephine did not pity him.

She nodded, her cheek on fire.

Mister walked in long steps down the sloping back hill of the yard, across the raw furrowed rows they had had no seed to plant. Jackson, the Negro overseer, watched over the others. Picking time, and the field just barely begun. Over at the Stanmores' they had hundreds of acres, dozens of slaves, and already the first tobacco leaves were finished drying and sent to market, the wagons rumbling by the house, the nut-brown bundles piled high in the back. Mister would always spit when he saw one pass by on the road to town.

Josephine watched Mister go. She wanted to bring her hand to her cheek, but she didn't. She spat a red streak across the weathered floorboards, rubbed at it with her bare right foot and then picked up her basket, stepped down off the porch, around the side of the house. There was a lightness in her, a giddiness almost. She walked down the slight slope, the grass cool under her feet, the sun a little higher now, the low mist burning off. *Run.* The word echoed thunderous in her ear and filled her head like a physical, liquid thing. *Run.*

Josephine had not been born at Bell Creek but she knew no other place. Riverbank, sink, fire pit, field, these had been the four corners of Josephine's world all seventeen years of her life. Missus Lu kept Josephine close, sent another to run the errands in town, took a hand servant hired from the Stanmores with her back when she used to travel. Josephine stayed behind. She knew the stream that twisted west of the fields, the narrow banks only a few yards across, sycamores and willows overhead, their branches trailing in the water. Here is where she'd do the wash, cool her feet, fish for brown trout and catfish and walleye perch. She knew the twists and turns of the bank, the mossy bits and where a large stone angled its peak out of the water and underneath spread dark and wide. She knew the fields in all seasons, brown and fallow, greening and ripe, and the grown tobacco plants rising nearly to her shoulders, the leaves as wide as her arms outstretched.

She knew the big house, built by Papa Bo's childless brother Henry back when the state of Virginia seemed blessed by both God and nature in the bounty of her riches. Henry's barren wife had devoted the fullness of her attentions to keeping a house sparkling and outfitted with the best that her husband's tobacco dollars could purchase or build. A wraparound porch in front, bedrooms many and large upstairs, full plate-glass windows in the parlor, a horsehair settee for sitting on when sipping from the bone china tea service marked with green ink upon the bottom of each cup. And a library, tucked at the back of the first floor, the books bound in red and brown leather, stamped with gold along their spines. They called the place Bell Creek and once it had been fine.

Now patches of white paint had molded to green, shingles slid down the low sloped roof, windowsills were splintered, the brick chimney cracked along the top rim. In the library, the books were stained with mildew, the pages stuck from moisture let in through a cracked side window that had never been mended. At night Josephine would listen to the scratching and burrowing of mice, squirrels, rats under the floorboards and behind the thin wood of the attic walls. Josephine slept on a thin pallet on the floor, the roof sloping low, the summer nights so hot she'd lie spread-eagle, no two parts of her body touching, her own two legs like strangers in a bed.

Josephine rounded the corner of the house and slowed at the sight of Lottie. She stood knee-deep in the side bed, weeding, picking purple veronia and pink cabbage roses for Missus' table. All around the house perimeters, sloping down toward the river and, on the east side, toward the fields, spread the flowers: morning glories, spring beauties, irises, purple pokeweed, goldenrod. Whatever design had once attached to the beds had been lost with time and inattention, but the plants themselves seemed none the worse for it. They flourished, encroaching onto the lawn, spreading their pollen down even to the road, where rogue roses bloomed every spring beside the trodden dirt path and latched front gate.

Lottie was bent at the waist, elbows pumping as she pulled and flung the weeds behind her into a heap, the flowers in a tidy pile beside her. A few stems of bluebell, Winton's favorite, were tucked under her apron strings. Lottie took small things here and there, bacon ends from the smokehouse, eggs from the hens, a sewing needle, a sweet; she never faltered and was never caught.

"Morning, Lottie," Josephine said, and she thought her voice would be steady but it cracked toward the end, the echo of Mister's blow still in her. Lottie raised her head, her gray hair tied up in a dark cloth, her skin shiny with sweat. A single horizontal line of worry creased her forehead as if a hatchet had been laid there once long ago.

"What? Child, what is it? You look like you seen a spirit." Lottie believed the restless dead of Bell Creek lived among the willows lining the river where the morning mist hung. Papa Bo, Lottie's own boy Hap, all Missus' dead babies, even Mister's mother and four sisters, their bodies buried back in Louisiana. Lottie saw them there on a summer's night, or just before the dawn, she said, dancing, laughing, wailing too, among the branches that trailed like a white woman's hair into the water.

Lottie dropped the flowers she held and moved toward Josephine. Her skirt hems dragged wet in the grass, and her gaze hardened as she saw the mark of Mister's blow. Taking Josephine's face in her hands, she turned it and laid one long finger on the tender spot. "Ah girl," she said. "You'll be needing chamomile on that. Or something cool."

"It's nothing," Josephine said, though the skin tingled and she felt a rising tenderness. "Lottie, it's nothing. Just a little thing." But she did not pull away. The chill of Lottie's hand, wet with dew, calmed her. Josephine leaned into Lottie's warm, tough bulk and she was again a child at night at the cabins, after Lottie and the others had finally returned from the fields, and all the day's sadness would fall from Josephine and into Lottie's yielding places: the flesh at her waist; the shoulder's curved hollow; an ample, muscled calf. Then as now, Lottie's body seemed sturdy and soft enough to contain all Josephine's hurts.

Lottie let Josephine fall against her and then she turned Josephine's face back around and took her in with a level gaze. "All right, then. It's nothing if you say it."

"It's nothing." Josephine shook her head quick, like shaking water from her hair. She squinted at the sky and then turned to Lottie. "I saw Nathan down back," she said. "He looked to be straining."

"He been laid up awhile, so he said. On account of his heels. Couldn't do nothing, couldn't stand or walk. They cut him too deep, is how he told it."

Mister had hired Nathan from Mr. Lowden, a neighbor six miles west, just for harvesting time, just to see them through. Nathan had run twice already and twice been caught and brought back to Mr. Lowden, whose tolerance for such goings-on had been sorely tested. Mister had hired him cheap on account of the history and Nathan's slow pace now that his heels were cut. He was still new to Bell Creek, Josephine had not spoken with him yet; she had not asked him where it was he'd been headed when he ran.

Josephine said, "What's he like, huh?"

Lottie paused, tilted her head. "He's fine. Seems fine enough. Got some sense."

"Mmm. Puts me in mind of Louis. Something in his person, way he stands." Louis had been sold off three summers past and this was the first time Josephine had spoken of him. It surprised her that her voice did not shake, that no tears came with the sound. *Louis.* The name hung weighty between them, a hope or a tragedy, neither of them knew which. He was gone, gone.

"Louis? I don't see no Louis in him." Lottie said this with a frown and a slow shake of her head, as if that decided the matter. "Josephine, what you want with Nathan?"

"Just wanted to say hello." Josephine looked down and stepped away, her bare soles marking 2-shapes in the mud. She had never lied to Lottie before and she did not like the feeling it gave her, a shifting underfoot, a drop in her belly. Tonight Josephine would ask Nathan to tell her the route north, tonight she would run. *Run.* The word still resonated within her and now took on a new pitch. Would Lottie come with her? Lottie and Winton possessed an unremitting belief in a salvation that would be delivered if they mustered faith true enough, if their path remained righteous. Lottie looked for signs of the redemption, like the two-headed frog Otis found by the river last summer, or the night the sky filled with lights falling and they shone so bright that everyone at the house and down by the cabins woke and stood on the front lawn, even Mister and Missus Lu, all of them together side by side, eyes open to that burning sky. These were all markers along the way, Lottie said, signs that Jesus be coming soon. She was waiting for Him. *You cannot wait another day,* Josephine wanted to say now. *Come with me, Lottie, you and Winton should come. Nathan will tell us the way.*

But here beside the flowers, the air heavy with their scent, the cool of Lottie's hand still on Josephine's cheek, the idea of running seemed too raw to bring out into the morning, into the sunlight, with tasks to be done, hours to be got through. The idea floated, not fixed or certain in its specifics, and she knew how easily an intention might go astray, how a path leading away might twist and return you to the place where you first began.

Josephine had tried before to run, one night some years ago. She had been no more than a child then, twelve, maybe thirteen, years old, with no understanding of the dangers or the true northward route or the way the shadows played tricks on the road. The journey back to Bell Creek had been long. This time she would not turn back. This time she would keep on, across the great Ohio River, all the way up to Philadelphia or Boston or New York, the northern cities that lived in Josephine's mind like Lottie's ghosts lived in hers.

Josephine said, "I got to be getting on. I'll come see you tonight, Lottie, at the cabins. We'll talk then."

"You come see me," and Lottie blinked her eyes slow, a softening at the corners of her mouth, the look Josephine knew so well in her, of cautious affection, a caring that Lottie always pulled up short before it went too deep. A muffled, distant kind of love. She'd been this way since Hap passed on, her last son, just twelve years old, proud as a peacock of his fiddling abilities, dead in minutes, with Lottie bent over his body still warm, lips and tongue puffed up, and on his arm a dime-sized redness where the bee had bit.

Josephine continued, down the low slope to the vegetable garden with its tangled rows and a thicket of raspberry and blackberry bushes grown together, fruit mostly for the birds because it reached too high and went too deep for Josephine to collect it all. Josephine thrust her hands into the brambles and pulled blackberries off their white fibrous posts. Last night Missus Lu had asked for berries with her breakfast. The thorns pricked Josephine's skin but she kept on. Today like any other day. Pick what needs picking, berries with breakfast, greens for Mister's supper. Do what needs doing. Like any other day.

Josephine gazed west at the small figures in the field, tattered scraps of dark moving against the tobacco green. Jackson alone stood motionless, a cowhide hanging ready at his belt. Even now with so few of them left at Bell Creek, he never flinched when whipping for a row dropped, a slow pace. He'd make a man eat the tobacco worm, Lottie had told her, the thick wriggling body with pincers at its head swallowed straight down. His wife, Calla, was stout and irritable, bought by Papa Bo years back from an itinerant trader. She never spoke of the children she'd left behind or the ones she'd lost at Bell Creek. There was a deep-down meanness in them both. Mister had no backbone for whippings, so Jackson did the work.

A thorn pricked Josephine's skin deep and she brought the fingertip to her mouth. The first time she ran, fear had seemed a physical presence, tall beside her on the road, and she tried but she could not run out of its shadow. Now the fear seemed different; it crouched and slithered and whispered within the berry bush and the tall grasses all around. It was smaller, trickier, more cunning. The sting of the cowhide. A twisted ankle, a summer storm. Would it thunder tonight, or would the sky be clear? The hounds, the rifles. She thought of Nathan's crooked walk. They cut the heels with an ax or a long-bladed hunting knife, the legs held fast under the weight of a man or within a vise like the one used for planing the new boards or just tied up with cord, bound as they bound the calves for branding. Two swipes of the blade would hobble both heels, but too deep and the wound would never heal, a leg swelled up and stinking or the foot itself dropped clear off.

A sudden cold descended upon Josephine and it seemed her legs turned dense and heavy, her breath caught deep within her chest. With shaking fingers she took another berry from the bush.

Like any other day. Do what needs doing.

A sound or a shadow took her away from the berries, and Josephine raised her eyes toward the house. A curtain rippled and she saw Missus Lu's pale face at the window, staring down to where Josephine stood. Like an apparition, if Josephine hadn't known better.

Hair dark and unsettled as a storm cloud, her eyes just shadows in her head. Missus placed a hand on the glass. Josephine nodded up at her and started back to the house.

A breeze came up and pushed at Josephine's back as she walked the path. *Run*, it whispered. *Run*.

Lina

The brief was not finished. Lina Sparrow, first-year litigation associate, took another sip of cold coffee. Her eyes flipped from her computer screen to the digital clock glowing red on the wall: 11:58 P.M. *Get it to me Wednesday,* Dan had said. *Counting on you to work your usual magic.* Never had Lina been late before, never, and yet here she sat, the last two minutes of Wednesday dangling just out of reach, her office a cave of paper and tented textbooks, the cursor blinking relentlessly on her screen. The brief: 85 pages, 124 perfect citations, the product of 92 frenetic hours billed over five ridiculous days, a document that would go to the judge, be entered into the official court record, be e-mailed to dozens of lawyers, to the client, to the opposing side. But was it *good*?

Lina's shoes were off—she always wrote barefoot—and as she stretched her toes, she wondered what precisely was her problem. Last year she had graduated at the top of her law school class, and she was now the highest-billing first-year associate at Clifton & Harp LLP, the preferred legal services provider for Fortune 100 companies and individuals of dizzying wealth. Lina had heard of other people's performance issues—time management, crises of confidence, exhaustion, depression, collapse—but never, in three successful years of law school and nine prolific months at Clifton, had she frozen like this. She rubbed her eyes with the heels of her hands and blinked fast. Her office vibrated in the cold fluorescent glare: beige walls, gray carpet, white particleboard shelving units of the kind found in college dorm rooms, office buildings, prisons. On her second day at the firm, Lina had arranged a careful selection of personal items: on her wall, the law degree and one of her father's smaller paintings; on her desk, the glass snow globe of a pre-9/11 Manhattan skyline and the photo of her parents circa 1982, both with longish hair and secret smiles. Each item represented a unique stamp on the exchangeable, impersonal nature of this space. *I am here,* the snow globe said. *This is mine.*

Lina picked up the snow globe now and shook it. Fake granular flurries settled over the city and she repeated the question again and again: Was the brief good? Was the brief good? Was it? Silently the clock shifted to 11:59. And as the deadline slipped away, Lina felt a rush like skiing, or eating sugar straight, or that icy morning a taxi had careened toward her as she'd waited on the corner of Fifty-first and Fifth and watched helpless, immobile, infused with a wondrous dread as it spun out inches from the curb. An intoxicating, brief adrenaline. 12:00. What was she waiting for? Resolution? Inspiration? The brief said exactly what it had to say: our client wants money and the law says give it to him.

Lina bent her neck hard to the left and heard her spine crack. She slipped her feet back into her high heels. Somewhere down the hall, the night cleaner's vacuum whined with the insistence of a mosquito. Of course the brief was good. Weren't her briefs always good? Wasn't this, the law, what she *did*? And she did it very, very well. Lina typed a signature line and beneath it: Submitted by, Daniel J. Oliphant III, Partner, Clifton & Harp LLP.

The strip lights burned and keyboards purred as Lina hurried the brief down the hall to Dan's office. Past the heads of the night-shift secretaries floating above the workspace partitions. Past a blinking, malfunctioning copier that sat abandoned, its various doors and flaps left open, awaiting the arrival of some jumpsuited Joe versed in the fixing of mechanical things. Past the coffee station, with its stinky microwave and humming soda machine. Past the row of half-open office doors through which Lina sensed more than saw caffeine-strung associates staring at computer screens or listening on mute to meetings under way in Hong Kong or Houston or Dubai.

At the corner office, Lina stopped.

"Dan?" She rapped a knuckle on the half-cracked door and pushed it open.

Dan sat marooned behind the island of his desk, his face glowing bluely from the computer screen. Floor-to-ceiling windows shimmered behind him, dark as a night sea. He was typing. His eyes shifted from the screen as Lina entered the room but his fingers remained in motion.

Dan was Lina's "mentor partner," a designation handed down by the HR department on Lina's first day at the firm. Lina had heard of him, of course. In the litigation world, Dan was a star. His perfect win record and lack of any obvious social anxiety issues distinguished him from the hordes of aggressively successful litigation partners at Clifton and throughout the city. A photo of two red-haired, pink-cheeked children sat framed in silver on Dan's desk. Lily and Oliver, Dan had told her. Twins. Lina had never met them, nor the wife (Marion) whose photograph hung behind his desk (tan, wan smile, one-piece).

"Sorry the brief is late," Lina said, checking her watch: 12:04. "I got a little carried away with the corporate veil discussion. These facts are just so *strong*. But here it is."

Dan blinked. With both hands he pushed away his prodigious hair: red, springy, tending to vertical. Some partners cultivated symbols of eccentricity like this, flares sent up from the Island of Same. One wore glasses with thick black plastic frames reminiscent of a Cold War Kissinger. Another practiced meditation in his office every afternoon promptly at four o'clock, the *oms* echoing down the hall.

"Brief?" Dan asked. "What brief?"

"The brief in the fraud trial?" Lina spoke carefully. Dan often feigned an attitude of happy indifference. He gave the illusion of a laid-back, generally affable person, a person who might, with a smile, service your car and charge you a fair rate or sit on a barstool and buy you a beer. But she had seen him take his blood pressure meds (a colorful assortment, one the size of a horse vitamin), she had seen the throbbing blue vein at his neck. She'd once heard him scream at a paralegal who'd stapled a document in the wrong corner.

Dan paused, then blinked again, faster this time. "Oh, yeah. Thanks, Lina. I remember—the brief. You're a little late." He glanced down at his watch (gold, glistening). "Throw it here on my desk." He pointed his chin vaguely toward the left. "So how did it come out?"

Lina hesitated, remembering those frozen moments in her office, her sense that something remained incomplete, undiscovered. But here, standing on Dan's expansive carpet, breathing the vaguely fragranced air (mint? licorice?) that seemed to permeate only the partners' offices, she pushed away any hint of uncertainty. "I'm very happy with it," she said. "The argument is persuasive. And I'm confident we've covered all the relevant case law."

"I'm sure it's great—your work always is." Dan paused, and then half-whispered, "You know, I probably shouldn't be telling you before the others, but we settled yesterday."

"Settled? Yesterday?" A coolness ran through Lina, starting at her eyebrows and ending at her toes, as though something warm and alive were departing her body.

"The client's been working on a deal for weeks. They signed the papers last night." Dan beamed. No trial, no possibility of defeat. The perfect win record, still intact.

"What about . . . ?" and Lina circled her hand in the air to indicate the brief she had just completed, the twelve sets of exhibit files copied and bound, the witnesses flown in from L.A. and London, the thirty-odd people working feverishly upstairs, their eyes red, their vacations canceled, their carpals tunneled. What about all of that?

"Yeah, I'll go up soon to share the good news. Got some stuff to finish off down here first." Dan examined a hangnail. "You know, it's always a good idea to wait until the ink is dry before you pull the plug."

"But our position was so strong." Lina shifted in place, tucked a restless lick of dark hair behind one ear. "So how much was the settlement?"

"Two-fifty." Dan lowered his gaze to the floor as he said this.

"Two-fifty! Jesus, Dan, that won't even cover the legal fees. We were *right*. We would have won."

Dan paused, tilted his head, and in the brief silence Lina read his disapproval, not of the settlement figure but of her outburst, her indignation. Rash. Unprofessional. She gave a chastised little nod.

"*Probably* we would have won," Dan said. "But you know, litigation is messy. It takes a long time. The client just didn't have the stomach for it. They're happy, Lina. They're satisfied." He exhaled long and low. "Look, this is what happens. I know, it's tough. You get caught up in a case, you want to go in there and win. But remember, the client calls the shots. We do their bidding. This isn't about us, it isn't about emotion or any sort of absolute . . . *justice*, or whatever you want to call it. At the end of the day it's about the client's best interest. What does the client want? What's best for their bottom line?"

As Dan spoke, Lina's gaze shifted to the darkened glass of his monstrous windows. Her own image reflected back: her blouse flared white, her hair a dark helmet, her face cast in shadow, the features indistinct, her body truncated and shorter (surely) than she actually was. And something in the position of her head, or the way the image seemed poised, hovering, disconnected from any solid ground, reminded Lina of the photo of her mother that sat beside her bed at home: Grace Janney Sparrow, dead when Lina was four, standing with bare arms and a forced smile on the steps of the house where Lina and her father still lived. In that photo, Lina's mother was square-shouldered, cock-kneed, paused, *waiting*—Lina had always wondered, what was she waiting for?—in just the way Lina was standing now.

Lina straightened, shifted in place, and her mother's image vanished. She shrugged her shoulders, settled her face to impassive—the look she so often admired on Dan, of calm reason, of dignified remove.

"Of course, the client's best interest. I'm glad they're happy. A settlement. That's great."

Dan nodded with gravity, with finality. Lesson imparted, lesson learned.

"And Lina," Dan said. "Glad you stopped by. There's something I want to talk to you about. A new case, something I think you'll like."

Instantly, the fraud trial and its beleaguered brief receded from Lina's mind. She needed a new case. There were so many hours in a day, all of them billable to a client, some client, any client. Lina allocated her time in six-minute intervals via a computerized clock that ticked away in the lower left-hand corner of her computer screen, silently reeling off the workday minutes in pie wedges of bright yellow. Another six minutes gone, and another wedge of that small clock flashed. At Clifton, time was an end in itself, the accomplishment of a task not nearly as important as the accurate recording of the minutes consumed by its execution. Lina felt sometimes, with an increasing frequency, that the clock existed inside her, all day, every day, the ticking away of minutes embedded in her brain, pulsing through her bloodstream. The idea of falling behind in her billables filled her with an amorphous dread.

"A new case sounds *great*," Lina said, and watched without one flicker of an eyelash as Dan picked up her brief and lobbed it into the trash.

"It's an unusual matter," Dan said. "We're taking it on for a big client. Important client. Keep him happy, you know. He's been threatening to take his business elsewhere so we're going the extra mile. We'll talk specifics tomorrow. But it's big. Historic. Controversial. What do you think about slavery?"

"Slavery? What do I *think* about it?"

"Yeah. First thoughts. First words."

"Bad. Civil War . . . umm, not good . . ." As she floundered, an image of Meredith, the six-foot blond litigation associate rumored to be dating a Yankees outfielder, danced through Lina's tired brain. Meredith sat ramrod straight in meetings; she spoke articulately, rationally, with apparent interest and keen insight, about credit default swaps, about sushi. Lina saw her as a nemesis of sorts, an otherworldly being who provoked Lina's competitive streak as well as her annoyance (Meredith frequently forgot Lina's name). Surely Meredith would have had some pithy, intellectual remarks on slavery. Even at one A.M.

Dan leaned forward in his chair. "And Lina, this case could be big for you. You're young, ambitious. This one has potential. *Big* potential. You may not know this, but we start associates on partner track pretty early around here." Dan raised his eyebrows. "And you are just the kind of person we'd like to encourage."

"Partner track?" The words pushed a button of delight within Lina's chest. "I won't let you down."

"Okay then. Tomorrow I'll reassign your caseload. You'll be full-time on the new matter. Now go home!" Dan looked at her and smiled, beatific as Santa Claus.

ONE OF THE FIRM'S CARS ferried Lina to Brooklyn, a silent silver Lexus, the driver fast and efficient down the expansive uncluttered avenues. The Midtown sidewalks were clear, the streets streamed with empty taxis. It struck Lina suddenly that this was the middle of the night. Even here, in the city that never slept, most people now were sleeping. Law firm time was like casino time, only instead of an endless darkened cocktail hour it was always a neon-bright afternoon. The dead center of the workday, all night long.

The car sped onto the Brooklyn Bridge, the river below like the sky above, shimmering constellations of boats and buoys and Lina in the middle, floating within the layers of light. Tonight's driver was a regular—a massive Russian with a shaved head and meaty knuckles. Igor, Lina vaguely remembered, was his name, an astrophysics professor before he immigrated west. Igor drove solidly, not too fast, and Lina relaxed against the plush interior of the backseat, the day's stress leaving her in steady increments measured by the distance traveled toward home.

Lina and her father, the artist Oscar Sparrow, lived in a Park Slope brownstone of the kind intensely coveted by a certain type of two-salary New York family. Four stories, a steep stoop, a brief weedy garden out back. The house had one functional (though still smoky, even after the cleaning) fireplace, two kitchens (first floor, fourth floor), three art studios (first, second, fourth), one walk-in closet (Oscar's), one claw-foot tub (Lina's). An ageless red oak rose mastlike from the backyard and in the front, nestled within a square of dirt cut from the concrete, grew a linden, the two trees roughly the same height as the brownstone. As a child, Lina often thought of the trees' roots intermingling beneath the floor of their house, holding herself and Oscar aloft in a living webbed cradle. In a strong wind, when the trees creaked and their branches scratched against the windows, she imagined that the house rocked within its root bed and the motion soothed her like a lullaby.

Oscar had bought the place decades earlier, when Park Slope was home primarily to drug dealers and poor lefty optimists. Throughout Lina's childhood and adolescence, his finances had seemed always to tilt toward ruin, and he had struggled to cover the mortgage payments. The obvious solution, one that they never discussed, was to rent out a bedroom, some studio space, maybe even the top two floors, themselves a spacious self-contained apartment. But they never did. Somehow—a painting sold, a teaching gig, some carpentry work—Oscar managed. Lina had started waitressing at fourteen, contributing what she could to keep the phone connected and the electricity on, and took over management of the family finances at fifteen, trying in vain to keep Oscar on a strict budget for paint, canvas, brushes, charcoal, and the various oddities (dusty taxidermy, amateur mosaics) he toted home from flea markets and tag sales. Lina questioned Oscar mercilessly about these purchases, cooking only cheap beans and rice for days afterward, but she never pushed him on the tenant question. Lina had spent her entire life here, through elementary and high school, then as an undergrad and law student at NYU. She too wanted the house all to themselves. She couldn't bear the thought of sharing with tenants. This was where her mother had once slept, cooked, painted, breathed, and Lina's memories of her seemed tethered to the physical space. The way a wall curved away, a washboard of light thrown by the sun against the bare floor, the sharp clap of a kitchen drawer slamming shut—all these evoked flashes of her mother and early childhood that seemed cast in butter, soft and dreamy, lovely, rich.

Lina held close a handful of these flashes: an image of dark hair falling down a pale back, like a curtain or screen. A smell of pepper and sugar. A quiet, secret laugh. A song with no discernible words and no recognizable tune, a hummed series of notes. *Da da dum da, da da dum da.* And a pervasive sense of contentment, of being cared for and watched over, as light played upon a yellow-painted wall, as a toy train sat in her dimpled hand. Were these memories? Or memories of memories? Or of what she desired to remember?

Lina let herself in through the heavy front door, the cold tiled entryway leading to tall double doors, each set with a narrow glass panel etched in curling lines and flowers. She clicked on the tall floor lamp and the living room was thrown into soft illumination. Above a long couch of cracked black leather hung Oscar's portrait of a six-year-old Lina: bright acrylics, Lina's hair in braids, her eyes astonished, in her hands a leggy green frog, one of several Oscar used to keep in the downstairs bathroom. Another, smaller portrait hung beside it: a dusky-hued oil painting of a dark-haired, moss-eyed young woman standing in front of an easel, paintbrush in hand, her body half-turned toward the viewer, no smile but her tidy, pretty features beaming with ease. This was Grace, Lina's mother, painted the year before Lina was born.

"Carolina, string bean-a, are you home?" Oscar yelled, using his favorite nickname for her, one Lina had forbidden him from uttering within earshot of any human being other than herself. But she secretly liked that he called her by her full name—Carolina. He was the only person she permitted to use the name, primarily because the Spanish-sounding pronunciation (*ee* in the penultimate syllable) always brought on too many questions about her background, and how was she to answer? Where had the name come from? She had no idea. *Your mother chose it* was all Oscar had ever told her.

Oscar appeared in the hall, his hair askew, a gash of red paint down one cheek. The late hour had no apparent effect on him, though Lina knew he'd been in the studio since seven o'clock that morning, working on pieces for his new show. He launched himself toward her, all six feet of him, enfolding Lina in a boisterous bear hug of the kind he delivered regularly. Physicality was part of his charisma—and he was charismatic, people often told Lina this—but there was something too in his large, clear blue eyes, a spotlight kind of interest in which people of all sorts—friends, colleagues, critics, women—would bask. Oscar had frazzled dark hair, thinning now into a sharp widow's peak, that matched his scrap of frazzled dark beard. Recently he'd been prescribed glasses, half-frame bifocals made of tortoiseshell plastic that he did not like to use for reasons having to do with vanity and age.

Lina looked nothing like Oscar. She had inherited her mother's slight build, dark eyes tending to green, straight black hair. Elfin, that was how Oscar described her when she was a child, a clever little elf. Lina had quick hands and hair cut sensibly shortish, falling just below her chin, a style she'd worn since high school and one she had no inclination to change. Her body was compact and lean, wiry in the legs and arms, an efficient tool that matched her able, precise mind. Since childhood, Lina had burned with a restless energy, a busyness that required an object, a project, whether mastering the monkey bars at recess, running cross-country in college, or understanding the church-state divide in law school. The current project, as she had told Oscar, was to make partner at Clifton & Harp before she turned thirty, an ambitious but not impossible goal.

"Ouch," Lina said. Oscar's glasses hung from his neck on a black cord, and Lina's chest was mashed against the frames. "Careful. I almost broke your glasses."

"Now that would be a shame," Oscar said.

Lina kicked off her heels, the three-plus inches she wore regularly at the office, and lowered herself, blessedly, wonderfully, onto the cool floorboards. She made her way to the kitchen. Oscar followed, humming.

"Carolina, can you help me with this?" he said, hand to the back of his head. "I've got something here." He turned and pulled from his scalp a thick lock of paint-stiffened hair.

"Not again," Lina said.

"Is it bad?"

Lina surveyed the damage. "Not like the last one. I don't think it'll show up too much."

Taking scissors from the side drawer, she cut out the half-dried paint, still sticky, taking as little of the hair as she could.

"Minimal damage," she said and ran a hand across the back of his head. "So have you eaten? Please say you didn't wait."

"Didn't wait. Made some pasta. A little mushy. Not bad."

"Whole wheat?"

"Yes."

"Greens?"

"*Yes.* Spinach. I'm a very healthy man. Look at this stomach." He patted his belly, which swelled with a small late-middle-age wiggle. "Fit as a fiddle."

Their three-legged cat, Duke (short for Duchamp), wove silently through the space between Lina's legs. Duke's right foreleg had been gone for years, amputated after nerve damage suffered during some furtive late-night cat activity rendered it useless and unfeeling, but he managed to glide just as gracefully on three, maintaining that essential liquidity of feline motion.

Lina fell into an old easy chair upholstered in riotous color, one of the mismatched four that flanked the table. Their kitchen was spacious and worn and Lina's favorite room in the house. A revolving assortment of Oscar's sketches and studies were pinned to the wall beside the fridge, along with the detailed schedules and charts that Lina compiled each month for grocery shopping, bill paying, Oscar's appointments, her work travel.

"So how did it go today?" Lina asked. Duke's purr revved, a little engine of happiness, as he pushed against Lina's legs looking for a scratch, and she reached down to the place he liked best, the triangle of short, soft fur between his ears.

"Really good, I'm happy to report." Oscar was beaming. "I think I'm ready."

"*Ready?*" Lina straightened up and Duke skittered away. Oscar had been working steadily for almost two years on the new paintings, working large-scale, using new techniques. No one had seen the pieces yet; no one even knew exactly what he was painting. Natalie, Oscar's dealer, had been a frequent visitor in recent weeks, anxious and lovely in her vintage dresses and tennis shoes, exiting the house with a small disappointed wave. The buzz, Natalie said, was growing.

For nearly all of Lina's life, Oscar had remained stubbornly un-fashionable, with his busy cluttered paintings (unironic, apolitical, neither minimal nor maximal), his refusal to go to the right clubs or cultivate the right friends. But when Lina was in law school, a wind had shifted, the planets aligned, trend or luck or who knew what. Now hedge fund managers and aging rock stars scheduled private appointments with Natalie, viewing with heads cocked and index fingers to chins certain canvases that Lina knew had once been stacked in precarious towers in the basement laundry room. Oscar had fretted, briefly, over integrity and mass appeal and selling out. But not for long. He switched galleries, from the loyal but staid Richard uptown to the glamorous and sharp-eyed Natalie in Chelsea, who told him to quit teaching part-time at City College and concentrate on making more pictures she could sell. Oscar consulted a financial advisor. He renovated the second-floor studio. He bought a pair of green leather shoes for $600 that he did not wear but kept on the kitchen table as a receptacle for loose change.

"So can I see the new pictures?" Lina asked, smiling too, caught by his excitement.

But Oscar's grin vanished. He hesitated, an anxious blink. "Carolina, I've been painting your mother."

Lina did not answer immediately. Oscar's words altered the feel of the room. He hadn't painted Grace since her death; he didn't talk about her or, as far as Lina could tell, think about her. Lina now experienced his revelation at a remove, her surprise muffled, her senses dulled. All at once she felt the exhaustion of her day, the 13.7 hours billed, the useless brief. "That's great," she said finally, but only because Oscar was looking at her and she could think of nothing else.

"I've been meaning to talk to you about it for months now. Truth is, I've been shitting my pants like a little boy. I don't want to upset you."

"Why should I be *upset*?" Lina looked up at him, his dark eyebrows, more gray than brown now, drawing together, his jovial handsome face serious and concerned. "Dad, really. *Upset*?" Grace's death had been so sudden—a car crash, Oscar had told her, ice on the road, darkness—and Lina so young. She remembered no suffering, no last good-byes at the hospital, no weeping or medicinal smells or shit-stained sheets. The event of her mother's dying had not marked her, and Oscar, of all people, should know this.

"It's just that we've never really talked about her, and some of these pictures might . . . I don't know, surprise you."

"We never talk about her because *you* don't want to talk about her, not me. Remember?" When Lina was sixteen, they had fought for the last time over Grace. Lina had asked, again, about her mother's family and Oscar had, again, refused to tell her. *I can't talk about Grace. I just can't,* he had said. Lina had screamed and raged; she threw a potted jade against the living room wall where it shattered with a bloom of ceramic shards and dirt, and then she ran to her room and cried, hating Oscar, hating how he had forced her to make up stories about her mother. Grace was from Florida, Mexico, Montana, Peru. Carolina was my grandmother's name, my aunt's, an old friend's. I remember her smell, her laugh, a bedtime story. I remember nothing at all. After that night, Lina had decided with a mix of embittered defeat and secret relief that she would never again ask Oscar about Grace. She had the house, full of her own half-memories, some photographs, a few of her mother's paintings; she didn't need anything more from Oscar. She didn't want to be angry at her father all the time. She didn't want to believe that he was hiding something from her.

"I know I haven't wanted to, but it's been twenty years," Oscar said. "That's a hell of a long time. Even *I* can change in twenty years." Now he grinned at her, but the smile seemed forced, an attempt at levity that Lina met with her lips pressed closed, doubtful. Where Lina's memories of Grace flickered indistinct as dreams, the weeks and months following Grace's death were burned in Lina's mind with vivid recall. A buzzy TV drone, the hot grease burn of pizza on her tongue, a parade of teenage babysitters—one faceless morph of ponytail and orthodontic glitter—and her father always there, always at home, hunched and shrunken, quiet, pale. Lina played, she watched TV, she had the run of every room; there were no rules, no schedules. As time passed, the sharpness of Lina's sadness faded, she learned how to carefully skirt the mental space occupied by her mother's death, and the avoidance quickly became a habit, unthinking, automatic. But Oscar did not seem to possess this tool of self-preservation. Even as a child, Lina worried. She sensed a danger in Oscar's inactivity, all the time indoors, the friends turned away at the door. What if Oscar's sadness continued? What if he did not return to himself? What if she were left truly alone?

"Are you *sure* this is a good idea? For you?" Lina asked.

"Yes, painting your mother is a good idea. It's the best idea I've had in years. Decades," Oscar said, and Lina heard no strain in his voice. "I'm okay."

"You're sure?"

"Yes. I'm sure. Jesus, don't worry! You worry too much." He grabbed hold of her hand and squeezed.

"And you want to show me the pictures? Now?" She glanced at her watch.

"I know it's late but you're so busy these days, Carolina Sparrow, attorney-at-law. Natalie's been breathing down my neck. I told her you had to be the first to see them. If you like them, if you're okay with them, I'm ready to show."

"Well, we wouldn't want to disappoint Natalie," Lina said with a weary edge of sarcasm that she knew sounded petulant, but she didn't try to correct it. Lina didn't really like Natalie, or rather she didn't like the package in which Natalie delivered herself: carefully mussed hair, artful quirky clothes, always a hand on your arm, a too-low voice that made you lean in closer to listen. And she particularly did not like the role Natalie now played in Oscar's life, of gatekeeper to the outside world, business partner and artistic confidante, even a bit of therapist and best friend, from what Lina had gathered from the snatches of conversation she'd overheard and the few extended periods she'd spent in Natalie's company. Lina stood and straightened her skirt. She tried to hide her exhaustion with a bright smile.

Lina followed her father upstairs to the second-floor studio. Oscar flipped a switch and the room was suddenly and brilliantly illuminated. Large canvases angled against the white walls, short stools sat around a trestle table like patient children. There was the murky, spicy smell of oil paint and dry plaster dust.

"Okay, here's the first one." Oscar stood beside a piece that reached to his shoulders. A swath of brilliant blue unfurled corner-to-corner across the canvas, bisecting a chaotic, colorful background. Within the blue a woman's body seemed to float, small, dark-haired, featureless, drowning. Lina listened as Oscar described the devices he had used, the screening technique and a collage of clippings from old New York tabloids. The piece was classic Oscar Sparrow—every inch of the canvas heavy with layered pigment and collage. Lina liked that Oscar's work was never simple, that each piece demanded of the viewer careful consideration of its disparate parts before consideration of the whole. Oscar's paintings were like arguments, in a way. Each painting had a point, but the end could be justified only by the careful accretion of facts, and those facts lay hidden within the canvas: a stroke of red, a small jagged shape of mirror, a paragraph cut from yesterday's newspaper, a pencil sketch of a dog. Oscar never gave away his intent. Deconstruction did not interest him.

Oscar turned away from the picture and Lina followed him farther into the studio. He stopped before three paintings propped against the wall. These were simpler, with stronger blocks of color, primarily abstract, though in one Lina thought she saw the image of a thumb, larger than her own head, and perhaps not a thumb at all. She didn't ask. Then in another, a knee, did she see a kneecap? And a scalp, a forehead, the line where the hair lifted from the skin etched in crimson paint. It seemed the paintings were of bodies, or one body, examined.

"Now this is where we start getting more figurative," Oscar said and he turned and pulled a sheet off an outsize canvas. Lina looked straight into the eyes of her mother, at twenty-four or twenty-five, when Lina was a baby. It was a portrait, the head and torso occupying the entire frame, stretching six feet high, five feet across, her arms folded in front, the posture stiff and formal, the face pale and mournful, elongated to the point of distortion, but the woman still unmistakably Grace: her long dark hair parted on the left, her lips full and swollen as though bitten.

Lina inhaled sharply. Twenty-four years old. Grace had been twenty-four when Lina was born, the same age Lina was now. It was ridiculous, the idea of Lina having a daughter, a husband, a house. Having them, and then losing them, or them losing her.

Oscar waited a beat, his eyes on Lina. "Ready to see some more?"

"Sure," Lina said. "Show me more." Her voice was casual, but her heart beat uncomfortably fast, the force of it pushing up into her throat as it did sometimes when she ran sprints.

Oscar moved to another canvas draped with a sheet. Lina remained in front of the portrait.

"Are they all of her?" Lina asked.

"Yes."

"The forehead? The kneecap? Those are her?"

"Yep. They're all Grace. The show is called *Pictures of Grace*."

As Oscar fiddled with the sheet, Lina examined the portrait. The painted eyes loomed large, dark as Lina's own. The hair was longer than Lina's but seemed to have the same heavy weight, the same near-black color. Grace's face appeared vast and complicated, the skin composed of multihued layers of pigment and collage.

Strips of newspaper cut into intricate swirls seemed to flutter at her throat, giving the impression of lace. Lina leaned in, but the overlapping text was nearly illegible, one sheet layered upon another and another. Finally she made out a single word in a small, no-nonsense, common font: "Enough."

Lina stepped back as if bitten. What did she know about her mother? Grace had been an artist too, though unsuccessful, not like Oscar. Lina had never met her maternal grandparents; she did not know their names, where they lived, or where Grace was born. She knew that Oscar met Grace in a bar in the Village, that they lived together in Brooklyn in the late seventies, married at City Hall, bought the dilapidated brownstone with the money from Oscar's first show. They made art and they struggled and they were in love and Lina was born. And then, the icy sweep of road, the crash. On a brilliant, cold sunny day, Oscar had scattered Grace's ashes at the Cloisters, a place she had loved for both its art collection and its sweeping views of the Hudson. Lina had not accompanied him; he had thought the task too upsetting for a child. As an adult Lina often wished she'd been with him that day, that she carried a memory of some physical act to mark Grace's death. Instead, Lina recalled only a vanishing, an absence, an ache.

Lina's gaze skated over the canvases—*Enough,* the crimson part, the kneecap, the small figure against the blue—and Oscar's open, expectant face as he stood before the next painting. But Lina didn't want to see any more. Duke lay at Oscar's feet, an old cat now, brought home from the animal shelter when Lina was ten. He was cleaning his face with little rolls of his one remaining foreleg.

"I didn't realize you were . . . ready. I mean, emotionally ready to do this," Lina said.

A tension appeared in Oscar's face, and he crossed his arms against his chest. "It's not like I just woke up one day and—*bam*— everything's okay. For so long I didn't want to think about her at all. But then, I don't know, the past couple years have been different.

I wanted to go back, to when she was young, and remember her. I loved your mother very much. I wasn't a perfect husband, I know that, but, Jesus, I loved her."

Lina watched Duke, and her own memories ticked by: a curtain of dark hair, the tuneless song, pepper and sugar.

"And look at you—you're an adult!" Oscar spoke nervously into the silence. "And I'm practically an old man." Here he grinned. "I wanted to . . . explain some things. Tell the truth. I'm better at showing than talking, you know that. These are for you, Carolina. I want to *show* you some things about your mother. Stuff we've never talked about. It's time you knew."

Lina looked again at the *Enough* portrait, her mother's elongated face—like an El Greco, she thought, one of those rapturous, wraith-like ghosts. Wasn't this what she had always asked of Oscar? *Tell me,* she would say. *Tell me about my mother.* But now she felt only an urgency to leave the room. Oscar had caught her unprepared. The reckless girl who had flung that pot across the room was long gone, replaced by a Lina who did not like surprises or this sinking sensa-tion of weakness and instability, like standing on sand as the tide pulled away. She needed time to consider Oscar's pictures, to ana-lyze and think through her reaction. And sleep. She needed sleep.

"Carolina, have I upset you?" Oscar asked, his voice tight. "Why don't we talk more tomorrow. You look exhausted."

Oscar's tone, and the way he was standing now, his shoulders slightly rounded, his stomach slack, provoked Lina's old concern. And of course—Natalie needed a show. In recent weeks the public-ity had been mounting, all tied to the mysterious subject matter of Oscar's new work: Why all the secrecy? What had Oscar Sparrow done now? Interviews with journalists, a spread in *Artforum,* all of it clever and enigmatic, Oscar deflecting questions with a bemused grin. It had pained Natalie at first, or so she said, but even she had to admit that, as a PR strategy, it worked. But now Oscar was reach-ing a critical point. An opening date for the show hadn't been confirmed yet and if they waited too long, Natalie had warned, people would lose interest.

Lina steadied her breath. "I'm not upset," she said, smiling as Oscar's eyes played across her face. "The pictures are fantastic. I'm so glad you finally want to talk about Mom." She did not want to lie to him, but she didn't know how to explain the thudding in her chest. "It's just . . . been a long day. I'll take a closer look tomorrow, but I'm glad you're painting her."

Oscar's shoulders relaxed, the muscles of his jaw gave way to a wide, relieved smile. He let out a whoop and swooped in to hug her. "Hallelujah. Okay then. I'm ready. I'll call Natalie tomorrow.

"And listen—" He pushed her out of the hug, hands on her shoulders. "I mean it, I want us to talk more about your mother."

"Sure. We'll talk more."

"Tomorrow."

"I'm pretty busy at work."

"Okay, the next day. Whenever you can."

Lina nodded. "Good night, Dad."

"Good night, Carolina." She leaned forward to accept his kiss, the scratchy brush of his beard against her cheek, and then she turned and moved toward the door of the studio. Her vision was focused to a fine, narrow point. A wedge of darkness loomed behind the half-cracked door, the glass knob smudged with half a thumbprint of blue paint. Lina reached out and pulled it open. Duke rushed past her, a blur of orange and white, and bounded up the stairs, his tail twitching.

Lina started up to her bedroom, past a series of photographs that hung above the steps. There were eight in total, taken on Lina's birthday from ages four to eleven. In each one she was standing in the same position, her arms at her sides, the camera aimed straight-on, her torso filling the frame. On her head perched a series of homemade birthday hats: ribbons and bows, a large plastic 8, peacock feathers, balloons.

Lina knew the photos by heart: smiling in years five and seven; serious in nine, ten, and eleven; crying in four; eyes closed and mouth open in eight. Every year it had been Oscar baking her birthday cake, inviting her friends, making her hat, positioning her against the wall, the same spot, the same anticipation, every year when she was a child. Every year, her father on the other side of the lens, clicking the shutter open and closed, freezing the moment in time.

Josephine

Josephine stepped through the back door into the kitchen and placed the basket, half full with berries, on the table. She felt Mister's slap still in the bones of her face, echoing down her spine, but she saw no mark when she checked in the glass above the washstand. She fixed herself with a stare: her eyes of shifting color, a shadow of blue here, green there, hazel and brown and gray, the colors fractured together and split. "Tonight," she whispered. The kitchen seemed larger with the word alive in the air, the stone floor pushing downward, the roof lifting toward the open sky.

She climbed the steps to Missus' room and clapped her hands before the closed bedroom door. "Missus Lu," Josephine called. "Got to get you up and dressed. Dr. Vickers coming today, coming from town."

For months Mister hadn't wanted to fetch a doctor. "He'll just rob us blind," Mister had said last October, after the first fit came, Missus Lu stiff and crooked on her bedroom floor. Josephine had never seen such a thing before. Papa Bo's trances at the pulpit had never gripped him with such demon force. Lottie sometimes fell to the floor with her praying, but her body stayed natural in its shape.

Mister said to Josephine, "Your Missus just having a bad spell. We'll wait on it."

But the spells went on and on, through the short days of winter, frost on the grass, and then snow on Christmas, the coldest Josephine could remember, the wash freezing stiff on the line, Josephine holding the flat-out dresses and pants close as a dancing partner as she brought them into the house to thaw. The willow branches froze too, touching the crackling ice of the river in a solid crystal sweep. Lottie said the cold made the spirits irritable and prone to mischief, and she saw Missus' troubles as play wreaked upon her by the babies and not-yet-babies Missus had lost. Sometimes a fit lashed long and hard, and Missus would sleep for hours afterward, a sleep so still and silent that Josephine would fear she had passed on and hold a mirror to her face to check for breath. But some mornings Missus woke up just right, speaking in her singsong voice of flowers that needed picking, mending that needed doing, where was that pillow-case I asked you to launder, the corncake I wanted for tea.

It was the New Year when Missus started to forget the names of common things. Bread, fetch me that bread, she had called to Josephine on that first day of the year 1852, and pointed a finger at her wrap warming there before the fire. Other mistakes followed, thick as fleas. Apple, she said, instead of comb. Door for fire, rag for spoon, milk for chair. Josephine tried to interpret Missus' requests, find a pattern in her new language, but none seemed to fit.

Snow melted, the red mud of spring came, and with it planting time. Mister was out of the house most days, working alongside his men. Missus shook her head at the shame of it, but they all knew there weren't enough to work the farm. With Hap dead and Louis sold off for money to buy seed, only Otis was young and strong enough to pull the plow, keep the pace from morning till night. Lottie and Winton and Therese worked slow with warped fingers and crooked backs. Papa Bo would have sold all three, bought just one more with the money and worked him dawn till midnight, but Mister didn't think that way. He never looked to change things, just struggled along with what he had. Missus called it a weakness, said it was something she hadn't seen coming until they were married and living already under the crumbling roof at Bell Creek.

Finally last week, the day so hot, Mister came back from the fields for his dinner, and he found Missus on the floor, Josephine there holding her head to keep it from knocking against the floor or a table leg. He saw how her body jerked, the eyes nothing but empty white. After the fit ended, after she had slept, Missus insisted on Dr. Vickers, down in Claremont, thirty miles south at least. Josephine remembered, it seemed a long time ago, Missus Lu's strong views on curtain colors, the names of her chickens, the way that Josephine wore her hair, a particular painting that must never be hung in the hall, only in the front parlor. "Dr. Vickers knew my daddy. He's the only one I'll consent to examine me," she had said, a rare brief return of that stubborn insistence about small things.

Always at the mention of Missus' daddy, Mister's mouth would set tight, his voice go low and strained. But on that day he had only nodded. "Tell Otis. Dr. Vickers in Claremont, and ride fast."

Now Josephine called again at the closed bedroom door: "Missus Lu, today's the day for Dr. Vickers coming. This morning, Missus."

No sound from inside, no call or creak of steps on the floor. Josephine opened the door and surveyed the unmade bed, the closed windows. A sticky smell of sleep hung in the air. But no Missus.

Josephine heard knocks from the room at the end of the hall, something heavy dragging—the easel, must be.

The studio was at the front of the house, four long steps from the door of Missus' room, with windows that looked west to the foothills of the Blue Ridge Mountains, the low mounds sloping soft as though drawn with a crumbling crayon. Josephine didn't know what the studio had been in brother Henry's time, but Missus Lu and Mister had envisioned it a nursery and painted the walls a pale blue with a border of yellow daisies at the top. The furniture that once had filled the room—an unpainted pine crib, a hanging mobile made of pressed tin and scraps of ribbon, a carved wooden horse that rocked on curved supports—had been burned years ago, Mister adding the pieces one by one to a bonfire out back. Since then, Missus Lu called it her artistic studio, where she pursued creative endeavors, painting and sketching mostly, some sewing and needlepoint. The walls were still blue, but the paint had dripped in long pale streaks down the plaster, and the daisies had bled to thumbprints of color.

Josephine knocked once and entered. Missus Lu's back was to the door, one arm raised and motionless before a canvas propped on the rough easel Mister had made from old fencing post. She wore a white cotton nightdress that hung too big on her now, the ruffled edge hiding her ankles, the fabric falling loose from her thin shoulders. Missus must have tried to do up her own hair because it hung in a messy topknot, stray dark locks cascading loose onto her shoulders and down her back.

A rough table with hewn timber legs was pushed against the east wall, its top piled with scraps of canvas and homemade paper, birch bark, jam jars and old brushes, pots of powdered color that Missus would buy every season from the peddler whether she needed them or not.

Missus Lu's canvases leaned against the north wall and hung by nails above: a half-finished still life of apples and pears beside a wooden bowl, the watercolors bleeding one into the next; a shapeless peony from the garden sketched in pencil; a self-portrait, Missus' brown eyes too large for her face, her mouth slanted open in a half-smile; small landscapes with the horizon cut short or the perspective tilted in such a way that they provoked in Josephine a mild nausea whenever she glanced at them hanging there on the wall.

In the far corner were piled Josephine's pictures. She painted scenes from the farm. Winton and Lottie standing beside their cabin, Louis in the fields, Hap playing the fiddle, Missus Lu and Mister side by side in their rockers on the porch, all painted on scraps of canvas or sketched on paper, or on wide lily leaves that Josephine would collect from the creek in summer, dry in the sun, flatten under the cutting block. Missus let Josephine paint some days, others not. On those other days, Josephine would fan Missus' face, or read to her from the Bible. Sometimes Josephine would sketch a form where Missus found herself unsure, the charcoal in Josephine's hand moving quickly, the apple or hillside or vase finished with confidence, and Missus would step to the picture again. As Missus labored at the canvas, Josephine would resume her fanning, her reading, but inside a restlessness would take hold, and a flush of herself, the joy in what her hands could do.

"Missus?" said Josephine. She inhaled the tang of turpentine mixed with the perfumed powder Missus used in the summer months to hide her own smell.

Missus Lu did not turn around as Josephine entered the room but spoke toward the canvas: "Your Mister. Your Mister knows God watches him, as I do. He knows what evil comes from licentious ways."

Josephine had grown accustomed to Missus' wandering mind. Topics started off and then abandoned midsentence. Stories from her childhood told as though she lived still with her sisters and brother in the big house in Mississippi, and the little dog that ate only catfish and peaches, it still nipped at her skirts. Always Josephine would nod, whether Missus' words were foolish or wise, wicked or kind.

Josephine nodded now. "Yes, Missus," she murmured.

Missus resumed sketching with the charcoal she held in her right hand, short quick lines, a form taking shape as Josephine watched. A child, a sleeping child, a lock of hair curled on its forehead, its lips slightly parted, and then another beside it, its twin.

"He stopped all that, years ago," Missus continued. "God saved him from himself, yes. There are so many worries that plague him now. He is a good man, like his father Papa Bo before him."

A good man. Papa Bo had carried with him always a cedar walking stick tipped in silver, dented and dark from dragging behind him along the ground. He'd use it for poking at things, tapping out the rhythm of his sermons, drawing figures in the dust and, once his legs gave way, banging on the floor beside his chair when he believed household attention to be improperly diverted elsewhere. Sometimes he used it on the field hands, though never at the house, except once on Mister that Josephine had seen. It was the sound that alerted her, and Mister crying out. The crack of wood against the hard places of his shoulder and upper arm and Mister's sharp grunt, an unsurprised sound that held in it a futility and an assent.

"Your Mister, he's drinking spirits again, isn't he?" Missus lifted her hand from the picture and turned toward Josephine. Her large dark eyes were wide and unfocused, and a flush lay across her fine nose and pale freckled cheeks. Josephine feared a fit was coming. "Isn't he?" Missus repeated.

Josephine paused. It took a moment for Missus Lu's question to truly register, for Josephine to quit watching her for a sudden jerk, eyes rolled up, and to consider the words. Mister drinking again? Josephine said, "I don't know, Missus, truly I don't."

"Papa Bo, he told me that Mister was not strong. The passing of his mother and sisters in Louisiana when he was a child, it hit him hard, Papa said. He said to me that I was the strong one, that I had to be strong for us both. That's what I have tried to do." Missus turned back to the canvas.

"Yes, Missus."

"God looks down and pities him. He pities us both." Missus pressed her lips together. "What does he do when he's gone in town two, three days? Do you know, Josephine?"

"I do not, Missus. I do not know."

"I can't help him now. And Papa Bo is gone. I fear for him. I fear for us all." Missus Lu's hand was trembling, Josephine saw the charcoal dance above the surface of the canvas. "I forgave him. Before," Missus said. "I never told him, but he knows. I forgave him what he did. A man cannot be held accountable for his conduct while drinking. Do you understand, Josephine?"

"Here, Missus, let me help you." And Josephine stepped forward to take the charcoal before it marked the drawing.

"Do you, Josephine? Do you understand?" Missus waved Josephine's hand away.

"Yes, Missus. Of course."

Josephine looked out the window to the road where one of Mr. Stanmore's boys was driving past. She could hear the driver calling to the horses, *Move on,* and the crack of a whip.

Mister, drinking again. The collar of Josephine's dress pressed too close, as though a hand tightened there.

There were days that had passed dark and quick, barely fastened now to her memory, hanging loose as the slate that sat crooked on the roof. After Papa Bo's passing, and another of Missus' miscarriages, the last, as it happened. And Mister never in the fields, always in the house. His heavy, slow footsteps outside her door. At night, the floorboards creaked and she would know it was him.

At night, with Mister there in her room, Josephine would look to the square bit of window that sat up high on the downward slope of the roof. Sometimes the moon shone full through it and sometimes it was the darkest gray of clouds and Josephine would try to mark its perimeters, where that square of sky began and the frame of the window left off. Who was she to tell? There was no one to tell, no use in the telling.

After those days passed on, that time ended and another began, and she gave it no more thought. Mister stopped his drinking and the narrow steps to Josephine's attic room were crossed only by herself. She gave it no more thought than she did a bee that stung her hard and then fell down dead to the earth, its stinger still embedded in her arm. She rubbed the wound and continued on her way.

Josephine's eyes went to the canvas, to Missus' picture. "Missus," Josephine said, "the second baby, its left cheek is flatter than the first." She pointed to the flaw.

Missus Lu turned back to the drawing. "Oh Josephine, come do this," she cried and threw the charcoal to the ground where it broke in two. Josephine retrieved the pieces and took the longer in her fingers. Her shoulders fell, her breath evened. With a steady hand she hollowed out the shadowing on the second child, then moved to correct another awkward angle on a third.

Missus watched for a moment and then her lips turned down, her face went slack. "I cannot abide this room another second," she said and walked out into the hall.

With a tipped head, Josephine focused on the picture Missus had begun. For Josephine there existed no greater joy than this. The faint pepper smell of the homemade paper, the gritty charcoal dust misting the space around her fingers, her fingers moving faster than her mind could determine where to draw this line, that shadow, the picture emerging from her in a rush as though no distance existed between the paper and her mind's eye, they inhabited the same interior space, the same intimate world that belonged to her and her alone.

Missus kept a set of books on the study of art that sat on a tall shelf in the studio. One of these was called *Artistic Technique and the Mastery of Painting* and in it Josephine had seen a portrait of Mr. Thomas Jefferson. He stood in his presidential office, his posture straight, his face solemn, and in the back was a tall chest, the wood burnished and gleaming in the soft oil light of the painting. The chest contained many drawers small and large, each fronted with a curved brass handle shaped like an elegant letter U with tendril ends. Josephine had studied this painting and found in it something of use, not for evidence of technique or artistic rendering but for the chest itself, a tall keeper of secrets. It was inside these drawers that Josephine put the feelings she could not have, the rage that would drown her or the disappointment that would crush her. Over the years she had learned to fold down rising emotion just as she would fold the clean bedsheets, the sheet growing smaller and tighter with each pass until all that remained of that wide wrinkled expanse of cotton was a hard closed-in square.

Each wrapped tight, packed away, corners folded over, a small firm bundle.

Inside those drawers: the smell of liquor strong on Mister's hot breath, the creak of the floorboards outside her door, the creak in his bones as he settled above her. All packed away, and Josephine closed that drawer with a shake of her head, a blink of her eye, a heartbeat slow and steady within her chest. She bent her body into the sketch of the children, bringing her face close enough to kiss its rough surface, and she began to draw another child, much larger than the others, its head almost double the size. With care she formed the child's lips, its sleeping eyes, round chin, and perfect scrolled ears.

Did Missus' dead babies sleep here in this studio, the room once intended for their use? Josephine did not believe in the spirit signs that Lottie looked for. But still, there was a magic in here, not entirely benign, not entirely wicked. A sharpness in the air, maybe from the turpentine Missus used to clean her brushes, or the acidic tang of the indigo powder. The light too radiated rich and clear, even after the sun had passed the windows and waned against the other side of the house. Even when the night's darkness came up through the hills and the valley with a soft graying and muting, the room still seemed aglow.

It was here that Missus had taught Josephine to read. Books brought up from the library, Cooper, Dumas, Dickens, Poe, the names written in gold, the covers cracked, pages spotted dark with mold but still Josephine touched them only with her hands clean, with reverence, savored every word written there, each one a small victory. Letters formed carefully, again and again, the paper burned in the grate afterward, but a few secret pages carried under Josephine's skirts, up the stairs to her attic room. "Don't breathe a word to your Mister," Missus would whisper. "We'd both be in a world of trouble."

Josephine stopped her work on the canvas. *This will be my last,* she thought. *The last picture made here in this room,* and she felt a bottomless sinking, a different kind of fear, not the fear of discovery, of the hounds, of capture and punishment, but of the deep unknown, the world beyond the latched front gate about which she knew nothing. For a moment it stretched forward in her mind as colors and light, chaos and noise. If Nathan told her the route, if she found her way north, where would she stop? What would hold her there?

Josephine's mother lay buried under a tall, sickly ash that grew in the slave cemetery, beyond the far wheat fields, to the east of the Bell family plot. Josephine had no memories of her mother though she had searched her mind, hoping for some image or smell, a song perhaps. Lottie said her name was Rebecca, carrying Josephine at her breast when Papa Bo bought them both at auction, and dead from a fever that would not stop in the months after her arrival at Bell Creek. A bad bargain, Papa Bo had raged. Josephine was six when Lottie first showed her the grave, just a rounding of earth, no marker, only the yellow ash leaves scattered about. Sometimes Josephine would go there, sit on the mound, listen for her mother's voice in the wind, but not once had she ever heard a thing.

Josephine left the charcoal on the easel and moved to the corner and her stack of pictures. Perhaps she might bring something with her when she ran. Could she carry a canvas rolled tight, a folded paper tucked within her bundle? Was it foolish to think she might keep them dry and safe? Each of these pictures had created in her an expectation, a hope for the day. Will Missus go to the studio? Will her mood be charitable or mean? Will there be an ocher made up, a new pencil to use? The completion of each picture, of Josephine saying to herself—*here, this is finished, I have done my best*—seemed a small passing, and she would mourn in a way. A lightness would be gone from her step, the pure tedium, the unrelenting weariness would return. Until she began another. And another. There were so many pictures to make, and the time was always short, the days when Missus allowed her to paint never enough to finish all the scenes that appeared before her.

Josephine paused at one canvas and picked it from the pile, a painting of Lottie over which she had labored for many days. Lottie stood before the cabin she shared with Winton, flowers in her hands. Behind her, Josephine had painted the sea, using as her model a picture she had seen in a heavy book she took from the library, *The Geography of the Sea,* by a Frenchman with a long and frothy name. Josephine had never seen the sea, and this book contained glorious plates of swirling blues and grays, complicated graphs that measured precisely the shape and volume of a wave, maps and text that spoke of the sea as a watch, its cogs and levers and wheels seeming mysterious to the casual viewer but operating to certain concrete principles that students and sailors alike might master. But still, the Frenchman wrote, unlike a watch, there existed always an element of wild, the great unpredictable passions of the sea that might rise up to foil the learned predictions. This was what Josephine hoped for Lottie, and why she placed a sea there in the most unlikely of places, behind a slave cabin in the landlocked county of Charlotte, Virginia. There, an ocean raged and in it the seeds of disorder.

"Josephine! Josephine! Where are you?" Missus Lu's voice came loud and insistent from the bedroom. "Josephine!"

No, the picture of Lottie was too large, too heavy to carry, but then another caught her eye, a drawing of Lottie and Winton together. And then one of Louis: gone these years now from Bell Creek but still in Josephine's thoughts, always there. And one too of a younger Missus Lu sitting on the porch, a sketch made before her illness, when Josephine was just a girl, giddy from learning her letters and the feel of the paint on her brush. Working quickly, she rolled the papers tight as she dared and slipped the roll up the sleeve of her dress, but it fell ungainly against her wrist. She pulled them out and placed them again on the top of her pile. Later she would return and spirit them away, fold them into her bundle or fasten them to the inside of her skirts. Later.

"Josephine!"

"Coming, Missus. I am coming."

Pale and watchful, Missus sat on her tall bed as Josephine entered the room. Missus' nightdress was streaked with charcoal dust from the studio, her feet were bare and dark with dirt. Silently Josephine wiped Missus' feet, hands, and face with a cloth wet from the jug, lifted her slender arms to wipe away the sour pungency beneath, and helped Missus to dress, easing first the petticoats then the dress over her slim hips, the tight arms, the bodice, and fastening the long back row of hook and eye. With both hands, Missus Lu lifted her hair away from the last fastenings, and Josephine inhaled sharply. A red lump rose from the back of Missus' neck, just below the hairline, the skin stretched tight into a rounded point like someone inside was trying to elbow out. The tip was small, the size of a currant, but the lump widened at the base, spreading out and underneath the skin.

Josephine shifted her eyes away to finish the hooks and then began to fix Missus' hair as she liked it, up at the sides, low in back. Her hands trembled. When had such a thing appeared?

"Hurry up, Josephine. Dr. Vickers'll be here soon and me not even dressed."

"Yes, Missus." Josephine sped the comb through Missus' hair, careful not to pull too sharp or to touch the lump.

"Dr. Vickers, he knew my daddy well," Missus Lu said in a conversational tone, tilting her head for Josephine's comb, seeming oblivious to the mark of sickness growing on her, and it was this ignorance that brought up a pressure within Josephine's chest. At that moment the vast spider's web of emotion she felt for Missus Lu was reduced to a single, simple strand of pity. "Why, I've known Dr. Vickers since I was just a tiny thing. Robert does despise him."

Josephine did not respond but kept on with Missus' hair, the strands heavy and slick with unwash. The last few weeks, Missus had refused to bathe, despite the heat. Water frightened her, she said. She believed it to be alive.

"Robert won't even come in to see Dr. Vickers. Too busy with the picking, so he claims. But you'll stay with me, won't you?" Missus turned full around to face Josephine, pulling out the half-finished updo, and grasped Josephine's wrists in her small, tight fists. "Stay with me."

Josephine nodded. "Of course, Missus. I'll stay with you." She placed a hand on Missus' shoulder and gently squeezed the thin muscle. "Don't you worry."

Missus Lu turned back, relieved, and Josephine finished with the hair, her eyes straying again and again to the knob at her neck. Mister was wrong. This was no passing spell. Missus would grow worse before she grew better, if she ever did—Josephine had seen prettier wounds than this lead to quick, ugly deaths. The pity twisted and burrowed in Josephine's stomach, and she pulled down at the hair to cover Missus' nape and wondered what marvels Dr. Vickers might summon to effect a cure for such an affliction.

Lina

The polished top of Dan's desk reflected a shimmering expanse of oily morning light. He looked refreshed, his shirt a glaring white, his tie a power red. His hair rose from his forehead in a freshly washed spirally frizz. A man sat in front of Dan's desk, his back to the door. He did not turn as Lina entered.

"Good morning, Lina. Take a seat," Dan said.

Lina sat in the empty chair to the man's right. Behind Dan's windows the sun hung like a curtain of heat and glare and unheard noise. The climate-controlled, custom-made, solid walnut bookshelves that housed Dan's collection of antique law books turned on with a gentle hum.

"This is Garrison Hall. He's a second year in litigation—have you guys met?"

Lina glanced across. She saw a straight length of nose, fullish lips, a clear smooth cheek, skin the color of a dull penny. Garrison Hall was gazing straight ahead, his body the model of careful attention, his head angled just so. Lina was sure he had gone to Yale Law; he had that air of casual intensity, carefully cultivated. She shook her head no, as did Garrison, without looking at her.

"So. Well." Dan shifted his gaze from Lina to Garrison and then back again. "We've got a new matter I thought you two might be interested in. It's something of a departure for the firm, but this came to us through an important client we'd like to be able to assist. And the marketing folks seem to think it will raise the profile of the firm in a positive way. You know, diversity." Here he smiled directly at Garrison, showing abundant teeth, more gum than Lina had seen on display before. Garrison nodded slightly, as though he understood what this was all about.

"So the project is this—we've agreed to assist a client, Ron Dresser of Dresser Technology, on a reparations claim, historical reparations. You may have heard about this stuff in the news. It's new legal theory, really groundbreaking stuff. Dresser Tech works primarily in oil and gas, as you probably know, engineering and logistics work. Big projects for the government, petrochemical companies, that sort of thing. This lawsuit is something of a departure for them, to say the least." Dan snorted a laugh, picked up a pen, and began to helicopter it with the thumb and index finger of his right hand. Lina watched the pen twirl.

"The claim is for slaves, I mean ex-slaves, ancestors of slaves, great-great-*great*-grandchildren of slaves, to claim money from roughly twenty private companies that benefited way back when from slave labor. We've cleared them all with the conflicts department, so long as we isolate you two. No discussing this case with *anyone*. Understood?" Dan's brow crinkled sternly. Lina nodded a solemn yes. "Now the federal government will also be an initial defendant, to maximize the monetary claim and for . . . well, for publicity purposes more than anything else. We'll be using an unjust enrichment theory, mixed with crimes against humanity to get around the time-bar problem. It's a stretch, of course"—Dan laughed, nervously it seemed to Lina—"but Mr. Dresser is pretty confident he wants to give it a go. And we're happy to help him. So long as he keeps paying us for all the deal work we do for him."

Dan pointed to one of the deal toys on his desk, *Dresser Technology* etched in italic Palatino across a leaping crystal horse, an easy $5,000 worth of useless corporate kitsch.

"And you two immediately came to mind—I mean, Garrison, I understand some of your um, some of your ancestors were once, at some point in time, enslaved?"

Garrison nodded, the movement almost imperceptible. Lina could not hear his breathing.

"And Lina, I know you enjoyed that asylum case you did in law school. So here's your chance for some more pro bono!" Dan looked at her brightly, eyebrows pushing toward the ceiling. "It's not straightforward pro bono, of course. If we manage to get a settlement, or even win it, we'll get paid. But we're not billing in the normal way, so it's *similar* to pro bono. It's in the same *spirit*, if you know what I mean."

"But I'll still get full credit for the hours?" Lina asked.

"Of course."

"And for bonus purposes?" This from Garrison.

"Obviously. Now, I'll be the partner on this. You'll be doing all the legwork but I'll be steering the project. We'll be meeting with Mr. Dresser tomorrow, eight A.M., to talk specifics." Dan glanced at his watch, then toward the door. "Sooooo—great! Any questions?"

Lina opened her mouth to speak—about charging dinners and cabs—but Dan launched again. "Oh, and one last thing—we're on a tight time frame here. Dresser Tech has a lot of ongoing defense-related contracts. It's a busy time. Mr. Dresser's got to stay in the good graces of the feds, but apparently he's gotten a green light from within the administration to go ahead with this case. They focus-grouped it, I kid you not. Something to shift attention away from all this Abu Ghraib, WMD, yadda yadda. But our window is *small*. I don't know all the specifics, only that we've got to get the initial complaint researched, written, and on Dresser's desk in just over two weeks. I know that's tight but"—he shrugged—"what can we do?

We'll get it done. It is what it is. Right, team? Great! Well, thanks for stopping by."

Dan picked up his phone, fingers poised over the buttons, and smiled at them: leave.

IN THE HALL, WITH DAN'S office door closed behind them, Garrison turned to Lina. He was tall and narrow as a pencil. The intelligence in him, the watchfulness, was sharp as one of Oscar's palette knives.

"Hi, Lina. Feels like we should meet again," he said, smiling, and stretched out his hand.

"Hi." Lina took his hand and eyed him, unsure about the niceness; unsolicited friendliness was a rarity at Clifton. He radiated authority and a measured calm, as though he were entirely unconcerned with what others might think of him. Lina thought that she might grow to like him, or hate him, or, more probably, she would never know him well enough to decide.

"You know, Dresser Tech does a ton of stuff in Iraq," Garrison said, his voice low. "Like Halliburton, but more below the radar."

"Hmm." Lina had not known this, though she did not want to admit it.

"He's tight with Cheney too, apparently. They're golf buddies. Or hunting. One of those. Dresser's taking a risk with this case, even with the green light. Suing the government? He must have a strategy worked out. I mean, don't shit where you eat, right?"

Lina nodded tentatively. "I see what you're saying."

"Hey, we should have lunch sometime this week." Garrison's confidential tone gave way to a friendly buoyance. "Looks like it'll just be the two of us working on this."

"Usually I just eat at my desk," Lina said.

Garrison stared at her blank-faced and Lina thought, without any degree of alarm, that she had effectively quashed his attempts at collegial chitchat. "You know, they do let first-year associates exit the building during daytime hours. The security guards won't tackle you. At least not if you tip them." He smiled, and all at once Lina's jaw relaxed, a coiled tightness within her loosened, and she returned the smile.

"Lunch would be great," she said. "Thanks for the invite."

"Okay then. My secretary will set it up." Garrison looked at his watch. "Crap, I've got to run. Conference call with London in five. See you later," and Garrison slid down the hall, hands in pockets.

As Lina watched him go, she felt strangely heartened by the encounter. It was not unreasonable to think she might have a friend at the office, was it? Since she'd started at Clifton, her professional life had been confined to billing hours, attending client lunches and firm events, keeping afloat with a frantic dog-paddle in the competitive fishbowl where she and the other junior associates circled, sharp-eyed and wary. But Garrison's calm chattiness seemed removed from all of that, as though he had worked out his own set of rules for navigating Clifton. Yes, maybe she could grow to like him.

Lina turned and headed toward the elevator bank. The layout of every floor at Clifton & Harp was the same. The secretaries, paralegals, and assistants sat in a warren of cubicle space located in the center of any given floor. The lawyers resided along the building's perimeter in square-box offices with doors that closed and one wall of floor-to-ceiling window that opened them up to sunshine and vertigo. Like a gnat on an SUV windshield, that's how Lina had felt when she first walked into her office. Like if she chanced too close to the glass wall, she would tumble noiselessly out into open air.

Lina exited the elevator and walked the east corridor toward her office. To her left, the secretaries buzzed and clacked and sipped. The secretaries were an exotic, unfathomable breed, prone to wearing elasticized waistbands and acrylic fingernails that clattered in a high-pitched musical way across a keyboard. The secretaries never asked questions. They deciphered the lawyers' scrawl as best they could, settled into their ergonomically correct workstations, suspended all independent thought, all personal convictions, and typed.

To Lina's right, half-open office doors allowed her glimpses of heads bowed over papers or fixed tightly to the glow of a computer screen or cradling a gray telephone headset between shoulder and ear. A whispery quiet prevailed. The wall outside each associate's office was adorned with a black plastic placard grooved in style-free white lettering that announced the resident of each particular zone, good solid names like Helen, Louise, Ted, James, Amanda, Blake. Lina's ex-boyfriend Stavros had interviewed at Clifton but had not received an offer, an event that had seemed mystifying and tragic for a few short weeks but that Lina now considered to be for the best. Stavros had gone to a small intellectual property firm in San Francisco and seemed happy there—at least that's what he'd said in the two e-mails he'd sent since starting work last fall. None of Lina's law school friends had ended up at Clifton either; most were at other firms in New York though she rarely saw them. Everyone was hectic, overextended with cases, deals, billable-hour targets. Although born and raised in New York, Lina often felt now like a solitary newcomer to a thrilling, strange city, the City of Law.

Lina arrived back at her office. The perpetually poised Meredith was speaking loudly about hedging the yen, her voice echoing out of her office and down the hall. Sherri, Lina's secretary, perched in her cubicle wearing a fluffy yellow sweater and large hoop earrings; she appeared to be reading the newspaper. Sherri's dark hair flounced over her forehead and ears and down her back in a series of complicated layers and curls, a thing so large and effortful that Sherri's head seemed more a display case for the hair than the hair an accessory to the head. Sherri was secretary to five other lawyers, all senior to Lina. Lina never asked much of Sherri, only to answer Lina's phone when she wanted to avoid speaking to someone and, once, to proofread a two-page letter for typos. (Sherri had found none.)

"Oh, Lina," Sherri called.

"Yes?" Lina paused by the entrance of Sherri's cubicle zone.

"Two things. One, the Yankee broke up with Meredith!" This Sherri mock-whispered, one hand held to the side of her mouth. "Just this morning, first thing! You should have heard the cussing!" And here she was: gleeful Sherri, joyful and enthusiastic, brown eyes bright, cheeks aglow. Only in moments like these, when juicy office gossip was in desperate need of dissemination, did Sherri's default posture of bored disinterest fall away. The secretaries had full access to the e-mail accounts of the lawyers for whom they worked and there seemed to exist an unwritten code of information sharing among them: any noteworthy matter, personal or professional, was dispersed cubicle to cubicle, floor to floor with the speed of an airborne tropical virus. The ethics of this were straightforward and unassailable: any lawyer fool enough to conduct their personal life via a work e-mail account deserved to have their secrets revealed to the Clifton & Harp populace.

Lina gave her stock gossip-response smile of part shock, part disapproval, part delight. "Wow, that was fast!"

"I *know*. Not even six months." Sherri's eyes widened.

Lina waited. "And the second? You said there were two things?"

"Oh, yeah." Gleeful Sherri vanished. With great care, she picked with a fingernail at a front incisor. "Dan phoned. You're meeting with Mr. Dresser tomorrow morning. Conference room . . . oh, which one was it? I can't remember. Call facilities and they'll have the booking." Sherri turned back to her newspaper; her brow furrowed immediately with grave concentration.

As always, Lina felt powerless in the face of Sherri's secretarial indifference. She had tried, how Lina had tried! Movie tickets, thank-you e-mails studded with exclamation points, vanilla lattes delivered to Sherri's desk. But all Lina's efforts were met with the same emotionless smirk and an apathy so clear it seemed manufactured from glass.

For a moment Lina lingered, and then, inspired by the amiable

Garrison Hall, resolved to try a new strategy. Lina would invite Sherri to lunch. A conversation, a shared meal, and afterward their relationship would blossom and Sherri would never again shunt Lina's phone calls to voice mail, or miss the FedEx deadline, or forget a conference room number. But before Lina could speak, a red light blinked on Sherri's phone and she answered the call. "Meredith Stewart's office," she said with authority, and began writing a lengthy telephone message in looping longhand.

Lina retreated slowly to her office. She picked up her phone, called facilities, and got the conference room number for tomorrow's meeting. Room 2005, twentieth floor. Eight A.M. Breakfast not provided.

FRIDAY

Three heads turned toward Lina as she opened the meeting room door. She was five minutes early and yet, apparently, the last to arrive. It was raining and she had not stopped at her office to unload her coat and bag and now, standing in the doorway, struggling out of her wet yellow slicker, she wished she had. The men watched her for a moment, then swiveled away and resumed talking.

Dan, Garrison, and, she presumed, Mr. Dresser sat at a small circular table with various firm paraphernalia arranged as a neat centerpiece. A coffee mug held a collection of pens and pencils, and beside the mug rested a stiff-billed baseball cap—all items emblazoned with the Clifton & Harp logo. A fourth person, a young blond man, blue-suited and glossy, sat off to one side with paper and a pen poised above it. Dresser's assistant, of course; men like Ron Dresser never came to meetings alone.

Small talk, Lina could tell. Dan speaking too loudly, Garrison murmuring in low pleasant-sounding notes. Mr. Dresser angled his head slightly at their efforts, the gesture of a man accustomed to being the subject of the desperate attention of others. All superfluous, his angled head seemed to say, Mr. Dresser was at ease. He wore a dark gray suit, a purple tie that glowed regally, shiny black leather shoes. His skin was coffee colored, coffee with much cream, and it was clear, even sitting down, that Dresser was large, not fat but rather monumental in length and width. His chair seemed barely able to contain him. Beside Dresser, Dan and Garrison looked like mini-men.

Lina slid into the only empty chair at the table. Mr. Dresser was the first to acknowledge her. "You must be . . ." and he looked down at a paper in front of him.

"Lina. Carolina Sparrow, but everyone calls me Lina."

"Mmm . . ." He looked vaguely unsatisfied with this response.

"Lina and Garrison are two of our brightest young associates," Dan said. "We are all really excited about this project. Now let's get down to specifics, shall we?"

Mr. Dresser leaned back in his chair, crossed right ankle over left knee, and moved the end of his tie to the side of his expansive stomach. "My friends, this will be the largest, most important case of your careers," he said. "I don't care if you've been a lawyer for twenty years, or if yesterday was your first day at this venerable institution. This is the one you've been waiting for. We seek to right this nation's largest, most enduring sin. We seek redress for hundreds of years of man's inhumanity to man, trillions—let me say it again, *trillions*—of dollars in unpaid wages. The plaintiffs number, at the very least, in the hundreds of thousands, and possibly in the millions. We seek not only to compensate them for their ancestors' sweat and blood but to memorialize, to remember. Who were they? Who were their oppressors? I want names named, on both sides. The truth telling, the testimony, the media attention that this litigation will generate—a public *reckoning*, so to speak—will allow these historic wrongs to finally be made right." Dresser uncrossed his legs and leaned forward. "You will help deliver the healing, the *truth* that this country needs. This lawsuit has the potential to, quite literally, rewrite history."

Dresser paused. His assistant's pen scratched across paper.

"And even if we don't make it to trial, we'll settle for a whole heap of money," Dresser said. "Now what's not to like there?" He chuckled and looked at Dan. "Right, Danny boy?"

Dan smiled broadly. "Right. Now let's talk about the plan."

For the next 4.2 billable hours, Lina listened while Mr. Dresser and Dan discussed the strategy for the initial complaint. They would use an unjust enrichment theory, arguing that twenty-two private U.S.-based corporations from various industries—tobacco, insurance, textiles, banking, transportation, energy, mining—had been unjustly enriched by using or benefiting from slave labor in the years before passage of the Thirteenth Amendment. The descendants of those slaves are the rightful beneficiaries now of compensation for the forced labor enjoyed by those companies from the first documented slave sale in 1619 until slavery ended in 1865. That was a 246-year spread. That was roughly, Dresser calculated with a Clifton & Harp pen on Clifton & Harp–embossed paper, $6.2 trillion, including compound interest earned over time at a rate of 6 percent.

The lawsuit would also target the federal government, Dan explained. This was where Dresser's green light came in. "I've gotten confidential confirmation that, after we file the suit, the government will agree to issue a formal apology for slavery," Dresser said. "We'll pull the government claim and then the feds will put some pressure on our corporate defendants to settle." He smiled. "It's a nice little distraction, you know, atone for sins of the past, maybe divert attention away from the perceived sins of the *present*. But it's the deep pockets we're concerned with here. The government gets to look like a good guy, and we get some real weight behind us."

"Money won at trial or received through a settlement will go into a trust to fund a variety of programs and institutions," Dan said, shooting glances at Dresser, who nodded in agreement. "A national slavery museum, a monument on the National Mall, college scholarships, educational programs, funds for minority-owned businesses, for community centers, for antiracism curricula in schools, the military, and the police. This is Mr. Dresser's vision, and we're here to help him achieve it."

Occasionally Lina or Garrison asked a question or made a remark that, generally, went unacknowledged by Dresser and Dan; even Dresser's note-taking assistant seemed oblivious to their presence. Sometimes Lina exchanged looks with Garrison, both of them in postures of interested silence and mutual understanding that their role now was this: to be present, to bear witness to the interesting and intellectually stimulating exchange between these two successful men, to absorb as if by osmosis their intelligence, experience, and wit (Dan cracked a few jokes).

Toward the end of the meeting, as Dresser was playing with some compound interest rate calculations, Dan asked a question.

"And why now?" Dan said, his tone neutral. "I'm not talking about statutory limits. I'm talking historically, generations after the slavery . . . situation ended. Why now?"

"Why *now*?" Dresser repeated and raised his gaze to a small window high on the east-facing wall that showed only a pale blue square of sky. He turned back to Dan. "Let me ask you something. American slaves built the White House, they built the Capitol building. Jefferson owned them, Washington owned them, Ulysses S. Grant—yes, the great commander of Union troops—*he* owned slaves. Eight presidents sitting in the White House *owned* African American people. And yet there is not one single national monument to our brothers and sisters in chains. Why is it that we have nineteen Smithsonian museums—nineteen, one just for goddamn postage stamps—and not one is dedicated to memorializing those people who lived in bondage and helped build this country? We would not be the world's superpower today if we had not had two hundred and fifty years of free, limitless labor on which to build our economy. Why now, you ask? What were their names, Dan? They were our founding fathers and mothers just as much as the bewigged white men who laid the whip against their backs. Isn't it time this country made the effort to *remember* them? And to calculate how much we *owe* them? It is *past* time, my friend."

Dresser eyed Dan steadily with, it seemed to Lina, a great dislike. Then Dresser smiled, and his teeth were very white and even as the edge of a straight razor. "I get riled up talking about all this, Dan, but no offense is intended. I know we're on the same team here. In my own family, we have a few names, a few details. As a child, my paternal grandfather was enslaved on a Mississippi cotton plantation, that we know. My maternal great-grandmother was taken away from her children, taken and sold off. What happened to that woman? To my great-grandfather? That history sits ill with me. It sits very ill indeed."

The room vibrated with an uncomfortable silence. The bare emotion of Dresser's voice, the earnestness, seemed to have cowed Dan and Garrison, and they each sat now with bowed heads, studying their hands with fierce concentration. Only Lina kept her eyes on Dresser. She felt a flush of possible understanding, an affinity with him having to do with her own mother's lost family and the nebulous desire to know. She wondered what else Dresser had learned about his history, the grandmother sold, the motherless children, and how he had achieved such success—Look at him! The watch! The assistant!—despite this constant, roaming absence. Despite a present identity perforated with giant person-shaped holes. She felt an urge, one she promptly suppressed, to grab hold of Dresser's hand.

Dan raised his gaze. "Thanks for that, Ron. I'm sure we all appreciate the history lesson." He turned his attention toward Lina and Garrison, and his hands came up, elbows on table. "Now, let's study the briefs that have been submitted in the other slavery reparations cases and the decisions that were handed down. Garrison, I want you to outline the primary reasons plaintiffs have lost before on summary judgment, and our arguments to get around these issues.

Standing and statute of limitations are the big ones. I have confidence you can put in some creative thinking.

"Now, Lina," and Dan pointed an index finger in the direction of her nose. "I want *you* to concentrate on defining the class." The finger descended to the table, jabbing for emphasis. "This is a biggie, and I think it's worth you looking at full-time. We need to nail this class down, and get ourselves a great lead plaintiff. Maybe a few to choose from. Think about the injury—what's the injury here, what is the nature of the harm? We need the face of *that*. We need someone to *show* us the harm. But be careful about sympathy fatigue. There are only so many sob stories people can hear before their eyes start to glaze over. Slavery was bad, yeah, yeah, what else? I want something stirring, a new angle, something *compelling*. And don't forget photogenic—these people will be on TV, they'll be in the papers, they'll be giving interviews. We need some great people, Lina, some great stories. The evils of slavery, of course, but also picking oneself up from the dust, yadda yadda, do you know where I'm going with this?"

Automatically, as she always did when Dan asked her a question with only one acceptable answer, Lina nodded.

"All right then!" said Dan. "Ron, we will get cracking *asap*."

At the door, Lina shook hands with Dresser. He placed his left hand on top of her right and clasped them together so she could not pull away. "Thank you," he said, looking directly at her for the first time. "I know this isn't an easy case. I know you'll work hard for our success."

"I look forward to working with you," Lina said. Dresser's skin pressed warm and dry against hers. His eyes flashed a bright hazel.

Lina had never considered the issue of slavery reparations before. It was not something she had studied at law school, it was not something that had ever crossed her mind. She was a twenty-first-century white girl from New York—what did she know about the enduring harm of slavery or $6.2 trillion in unpaid wages? The dozens of briefs she'd written to date at Clifton marched before her in a mental parade, each case and client distinct but essentially the same. Each client an LLP or PLC or Ltd. or Corp. Each complaint a variation on the same broken-contract theme. But Dresser had brought to Clifton something utterly new. Two hundred and fifty years of nameless, faceless, forgotten individuals. Yes, they were America's founding fathers and mothers as much as the bewigged white men who laid the whip upon their backs. Why *didn't* Lina know their names? Why *hadn't* she studied their histories? Where was the monument? Where was the museum? What had they wished for and worked for and loved?

Josephine

At half past nine the doctor's coach rattled into the yard. Josephine and Missus Lu had been waiting on the porch since just after breakfast, stains widening under the calico arms of Missus Lu's dress as she rocked in her chair. Josephine fanned a hand in front of her face, feeling the sweat dry coolly on her upper lip. Her legs ached from standing, her mouth was sticky with thirst.

Dr. Vickers climbed down from the carriage bench and removed his hat with great solemnity. The horse twitched its ears at a snarl of flies as Dr. Vickers stood for a moment gazing up at Missus Lu on the porch. His bald head gleamed shiny as a peeled potato, his belly round, his back slightly stooped, and too-short legs bowed away at the knees like a chicken's wishbone. His face had the look of a carved apple left to dry in the sun, the skin pinched and pulling into itself, eyes wide set and dark. "Good day, Mrs. Bell," he said.

At once the doctor's face and voice flared familiar, and Josephine's breath caught as a drawer opened, a memory released. The bald head like a peeled potato, and Josephine returned to the night she had first tried to run, when she came back to Bell Creek with a pain deep in her belly, so sharp that she could not breathe. The pain: this was why she had returned. It had been dawn, there had been rain, a crow at the window. Josephine had lain atop a tall bed,

Missus Lu sitting beside her and a man she did not know moving about the room, his thick-fingered hands probing at her, touching.

Dr. Vickers stood now in the dust of the yard, a trickle of sweat running the length of his face with the speed of a caress. This was the man.

Josephine pushed the memory away and looked to where a crow had landed at the bottom of the porch steps, striking its hard beak into the dirt. The doctor's horse flinched and sidestepped away as the crow hopped closer to its hooves, pecking the packed earth. The horse grunted and the crow flapped low into the air, something small and black trapped in its beak.

The doctor started up the stairs. His body swayed side to side and the banister creaked with the strain of his weight. He held a cane in his right hand but he did not use it. With arms spread wide, he approached Missus Lu.

"My dear Lu Anne, it has been many years. It is wonderful to see you again." His voice was liquid in its low notes, smooth and sugary.

"And you as well, Doctor. How long it's been!" Missus Lu stood to greet him, her hair damp and matted around her forehead and neck, her dress dark down the back where it had pressed against the porch rocker. She swayed as she bent her knees in a vague approximation of a curtsy.

"I was so very sorry to hear of your recent troubles," the doctor said. "The barn. And of course your failing health."

"Oh, it is nothing, really, nothing to bother you over. I am so very sorry you've had to travel all the way out here, into the wilds of Charlotte County, to see just one poor patient! Please, come inside out of this heat."

Missus Lu led the doctor to the front parlor, a rarely used room that persisted in smelling of mold despite Josephine's efforts with rose water and brush. Missus gestured for Dr. Vickers to sit, and she joined him, the two on opposite ends of the square-backed set-tee that was covered in a chocolate-brown cloth, the edges tucked against the wood with round brass tacks that ran across the back and down the armrests in two unbroken rows. As a child Josephine had loved to run a finger along their smooth tops, almost like counting money in your hands.

The room held a collection of furniture and ornaments that brother Henry had purchased or paid others to make, the finest workmanship, the latest fashions of fifteen years past. Nothing had been removed or replaced since Henry passed on and Papa Bo took his inheritance. Two small tables of dark-brown walnut waxed and polished to a high shine stood at either end of the sofa, two straight-backed chairs with slender legs placed to either side, framing a place for sitting and conversation in front of the wide brick fireplace. On the mantel rested a series of ceramic figurines, scenes of a bucolic nature: a deer and her fawn, a small flock of white sheep, a black-faced slave tending a brown-spotted cow, as well as a small bowl of clear blue glass, a bubble suspended at the centermost bottom point like a giant frozen tear. Every week Josephine would hold these ornaments in her hands and wipe clean the wooden mantel beneath them. She would rub a cloth over their brittle painted faces, the deer's snout so realistically drawn, the cow's hooves black as the man's face, the blue glass thinning to such a fine edge that once Josephine cut her thumb and it felt as if she had drawn it against a blade.

Missus Lu sat with back straight and shoulders squared, her hands folded palm to palm in her lap. Josephine had known no other mistress but had seen the daughters of Mr. Stanmore as they rode by on their sable mares, and Missus Lu's posture recalled for Josephine now their riding stance. They shared the same confidence in bearing, bred from privilege and a certainty in their place in the world. Hardship with Mister had not bled it out of Missus.

"Josephine, fetch the good doctor some lemonade, or perhaps sweet tea, Dr. Vickers?" said Missus Lu.

"No, nothing for me, thank you, Lu Anne," said the doctor. He paused and then added gently, "May I ask how your symptoms have been?"

"Doctor, I've been right as rain, not a care in the world." Missus Lu smiled broadly, but her eyes were unfocused and a twitch lifted the right corner of her upper lip as she spoke.

"Yes. But come, let me examine you. If I may."

Missus Lu hesitated, her mouth twisting again with the tic. "And is it absolutely necessary?"

"I'm afraid so, my dear."

"If you must . . ." she said and gazed away from the doctor, out the parlor window bright with sun. "But Doctor, I'm afraid that Robert is not able to see you today. You are to speak your conclusions to Josephine. I am terribly forgetful, you see." Missus spoke these words slowly, with a childish purpose, as though afraid of the scolding she might get if she did not say them right.

"Oh, that is a pity. He cannot spare a moment?" Dr. Vickers spoke with irritation and glanced at Josephine, a sideways lifting of a lid, and that gesture provoked another memory: of the doctor's fleeting attention, an impatience and disguised aggravation at the untidy way of things. His thick fingers, rough and careless. "Not even a moment?" he asked again.

"No. Robert gives his apologies." Missus Lu stood and gave a small shake of her head. "He is very busy."

The doctor pushed himself up from the settee. He did not look again at Josephine.

DR. VICKERS WAITED IN THE hall as Josephine helped Missus Lu remove her dress and place it across the screen painted with flowers that shielded a corner of the room. Missus' high narrow bed sat against the east wall, a wash table and jug beside it. There was no rug and the windows were hung with heavy dark curtains that gathered dust and small flying insects in their folds. Missus' clothes were kept in a paneled wardrobe of cherrywood that had gone dark over the years. Though situated at the back of the house, this had been the room Missus Lu insisted on calling her own because the bank of west-facing windows afforded a view of the setting sun, an event Missus preferred to consider while reclining upon the bed, her head propped by pillows.

"Ready," said Missus Lu, and Josephine fetched the doctor from the hall. Missus stood in her petticoats and chemise, no corset, her skin pink and rough-looking, and submitted without protest to the doctor's prodding and taps. The markers of Missus' illness were plain: her sunken chest, the rough rasp of her cough, the spray of pink spots across her back. Dr. Vickers turned Missus' body and placed his fingers around the nape of her neck, examining the red lump.

A shiver ran through Josephine. She looked away, her breath suddenly turning fast and hard, her heart thundering. Memories rushed through her with the speed and force of a locomotive, she could not stop their forward thrust. That first time, she had waited too long to run, all those long months of not understanding, not wanting to understand, hiding her changing shape behind heavy skirts, her long apron. She had returned to Bell Creek as the pains came, her belly hanging low and heavy, a twisting inside; Josephine had known her time was soon, she would not make it far on foot.

She had lain atop a high bed—Missus' bed?—with Missus Lu beside her and the doctor there, his bald head, his impatience. And the pain finally had ended, and in its place there was silence. She heard no baby's cry, nothing of that breathless high wail she remembered from Calla's newborns. Only silence, heavy and full, and she listened to the sound of nothing and the beating rain. It seemed the natural course, her baby born dead, as all babies were born at Bell Creek, perhaps the air not ripe enough to sustain new life, or perhaps the spirit others would not tolerate one wet and screaming and so they took it for their own.

Afterward, the doctor left her, and Missus Lu stayed for a time and stroked Josephine's hair and held her hand and then she too left the room, the door closing with a sharp drop of the latch. Josephine was alone and she had wept until her body seemed dry and hard as a stone in the sun.

Mr. Jefferson's chest of drawers had opened and Josephine struggled to close it again. She pushed her fingernails into her palms and focused on their bite until the knuckles felt they would crack or the skin split apart. She directed her gaze out the window, the sky a whitewashed blue, the treetops still on this windless day. The view here was a pleasing one, looking out over the green tobacco fields, and beyond those the gold shimmer of the wheat backing into the far distance and, against the gold, a sturdy line of dark evergreen. Above the trees two hills rose gently, the slopes meeting in a dark convergence that gave the land the look of a woman lying back, her legs crossed, and the perspective as if Josephine stood at the woman's toes. She thought of her mother's spare grave, the small rounded mound, and now imagined her mother as monumental, her body carved from the mountaintops and valley, her hair the clouds, her skin the smoothness of a young green leaf. How to paint such a scene, of a woman's body curved within the hills?

Josephine released her clenched fists. She watched a sparrow alight on an apple branch, flit away beyond the window frame, then back again, to a different branch, and away, and back. Over and over, the sparrow's underwing flashed white, its head pointed like an arrow. Josephine heard the distant low thrum of the field hands singing at their work. *Tonight I will run. Tonight.* Silently she spoke the words again and again and again.

Dr. Vickers finished the exam and bade Missus Lu get dressed. Josephine moved from the window to help her and the doctor paused for a moment, sunlight now piercing the room. He stepped closer to Josephine and narrowed his eyes, appraising her or perhaps merely in response to the glare. "I will wait in the hall," he said.

Missus Lu was docile and calm after Dr. Vickers's exam, her

gaze never straying from the window as Josephine removed the old petticoats and dressed her again in clean garments. She lifted her arms, turned her body as Josephine directed. Was a fit coming? Josephine worried, with the heat of the morning, the doctor's visit. "After, we'll sit in the shade, down by the river," Josephine whispered to Missus Lu. "I'll read to you."

Josephine left Missus Lu sitting on the bed. "I'll be just a moment," she said and closed the door behind her. She turned to face the doctor, who waited just paces from the door, his cane tapping impatiently against the floor.

"Your mistress's condition is very grave," he said. "Is she resting? Does she eat well?"

"Yes—yes," Josephine stammered. "Her appetite is good. Rest, yes, she sleeps moderately well. Though the fits sometimes disturb her."

"I will need to bleed her, and I have not brought my mercury. I did not believe the tumor would be this advanced." He was speaking to himself now, his eyes distant, gazing toward the window at the end of the hall, over Josephine's shoulder. He shifted back to Josephine: "You must keep her calm, but keep her spirits lifted. She has a melancholy nature and a fragile composition. The combination is not good for a life of hardship on a farm such as this, and it is imperative that you keep her mind focused on happy thoughts, frivolous things." The doctor's eyes scanned the hall, the bare floorboards, the mended curtains at the far window, the patches of stained plaster mottling the walls. "It is a rough road your mistress has chosen," he said.

In deep Mississippi, Missus Lu's family farmed cotton on a sea of rich land, where Missus and her five sisters and one brother had been raised. She spoke of it often to Josephine, the dresses she once wore, the dancing and music at the parties her family would host, a bracelet she'd been given on her sixteenth birthday, a slender ribbon of gold she wore every Friday evening for supper with her parents.

"I left it behind, Josephine, when I married him," Missus had said, before her illness. She had spoken in a factual tone, the reporting of events long gone. "He cut a fine figure then. He talked so sweet and shy, and his eyes were indigo blue."

The doctor took a step and leaned in closer to Josephine. She smelled the mustiness of unwash and a strong medicinal bitterness.

"I know you, girl," he said. "Do you remember me?"

He tilted his torso forward just slightly, and she saw a darkening on the inside of his collar, a glimpse of the gray-yellow skin of his neck and a scabrous redness edging up from his chest. His smell turned rank in the closeness of the hall.

"No, Doctor," Josephine said, backing away. She wanted nothing more to do with this man. She wanted him gone from Bell Creek, with his cane and his inquisitive hands.

"Don't you? I think that you do."

Josephine shook her head no but she saw the way he looked at her, the certainty in his eyes and a curiosity, cold and clinical.

"Yes, well, it is to be expected," he said. "You were very weak, and so young. I administered a sedative." He tilted his head back and his stance shifted, his chest pushed forward. "The whole affair, it was a pity. A disgrace." Dr. Vickers spat out the word. "Your mistress has shown you such kindness, more than any other would, I can assure you of that. You'd be sold away, gone, or at the very least in the fields, out of her house. I don't know why she does what she does. She has always been headstrong."

Josephine lowered her gaze, careful not to meet his eyes or make any motion that might prolong this encounter. The doctor's white knuckles curved along the handle of his cane.

A faint rustle of movement came from inside Missus' room, a creak of floorboard, the hush of petticoats moving behind the closed door. Distracted by the sound, Josephine turned her head and Dr. Vickers stepped away down the hall.

When the doctor spoke again, his voice was efficient and direct.

"Your mistress, I believe she is dying. It seems there is a tumor; that is the source of the protrusion at the back of the neck. The question is really one of time. It is difficult to know how long it will be in these cases. The illness has persisted for so long already, and her mind is not strong. But she may very well surprise us all, find an inner reserve." He lowered his chin.

"Tell Mr. Bell all that I have told you. I will call again in two days' time. If anything should change in her behavior, Mr. Bell must send for me at once. Do you understand?"

"Of course, yes. I understand."

Dr. Vickers's eyes were heavy-lidded, unblinking. "I will see myself out. Stay with your Missus." He turned to make his way down the creaking stairs, the tip of his cane held high, never once hitting a step.

JOSEPHINE REMAINED IN THE HALL long after Dr. Vickers had gone, waiting for Missus Lu to summon her. Missus Lu, dying. The doctor's words settled into Josephine, taking possession of her heart, and she felt her resolve falter. After she was gone, who would care for Missus Lu? Who would hold her down when she shook, comb her hair, fetch what she needed, see that she ate? Mister would never do such things. He had no money for another house girl. Lottie, Therese, Calla, none of them knew all that Josephine knew of the house, of Missus and her ways.

Josephine watched the sun on the floorboards, the shadows cast by the clouds moving like water across the wood, and she thought of an earlier time, when she was a girl but not a child. Her bare feet slapping on the stones of the kitchen floor as Missus sang a tune in the parlor. Books taken from the library and ferreted up to her room, and the night hours full of the marvels they contained. There had been a lightness then. Before the bee sting that killed young Hap, before Missus' fits, before Louis got sold away. Louis brought Josephine flowers once, just before he left. A handful of the goldenrod

Lottie would pull as weeds, left at the back door; Josephine had known who they were for and who had left them. He was quick on his feet, long and lithe, a handsome curl to his upper lip when he smiled, which he did freely, with an eagerness to please her.

He talked of running. It was Louis who first made it seem to her like a thing that could be done. When she visited with Lottie and Winton late in the evenings, with the musty smell of wet woodsmoke from the fire and the spray of red sparks when Winton poked a log, Louis whispered to Josephine of how, one day, he would run. *Philadelphia,* he said. *Boston. New York.* And he had spoken the names of northern cities as if they were sweet drops rolling in his mouth. *Come with me?* he asked and he had thrown back his head and laughed as though it were a plan they could make, to go for a picnic, to run for their lives.

The last time Josephine saw him, he lifted his brows, inquiring as to how she had been keeping. Josephine in the house, Louis in the fields and the cabins; only yards separated them, but rarely did they pass each other to speak. They had never touched. It was late morning, Josephine sent out to fetch Mister, and Louis had stepped away from his row when Jackson's back was turned. *Watch me go,* he had whispered to her. *Soon. Philadelphia. I'll call outside your window. A dove, they don't call at night. You'll know it's me.*

I'll know it's you, Josephine had said. This was before Mister and his drinking, before Josephine's breasts grew so tender, before her belly began to swell, and she had imagined the streets of Philadelphia, she and Louis side by side amid the crowds, just another boy and girl making their way along the road.

A few days later, Louis was sold off. Sometimes at night she'd listen for the dove's call, but it never came. Doves don't call at night, she knew as much.

Not long after Louis got sold, Hap died, and it seemed all the light of the world was snuffed out for a while, those two strong boys gone in an instant, and the women and old men left weeping. Josephine mourned in her own way. She did not kneel down with Lottie, she did not visit the place where Hap was buried. Lottie asked her: Why do you reject His light? Why do you scorn Him? Lottie's religion was grounded in Papa Bo's sermons and the tragedies she herself had suffered. A man she once loved taken from her in a way that Josephine had never learned, Lottie never told of its particulars; Lottie's mother and the three little sisters, scattered somewhere in the cotton states, so Lottie supposed; other children, Lottie never spoke their names, born before she came to Bell Creek, Josephine could only guess at their number; and then Lottie's last, her beloved Hap, a spot the size of a dime. It was only the Lord who would not leave her.

Josephine had pondered Lottie's faith. She had stood beside Lottie and Winton in the old meat house as Papa Bo preached and moaned, shook, and sometimes fell to the ground. Time and again Josephine had tried to feel their fervor but she had looked upon them and felt nothing. Missus too believed. Josephine had seen her lips move without sound as her finger traced along a gilt-edged page. But Josephine was not transformed; she had never felt an ecstasy or heard a call. Her body was hers alone, not belonging to Mister or Missus Lu or to the Lord above. And it was only with this true belief that she could tolerate the putting of one foot before the other, the drawing of another breath and another and another.

Standing in the hall, the sun lengthening across the floorboards, Josephine saw her mother's body stretched across the hills, and Lottie on her knees at Hap's grave, and the sheen of Louis's skin by firelight; she heard the doctor's words: *It was a pity. A disgrace,* and that terrible breathless silence. The things you can control and the things you cannot. And Josephine knew she could not wait, no, she would not stay for the dying Missus Lu. *Run.*

Lina

Eleven thirty P.M. and Lina was working at home. Conversation fragments, laughter, and hoots filtered into her room from the sidewalk below, but for Lina the weekend seemed as distant as the moon. She sat in bed, a pillow on her lap, a book on the pillow, and read. As promised, Dan had shifted all of her client work to other attorneys. During the course of the meeting with Dresser, Lina's desk had been cleared of all papers relating to her old cases and a pile of books and binders had replaced them: information on class action lawsuits, histories of U.S. slavery, economic treatises, financial models of farm worker wages and earned income, and case precedent—reparations for Holocaust survivors, for Japanese Americans, for East Germans post-reunification; decisions from the International Court of Justice, the Nuremberg Tribunals, the British Foreign Compensation Act.

To begin her research, Lina had lugged home a briefcase full of transcripts from interviews conducted in the 1930s to record the memories of the last surviving American slaves. The nature of the harm, Dan had said. One individual's experience to represent the experience of the many. Lina was hoping some potential leads might emerge from the interviews. Using census data, public historical records, and the biographical information contained in the transcripts, it would be easy enough to track the descendants of an interviewee. And Garrison had offered to put her in touch with some friends who had already traced their antebellum family roots. He'd stopped by her office after the meeting with Dresser, standing in the doorway, a pen behind one ear. "They'll be happy to talk to you. Just use my name," he'd said, and winked.

Tomorrow Lina would make some calls, arrange some meetings, and by early next week she would have a few candidates for Dan and Dresser to review. This would not be a tough assignment, Lina thought, and she felt a flash of pity for Garrison.

Lina's bed was king-size, a giant white raft positioned in the center of the room, facing three large sash windows that looked out over Sixth Street and the linden's sturdy gray trunk. Only the gooseneck lamp on her bedside table was lit, but the circle of light was wide and bright at the center where Lina sat. The rest of the room—the painted white dresser bought by Oscar when she was seven, the potted ficus grown nearly to the ceiling, the forgotten guitar in its dusty case, the overflowing bookshelves—remained in shadow.

Duke wandered into Lina's room, eyed the bed appraisingly, and jumped. At the foot, he circled out a nest in the blankets and began to clean himself with long sweeps of his precise pink tongue. He finished with his left foreleg and moved to the phantom right, his tongue licking air, his empty shoulder moving in circles.

On the open page of her notebook Lina wrote, "Nature of the harm—slavery." She turned to the transcripts, beginning with the index of slave interviews. The listed names were musical and endless: Larkin Payne, Millie Barber, Sarah Odom, Sidney Bonner, John Payne, Lina Anne Pendergrass, Cella Perkins, Marguerite Perkins, Andrew Boone, Amanda Oliver, Robert Bryant, Rachel

Perkins, George Washington Buckner, John Coggin, Neil Coker, Amy Perry, Lizzie Davis, Louisa Davis, John B. Elliott, John Ellis, Helen Odom, John Ogee, Lewis Ogletree, Daniel Phillips, Nathan Gant, Clayborn Gantling, Jenny Greer, Henderson Perkins, Andrew Gregory, Benjamin Henderson, Molly Hudgens, Carrie Hudson, Jesse Meeks, Nathan Neighten, Sam Kilgore, Lucy Key, Ella Johnson, Edward Lycurgas, Ballam Lyles, Jane Oliver, Annie Osborne, Victoria Adams, Dolly Whiteside, Belle Robinson, Ellen Polk, Dina Beard, Nathan Beauchamp, Irene Poole, Harrison Beckett, Annie Beck, J. H. Beckwith, John C. Bectorn, Prince Bee, Mary Poe, Enoch Beel, Welcome Bees, Matilda Poe, Anne Bell, Oliver Bell, Cyrus Bellus, Sam Polite, Carrie Pollard, Edgar Bendy, Minerva Bendy, Allen Price, Willis Bennefield, Carrie Bradley, Logan Bennett, Fannie Berry, Kato Benton, Henry Probasco, Ellis Betts, Jack Bess, James Bertrand, Alice Biggs, Jane Birch, Jenny Proctor, Carrie Binns, Ransom Simmons, Rosa Simmons, Andrew Simms, Millie Simpkins, Ben Simpson, Fannie Sims, Senya Singfield, James Singleton, Billy Slaughter, Alfred Sligh, Peggy Sloan, Samuel Smalls, Arzella Smallwood, Sarah Smiley, Anna Smith, Clay Smith, Francis Black, Ank Bishop, Nelson Birdsong, Josephine Stewart, Elvira Boles, John Price, Marshal Butler, Titus Bynes, Annie Stanton, Tanner Spikes, Solbert Butler, Laura Sorrell, Nathan Byrd, Granny Cain, Rosa Starke, Maggie Stenhouse, Charlotte E. Stephens, Laura Caldwell, Jeff Calhoun, Mariah Calloway, George Scruggs, Abram Sells, Sarah Sexton, Alice Sewell, Roberta Shaver, Mary Shaw, Nelson Cameron, Chaney Spell, Jessie Sparrow, Easter Campbell, Patience Campbell, Patsy Southwell, Elizabeth Sparks, Fanny Cannady, Sylvia Cannon, James Cape, Tille Caretaker, Susan Snow, Albert Carolina, Cato Carter, Frank Reed, Esther King Case, Charlie Rigger, Julia Casey, Susan Castle, Zenie Cauley, Ellen Cave, Dora Richard, Lula Chambers, Amy Chapman, Charity Riddick, Ce-

celia Chappel, Harriet Cheatam, Alice Rivers, James Childress, Mary Anne Patterson, Solomon Pattille, Carry Allen Patton, Martha Patton, Amy Penny, Sallie Newsom, Pate Newton, Lila Nichols, Margaret Nickens, Margrett Nillin, Fanny Nix, Cora Torian, Neal Upson, Dolly Whiteside, Sam T. Stewart, Mark Trotter, Ellis Strickland, Jim Taylor, Luke Towns, Addie Vinson, Charlie Van Dyke, John Wesley, Ophelia Whitley, Alice Rivers, Susie Riser. The names went on and on and on.

As with every one of her cases—breach of contract, restitution, fraud—Lina began with a chart. Within neat rows and tidy columns, the facts became more than just a list of names, a catalogue of tragedies and mistakes; they became usable, valuable, revelatory. Was there a pattern? An anomaly? How did events unfold? Who were the key players?

Lina titled her chart "Nature of the Harm" and labeled the columns with general types of harm as she found them in her reading.

Nature of the Harm								
Difficult, repetitive work	Poor living conditions	Children separated from parents	Husbands separated from wives	Physical abuse	Sexual abuse	Education denied	Personal relations denied (e.g., legal marriage)	Murder

As she located a specific example of a type of harm, Lina wrote the initials of the individual involved and the relevant page number. She skimmed as she read, not dwelling on the facts she found. *Law is the bastion of reason,* Lina's criminal law professor had always liked to say. *There is no place for feeling. As lawyers, we reason, we observe, we analyze.*

At three thirty A.M., Lina examined her work.

Nature of the Harm								
Difficult, repetitive work	Poor living conditions	Children separated from parents	Husbands separated from wives	Physical abuse	Sexual abuse	Education denied	Personal relations denied (e.g., legal marriage)	Murder
LP, 2;	HK, 2;	HK, 2;	JK, 10;	RY, 8;	CH, 4;	CH, 4;	JC, 2;	CS, 9;
HK, 2;	EN, 3;	OK, 3;	RY, 10;	VIM, 11;	JK, 10;	DP, 8;	CH, 4;	WN, 13;
CH, 4;	CH, 4;	CH, 4;	VIM, 11;	CD, 18;	DK, 14;	HK, 10;	DP, 8;	RKW, 19;
DP, 8;	SP, 5;	DP, 8;	CD, 18;	RKW, 19;	19;	JK, 10;	JK, 10;	TLP, 20;
RY, 8;	DP, 8;	JK, 10;	EY, 23;	FG, 19;	HK, 16;	WN, 13;	VIM, 11;	PE, 20;
JK, 10;	BR, 10;	MS, 17;	OU, 23;	OU, 20;	MS, 17;	DK, 14;	WN, 13;	SY, 21;
WN, 13;	JK, 10;	WN, 17;	OW, 28;	NT, 23;	WN, 17;	MS, 17;	MS, 17;	VO, 31;
JS, 16;	LT, 12;	CD, 18;	110, 114;	VC, 23;	CD, 18;	WN, 17;	CD, 18;	TK, 32;
MS, 17;	WN, 13;	NT, 18;	TK, 32;	CU, 26;	RKW, 19;	NT, 18;	TLP, 20;	NK, 33;
CD, 18;	MS, 17;	RKW, 19;	NO, 33;	AP, 27;	CU, 26;	CD, 18;	PE, 20;	KP, 34;
FG, 19;	CD, 18;	TLP, 20;	TN, 33;	ES, 28;	AP, 27;	DW, 19;	AR, 22;	OK, 37;
PE, 20;	RKW, 19;	PE, 20;	TT, 33;	NO, 33;	OW, 28;	RKW, 19;	AK, 22;	JS, 42;
TLP, 20;	SY, 20;	AR, 22;	NO, 33;	TN, 33;	110, 114;	AR, 22;	MP, 27;	CI, 55;
AR, 22;	AR, 22;	AK, 22;	UV, 34;	GL, 33;	ES, 28;	CU, 26;	VO, 31;	DP, 55;
AK, 22;	AC, 22;	CU, 26;	KP, 34;	NJ, 34;	HK, 32;	OW, 28;	TK, 32;	NO, 63;
VC, 23;	AK, 22;	VO, 31;	BN, 35;	LT, 38;	TN, 33;	110, 114;	NO, 33;	LL, 72;
OW, 28;	TK, 32;	TK, 32;	OK, 37;	LE, 39;	GL, 33;	TT, 33;	NK, 33;	CIE, 73;
VO, 31;	KP, 34;	GL, 33;	LE, 38;	48, 55;	NJ, 34;	TN, 33;	SP, 40;	EC, 80;
GL, 33;	OK, 37;	NK, 33;	LT, 38;	LK, 47;	LE, 38;	GL, 33;	CAP, 40;	ES, 85;
NK, 33;	PK, 38;	KP, 34;	48, 55;	AP, 47;	LT, 38;	NJ, 34;	MP, 41;	TC, 90;
UV, 34;	NN, 52;	NJ, 34;	LK, 47;	TT, 49;	AP, 47;	UV, 34;	LK, 47;	NV, 90;
OK, 37;	EV, 72;	OK, 37;	OF, 44;	LV, 56;	48, 55;	BN, 35;	NL, 49;	PS, 108;
LT, 38;	LL, 72;	DP, 55;	LK, 47;	ZI, 71;	ZI, 71;	OK, 37;	TT, 49;	FC, 110
MB, 40;	CIE, 73;	CI, 55;	AP, 47;	NO, 80;	CIE, 73;	LT, 38;	DP, 55;	
AP, 47;	DS, 78;	ZI, 71;	TT, 49;	OI, 88;	NV, 90;	LE, 38;	CI, 55;	
48, 55;	KL, 82;	LL, 72;	LV, 56;	CT, 98;	CT, 98,	OF, 44;	TL, 63;	
TT, 49	UK, 90;	CIE, 73;	SI, 57;	AL, 98;	101	AP, 47;	ES, 68;	
GC, 50;	TC, 90;	DS, 78;	NT, 66;	VB, 98;		SS, 48,	DS, 78;	
CI, 55;	NV, 90	NO, 80;	LO, 71;	TT, 99;		55;	JT, 81;	
DP, 55;		TC, 90;	LL, 72;	CS, 101;		SI, 57;	LT, 85;	
LV, 56;		NV, 90;	CIE, 73;	CVD, 114		ZI, 71;	AV, 92;	
TB, 60;		TC, 90	POV, 78;			CIE, 73;	AL, 98;	
NY, 66;			TC, 90;			POV, 78;	SN, 101	
LL, 72;			NV, 90;			NO, 80;		
DS, 78;			KP, 94;			TC, 90;		
ES, 85;			CT, 98;			NV, 90;		
EB, 91;			101;			CT, 98,		
TS, 92;			VB, 98			101		
RS, 96;								
AL, 98;								
VB, 98;								
CS, 101;								
MS, 108;								
FC, 110								

The once neatly organized transcripts had become a sprawling white paper landscape across the bedspread and over the floor. The chart alone remained ordered and clean. Lina studied the names, the frequency and types of harms; she cross-referenced gender and location, age and origin. But no pattern appeared. The harm was everyone and everywhere.

Lina's eyes hurt, her fingers hurt, her laptop lay heavy and hot against the top of her thighs. A waking dream of all that she had read flashed in colorless cutout silhouettes across her vision. Lina wrote on her yellow legal pad: *The harm is* <u>*immeasurable*</u>.

Outside a car passed; the arc of its headlight roamed the ceiling and disappeared. From above came the dull thumps of Oscar's footsteps as he wandered the fourth-floor studio. Lina had not seen or spoken to him since the night before; she had tried not to think about the pictures of Grace. The dinner-plate eyes with the empty centers.

Enough.

On Lina's wall hung a series of pictures Grace had made before Lina was born. Four small pencil sketches, portraits no larger than an apple, but the detail extraordinary, each wrinkle and eyelash precisely drawn. An old woman pursing her lips, annoyed, her hair a helmet of tightly wound curls. A teenager with a Mohawk and a row of earrings, a placid, satisfied smile curling his lips. Each was labeled with an obscure family reference scripted in elaborate scrolling letters: *Sister's Nephew's Son, Fourth Cousin Once Removed, Grandmother's Uncle.* Lina had no idea if these people were actually Grace's relations, and thus also her own, or Grace's friends, neighbors on their block, or people Grace had passed once on the sidewalk. Lina grew up envying these strangers, for they had been the subjects of Grace's attention in a way that Lina had not: Lina had never seen any pictures of herself made by Grace, a fact that still managed to cause a mystified little jolt of hurt whenever she considered it.

Upstairs, the studio door opened and closed, followed by the sound of Oscar's feet on the stairs and then moving down the hall to Lina's door.

"Come in," Lina called before Oscar had a chance to knock on the half-cracked door.

Oscar pushed the door fully open with a creak of old hinge and leaned against the frame, hands in pockets. He looked disheveled and tired. "Just wanted to say good night. Working hard?" and he pointed his chin toward the papers and books that covered the bed.

"New case," said Lina. "I'm trying to get up to speed."

"Hey, I've been meaning to ask you—whatever happened to Stavros?" Oscar said with careful indifference. "I haven't heard you talk about him in a while."

"We broke up." Lina turned back to the papers. Stavros, with his wire rims, the unprotected nape of his neck, how Lina had thrilled at the sight of him in the beginning. Neither of them had changed, not exactly, it was just circumstances—this is what they had told each other—and timing. That one long phone conversation (four hours? five?) and neither of them had cried or yelled, the decision was made mutually, amicably, responsibly. She knew she should have told Oscar about the breakup months ago. He had always liked Stavros, despite their vast differences in political beliefs and chosen professions.

"I thought you guys were pretty serious," Oscar said.

"We were, I guess. I mean, four years is a long time. But it just didn't make much sense. He's in San Francisco. We're both working so much."

"Love doesn't always make sense, Carolina."

"Dad. Please. You sound like a greeting card." Annoyed, she looked up at him and was surprised to see his face so drawn. His eyes roamed over the papers on Lina's bed, the piles of books, the open notebook with all her scribbling. "I'm fine, you know," she said quickly. "Maybe I'm just waiting. Waiting for something like you and Mom had." Lina wanted her father to know that this wasn't all she expected out of life, work and late nights and a burning laptop, but somehow these words landed wrong. Oscar's face registered a hurt shock and then closed up, and Lina immediately regretted having mentioned her mother.

Oscar shifted away from the doorframe, and his eyes went to the floor. "Well, I will take my greeting-card self downstairs to bed then. Good night, Carolina." He did not blow her a kiss, as Lina was expecting. He shut the door behind him.

"Good night," she called after him, feeling as if she should apologize to him, though for what she wasn't sure. The breakup with Stavros? The greeting-card remark? The choices she had made, was making every day, to build a life so different from his own?

Turning to her bedside table, Lina picked up the photograph of Oscar and Grace, the original of the reprint that Lina kept in her office. In the photo, her parents sat at a restaurant, the curving mouths of two wineglasses just visible at the bottom of the frame. Oscar's left arm circled Grace's shoulders; Grace's hands were hidden but Lina had always imagined that they must be holding Oscar's right hand under the table—look at how closely they were sitting, look at the intimacy. Oscar seemed so young—no beard, his hair shaggy and falling into his eyes, his smile exuberant. Grace was turned toward him, a smile there too, one visible eye shining, looking up at him with love and pride. The photo was taken after Oscar's first important show, a group show, but the gallery was trendy, and he had sold a painting. One painting! It had seemed impossible, amazing, like they were on their way, Oscar had said. Nine months later, Grace was dead.

A wintry sweep of road, going where? The car—what kind? A tree, a telephone pole, a concrete divide. Grace alone. Had she been alone? Blood on the front seat, a splintered windshield, a body thrown, dark hair fanned across red-spotted snow. It had been years since Lina had thought about her mother's death, really wondered about the specifics that once had seemed so essential to know. But Lina's imagination now unfurled these images in vivid color and excruciating detail.

For years, from late childhood and into her early teens, Lina had followed dark-haired women she passed on the street or saw on the subway. She looked for those who seemed about the age her mother would have been—mid- to late thirties—and she stalked them quietly, harmlessly, down Manhattan sidewalks, into the post office or the bank, as they shopped for groceries or sat in a café with friends. It was something she did with a complicated thrill of fear and excitement and guilt. She never bothered them. She took nothing from them. She spoke to only one, a woman wearing a long dark-green coat whom Lina followed one late afternoon of the winter she turned fifteen, a bitterly cold day, the air heavy and gray and smelling of metal. She had seen the woman first on the subway, exited behind her to the street and followed her east along Seventy-seventh Street in Manhattan. Snow was falling, restless flyaway snow that scattered across the sidewalk and onto the arms of Lina's coat and her bare head. She followed the woman as the sidewalk disappeared under shifting layers of snow and Lina's hair crackled with ice. Suddenly the woman stopped and turned to face her. The block was empty, apart from the two of them, and the woman's eyes were wide and frightened.

"Why are you following me?" she asked.

Lina had been so startled by the sound of the woman's voice—high and nervous—that she almost turned and fled. "I'm—I'm not following you," she stammered.

"Yes, you are," said the woman, seeming less afraid now. "You've been behind me for blocks. I saw you on the subway. I saw you looking at me. Why are you doing this?"

Now that the woman faced her, Lina could see that she was in fact much older than Grace would have been, hair threaded with gray, her face lined around the mouth and purple beneath the eyes.

And it was this that made Lina say, "It's nothing. I have to get home now," and she turned and walked back, past the silent brooding brownstones of the Upper East Side, to the subway stop where she had first exited, some five paces behind the woman, wanting to see where she would go, wanting to see the life that she—this woman who looked like Grace—was leading.

The sound of water rushing through creaky pipes filled Lina's room—Oscar brushing his teeth—followed by muffled thuds from below of drawers closing, floorboards groaning as he prepared for bed. Lina heard the oddly distinct click of his bedside lamp turning off, and then silence. Again she looked at the photo of her parents, at her mother's shining gaze. She remembered the snow on that day, and the shock at seeing the lined, frightened, tired face of the woman and realizing that no, this woman was not her, this woman could never have been my mother.

Josephine

Josephine became aware of Missus' voice, a faint repetitive calling, almost like a bird, but with a sharp insistence. "Josephine! Josephine!" The sound startled her, and she could not say if this was the first time or the tenth that Missus had said her name.

Opening the bedroom door, Josephine found Missus sitting on the bed, her back to the door, long hair loose on her shoulders. It was close on midday now and sunlight filtered in through the two south-facing windows directly opposite Missus, the ones Josephine had looked to from the garden earlier that day; two others on the west wall were dark with the curtains drawn. Only the window closest to Missus was open and the room still breathed with the smell of Dr. Vickers and his poultices.

"Dr. Vickers has gone, Missus," Josephine said. "It's coming up for dinnertime. Let's get you back in your dress."

Missus nodded vigorously, the uneven ends of her dark hair rising and falling across her back. "Yes, yes, the doctor. Josephine, I am not right today, not right at all."

She turned and Josephine saw blood on her face, a deep cut horizontal along the curve of the left cheek, the gash ugly and open and bleeding. A look of satisfaction or pride flashed across Missus' eyes, and then it was gone and there was fear and pain.

"Missus, what's happened?" Josephine ran to the bed and took

Missus' face into her hands. Bone flashed white underneath the blood and Josephine pushed the edges together. The cut was straight and true and they met neatly like two broadcloth seams for sewing. Josephine pulled a corner of sheet off the bed and ripped a strip of cotton, the tearing sound loud and awful in the room. She held the strip to Missus' cheek, pushing against the cut, but the bleeding went on and on, drips running down Josephine's wrist and into the sleeve of her dress. Throughout, Missus Lu remained silent, surrendering herself to Josephine's ministrations, her eyes blank, her breathing shallow.

Finally Josephine released Missus Lu's face and gingerly removed the strip of sheet, now heavy with blood. "Did the doctor do this?" Josephine asked.

Missus Lu said nothing, just gave a long deep sigh, and then, "Josephine, you are a dear girl. Who do you think did this? Who do you think?" She smiled with a slyness that Josephine had not seen before. "It was me. Who else? I have no need for this face anymore. I heard what the doctor said. I listened by the door, I heard the things he said to you. I am dying."

"Missus, don't—" Josephine began but found she could not continue. She went to the bowl and jug and washed her hands, wrung out her dress sleeve as best she could, wet a cloth for Missus. It was words of comfort that Missus wanted. She wanted Josephine to contradict her, to say, "No, Missus, you heard wrong what the doctor said. He said nothing wrong here, no need for my services here." Perhaps on a different day, Josephine would have said this. She had done so in the past, at other times when comfort was needed. She had smoothed Missus' hair and held her hand and rubbed her back, like a sister or a mother or a daughter would.

But today Josephine's mouth could not say the words. She felt herself separate from the room, from Missus Lu, from the sun on the floorboards, from the bloody residue still sticky on her fingers, as though she lived according to a set of principles that applied only to her, the principles having to do purely with escape. Every nerve was tensed and every muscle flexed toward this one goal, flight, and the simple tasks she did every day, the things she touched, the words that came from her mouth—*Yes, Missus; Yes, Mister*—all bound her to this place, and she wanted to shed them all, shake them from her as a dog shakes water from its coat. Part of Josephine was already gone, through the gate, turning left on the road to town. As the sparrow did, Josephine would point her head like an arrow and fly there.

Josephine brought the wet cloth to the bed. She sat close beside Missus and took her face in hand to clean the cut. The blood had not yet dried and it came away easily, leaving the skin raw pink and puffy. Missus Lu winced from the scrubbing but did not pull away. "I used to be a great beauty, you know," Missus said. "My sisters all despised me for it. My mother and daddy, oh, they were so afraid when they saw me in my birthday dress. At thirteen, I was irresistible. Thirteen, can you imagine?"

Missus pushed Josephine's hands away and rose from the bed. She walked to the end of the room and threw open the curtains of the far windows, bringing a sudden rush of light. Josephine's eyes narrowed and she put a hand out to shade them as she looked down and away from the glare. Her gaze went to the windowsill. There, a kitchen carving knife, the blade streaked red. This was what Missus had used, a knife from her own kitchen.

From across the room, Missus Lu's voice was measured: "I have lived more years here than at my daddy's farm. Did you know that? My, how it smarts." Missus shook her head. "I have wasted so much. Almost everything, I know that's true. I have a little beauty left and this I will pass along to you. Pass it to you, Josephine. There is no one else." As she spoke, she walked slowly back toward Josephine, her fingers trailing against the wall and then against the glass of the windows as she passed each one. "My face was a beauty, wasn't it? I was a great beauty."

Missus Lu neared the last window and then lunged toward the knife on the sill, fingers grasping for the handle. Josephine was ready. She jumped from the bed and grabbed Missus' shoulders, pushing her away from the window, back against the wall, and she held Missus there as she struggled. Josephine's breath came fast with the strain but she knew she could keep her. Missus surely weighed no more than a child. Nothing more than sinew and bone.

Missus Lu stopped struggling and let her head hang down, but her breath still raced, and Josephine did not release her. They stood like that until Missus Lu crumpled to the floor, crying softly. "You don't understand," she said. "That's all I have to give you, Josephine. There's nothing more."

Leaving Missus Lu against the wall, Josephine walked to the open window. She picked the knife off the sill and threw it long and hard through the window, onto the front lawn. It landed blade down, the carved bone handle poking from the long grass, nearly obscured. She watched it for a moment, until a breeze stirred, the landscape shifted, and the handle disappeared into the green. Josephine turned back to Missus.

"Come now, let's get you cleaned up for dinner."

"Leave me, just leave me here. I am so very tired." Missus' legs were bent beneath her. The neck of her chemise gaped wide and exposed the thin jut of her collarbone.

Again a shadow of pity passed across Josephine's vision and she blinked her eyes fast to clear it. She went to Missus Lu on the floor, helped her to stand and led her to the bed.

"Lay back," Josephine said, and sat beside her. Josephine re-wet the cloth and wiped away the remaining blood from the cut. Carefully she held Missus' face in her hand, turning it to clean the skin thoroughly, until it shone wet and new. Missus closed her eyes.

"No more of this, Missus."

"Yes, Josephine."

Missus lay back against the pillows, her breath evened out, her features softened. Missus Lu now was so altered from the Missus who had walked down the path to fetch Josephine those years ago. The cheeks more hollow, the hair more sparse, her whole person washed and wrung out in the muddy shallows of the river. Josephine did believe what Missus had said; she could still see the beauty that had been there. The bones of the face, the ripeness of the lips. Those things would be with her until she died.

What Josephine felt for Missus now was sour and sweet, hot and cold, a flash of tenderness so sharp that Josephine longed to slap her across the face, or dig her nails into the softness of Missus' arm, the skin pink beneath a screen of fine dark hairs. Missus was not Josephine's protector, not her confidante, not her friend. But Missus had taught her to read, she had washed the sweat from Josephine's face when she was eleven years old and so feverish she had collapsed in the kitchen, her cheek pressed against the coolness of the stones. A dress that Missus had grown tired of, she gave it to Josephine. Cotton with small blue flowers and stems of green printed in rows. Josephine had worn that dress every Sunday until the buttons would not close along the back, no matter how deeply she inhaled and pressed her breasts and stomach down to flatten them. She had wept when the buttons would not close, for the dress was the prettiest thing she had ever held in her hands.

Josephine never knew the name of her daddy. Lottie always said it must have been a white man on account of Josephine's tawny skin and the blue threads in her eyes. Missus Lu brought Josephine up from the cabins at seven years old, after Missus had lost another baby. The farm had still been producing well then; Mister had twenty-one field hands working the tobacco and wheat, a barn that housed eight cows and five horses, and beside it the curing barn for readying tobacco for sale. Mister hadn't wanted Josephine; he wanted to buy a new house girl and put Josephine in the fields. But Missus had insisted.

Missus Lu used to go down to where the field-hand children played, over by the tall oak with the roots that rose and twisted away from the earth so there were places to hide underneath, cool and dark. Missus would sit on a root and clap her hands with the children, sing songs, play hidey seek. Josephine was the one Missus would look for longest. After all the others had tired of the game and wandered away, Missus would circle the tree again and again, calling, "Where are you, Josephine? Where are you?" She would give Josephine the largest biscuit, or a new shirttail, once a rag doll, and the other children teased her for it, even shunned her sometimes in their games, once Missus Lu had gone back up to the house and they were left alone again.

Lottie would tell Josephine that the others were only jealous, and she should use Missus Lu's attention. More and better food, something warm for wintertime, extra blanket for her bed. Lessons maybe.

And so Josephine had gone up to the house without tears or tantrum the day after Missus Lu came down to the cabins. Lottie and Winton had just returned from the fields, Lottie heating collards and salt pork over an open fire in the yard, and Winton on the cabin steps carving at a piece of birch, making a spoon or toy that perhaps he'd sell on Sunday to white folk for a penny. Josephine sat on the ground beside the fire, smelling the supper, her stomach rolling in anticipation, waiting for Lottie to be finished and a steel plate to be passed her way. Winton and Lottie saw Missus first; they looked up in unison at her. Josephine's eyes were intent on the black pot, so she only saw Lottie's head turn and thought with dismay that something would now delay the meal.

But then Josephine heard the voice, soft and wavering, apologetic in a way but stating a fact, not an item for debate, not something that could be questioned. "Lottie, Winton, we're bringing Josephine up to the house, train her as a house girl. Tonight will be the last she'll sleep down here with you." Josephine looked up at Missus Lu, so much like a creature from a storybook, her dress a pale yellow, and silk slippers that winked out from beneath her skirts.

"Why yes, Missus," said Lottie, without hesitation, as though she'd been asked for the use of Winton's old rake, standing there against the side of the cabin.

Josephine heard what Missus said, the words like a hard pinch. But then came Lottie's calm approval, as if letting Josephine go would mean nothing to her, as though she were just a child who slept on her floor, ate from her pot. Josephine wanted to cry out and run toward Lottie and shake her, shake sense into her that no, Lottie could not let Missus Lu take her away. How could she do such a thing?

But Lottie turned slowly to Josephine and nodded her head just so, and Winton resumed carving the birch piece in his hand, the sound of wood chips hitting the dirt. Missus Lu stood awkwardly in her toy slippers just a few steps from the pot, which was bubbling now on the fire, ready to be eaten. All this told Josephine in a matter of seconds that she would go, there was no stopping it. Some things there was no stopping, most things in fact.

Josephine looked at Missus Lu. "Yes, Missus," she said. "Thank you, Missus."

Missus Lu turned to leave and they all watched her go. Just as the path turned back up toward the house, Missus Lu slipped in the spring mud and nearly lost her balance. Neither Winton nor Lottie moved to help her and Missus didn't look back as though expecting anyone to, just righted herself, her skirts now muddied at the hem, and continued on.

The next morning Lottie had sent Josephine up the path to the house alone.

Lina

Lina woke late and went down for breakfast. Oscar was standing at the stove in jeans and a paint-stained CBGB T-shirt. Positioned on a burner glowing red was Oscar's favorite piece of domestic equipment, a cast-iron waffle maker circa 1951, a time when household appliances required careful handling. Oscar enjoyed the danger inherent in the thing and liked to show off a thick straight scar across his left palm where once, years ago, he'd hastily gripped the hot iron handle. This was Oscar's sole contribution to their meals: every Saturday morning, for as long as Lina could remember, he made waffles.

For a moment, Lina stood in the kitchen doorway. Nina Simone was playing and Oscar hummed along as he lifted high the bowl and poured batter onto the waffle iron, the sizzle and steam and baked butter smell rising into their colorful, sunlit kitchen. The scene pulsed with a comfortable rhythm and yet Lina sensed a tension, some kind of nervousness, maybe in Oscar's shoulders, or the way he remained at the stove, not turning to face her. Or maybe it was just her, still half-asleep, still vaguely guilty from the night before—

the greeting-card comment, not having told her father about Stavros. With a loud yawn, Lina stepped into the kitchen.

"Morning, Carolina," Oscar said, turning finally to face her, and planted a quick kiss on her cheek. She took a juice glass from the cupboard, fork and knife from the drawer, and sat at the table. Oscar's back was to her, his head down. The song ended and the only sound was the faint silky pour of syrup from bottle to jug. Lina scratched her ankle and waited for the waffles.

Her father turned toward her and, yes, there was a nervousness in him. He cleared his throat, his eyes darted away and then returned to her. "Carolina, about the paintings—do you want to talk? I meant it the other night, I want to tell you about Grace. You can ask whatever the hell you want to ask. You don't have to worry, I swear."

The pictures came back to Lina with immediate clarity, as though Oscar had hung them here, in the kitchen, above the sink, and she had only now noticed: *Enough,* the woman drowning within the blue, the kneecap, the scalp. And along with the pictures came the same raw, splintered feeling that had so overwhelmed her that night. She hadn't known what to call it then, but now she recognized the feeling for what it was: fear. Lina rarely acknowledged a fear of anything, spiders or darkness or death, but now she took it in, this understanding that she was terrified of what her father might tell her. The quiet laugh? The tune? What if none of that were true?

Lina dropped her gaze to the checkerboard linoleum floor, the table with the curved wooden legs, scarred with age and cigarette burns from Oscar's long-gone parties. How many times had Lina sat at this table? On how many Saturdays had she eaten Oscar's waffles and maybe they would go to a movie afterward, or walk across to Prospect Park, or Lina would go running, Oscar head to the pool? Lina had lived so many days without knowing about Grace. She had never needed the truth. Look at all she had achieved, and now she was poised to climb to the top of another ladder, this one bigger and better than any that had come before. Clifton & Harp LLP, partner track, and each year would bring her closer to the prize: a seven-figure salary, a corner office, a solidly successful life that no one could take away from her.

Raising her head, Lina met Oscar's gaze. "I'm ready for some waffles," she said. "Two—no, three if you've got them."

Oscar looked at her for a beat, unsure, and then lifted a piece of foil off a platter and forked three waffles onto a clean plate. Leaning over the table, he placed one hand on her shoulder and set the food before her.

"I have a new case," Lina said brightly and shrugged off his hand. "Reparations for slavery. A class action."

Oscar stood unmoving for a moment, and it seemed they both hesitated, uncertain how to proceed. Their days together had never included Grace, not the image of her, not her name. Lina looked up at Oscar, his lips thin, his cheeks a little red from the heat of cooking, and she understood that he did not know how to do this either; they had waited too long.

"You've got to be kidding," Oscar said at last, and he grinned, the nervousness gone, and Lina recognized his relief because it matched her own. "Good old Clifton & Harp is looking into reparations for *slavery*?"

"There's a big client who's funding the case."

"Of course there is. Oh, my lovely Carolina, I will never understand why you choose to spend your days with a bunch of money-hungry corporate bozos."

"As compared to your unemployed artist-friend bozos?" Lina flashed a smile; she had heard this particular rail before. Oscar was a proud subscriber to *Mother Jones*. He talked often of retiring to Sweden.

"Point taken. Some of my friends are indeed bozos, but they are at least *nice* and *poor* bozos." Oscar placed the syrup on the table. "But I mean, what is Clifton getting out of a reparations suit?"

"Well, money. A lot, if we get a settlement or win. But there's more to it than just that." She described the case to Oscar in the terms Dresser had used. Truth. Justice. Reparations paid into a fund for scholarships, education, memorials, community building. Naming the names, clarifying the past. Celebrating those who had died as slaves. Honoring them. And Lina's immediate task: to find a lead plaintiff. Someone (photogenic) whose ancestors were slaves and whose injury was representative of the injury suffered by the class.

Lina finished. Oscar, surprisingly, had listened without comment or critique.

He said, "You know, that's actually the most I've heard about any of your cases since you started at Clifton. I withhold all judgment. It's nice to see you this enthusiastic."

Lina smiled around a mouthful of waffle. Oscar was sitting at the table now, working at his own plate of waffles amid the general mayhem of a deconstructed *New York Times*.

"Carolina, look at this," Oscar said with sudden focus. He handed her the Arts section, folded over to a headline: LU ANNE BELL—GENIUS OR FAKE? "This reminds me of something. Hold on." Oscar jumped up. As his slippers shushed down the hallway and into the living room, Lina skimmed through the article: masterpieces, Lu Anne Bell, house girl, mistake, fraud. Oscar returned, holding a thick white envelope.

"Here. This might interest you."

Lina set down the newspaper and lifted the envelope's flap. Inside was an invitation: heavy cream paper embossed with the name *Calhoun Gallery* in dark-red ink. Lina knew the gallery, a storefront in Chelsea painted lacquer red, its owner, Marie Calhoun, an old friend of Oscar's. The invitation read:

THE ART AND ARTIFICE OF LU ANNE BELL

Much has been written about the early death and turbulent life of the southern painter Lu Anne Bell. An artist with no formal training, she rendered masterpieces of everyday life on the failing tobacco farm where she lived and died. Her work provokes questions of class, race, poverty, and the pernicious effects and moral bankruptcy of the "peculiar institution," slavery in the antebellum South. She has been embraced by modern feminists and civil rights activists as a woman who, due to the constraints of the society in which she lived, expressed her beliefs in the only way she could: through her art.

Or did she?

Art historians now question the true authenticity of the Bell oeuvre. Famously, Lu Anne Bell signed none of her art. New evidence strongly suggests that the author of the masterful Bell works was not Lu Anne Bell but in fact her house girl, the adolescent slave Josephine. Josephine Bell's parentage remains unknown, as does her fate following Lu Anne Bell's death in 1852, but her legacy may live on.

The Calhoun Gallery is proud to present this compelling exhibition, The Art and Artifice of Lu Anne Bell. *On display for the first time anywhere will be newly discovered paintings now believed to be the work of Josephine Bell. Alongside them will be major works previously attributed to Lu Anne Bell. We will have on hand art historians and authenticity experts to lead discussion and evaluation of the new and previously known works that will permit you to reach your own conclusion: Who was the master? Lu Anne Bell or Josephine Bell?*

Please join us for this landmark show.

On view will be the iconic Bell paintings Lottie, Jackson with Whip, The House at Dawn, *and* Children No. 2, *as well as other rarely seen Bell works from private collections.*

*Special lecture by Porter Scales, critic, art historian, and
expert on the work of Lu Anne Bell.
Opening night, June 24, 2004
7:00 P.M.*

Lina knew of Lu Anne Bell's work from a college art history
class. A woman born into privilege on a Mississippi cotton plantation. No formal artistic training. Disowned by her family after she
eloped with a man deemed unsuitable, Robert Bell, the son of an
itinerant fundamentalist preacher. She died young, only forty-three
years old, after a debilitating illness, childless, living the last years of
her life in virtual seclusion, never reconciling with her family. Her
paintings were said to portray the humanity of the slaves her husband owned, a tacit challenge to the southern plantation society into
which she had been born.

"What do you think?" Oscar said. "Maybe there's something in
there for your case? A Josephine Bell descendant for your plaintiff?"

Lina gave a tentative nod. "I could see Dan getting into this," she
said. "He likes controversy, and publicity. But it doesn't say if Josephine had any children. Or if she's got any descendants alive today."

"I can call Marie, if you're interested. I'm sure she'd know."
Oscar pushed himself up from the table. "I haven't seen Marie in
years," he said, half to himself. "It would be good to reconnect." He
began to clear away the plates, sticky with syrup, and Lina jumped
up to help him.

UPSTAIRS, STILL IN HER PAJAMAS, Lina opened a search on
her computer and typed: Lu Anne Bell; Josephine Bell; Virginia.
Pages of information about Lu Anne appeared. Scholarly articles,
reproduced images, art journal pieces, feminist theories on her life
and work, fan websites, even a site apparently established by and
for artistic, angst-ridden teenage girls. Finally Lina brought up the

website for the Bell Center for Women and Art, a museum and artists' retreat located at Lu Anne Bell's former home in Lynnhurst, Virginia. Lina clicked through photos of Bell paintings and the Bell Creek grounds, biographical information about Lu Anne, and financial statements released by the Stanmore Foundation, the organization that funded and operated the Bell Center.

But in 2.7 billable hours of research, Lina found only a few passing references to Josephine Bell.

And one photograph.

Lina stopped her mouse and narrowed her eyes. The pixelated screen glowed silver. It was a black-and-white image, degraded as though covered in dust or viewed through a screen. The caption read *Lu Anne Bell and house slave Josephine, Bell Creek, 1852*. A dark-haired white woman sat in a rocking chair on the porch of a house. Her dress was pale with voluminous skirts folded around her, her hair parted in the middle and gathered up in an elaborate style, with a forward curling section on each side, covering her ears. Lu Anne Bell wore the barest of smiles. Her hands were clasped tightly in her lap. Next to her stood a young black woman, her hair pulled completely away from her face, her brown skin clear, the face broad, with high cheekbones and full lips. Even in such a poor reproduction Lina could see the beauty there. The eyes had a lightness to them, as though colored blue or green, and a sense of movement. Josephine's shoulders were straight and square, rigid with a sense of anticipation. Josephine did not smile; she looked levelly into the camera, her face inscrutable. The camera had been placed so that the entire front of the house fit within the photographic frame, and it seemed that it was the house, not the women, that the photographer had sought to capture. The women had been there, on the porch, they had stopped where they were, not with any enthusiasm but perhaps with a sense of duty, a wish to not be bothersome. *Yes, we will remain still. Yes, we will direct our gaze toward the camera.*

Lu Anne Bell died in 1852, the same year the photo was taken. According to the Calhoun Gallery, nothing more was known about Josephine after that date.

Had Josephine known then, standing on the porch beside Lu Anne, that her world was about to change? Josephine's head was poised and erect, held carefully, perhaps at the request of the photographer or perhaps because she had reason to move through her days with care. Josephine's hands were clasped before her, the fingers tensely intertwined as though one hand pulled the other from a turbulent sea. Her eyes were fogged as if in motion. Perhaps she had looked beyond the photographer. Perhaps she had contemplated the road ahead.

Josephine

Hot strong sun came through the bedroom windows as Missus Lu slept, the cut on her face still red and raw.

Dinner, thought Josephine. Mister would be coming in soon for his dinner and nothing yet prepared. *Today like any other day.* Josephine rose from the bed and started toward the door, but her eyes caught and she stopped. There beneath the half-opened wardrobe door, cast half in shadow, were Missus' good boots, the ones she wore for trips to town, calling, church.

Josephine would need shoes. She had not worn them the first time and it had been an error she remembered for many weeks upon her return, hobbling on tender soles.

Josephine eased herself back into the room, to the wardrobe, and with a quick hand snatched up the boots. They were short, made of brown leather with pewter buttons that fastened off-center, a low heel, good for walking, the bottoms worn but not cracked. Missus had her house slippers, and soon enough she'd be wearing her winter boots, the ones lined in gray flannel. These others she would not miss, surely not for today. Josephine would keep Missus indoors for the afternoon, under Doctor's advisement. Rest, frivolous things, perhaps they would read aloud together or Missus might sit with embroidery on her lap. Boots would not be missed.

Josephine glanced quickly at Missus, who sighed and turned from her back to her side and then was still.

The boots were too bulky to fit under Josephine's apron or skirts so she carried them low with one hand, her arm straight, her eyes pegged to Missus' sleeping form, as she left the room. She would ascend the creaking flight up to the attic. She would walk slowly, avoid the weak spots where the wood had gone soft and complaining, careful not to disturb Missus with the noise. Under her sleeping pallet, she would hide the boots for later.

Josephine stepped to the attic door and at that moment heard outside the rattling of a horse and wheels on dirt. No one was expected. Callers were rare at Bell Creek, and the peddler had passed already for the season, his cart loaded with wares for the winter, harness bits and wool, tallow candles, poultices, spices and sweets. Perhaps the doctor had returned? Or a slave from the Stanmores, sent to borrow a bucket or a scythe?

Gazing out the hall window, Josephine saw beside the barn a buggy she did not recognize and a woman's figure descending from the bench, a dark dress and white petticoats hanging low as she angled herself down to the ground. The woman wore leather riding gloves that she removed, picking at each finger with strong little pulls and glancing all around her, at the barn, the gate, the row of fruited apple trees. The woman's body was short and rounded in the chest, at the backside, and her waist was stout so that the cloth of her dress seemed to strain to contain the all of her. Josephine did not immediately recognize the caller, and she narrowed her eyes to better make out the face, but a bonnet cast the woman's features in shadow.

The woman walked with purpose up the path to the front door and Josephine heard knocking and the woman's voice, shrill and frilly, "Yoo hoo, it's Melly Clayton, come to call."

Josephine looked down at the shoes in her hand. She could not now go upstairs to her room—the caller might wake Missus with her shouts, or Josephine would with her hasty up-and-down the steep attic steps. Josephine placed the shoes just inside the studio door, unobtrusive, half-hidden in shadow. Later, she would pass this way and retrieve them.

Josephine hurried downstairs and opened the front door.

"Good day," said Melly Clayton, looking beyond Josephine. "I've come to see Mrs. Bell. I passed the doctor on the road this morning and he said she was most unwell. Is she accepting visitors?"

Melly Clayton did not wait for an answer but stepped into the house. She untied her bonnet and handed it, limp with damp, to Josephine. Now Josephine could see her face well: rosy in the cheeks, blond hair darkened around the crown with sweat, not young but not yet old. Her round pale eyes were set too close together and gave her a cunning look, like a ferret or a stoat, and her chin sloped away at a lazy angle into the doughy flesh of her neck. No, Josephine decided, this Melly Clayton had not called before at Bell Creek. She watched as the woman's too-close eyes roamed over all that could be seen in the entry: a portrait of brother Henry Bell done in dusky oils that hung at the foot of the stairs, the small chandelier missing dozens of its crystal pieces but still it glittered like a night sky, the umbrella stand, and beside it the small table with its single drawer.

"Mrs. Bell's asleep upstairs," Josephine said. "I'll tell her that you called. Perhaps you can come again tomorrow?" She said these words with little hope that Melly Clayton would indeed leave. The woman had in her something sly and determined, a purpose that would not easily be put off.

"Oh, no, why don't I wait. A midmorning nap never lasts more'n a few minutes. And I am very eager to express my condolences for her condition, and to see if there is anything that I can do to assist. Dr. Vickers instructed that I come here straightaway and I do not intend to cross him!" Melly gave a sharp, high laugh and wandered into the parlor. She turned and stared at Josephine. "Tea?" she said.

Josephine left the room. In the kitchen, she set the kettle on the hot coals for Melly Clayton's tea and placed a cup and saucer on a painted wooden tray. In the cupboard there was a tin of store-bought biscuits that Mister had brought back from Richmond last Christmas. Missus Lu would present them to callers, arranged prettily on a plate, each in its own red wrapper with the ends twisted. Josephine had never tasted one but the discarded papers smelled of almond and butter and a faint bitterness, like the rind of an orange. She opened the tin and inhaled deeply as she always did, and this was almost enough, the smell so full and rich. Just a few remained and Josephine wondered, did Melly Clayton merit such attentions? No, not with her coarse manner, those plump hands and calculating eyes. Josephine replaced the biscuit tin in the cupboard and looked for a moment upon its half-filled shelves.

Quickly, she took out three short biscuits, an apple, ashcake, salted pork, a half-loaf of bread. She pulled a tea towel from a drawer and spread the cloth on the long, low cutting table built from oak planks taller than a man, the table she had used for husking corn, cutting meat, skinning fish and rabbits, opening oysters, cracking eggs, kneading bread. And now, here, food for her journey. She folded the checked square end-over-end, knotted the corners together, the food inside. The kettle began to rush with steam, and Josephine plucked it from the coals and poured the tea. And what to do now with the bundle? She surveyed the kitchen she knew so well, every pocket and corner, but each hiding place seemed only to trumpet her theft. Then her eyes settled on a spot. By the back door was a table, a nest of gourd bowls upon it, a place easy to pass by unnoticed, where later she might pause for a moment, reach out a hand, then glide silently out the door. Josephine placed the bundle there, behind the bowls.

She smoothed her skirts and the frizz of hair around her face that had escaped from the tie and then carried the tea tray into the parlor.

"Ma'am?" said Josephine. She stood in the doorway of an empty room.

"Yes, I'm here." The voice came from below and Josephine dropped her gaze. Melly was in a corner, on her hands and knees, the edge of the rug flipped up. She appeared to be examining its underside. Josephine caught a hint of its smell—of distant lands, a spiciness, pepper and smoke—as Melly flipped the rug over right-ways, displacing a sudden plume of dust that hung brief and radiant in a shelf of sunlight.

Melly scrambled to her feet, her pink cheeks shading pinker. Without a word, she sat on the brown sofa, the same spot where only hours before Dr. Vickers had been. Josephine placed the tray on the table in front of Melly, who immediately picked up the teacup, a line of black grit visible under each of her fingernails. Her eyes again roamed the room, seeming to appraise each item as a merchant might. A long time ago Josephine had learned to watch without watching, to dislike without any evidence of it showing on her face. What to do with this Melly Clayton? How to persuade her to leave?

But a bell rang then, the large brass handbell with a hickory handle that Missus used to summon Josephine when her voice was too tired to call.

"Ah, is that Mrs. Bell?" Melly asked.

"Yes," said Josephine. "Just a moment," and she left the room. With a sinking dismay, she realized that Melly Clayton would stay for a morning visit, then Mister would come in from the fields for dinner, then a quiet activity for Missus, reading to or embroidery. Or again in the studio? The elements of the day stretched before Josephine, all in upheaval due to Melly Clayton's visit, minutes knocked against minutes, task against task. Soap making, canning the blackberries, washing and mending the torn, bloodstained sheets. Retrieval of the food and shoes stretched far from her reach. And what if Missus saw the shoes there? Or Mister? Shoes were precious things. They did not sit in the low shadows of doorways.

Josephine entered Missus' room to find her sitting up in bed, still in her slip, pushing the dark mass of her hair into some approximation of an upsweep, but without pins it kept releasing from itself and falling back onto her shoulders.

"Josephine, who is here? I heard a woman's voice. Who is it?"

"Miss Melly Clayton," Josephine said evenly.

"Melly Clayton?" Missus' eyes narrowed, her face pinched up as though she were straining to push the memory forward with the same force applied to a physical thing, a stuck window or a stubborn cow. "Melly Clayton. The schoolteacher? Whyever is she here?"

"She said Dr. Vickers told her to call, to offer her assistance to you. And her condolences."

"Condolences?" Missus let her hands drop from her hair.

"That's what she said, Missus."

"Condolences. My word, I am not dead yet. Josephine, help me get dressed."

MELLY ROSE AS MISSUS LU entered the room, Josephine walking behind. "Oh my dear Lu Anne, look at you!" Melly's eyes went straight to Missus Lu's cut cheek, but she said nothing. "You look healthy as a spring calf, shame on Dr. Vickers for telling me different."

Missus smiled and looked to the empty teacup and saucer on the table. "You are too kind, my dear. What a lovely surprise to see you! Please sit. Would you like more tea? I have some lovely store-bought biscuits and we still have some of that molasses cake, don't we, Josephine?"

The two clasped hands and sat. Melly began recounting the details of meeting Dr. Vickers by chance on the road, his concern for Mrs. Bell, his admonition to Melly that she must call at once.

In the kitchen, Josephine fixed the tea and placed the last remaining biscuits on a plate. When she returned, Missus said, "See how well she takes care of me?" as Josephine placed the tray on the table, and the words were spoken as though Josephine's caregiving had been the subject of discussion.

"Oh, but surely you need a nurse? Someone with skills? Or a family member even?"

"No no, Josephine's been with me since she was just a little thing. She knows all my needs. I swear, sometimes I think she knows me better than I know myself."

"You spoil her, you do. I can hear it in your voice, Lu Anne. Look at this room, she is not keeping house here very well. Why I took just a casual look round, and there is dust everywhere. Everywhere you place a finger, it comes back gray."

Josephine stood beside the door and watched as Melly Clayton's moist mouth spoke these words to Missus.

"Oh, not at all, Melly," said Missus, but her voice faltered. Josephine could not see Missus' face but her hands were twisting in her lap, the fingers uncertain in their grasping.

"I am afraid that your condition perhaps has made you too . . . too forgiving. Please, would you humor me, let me peruse your good home, just so I can assure myself that you are being properly looked after?"

Josephine could not fathom the motive in Melly's request. But this woman with her crimped eyes and small round shoulders might see what the ailing Missus Lu would not. The food. The shoes. Josephine's rolled canvases. Items pocketed in corners of the house for Josephine to retrieve later, after Missus and Mister had eaten their dinner, Missus busy or napping, Mister back in the fields. Today like any other day, do what needs doing, until the night, until she visited Lottie and Winton at the cabins. Until she spoke to Nathan about the northward route.

Missus hesitated, her hands knotted together now in her lap. "Well," Missus began. "Well, I don't see what could be the harm. You have only my best interests at heart, I am certain of that, Melly." And Missus stood and turned to Josephine and looked beyond her as though she were another polished table, silent, sturdy, ready for use.

Josephine trailed behind Missus Lu and Melly as they walked the hall in the direction of the kitchen.

Abruptly Melly stopped. "Lu Anne, what a charming picture!" She pointed to a small watercolor hanging on the wall, half-hidden in the shadow cast by the underside of the stairs, one that Josephine had painted some years previously of Bell Creek in early summer, the flower beds awash in color, the sky a flawless blue. Josephine remembered her satisfaction at having captured the flowers in their full glory during those short weeks before the blooms began to droop from the heat, when all was still lush and bright. "You are quite an artist if I do say so. However have you kept it such a secret?" Melly turned to Missus Lu with a primly turned-down mouth, a look of mock disapproval that Josephine imagined she must use on her fearful young students.

"Well, it's just something I do. To pass the time." Missus' face flushed and she gazed to the floor, embarrassed, it seemed, by Melly's flattery. Then she raised her head with a surer smile; she did not look to Josephine. "But thank you, Melly, I do enjoy it. I'm so glad you find my little hobby pleasing to the eye."

"Oh, but I do! Now you must move this to a better position, where anyone might admire it. Such modesty." Melly linked her arm in Missus' and the two progressed to the kitchen, Missus leaning comfortably against Melly, the two of them fast friends now.

As Josephine passed the watercolor, she too paused to look upon it. At Missus Lu's acceptance of Melly's praise, a familiar bitter emptiness sounded within Josephine. An awareness came to her, as it had countless times before, that she possessed nothing, that she moved through the world empty-handed with nothing properly to give, nothing she might lay claim to. *See, you have nothing. See, you are nothing,* said a voice inside her head, and it was not Mister's or Missus Lu's, it was her own voice that said those words. *See, you foolish girl.* For one more moment Josephine stood before the frame and in the dim light of the hall she felt herself fading away, diminished as a shadow or a ghost, and it seemed an impossibility that once she had held a brush, chosen a color, put hand to canvas to make anything so material and fine as the painting that hung there on the wall. Perhaps she had been mistaken. Perhaps it had been Missus Lu all along. The blooms pulsed with color across the canvas.

Josephine turned away from the picture and hurried to join the women in the kitchen. As she entered, Melly was circling the room with a slow, methodical pace. The earlier chatter had been replaced by a taut silence that struck Josephine in a physical way, as though she had entered a room filled with water or sand. Missus Lu watched Melly with a look of fearful suspense, and Josephine found herself in strange admiration of this woman, who managed to arouse in others such a desire to please, to not be found wanting.

"It seems tidy enough in here, I suppose," Melly said as she paced, tracing one finger along the cutting table, the rows of knives stored there in notches in the wood. One notch empty. Melly stopped. "But Lu Anne, where is this knife?"

For a moment Josephine and Missus Lu both froze, both guilty in the shared secret of Missus Lu's madness, the cut face, the intended gift from the mistress to the slave. How to explain such a thing?

Then Missus spoke. "Melly, Melly. Robert took that knife to the tool shed." Missus' lie was so effortless that for a moment Josephine herself could imagine Mister selecting the handle, testing the blade, striding outside with some purpose in mind, to cut a length of rope, to slaughter a calf. "Please, Melly, let us sit on the porch to visit," said Missus. "The heat in here is stifling." She waved a hand toward the embers glowing red in the wide stone hearth. The day neared one o'clock and the sun entered in hard, slanting angles through the back windows. Missus' cheeks flushed too pink, her brow glistened with an unhealthy sheen.

"Of course, my dear Lu Anne," said Melly. "I do apologize. How foolish of me!" Her eyes still roamed the room but she began making her way toward the hall.

With weary relief, Josephine started out the door, and then Melly's voice came, quiet and sure in her success. "And this?"

Josephine turned back and Melly stood with the bundle of food in her hands, prying open the knots, sniffing at the inside. "Is this one of your supper napkins, Lu Anne? And why is good food all done up? Do you think she's fixing to take it to the field hands? Steal right from under your nose? You know, my mama says they're all thieves, every one."

Josephine saw on Melly Clayton's face the clear fact that she loved the sport of this. Perhaps there was a reason for the inspection deeper than pure enjoyment, but for now it was only that, the pleasure of watching Josephine squirm and twist, the pleasure of controlling the destiny of another with nothing more than a suggestion, a whimsy of a passing thought.

Missus examined the bundle with a frown. "Josephine, what is the meaning of this?" she said. "Why do you keep a bundle of food, just here by the door? Who is this for?"

Josephine stood in the doorway, the heat of the kitchen in her face, Missus Lu and Melly in postures of waiting. Josephine felt her cheeks burn, and then her lie, as effortless as Missus Lu's from a moment before. "It's for Mister," Josephine said, her voice level, her posture sure. "He asked for a bundle made, I don't know the particulars of why."

Melly narrowed her eyes. "You can ask him yourself soon enough," Melly murmured to Missus Lu. "Then you'll know the truth of it. But looks to me that's the face of a guilty Negro."

Slowly Missus Lu shook her head. "And where are my boots, Josephine? My boots?"

Melly inhaled. "Boots? Are you missing your boots, Lu Anne?"

Now Josephine felt a panic rise up, a heat greater than the kitchen and its engulfing sunlight, greater than the red embers themselves. She felt the prickling of fear and a loosening too, as though she might urinate there on the floor while the two ladies watched, a hot stream running down one leg and onto the wide flat paving stones, evidence more than any other of her guilt. She imagined Melly's triumph, the smile that would unfurl.

Josephine could not speak and the three of them, a tableau of accusation, confusion, terror, stood for what seemed like many minutes or perhaps only a single breath, the time it might take a pair of lungs to empty, to fill again. Josephine said, "Missus. You know yourself Mister took your boots for resoling. He left them with the cobbler's in town and the cobbler will send them straight back when they are good and done. You must've forgotten, Missus. The doctor said it was to be expected, what with your illness, you turning forgetful."

Neither woman reacted immediately. Josephine did not advance toward them or retreat farther into the hall. Melly turned to Missus. "I—I—I," said Missus, faltering, as though sure of nothing beyond the fact of her own mere existence. She put a hand on the cutting table and leaned against it.

Melly's eyes widened. "My dear, I am sorry to be bringing all this up." She stepped toward Missus. "My senses must have left me. Let's go on outside." She half-turned to Josephine. "Girl, get your Missus something cool to drink. Be quick."

Melly and Missus Lu left the kitchen, stepping around Josephine, and she stood for a moment in the doorway, listening to their footsteps in the hall, the open and shut of the front door, the murmur of Melly's voice. Outside, a horse neighed and Josephine became aware of the tireless, brittle barking of a far-off dog. Josephine moved. One foot, two. She opened the cellar door and descended on narrow steps.

Downstairs in the semidark, muffled by earth and the floorboards overhead, she poured a glass from the cool water jug for Missus. The task took far longer than it should have. Her hands shook and the water spilled again and again over the lip, leaving a mottled dark stain on the cellar's dirt floor.

Josephine brought the glass to Missus on the porch, who accepted it without a word, and then she stepped back and waited. The air hung heavy over the road and the dry yellowed grass had begun to shimmer as it did in the hottest part of the day, the sun causing it to buckle and bend. Josephine's heart knocked hard against her chest and she felt a snaking poison in her blood that worked with the heat upon her muscles and her mind like a drug of dismay. The shoes, the food, her small pictures, these were hardly enough to sustain the journey she must take. Who was she to think of escape? Who was she to imagine a world beyond Bell Creek? *You foolish girl.* Standing on the porch, the sharp smell of a distant fire, her dress stiff with dust and damp, the groan of old wood as Missus Lu leaned the rocker forward and back, forward and back, and Josephine felt as though roots had long ago forged themselves beneath her, securing her forever to this small piece of earth, and it was not within her power to release them. Only when she, Josephine, died would these roots wither and die with her.

Missus Lu laughed with a sharp bark and Josephine's attention returned to the women. They were talking now of Melly's prospects, the disappointment of a departing suitor, a blacksmith in town who had it in him to try California and the gold said to grow in the rivers there, set in glistening clumps like eyes on a school of fish.

"You must be so happy here," Melly said, placing a hand on Missus' arm. "Such a well-appointed home. And a handsome husband."

"Mmm. Happy, yes, of course," said Missus. The tone was airy, far-off. Josephine could tell Missus was tiring.

"Is Mr. Bell in town for the day?" Melly said.

"Why no, he's—he's attending to some business here. He's in the fields."

"Oh? Well, that's a comfort. Widow Price has had troubles

aplenty. They run her every which way, with no man to take charge. Soon as the master's off, it's like a week of Sundays in the fields."

"Is that so?"

"And runaways. Widow Price has had three gone in the last few months. And that boy over at the Broadmoors', a patroller hauled him back just last week, but you know how the taste for it gets under their skin. He'll run again, no doubt. Mrs. Broadmoor says they keep him in shackles day and night. She can hardly abide the racket they make."

"The Broadmoors? Do you mean Louis? We sold that boy on. I didn't know he'd run."

With the name *Louis,* Josephine's heart turned and, in that instant, her heaviness lifted and she became a sensitive, waiting, listening thing, every inch of her attuned to the women's conversation, to the timbre of their voices, the rise and fall in Melly Clayton's tone. Louis, her Louis. She recalled Mrs. Broadmoor from calls to Missus Lu, a tall, gangly woman, too big in the knees and the elbows, a horsey face and coarse dark hair. Sickly too, with a dry persistent cough. She had seemed neither kind nor horrid, so far as Josephine could remember. That was where Louis had gone, sold to the Broadmoors. Carefully, Josephine inclined her head toward the women and inched her feet forward half a step.

"He didn't make it very far. Josiah picked him up just outside of Lynnhurst town," Melly said, seeming pleased to possess information that Missus Lu did not.

"Oh, that's lucky then," said Missus Lu. "He's a very good worker. I'm surprised he'd ever do a thing like run." Josephine saw a flash of Missus' brown eyes as she glanced sideways at Josephine.

Again Josephine found herself beside Lottie's fire with Louis, the soft pink of his tongue as he opened his mouth wide with laughter. *Come with me?* he had asked.

"Oh, but don't you worry, Lu Anne." Melly waved her hand in

the air. "I can scarcely believe yours will give you and Mr. Bell any trouble."

"No, I'm sure they won't," said Missus Lu.

"Mr. Bell seems a fine master, very efficient. Very circumspect," said Melly.

Mr. Bell. Josephine realized then Melly's interest, her cataloguing and snooping. Her attention to Missus' illness. Perhaps Dr. Vickers had spoken of her prognosis. Perhaps there had been only a suggestion of gravity, but Melly nonetheless had smelled it out. Melly knew that soon Missus Lu would be gone, and Mister still young enough, a landowner, a slave owner, a fine catch.

Missus leaned back in the rocker and closed her eyes. The chair just moved with the barest push of her toes.

"Well, I should leave you now," said Melly, discomfited, it appeared, by Missus' silence and the purple-blue tint of her eyelids.

Missus drew open her eyes and gave a slow nod. "Yes, thank you for calling, Melly. May Josephine help you to your buggy?"

"Oh no, no," Melly said, too fast. "No need, really. It's scarce ten paces. I shall be fine on my own." She leaned to kiss Missus Lu's cheek and then descended the porch steps, down the side path toward the barn where her buggy waited. Otis had watered and fed and then rehitched the horse. It watched Melly approach with an air, it seemed to Josephine, of placid disappointment.

"That woman is nothing but clay-eating trash." Missus' voice rose razor sharp from her chair. Her eyes were open and watchful as Melly seated herself on the bench, took the reins, and waved a tightly gloved hand in farewell as the horse began its plodding toward the road.

"A spinster. She sniffs around here, seeing to me. Condolences. Do not allow any other visitors to enter this house. Do you understand, Josephine? I will see no one." Missus did not look at Josephine. "Now, go fix up Mister's dinner. He'll be coming in soon."

•   •   •

JOSEPHINE LEFT MISSUS ON THE porch and stood for a moment in the entry, seeing if she might follow inside. But no, she heard the soft creak-creak of the rocker, regular as rain. Walking high on the soft pads of her feet, Josephine darted first to the kitchen for the bundle of food, then up the stairs to the studio. With one hand she grabbed the boots by the laces, with the other she plucked the roll of canvas from her pile. In her attic room, Josephine placed these treasures under the sleeping pallet. The material bulged with the bulk of them, but there was nothing else to be done.

Josephine started down the stairs and to the kitchen. With Louis's name spoken into the day, Josephine felt the world shift toward brightness. He had run once, he would run again, Josephine had no doubt. *Philadelphia,* she again heard Louis's voice form the word, each syllable sweeter than the last. She did not think of the mechanics of finding him, the likelihood of their success and reunion. It was merely the knowledge that he lived that made herself seem suddenly more alive, and stronger too, capable of running away because wasn't she running toward something? Wasn't there the picture now in her head, however fantastic, however unreal, of walking with Louis along a broad busy street, of a city where she might find a beloved face, and in that face find her home?

Lina

Lina and Oscar waited outside the Calhoun Gallery for Marie to return from a pedicure appointment. They sat in silence on Parisian-style black lacquered chairs under the shade of the gallery awning and sipped iced coffees bought from the grocer on the corner. The morning was hot and Lina felt sweat beading on her upper lip and her shirt dampening where it met the chair.

Marie arrived wearing flimsy pink paper flip-flops and a green silk sundress that reminded Lina of 1940s movie stars in the way it floated across her body and shimmered in the sun. She sat down beside Oscar and lit a cigarette.

"I am so very *paranoid*," Marie said with a dramatic exhale of white smoke. Her voice was nicotine-hoarse, the French accent strong. "No one is allowed to see the new paintings until the opening. Only you, Oscar. Only for you would I do such a thing. And your lovely daughter."

Marie leaned forward, directing her attention now to Lina. "We have no information on Josephine's family," she said. "Nothing. From what we know, she had no children, no brothers, no sisters. After 1852, she disappeared from the face of the earth. Just"—and here

Marie snapped her fingers—"gone. And to be honest, that is fine with us. We have no familial estate contesting ownership of the works. It's a windfall. It's the largest windfall in the history of windfalls! The owner is an amateur collector, a man from the South— South Carolina? Or South . . . West Virginia? I never can remember. He bought all the paintings—fifty-two! For fuck's sake! He bought them at an estate sale, an old lady who died with no will, no kids herself. But a white woman, very white. No actual relation to Josephine Bell, so it would appear."

Marie dragged long and hard on her cigarette. "This . . . collector, he is looking at significant sums. Big money. He is happy as a little clam. I won't even tell you how he came to me, it is a funny story." Marie Calhoun rolled her eyes and smiled, more to herself than to them, and stubbed out her cigarette. She checked her toenails and slipped out of the paper shoes, changing them for a pair of vertiginous heels she fished from a purse as big and round as a man's head. "Now. Shall we go inside? You must not tell anyone you have seen the pictures. Mr. South Virginia will be very upset." Marie giggled, her mouth circled by little smoker's wrinkles and colored a brilliant red.

At the gallery entrance, beside the empty receptionist's desk, a tripod easel displayed a posterboard printed with a black-and-white headshot of a smiling man, his thick gray hair well coiffed, his teeth gleaming white. THE ART AND ARTIFICE OF LU ANNE BELL, LECTURE BY PORTER SCALES, JUNE 24, 7 P.M. was printed in large type beneath the photo.

"It is Porter who first questioned authorship," Marie said to Lina as she paused to examine the poster. "He has spent many, many months examining these works. The new, and the old. But it is always hard to change people's expectations. Change what they have so long believed." Here Marie gave a quick frustrated shake of her head, and then turned to Oscar. "Oh Oscar," she said, her tone now teasing. "Will you be here for Porter's talk?" Marie gave a sly grin.

"I would answer that in the *negative*," Oscar said with more force than seemed necessary. Lina tried to remember why the critic's name rang a bell, and then she had it.

"Wait—isn't he the one who called you *fidgety*? Who gave you that awful review?"

Oscar nodded once. "That would be him, yep."

"Porter and Oscar have a—how should I say it?—a *long history*," Marie said, turning to Lina. "But he is a very brilliant man. He knows everything about Lu Anne Bell. About many things in fact. He is very learned. An intellectual."

"The guy's a hack, Marie," Oscar said. "He was born with a silver spoon in his mouth, never had to work a day in his life. Couldn't paint to save his ass so now he just criticizes what real artists do." Oscar moved into the gallery, his boot heels echoing loudly in the empty room. Marie raised her eyebrows at Lina and followed him inside.

The show filled all three of the gallery's white-walled rooms. Some of the pictures hung in simple frames; others leaned against the wall, waiting to be placed. There were primarily paintings, both watercolor and oil, but also some pencil and charcoal drawings, a few wood engravings. Veering away from Oscar and Marie, Lina started at the back of the gallery, where a row of landscapes hung, watercolors and oils of the tobacco fields, the Blue Ridge Mountains that surrounded the Bell farm, and numerous studies of the main house seen from different angles at various times of day and evening. In one image the house seemed monstrous and foreboding, and Lina stopped to examine it. *Bell Creek at Dawn* (1848) the label read, though the light seemed too murky and bleak for dawn. A flock of crows quivered in the upper left corner and a small group of slaves hovered on the lawn, seven of them, their figures dwarfed by the looming house, their faces indistinct. The stillness of the scene invoked in Lina a sudden and sickening claustrophobia.

She turned away from the landscape to a wall of portraits. Each of these was in oil, each of a slave, half-length and full face, realistically rendered, each devastating in its own particulars. *Winton, Lottie, Jackson, Calla, Therese, Otis.* The names were printed directly onto the gallery wall beside each painting, the dates ranging from 1845 to 1852.

"It is the imperfection, the authenticity, that is so striking in the Bell work," Marie whispered, standing at Lina's ear. "That woman, her name is Lottie. I have always found this to be the most moving of the portraits." Yes, Lina could see why. Lottie's hands, gnarled and bent as the roots of a tree, were clasped before her, holding a bouquet of flowers. Lottie's eyes looked patient. She looked as if she were waiting for something, or someone, but with no expectation that it or he or she might ever arrive.

"None of the Bell works are signed, but the names of the subjects are written on the back of each portrait," Marie said. "Handwriting. This will help us prove it was Josephine who made them, not Lu Anne. As soon as we have access to the full Bell archives."

"What's the problem?" Lina asked.

"Well, the Stanmore Foundation, they own nearly all the Bell works, of course, and it is a very dramatic shock to them, the idea that Lu Anne was nothing more than a fabricator. A liar. So they are not as . . . *cooperative* with us, with Porter, as they should be. That is why we are having the show now, to push the question. To take it public."

Lina nodded. This was a strategy she understood: wasn't this what Dresser was doing with the reparations claim? Pushing the question. *What were their names? Isn't it time we made the effort to remember?*

Lina continued farther into the gallery, through a wide archway to an open middle space where a large drawing was displayed alone. *Children No. 2* read the title on the wall. It was in charcoal, done on rough, perhaps homemade paper. Several heads of babies and children floated disembodied in the background, a row of them, all similar in appearance but none of them quite the same. A larger head of an older child dominated the foreground. Lina guessed the child to be three or four years old; his (her?) face was expressive, full of an expectant joy, but the eyes were closed. It was an odd juxtaposition—the face conveyed a strong emotion, it made Lina's throat catch, but the closed eyes cut the viewer off from sharing the joy or understanding it.

Suddenly Oscar was there, standing beside her. "Just look at that," he said. "She must have been warming up, experimenting with the smaller ones. Studies, looks like. But that face, holy shit, she nailed the bigger face. Look at that kid, Carolina. Just look at him."

Lina looked. The closed eyes, the smooth full cheeks, the lips turned in the barest suggestion of a smile, and the picture hit Lina with a force she wasn't expecting, in a way her father's paintings never had. Her reaction here was emotional, not intellectual, and for once she wanted to leave it at that, without searching for clues to analyze, references to dissect. She couldn't explain why this boy's enigmatic face captivated her, nor did she want to explain it. Looking was enough.

Just then a phone buzzed from across the room. Marie answered in clipped urgent syllables, then hung up and clicked across the gallery expanse toward Lina and Oscar with her arms held wide.

"Darlings, I'm afraid I must be off." She raised herself up on tiptoe and kissed Oscar on each cheek, then stood for a moment holding his face with both hands. He looked down at her and smiled, it seemed to Lina, with a rueful, half-there apology, but also with delight, and an energy, a look passed between them. Lina felt as though she were watching the scene through a peephole, something she should not see, and yet fascination held her gaze steady: this unknown sliver of her father.

Oscar dated, of course he did, but Lina never met them, never saw them. These women existed for Lina only as a stray blond hair across the back of his jacket, a feminine voice on their answering machine, and, once, a photograph of Oscar and a leggy brunette in one of those free, glossy Manhattan magazines. But Marie—Lina remembered her from Oscar's parties, the ones he used to throw regularly with a pauper's abandon throughout Lina's childhood; she'd heard Marie's name spoken over the years, a gallery move, a marriage, a divorce. Lina felt now as if she'd missed something vital, a clue to Marie's significance. And what else had she missed?

The night Oscar had shown Lina the Grace pictures, he'd said, *I'm okay, Carolina,* the words flying naturally from his mouth as though he had said them a thousand times before. After all these years, and Lina's constant, lurking worry. *I'm okay.*

I wasn't a perfect husband, Oscar had told her.

That small word etched at Grace's throat: *Enough.*

Marie released Oscar's face and turned then to Lina. "Carolina, my dear. You are a lucky girl, you look nothing like your father here." She gave a sideways wink to Oscar. "You have grown into a beauty, just like your mother. I am so very glad to see you again after all these years. Good luck with your case." She pulled Lina close and made a quick pass to the right and to the left, planting a dry kiss on each cheek.

Marie turned, fishing through her bag for her keys, and then she disappeared out the front door, Oscar behind her. Lina paused for a moment in the empty space and focused again on the drawing of the children. The child with closed eyes seemed older than the others, sketched with more skill and more detail. It was only this one that truly demanded the viewer's attention. What was that child thinking? What did he not wish to see?

With reluctance Lina turned away from the drawing and followed her father outside. She emerged from the gallery, squinting with the sudden rush of sun, and stood silently beside Oscar as Marie locked the door with a hard twist.

"Lina, I hate to admit it, but I hope you do not find any of Josephine's relations," Marie said. "It would make life much more complicated for me. Bye now!" And Marie Calhoun ducked into a waiting car, a suited driver closing the door behind her.

OSCAR AND LINA CAUGHT A cab back to Brooklyn. There was no air-conditioning and all four windows were opened wide, the rush of the wind flinging Lina's hair around her face. She wanted to ask her father about Marie, not because she really wanted to know but because the alternative—wondering, imagining—gave her a hollow ache in the back of her throat.

"Dad, what is *up* with you and Marie?" Lina asked, shouting to be heard above the wind. She tried to make the question into a joke, hoping that he would reply with a laugh, some funny story.

But his reply was serious and guarded. "What do you mean?"

"I don't know, it just seemed like you guys had some kind of connection."

"We're old friends." Oscar turned away from her, toward the window, and the breeze pushed his hair away from his face and flattened his beard, leaving the bones of his cheeks, his forehead, his skull exposed.

"Just friends?"

A hesitation. A beat. "Just friends. Yes," he answered.

"And she knew Mom?"

"Yes, they were good friends."

The cab stopped at a red light and the air around them quieted. Lina became aware of the tinny beats of an Indian pop song trickling from the driver's cracked radio, the smell of roasting peanuts from a vendor on the corner. Oscar gazed out the window, his face visible to her only in profile, the long slender fingers of his right hand resting lightly on his jeaned thigh, one blue eye that gazed away from Lina, toward the peanut vendor and the endless stream of strangers on the sidewalk. She saw the tension in his shoulders, a sharp blink, the way his lips pulled down at the corner.

"But listen, Carolina—you heard Marie," Oscar said, and he turned to her, his cheeks pink, his eyes alight now with enthusiasm. "She didn't look that hard for any relatives. It's better for the gallery if there's no contested ownership. Nothing to slow up sales from the show. Start looking, Carolina. The picture of that kid, it just—I don't know. I think you'll find something."

The light flipped to green, the cab roared ahead, and Lina's heart quickened, her hair flurried at her cheeks, and the sudden wind in her eyes made them tear. Any impulse to push her father on the Marie question disappeared into the noise and distraction of the car and Lina felt a shaky kind of calm, as if she had only just dodged something unbearable. She let herself be taken from her moment of suspicion. *Show us the nature of the harm,* Dan had said.

How might she find Josephine's descendants? It would be difficult, perhaps impossible. Nothing was known about Josephine Bell following her mistress's death in 1852. There might be no descendants; she might have died without leaving anyone behind. Dan might hate the idea, Dresser might hate it. But a rising certainty took hold of Lina, as the cab hurtled down Broadway, past the federal courthouse, past Ground Zero, catching all the green lights as the long avenue unfurled evenly beneath them. She had twelve days to find a plaintiff. She would find Josephine.

PART TWO

Lina

Josephine

Dorothea

Lina

LOTTIE*

By Porter Scales

Do her eyes accuse you? Do they question? Do they blame? What, in the end, does she want? It is impossible to gaze upon Lu Anne Bell's masterful *Lottie* without posing these questions. We know that Lottie was a slave owned by Robert Bell, Lu Anne's husband. We know that Lu Anne Bell painted Lottie in 1849, some thirteen years before the Civil War began. We estimate Lottie's age at perhaps fifty? Sixty? It appears from her homespun dress, her thick cracked fingers, that Lottie was a field hand and would have worked the tobacco, wheat, and corn fields of the Bell Creek plantation. In her hands she holds flowers—some bluebells, a branch of magnolia, lilies, all types native to Bell's Virginia—and the paint here is heavy, the canvas saturated with hue.

The viewer's eyes are drawn inevitably, irresistibly, to Lottie's face; it is an extraordinary face. The cheeks are full, the lips thick and slightly parted, a sliver of inner pink visible, as though Lottie were about to speak, as though she had something to tell us. A horizontal crease marks her forehead and the eyes are a deep brown, the lids heavy but the gaze expressive. She looks directly at the viewer and there is something uncomfortable in this gaze. For a moment we turn away from her eyes, to the weathered wood of the cabin before which Lottie stands, and to the fields beyond, which seem restless and awhirl, as though the tobacco plants danced in a strong wind. We examine the details of Lottie's immediate surroundings: the spider on the cabin wall, the suggestion of a low-hanging sun, the thin, shadowless clouds in the far sky.

Only then do we return to Lottie's gaze. We look and we find her without pity, without judgment. She is not a worker, she is not sexualized, she is not a benignity with the presence of a child. She is a woman, flesh and blood, with hopes and fears there on her face, in her eyes, in her hands that hold the flowers. In painting her subject, a slave, in such a way, with tenderness and hope, Lu Anne Bell has given us a portrait of humanity itself.

As with any great portrait, we are left wanting to know more about the subject and about the circumstances of the work's creation. Robert Bell owned dozens of slaves over the course of his marriage to Lu Anne. There is no way for us to know now, some 150 years after Lu Anne Bell's death, why she chose Lottie for such a luminous examination. Was Lottie dear to Lu Anne? What were the precise parameters of their relationship? Likewise we can only guess at the mechanics of the creation itself. Did Lu Anne compose the painting from memory? Did she pose Lottie before the slave shack, place the flowers into her hands, prop an easel there in the mud?

In the end, our ignorance as to method and reason is, I would argue, wholly inconsequential. What we are left with is the artistic experience at its most innate, its most sublime. There is no cleverness or theory or striving for us, the viewers of art, to contend with. There is nothing to be got through. There is nothing to feign. There is only Lottie, this powerful visitor from a time and place so removed from our own, so wholly foreign to our experience, that we will never understand her. And yet we try. We meet her gaze and the modern world falls away. We are standing with her in Lynnhurst, Virginia, in the year 1849, on a sunny day, a day like any other. Lottie invokes a calm, a pure and unparalleled call for empathy that should not be ignored or forgotten. Her gaze holds us. We cannot look away.

* *This essay first appeared in* Artforum, *March 25, 2000.*

⁂

LU ANNE BELL'S *CHILDREN NO. 2**
By Porter Scales

The children themselves are, in many ways, unremarkable. There are six, the largest positioned in the foreground and five smaller in the back; none looks straight at the viewer; each appears in profile or semiprofile; the eyes of the largest are closed. They have been sketched in seemingly quick and confident strokes of charcoal. The paper is rough, homemade; the edges, if one could see them beneath the wood of the frame, would surely be frayed and irregular. The children's heads are disembodied, floating as if through space and time, but in all other immediate respects they tend to the regular, to the typical; they might appear in, say, a particularly well-illustrated child's storybook or the portfolio of a talented commercial portraitist. But then one looks closer, at the shadows beneath the eyes of the largest child, at the complex beauty of the whorled ear on the third, at the fine line of the arched neck on the smallest. The details call to the viewer softly, in whispers of simplicity and effortless technique. Here is the work of a master hand; here is something to behold.

But what, exactly, do we see? This is where context becomes so critical. These children: are they black or are they white? It is impossible to tell. This question of race—which must pervade the work of

Lu Anne Bell, which cannot be ignored given where and when and how she lived—is utterly absent. On the faces of the children, on the surface of the drawing, there is the black of the charcoal, the white of the paper, but the racial identities of these children remain opaque. Of course, critics and historians have tried to affix labels. Hawkins and Jeffers claim the child in the foreground is African American, the others, Caucasian. A more recent study by a French historian, Martine Cloussoud, contends that they are all Caucasian, depictions of the many children lost to Lu Anne Bell in the period 1840–1850.

Another interpretation, I would argue, presents itself: this is an examination by Lu Anne Bell of the children so often born to black women, fathered by their white masters. By law, the status of such children followed that of their mothers: they too became slaves. And the child produced from a further master-slave union again remained enslaved. And so on, and so on, and so on. Over the years, generation after generation, the physical markers of racial identity became virtually meaningless. Who is slave? Who is free? In this context, the picture becomes illustrative of a larger phenomenon, one that occurred throughout the antebellum years and beyond, that of passing. There exist many historical examples of former slaves passing into the white world, leaving their African American identities—whether such an identity was imposed or deeply felt—behind. How common was this occurrence? How many today find themselves with gaps in a family tree, missing ancestors, unknown histories?

Lu Anne Bell's interest in this issue may have been motivated by the circumstances of her own marriage. We know that Robert Bell, Lu Anne's husband, went on after her death to remarry and to father children both by his second wife, Melly Clayton Bell, and by at least two women he owned as slaves in Louisiana. We do not know if he conducted himself likewise while at Bell Creek and it is possible, of course, that he did not, or that Lu Anne Bell herself was never aware of her husband's behavior. Yet it seems equally possible—and, I would argue, likely—that such hard truths informed her rendering of these floating, isolated children.

It is Bell's triumph, then, that the work transcends so fully the personal to stand as a powerful artistic achievement and social commentary. With clarity and compassion, *Children No. 2* remarks upon the nature of the race line during a time when that divide carried such determinative weight. To be identified as white or black was quite literally a question of life or death. Lu Anne Bell portrays for us the arbitrary nature of that divide and, I would argue, raises questions about the wider implications for the enslaving whites. Who is slave and who is free?

The enslaving whites deprived their slaves of the opportunity for basic self-identification, self-realization. The exercise of this determinative power created for the enslavers a different sort of prison, a prison of their own devising but a fatally confining one no less—economic, social, spiritual, moral.

Did Lu Anne Bell see this? Did she understand the essential unsustainability of her way of life? Did she sense the ruin to come?

I suspect that she did.

* *This essay first appeared in the* New Yorker, *November 15, 1997.*

MONDAY

Lina had arrived early at Clifton to conduct further research on Josephine Bell before the phones started ringing, before the secretaries trooped in. Sometimes, without people, the office seemed almost restful, a blank neutral expanse, like an airplane hangar or a meadow. Lina was clicking through Porter Scales's slick but serious website: the same headshot she had seen at the Calhoun Gallery and, beside it, a catalogue of essays and reviews previously printed in *Artforum, Art in America,* the *New York Times Magazine,* the *New*

Yorker, Vanity Fair; also some lectures he had given at Columbia, where he held an endowed chair, at Yale, at Cambridge, to audiences at MoMA and the Guggenheim. Porter Scales's field of expertise was nineteenth-century American art, it seemed, although his writings addressed twentieth-century work as well. A one-stop shop for American high culture of the past two hundred years.

As her digital clock shifted to 9:00, Lina closed down Porter's site. Sounds of arriving secretaries now bounced along the hall and into her office, elevator pings, swishing slacks, the smell of coffee and sweet doughy things. She heard Sherri arrive and immediately begin a phone conversation that involved long breathy silences and sudden jarring hoots of laughter. Lina rose from her desk and quietly closed her office door.

Over the weekend, Lina had compiled a list of companies and professional genealogists that specialized in tracking African American ancestry. She started with AfriFind, the largest and seemingly most professional of the fee-charging services; its website promised to "reunite African American families, discover historical roots, acquaint you with the ancestors you never knew."

The woman who answered Lina's call was a full-time genealogist, she said, and happy to speak with Lina about her search.

"I have some recently discovered information about a . . . family member," Lina improvised, "who was a slave on a tobacco farm in southern Virginia, but no one knows what happened to her after the year 1852. I'm trying to confirm the family connection, track from here to there. But I'm working under a tight time frame."

Any results would take six to eight weeks, perhaps longer, the woman said. The only faster option was for Lina to conduct the research herself. Lina could check the private papers of the farm where her ancestor was enslaved. Slave owners often kept detailed records of their holdings, which might indicate if the woman died, was sold, or ran away. If she had survived the Civil War, she might turn up in national census records, although African Americans were not listed by name until the 1870 census, and even that was problematic because freed slaves often took on new surnames.

"Farm records can be very hard to find," the woman explained. "They're scattered across the state in local historical societies, community centers, that kind of thing, or at the old plantation houses themselves. That's why any search takes such considerable time."

Lina was silent. Six to eight weeks. Scattered across the state of Virginia.

"What county did you say again?" the woman asked.

"Charlotte, in southern Virginia."

"And you say she disappeared in 1852?"

"Yes. We have a photo dated 1852 that shows her on the farm, but nothing after that date."

"Well, there was a very active Underground Railroad station around that time in the town of Lynnhurst, in Charlotte County. The Rounds farm, a white family, which was unusual. Most of those active on the Railroad were free blacks, and most of the ones we know about were farther north. But there's some good documentation on the Roundses. It's very possible that your ancestor used the Railroad to escape."

The woman paused on the line. Lina heard taps on a keyboard, the rustling of some papers.

"There are some relevant documents in the archives of the Virginia Historical Society," the woman continued. "Though it looks like there's not a lot available online. The Historical Society is in Richmond. You might want to head down there to see what you can find."

The Rounds family. Lina asked for their names: Horace Rounds; his wife, Evie; their daughters, Kate and Dorothea; and a son, Samuel. Horace was a carpenter and the town's informal undertaker, the woman told her, when undertaking was still a new profession. Not a wealthy family, though educated, even the daughters, who were taught at home.

For the next 4.8 billable hours, Lina searched online for Horace Rounds. The information she uncovered seemed promising but inconclusive. An estimated thirty-two fugitives passed through the Rounds farm in 1846, over fifty in 1847, and eighty-three in 1848. Passage of the Fugitive Slave Act in 1850, with its harsh new penalties for aiding fugitives, forced many conductors to increase the secrecy of their activities, one website said, and figures after that date were impossible to verify. Lina found nothing more on the family's activities for 1849 and beyond, although the eldest daughter, Kate Rounds Sterrett, kept popping up on websites dedicated to the suffrage and abolitionist movements of the late nineteenth century.

The Rounds farm was located just twelve miles from Bell Creek.

Next, Lina brought up the website for the Virginia Historical Society. She scanned the index of online documents and, amid a list of newspaper articles and abolitionist speeches, she found something that made her stop: "Rounds, Dorothea: Correspondence 1848." Dorothea Rounds, the youngest daughter.

Lina opened the link, and a fuzzy scan materialized on her screen. A letter, the handwriting small and precise. Narrowing her eyes to focus, Lina began to read.

April 9, 1848
My Dearest Darling Kate,

    The wedding flowers have only just begun to wilt & here I sit down to write. How I miss you already! The house is not the same. I have found myself in these last few days arriving at the door to our room, half dreaming that I will push it open to find you there, in your familiar pose, seated at your desk looking over the apple trees, pen in hand. I hope you continue your writing in your new home. Is Gareth an avid reader? Does he bite his lip & cluck his tongue, as I do, over your mistakes in spelling?

And how do you find New York? Are the streets as wide as we saw in the picture book? Do all the women wear their hair in curls & smoke in public company?

And tell me about your house! Where am I to sleep when I come to visit you? I am bursting with questions & cursing the post that will take so many weeks to bring me your reply.

I should tell you about Mother & Father. They are both well, although each sad in their quiet way to have you gone. At mealtimes Mother looks to your empty chair with such concentration, as though hoping to conjure you out of air. Pastor Shaw's friendship with Father continues & I am grateful that Father has an abiding influence, a spiritual advisor & confidant. Father visits with him often & many nights the Pastor is at our table. You know already my views on the Presbyterian teachings, but Father's faith supported him in our family's darkest time, where mine failed, & I am grateful that Father continues to find solace there. Indeed I wish that I were so fortunate. The heaviness still remains in me, Kate, even two years now already gone. I think of Percy every day.

Father of course is busy with his undertaking. I wish that I could assist him but he is adamant that it is not work for women. Yesterday there was a young boy come to the house whose mother had passed on. His father had been gone in town 3 days & not yet back. The boy had nowhere to turn. Only 7 years in age, still in short pants, he'd used up all the eggs & flour & butter to be found at home, all the while his poor Ma laid upstairs.

Mother took the poor boy inside—what else could she do?—and gave him oatcakes & milk. He spoke not a word but cried as he ate. This is such the trouble with Father's work, why I both admire him for it & despise the toil it brings us, especially to Mother, every day. Why could he not have kept on with the carpentering alone, as before? I know that he aids those suffering at their time of greatest need & he has spoken so often of the satisfaction deriving from his efforts, but I cannot help but imagine someday this will all come to be too much, that we will not survive ourselves the constant exposure to death & tears & hardship.

I am sorry to end on such a dismal note. Next letter I promise will be full of laughter.

Your most loving sister,
Dorothea

April 10, 1848
Dearest Kate,

I don't suppose you have received yet my last letter & already I am sending you another, testimony to how greatly you are missed. I feel also that I should dispel from your mind the words with which I left off in my last—please forgive the dreary tone. The boy (his name is Samuel) had just come to the house & his soft white cheeks & dark curls put me in mind of our own dear brother. I think Mother too could not but look at him & see our Percy. The similarities lie not just in their height & boyish ways but genuinely in other aspects as well: his nose, upturned like an elf's, and his voice, a high little pipsqueak, trilling forth like a waterfall. He is staying with us still, Samuel, sleeping in the extra room downstairs. Mother has moved the sewing things & the extra armchair into the front room, & made up a bed of sorts from various cushions laid on the floor. Samuel is comfortable enough, so he says, & he eats well.

There has been much talk of the escape of a field hand from the Price farm & the search that ensued. Even with Widow Price 20 miles off, still we were visited by the Patrollers, asking questions & looking round the barn. Father volunteered to join the patrol but there were sufficient townsfolk already engaged. In truth I was glad Father did not search. In recent weeks the coffles have gone past with such regularity, it must strain even the hardest heart to see the chained Negroes shuffle along these long dusty roads.

Justin Broadmoor has stopped his calling. I am perplexed but not distraught. His dark hair grew so coarsely from his head, putting me to mind of a hedgehog, & his voice rang out so loudly—do you remember how our heads would ache after his visits? Mother says he is a fine boy & would have made a good husband, but surely my voice would have soon grown hoarse from trying to make myself heard above his shouts. Mother says now that I am 17, I must turn my attention to such matters, but I find it so tiresome.

Do you recall Jack Harper? I saw him yesterday in town & he sends his regards to you. I had not seen him since he & his brother Caleb left school. His appearance is quite altered, though pleasingly so—scarcely did I recognize him.

I hear Father calling for me so I will end this letter forthwith. I hope you are well, & my love to you & to Gareth,

Your sister,
Dot

** Further documents related to the Rounds family, the Underground Railroad, and Lynnhurst, Virginia, are available at the Virginia Historical Society, Richmond. Call or e-mail for an appointment.**

Lina felt her pulse race, her foot tapped out an excited staccato beneath her desk, and part of it was due to the buckets of caffeine she'd consumed that morning and part of it was due to those faint spidery words still glowing on her screen: *An escaped field hand,* Dorothea Rounds had written in 1848. If she wrote of the family's later involvement in the Railroad, she might have recorded information about Josephine Bell. Or perhaps her father, Horace Rounds, had maintained his own records?

LINA RODE AN EMPTY ELEVATOR up to Dan's office. In the reflection of the polished steel door, she rehearsed her words and pitch. A two-day trip to Richmond would advance the search for a lead plaintiff quickly and efficiently. Travel costs were minimal. A Josephine Bell descendant would have a fantastic backstory.

"I have an idea about a lead plaintiff, the perfect plaintiff, with a very compelling backstory," she said, standing in the open doorway of Dan's office. "But I need to do some additional research, and I need to do it in Virginia. The Virginia Historical Society in Richmond. Maybe some of the old plantation houses too."

Dan looked up from his desk. He gripped a pen in one hand; a pile of papers, red ink scrawled along the margins, rested on the desk before him. He wore a suit but no tie, and his collar buttons were open. The skin at his neck glowed white as paste. As Lina advanced into the room, she smelled stale coffee and just a hint of sweat.

"You know, I didn't ask you to find the *perfect* plaintiff. I asked you to find a few potential lead plaintiffs, some folks that fit our needs for the lawsuit."

"I understand," Lina continued, the caffeine excitement still coursing in her. Surely Dan could be convinced to feel it too. "But this particular angle is powerful. I've been researching a woman named Josephine Bell, an African American artist enslaved in

Virginia in the mid-nineteenth century. She disappeared in 1852, and it seems likely she escaped using the Underground Railroad." Lina paused, waiting for some sign of Dan's interest in her brilliant idea, but his face remained an inscrutable blank. From beneath the desk came the unmistakably agitated *tap tap tap* of Dan's foot. Lina hurried along. "And even if I don't find anything on Josephine Bell's descendants, the state archives will lead me to a plaintiff. An incredible plaintiff, someone descended from a runaway, one who used the Underground Railroad and made it to freedom. Picking oneself up from the dust . . ." Her voice trailed off.

"Lina, do you actually have someone in mind, I mean someone alive now?" Dan's voice was razor sharp.

"Not exactly. But—"

"It sounds ridiculous. Sending you to Virginia. You can do the research here in New York."

"Dan, I—"

"We don't want to waste Mr. Dresser's good money on some wild-goose chase."

"But I would—"

"Why don't you put your head down and start *thinking*." Dan reached out an arm and checked his watch. "I have a lot of work to get through tonight." He picked up his pen and resumed reading. With a frown, he marked a straight line across the page.

Dan had never spoken to her like this before; to others, yes, but never to her. His words evoked in Lina a combination of indignation and shame. Gone was her excited buzz, and in its place a creeping nausea. Lina stood there in front of him, motionless, waiting for him to raise his eyes again so she could—what? Defend herself? Argue with him? No, she couldn't. Those kinds of exchanges didn't happen at Clifton, at least not between a partner and a first-year associate. She marveled at Dan's poise, the unapologetic exercise of his presumed right to be an ass.

"Okay, Dan. I understand," Lina said, hating the surrender in her voice. She turned and left the room, closing the door behind her with a soft click like the sound of teeth. The carpeted hallway stretched long and silent before and behind her, empty but for a man perched atop a ladder, his upper torso installed within a dark gap in the ceiling tiles. He wore a blue jumpsuit that bagged at the knees and heavy work boots of yellow, new-looking leather, and his waist twisted, his heels lifted, as though occupied by some laborious task within the ceiling innards. Lina edged around the ladder, resisting the urge to call up to him, and then continued along her way to the gleaming elevator bank with all its pinball buttons. Somewhere a door slammed, a woman coughed. Lina pushed the down button. She waited. All around her, the walls breathed with the hush of work, the muffled tap of keyboards, the murmurings of secret conference. The deafening noise and mysterious purpose of gray carpets and beige walls.

LINA LET HERSELF INTO THE house and called into the dark for Oscar, but only silence came back. She moved through the still air of the entryway, turned the switch on a table lamp, checked the mail, then started up the stairs, her steps muffled by the red padded runner. The earlier exchange with Dan, his casual dismissal and her readiness to accept it, had fueled a restlessness in her, a frustrated spark. In her head, she replayed the scene with Dan again and again. Why hadn't she told him more about Josephine Bell? Why hadn't she stayed to argue her case?

She walked the dim hallway to her room and paused, then ran down the stairs again to the second floor. An idea was beginning to form and it seemed as much a response to Dan's dismissal as it was to Oscar's invitation to talk about Grace. Paralysis had gripped her both times, both times had left her feeling vulnerable and irritated, with herself and with them. What was she so afraid of? It seemed she should be able to shoulder her way through Dan's condescension, Oscar's mysterious new candor. Push them open, take what she needed.

The idea took shape, and she wanted to execute it quickly, before Oscar came home, before she lost her nerve. Lina stopped in front of the closed studio door. She knocked once, twice, though she knew her father wasn't there. Tonight she would look at Oscar's pictures of Grace, without him standing beside her. She would examine them carefully, take her time. Perhaps without the pressure of her father's expectations, the pictures would make sense to her.

The whole house creaked and moaned in the way it did at night, mysterious settlings, the banging on and off of instruments meant to keep them warm and watered. The hallway felt cold and stark, lit only by a bare bulb hanging overhead. For the first time, Lina noticed the unpainted skirting board, the rough doorframe, the paint-speckled floor, the various to-be-done details left from the studio renovation that she knew Oscar would never finish. And his sloppiness struck her suddenly as a larger failing: look at how little care he took with all that he had.

Lina opened the door. The room was messier but emptier than it had been last week. Much of the wall space was now clear—most of the big pieces must have already been moved to the gallery. As Lina wandered through the studio, she uncovered a blank canvas, and then another; a pile of sketches on the table showed only Duke, captured in three-legged motion. There seemed nothing left of the Grace pictures and Lina looked around her with a sinking disappointment, that she hadn't before realized the opportunity—what those pictures might tell her, what they might mean—and now it had passed.

At the far end of the table rested a tall pile of books Lina hadn't seen before in the studio. She picked one off the top: *Women in Love* by D. H. Lawrence, the cover showing two female silhouettes, like featureless heads in a cameo brooch. Lina had read the novel once in college, though she didn't recognize this cover as one from her or Oscar's bookshelves. Where had it come from? A bite of curiosity displaced her disappointment and she opened the book. On the first page, in a neat feminine script, Lina's mother's name was written: *Grace Janney Sparrow,* along with their Park Slope address and home phone number. Scraps of paper sprouted from the top of the book and Lina opened to the first of them. In the same handwriting, her mother's, Lina read in the margin of the page: *Why does Gudrun love? What does Gudrun need?*

Lina traced her fingers over the depression the pen had made in the paper. Her pulse in her throat, she turned to the next marked page. In a blank space where the chapter had ended, Grace had written:

- *Art—creation—is this enough?*
- *Reason?*
- *Desire?*
- *What gives meaning?*
- *Who is free?*

Lina read the words, and then again, and a third time. And then she pulled out a stool. She did not wonder why these artifacts were here, tonight, in Oscar's studio, or why she had never seen them before even though she knew every inch of this house, every corner and closet, the contents of every drawer and cubby. She felt only a pure urge of possession, that she must touch the papers and books, place her hands where her mother's hands had once been. Lina brought the book to her face and inhaled, breathing in its smell of mildew and dust, the deep underlying odors of age and decay.

For the next 1.7 hours, she worked her way through the stack, turning to each bookmarked page, reading the notes her mother had made.

This is what she found:

- From a 1979 datebook, the year before Lina was born:

  June 7, gallery; June 19, show at Lize's; June 28, L's party; July 4,
  whose birthday is this?!; July 13, meet Porter; July 26, doctor 10:45;
  July 31, hot hot hot; August 7, Porter at 7:00.

- Inside *Paul Cezanne: A Biography,* on the inside cover, a
  small drawing of a person pulling a frown and beneath it, in
  pencil:

  I am so sorry. Love, G.

- A birthday card, a black-and-white photo of a small funny-
  looking dog and a woman's feet in old-fashioned lace-up
  boots. The card read:

  My dearest darling O
  I love you you you, only you.

- Inside a green notebook of white lined paper:

  O more than anyone deserves it. He does of course he does.
  . . .
  Listen to the pigeons, they chatter and gossip and spit.
  Can't work, can't think, can't breathe.
  . . .
  Is it so much to ask for? Is it so much? O does not understand, he
  cannot. Always something appendaged to me, always this noise, or
  this fear of noise. Be cautious, quiet, still. What if I want to scream
  too? What if my hands feel too heavy to lift even the slightest weight,
  a paintbrush or a baby?
  . . .
  She is the loveliest thing I have ever seen.

- A sketchbook with a hard black cover and creamy sheets of thick paper. Inside, small pencil sketches of faces done in the same style and with the same familial labels as those hanging in Lina's room.

Joy, my favorite person my favorite name—Sister's cousin
Porter, my anti-O—Cousin, brother, twin
Lark, a beauty—Cousin thrice removed
Tisha, too much like me—Niece's nephew's daughter

And a series of rough sketches of a baby, only a few months old, indistinct in the way small infants are, but Lina recognized them as herself and her breath caught. Below each, Grace had written simply:

Daughter. Daughter. Daughter. Daughter.

On the last page, no sketch, only the words:

Nothing is as I see it. What do I see?

- Four loose pieces of paper, undated, all written in Grace's neat curling script. The first of them read:

Oscar,
If you want to keep the fucking frogs, keep them in the plastic tub
not MY tub. I do not like their fucking sliminess.

The second:

19 weeks, so I am told. My belly is getting big.
O happier than I've ever seen him, perhaps this is enough.

The third:

Lydia
Laura
Aurelia
Zephyr?
Caterina
*Carolina

The last, a scrap torn from a longer document, the final sentence incomplete:

I cannot bear to leave her. I cannot bear to stay. I am—

Lina heard a sound, the grating of the lock downstairs, the front door closing and her father's footsteps in the entry, the dull weight of him moving through the living room, into the kitchen. She rose from the stool. She did not want Oscar to find her here; it seemed a trespass. She should not be reading these notes, they had not been marked for her. Quickly she replaced the loose pages into the sketchbook, reordered the books on the table, and left the studio. The noise from downstairs stopped, and Lina tiptoed silently to her room. Inside, she leaned against the door and it seemed she held a bowl of water on her head and must move carefully, breathe slowly, or the bowl would dislodge and come crashing to the floor. *Nothing is as I see it. What do I see?*

Josephine

Josephine started on dinner, the pork sausages she'd finished making last week, ready for Mister when he quit the fields. Mister would come inside but the rest would squat to eat among the tobacco plants, the food barely past their mouths before they'd take up picking again.

The sausages frying on the griddle, a pan of hoecake baking in the coals. *Tonight.* An image of Louis came to her, the sound of his voice gravelly and deep as a man's but shot through with high notes, little squeaks that had made her giggle, and he had smiled too, powerless to stop them. How many days had passed since that day? How had he changed? And how had she? Would he still look at her as he did then, with a shy wonder?

Josephine pulled the last two ears of summer corn from the basket under the table and they felt small and light in her hands.

Right now Nathan labored in the fields, sweat running off him, his hands chapped and cut from the thick tobacco stalks. It was hours still until Josephine might steal down to the cabins to speak with him about the undertaker and his daughter.

Josephine husked the corn, pulling the green leaves down to reveal the pearly kernels hidden there, some starting to wrinkle and pull into themselves now, so long after picking. Steam rose from the pot and she dropped in the ears with a splash and a hiss of water hitting the coals. At that instant, a memory descended upon her, a memory of an ear of corn in an apron pocket.

Josephine closed her eyes.

It had been high summer when she ran before, an August night sticky and close, a full moon casting the road and the fields in bright relief. She had left without shoes, but had thought to pack some oatcake stolen from the pantry, and an ear of corn, so abundant at that time of year, Missus would never notice just one gone. An ear of corn in an apron pocket.

She had taken the main road toward town, ignorant of the regular patrols that searched that way for runaways. Somehow she had passed unseen, scrambling down the bramble-filled bank only once, when dust thrown by a fast-approaching horse appeared in the distance and she thought surely no good could come of a man in a hurry. The white man rode past her in a fury of hooves and flying dirt, pebbles and earth showering over her as she crouched in the bushes. She had dusted off and continued walking, sure now that she must be close, close to somewhere.

But the road continued, bordered on both sides by undulating fields of corn, wheat, some tobacco too, only the *chirrup* of night crickets to remind her that other living things existed in this desolate plain. Josephine would have walked all the way to the center of town, or surely been set upon by patrollers, but she heard a voice.

"You, girl, over here." It was a boy's voice, almost feminine in its high-pitched notes, but hoarse as though talking was something to which he had grown unaccustomed. She turned her head, narrowed her eyes and saw, standing in the field alone, a boy no older than herself. He stood shirtless, straight-backed and rigid, his neck in a wooden yoke, his hands fixed in holes to the side, one at each ear. Just above his knees a second yoke held his legs, and this board was wide such that the boy could not walk or sit, only stand or fall in that one place amid the tall green corn. Heat and sun had weathered him harshly, his hair was matted thick with dirt, traces of salt marked his skin white where the sweat had run and dried. His hands hung like alien things, the fingers bloated, the skin purple and blistered.

"Come here, girl. Scratch my back, would ya please. It itches like the devil. Please." Josephine looked around her, thinking there must be someone keeping watch, but she saw no one, only the corn stalks, and a bat flapping black against the silver sky.

She did as he asked, as best she could; she ran a finger down the flayed flesh of his back, hardly a ribbon of skin left, and it seemed to soothe him. Her finger came back sticky with his blood and she wiped it against her skirt. He let out a sigh.

"You done a good deed for a dying boy," he said and laughed. "You can sleep easy now, rest a your days. You're heaven bound." He grinned at her, his mouth a graveyard of dark space and gray stone.

"What'd you do?" Josephine whispered.

"Nothing. Not a thing. I ain't done a thing since I been born," the boy said, and laughed again, loud and raucous until it ended in a flurry of coughs, his throat straining against the yoke as his head pitched forward with the force of them. "You best get moving along," he said finally, and he glanced at her stomach, full and round beneath the apron. "Patrollers come by. I seen them two, three times already tonight. They don't pay me no mind but they'd chase you down, oh they would indeed."

"I don't know where to go," Josephine said. This realization was sudden in her, the boy's blood sticky on her hand, his suffering absolute. The field was open, exposed, and the moon bore down like a face watching from above. Fear swept over her, drying her mouth, weakening her legs where before they had been steady.

"Go to the undertaker's. The undertaker and his daughter. You can make it there 'fore morning. Take the right fork in the road, you'll see his wagons. There's help to be found there. But you better run, run, run! Run! *Run!*" And the boy started screaming, his voice emptying into the fields and the road and beyond.

Josephine left the boy behind but the sound of his voice stayed with her, echoing beside her for miles. As she walked, she whispered to the boy, soothing him as he stood condemned in the cornfield, and soothing too the child within her. A girl, she believed it to be, and she felt strong twists and turns within her belly, rounded pokes of small elbows and knees as she walked on. She continued in her whispering, patting her belly with her right hand to keep the time of her steps and to assure the child that soon they would reach the undertaker's barn, just as the boy had told them. Help could be found there; soon they would be safe. The moon above revealed her, the misshapen curves of her shadow falling long on the road. There is nothing to fear, she whispered to the boy in the cornfield and to the baby inside her, but her voice shook in its whispering.

Night progressed and the sky clouded over, the moonlight dropped away, and Josephine reached the fork in the road. Take the right, the boy had told her, and so she did, pausing only once to look behind her into the gray dark. As she stopped, a single drop of rain fell onto the road. She saw the blackened spot it made, and a cool breeze rose up, chilling the sweat on her face and arms. Josephine hurried along, her hand patting faster against the underside of her belly. The baby no longer twisted but now, she supposed, slept with the rhythm of her steps, her bare feet moving faster, faster over the pebbles and dust.

At last she saw it, yellow as a second moon: a lone lantern in the cool, prestorm night. A barn, the wagons, just as the boy had told her. Josephine approached silently across the grass, not using the path to the main house, and then she saw the wooden boxes laid out against the side of the barn, just under the eaves, stacked one atop the other. Caskets. *The undertaker and his daughter.*

Softly Josephine knocked on the barn door and it swung open wide. A young white woman stood in the doorway, her eyes soft and brown as a horse's flank, and Josephine stood for a moment outside, the woman inside. Worlds separated them, it seemed to

Josephine, and how was she ever to cross that divide, the threshold between the barn and the night? But without a word the woman nodded and smiled and took Josephine's hand, and pulled her inside. There was a man in the barn, his eyes like the woman's, the sleeves of his shirt rolled to the elbows, his forearms strong and brown from sun, and he looked once at Josephine, his eyes going to her stomach, and his face changed in a way Josephine could not determine, whether from soft to hard, from certain to hesitant, she couldn't say, the light was too dim. Then the woman took Josephine's hand and laid her down to rest on a pallet of straw, the smell of animals comforting and close. This must be the place the boy had spoken of, Josephine had thought. It must be that help could be found here. Josephine had continued in her whispering but now it was the young woman to whom she spoke, not the boy or even the child inside, and the woman looked at her with those soft eyes and stroked her hair, nodding as Josephine told of Bell Creek and her journey away from there. Josephine talked until exhaustion overcame her and it was the woman's face she saw last as her eyes closed.

On that long-ago night, Josephine had fallen asleep in the undertaker's barn as though she were rolling off a cliff, a silent and complete surrender, trusting that someone below would catch her.

JOSEPHINE PLUCKED THE COBS FROM the hot water and set them, steaming yellow, onto a plate. Inside Mr. Jefferson's chest of drawers, just a small one, Josephine kept the face of that boy in the field and the sound of his screams. She kept the feel of her own rounded belly, the ghost memory of those movements inside her.

Mister walked through the door, the stench of sweat and earth reeling off him in waves as he moved through the kitchen and into the dining room. Josephine followed him and placed the plate on the table next to the sausages already there. She turned to fetch Missus Lu. Mister and Missus always ate the midday meal together. It was the only time they sat face-to-face, the only time they spoke a word to each other, that Josephine could tell.

"Leave your Missus be for now," Mister said. "Tell me, what did the doctor say?"

Josephine stopped in the doorway and turned back to face him. Mister's hands were in his lap and sunlight from the windows cut across the long table and hit his face so every line seemed drawn there with Missus' sharp pencil. There was no color in his skin, only the grays and browns of exhaustion and physical labor under the sun. His eyes merely suggested blue, the color tending to navy, not the indigo that Missus Lu had spoken of, that had once so bewitched her. Papa Bo's eyes had been a deep brown; the blue must have come from Mister's mama. Josephine never heard talk of Mister's mama, or his dead sisters.

"The doctor, he said Missus is almost certainly dying. He believes she has a tumor, here," and Josephine touched the back of her neck. "He can't say how much longer she'll have, maybe months, maybe more or less. He'll return in two days and we're to send for him if her condition changes. We're to send for him at once."

Mister said nothing. Steam rose from the corn in great white billows. The smell of the sausages, their drippings visible on Mister's plate, made Josephine's stomach grumble, the pangs loud in the silence of the room, the air thick with Mister's contemplation.

Josephine thought of Lottie's ghosts who danced by the river. Did Papa Bo dance there too? Did he carry his stick, the one tipped in silver? The one he used to beat Mister? Again her stomach rumbled, or perhaps it was the blood rushing in her ears. Mister's shoulders bent over the plate, and she saw Papa Bo there with his stick, raising it high above his head to bring it down across Mister's back.

Mister cut into the sausage and raised the fork. He opened his mouth but then stopped and threw the knife and fork down with a clatter that made Josephine start. He pushed his chair away and stepped toward the door, looking up at Josephine with a deep confusion, as though nothing she had said could be true, as though the world that had once seemed so bright—a lovely young wife, an inheritance, a farm of his very own—was now shrouded in mist and peopled only with ghostly apparitions.

He is a good man, Missus Lu believed. Josephine did not know how goodness came to a person. Papa Bo's preaching voice had rung loud and heavy day in, day out, as if a battle raged within his chest between God and the devil himself. Was he now up in heaven with the angels and the Lord? Had he found his salvation in the end? Perhaps if Mister's mama had lived, perhaps if he had not come to Virginia, to Bell Creek where the earth was worn out, where Missus would never be happy. Perhaps if he had never married Missus, never even glimpsed her round cheek, the sly arching brow of her at sixteen, itching to flout her daddy's will.

Mister was beside Josephine and then gone, her skirts ruffled by the breeze of his passing. She heard the rattle of the door latch and his boots booming across the porch and down the front steps to the dirt path. Josephine followed and watched as he emerged from the barn, leading his horse. He mounted and spurred the horse along the road to town.

As he disappeared from view, she heard Missus' voice calling from inside, "Josephine! Josephine! What has happened?"

Josephine returned to the hall and Missus was descending the stairs. She had combed her own hair and fixed it up in back.

"Whatever happened? Why all this slamming?" Missus had returned to herself. Though the cut blazed raw on her face and the back buttons on her dress were not fully fastened, she spoke now as mistress of her house. "Josephine, why did Mister see fit to gallop away like the hounds of hell chased after him?"

Josephine hesitated. How was she to answer? *Keep her calm*, Dr. Vickers had said. Josephine searched her mind for an explanation that would not see another knife gone from the kitchen, another afternoon of fits and rages.

"He was sorry at having missed the doctor's visit, not having time to see the doctor," Josephine said with care. "He wished to see Dr. Vickers himself."

"And what will your Mister do then? Shout and scold? It will do no good, I will still be as I am now."

Missus gazed out the open front door, at the spot by the barn where the dust thrown by Mister's horse still lingered, clouding the air. "The weather is fine today for working," she said. "Jackson is keeping them in the fields then?"

"I believe so, yes, Missus."

"Widow Price has had troubles aplenty, so I hear." She turned to Josephine. "I want you to go to Jackson, tell him they are to work as usual, there is to be no relaxing just because Mister has left on an urgent errand. Tell him Mister has left on an urgent errand, and he will return shortly . . ." Missus' voice trailed off. "Go, Josephine. Now."

THE FIELD HANDS WERE WORKING some distance from the house. A hazy sun shimmered overhead and the day's heat lay heavy across the fields as Josephine struggled through the rows of leaves, a forest of green tobacco stalks reaching almost to her shoulders. All the field hands were there, even Therese, whose back bent almost parallel to the ground, a dark blue cloth wrapped around her head so that Josephine could not see her face. Her working days could not be many more, Josephine thought, and then what would become of her?

Josephine called to Jackson and he lifted his head. He stood beside Therese, who lagged behind the others at the far end of the row.

Jackson called, "Nathan!" and pointed to Josephine, as though his business with Therese could not be interrupted by traversing the length of the field to where Josephine stood.

Nathan laid down his bundle of leaves and walked to her, flicking sweat off his face with the fingers on his right hand. He limped with slow jerky movements as if learning to walk anew with each step. The others kept on, backs stooped, arms pumping in a constant awkward rhythm of *grasp pull drop*. Winton moved between the rows, picking up the stacks of leaves, twisting the stems to secure each bundle, each like a fan of many hands, palms pressed together and wrists tied.

"Uh-huh," Nathan said.

"Missus wants me to say that Mister's been called away on an urgent errand, and y'all should stay in the fields till suppertime as usual. She wanted me to tell Jackson that."

Nathan nodded and looked to her with dead eyes. Josephine said, "Nathan, I heard you ran before. Did the undertaker help you?" The recklessness of saying these words here in the fields with Jackson so near made Josephine's face hot and her throat ache with a stiffness as though she'd tried to swallow something too big to go down. She scratched at the inside of her right wrist, shot a glance to Jackson who stood with one hand on hip, one knee bent, his eyes on Therese. Certainly Nathan must hear the pounding of her heart.

Nathan tipped his head to the side a little, shifted his weight with a wince of pain. "I ran before but no more, they cut my heels." He spoke slowly. "I ain't got nothing to say to you, girl. Go on back." Josephine held his eyes for just a moment, hoping for a nod, a blink, some encouragement that she should try again, that he had something more to tell her. But he looked back at her stony and mute, then turned and limped away toward Jackson. She could not hear Nathan speak but Jackson looked to him as though listening and then shifted his gaze to Josephine. She nodded but he did not respond, only stared at her for a moment more and then down again at Therese as she bent to pull a leaf away.

Josephine crossed again through the tobacco and toward the back of the house. She would speak to Nathan tonight, down by the cabins. Of course they could not speak in the fields, with Jackson so close. It had been foolish of Josephine to try. What if Jackson became suspicious? What if he spoke to Missus? Josephine waved away an insect that buzzed in her ear and wished she could return to the moment with Nathan and take back the words she had said, stop her carelessness before it happened, and she scratched again at the inside of her wrist until her fingernails drew blood.

Once out of the tobacco Josephine stopped. She did not want to return to Missus Lu, to whatever mood might have struck her in Josephine's absence and the tasks that lay ahead for the day. Impulsively she left the path and cut through the tall grasses of the far lawn and around toward the front of the house, toward the road and the open plain of wild grass beyond. Her feet were already restless, reckless, and speaking like that to Nathan—the foolishness! What if her chance already was dashed? Without a backward glance, Josephine crossed the dusty road. She strode farther and farther away from Bell Creek, the grass growing wilder with brambles and ivy, a persistent deerfly buzzing at the sweat on her bare arms, her face and neck. The air seemed wilder here too, smelling of dry grass and old manure, nothing of the flower beds' perfume or house smells—lye from the wash, grease from the cooking.

Finally, her breath labored, Josephine turned and looked back at Bell Creek, the only place she'd ever known. The white walls, the gray-green roof, the slope of the earth so familiar to her, the way the house stood up just a little from the surrounds, the porch jutting out like a bottom lip from a face. The flower beds looked frivolous and showy, flouncy skirts around a stout middle. The close-together windows of the second floor were so many eyes staring out toward the windblown treetops and far-off foothills.

For a moment Josephine watched Bell Creek and she imagined that if she ran now, the house surely would lift from its foundations and chase her down. Those window-eyes saw her standing there, so far from her usual places, well beyond the permissible limits of where she might go. The house's gaze was reproachful and accusing. It beckoned her back and Josephine lifted one foot, then the next, retracing her steps through the field.

As Josephine walked, the full memory of the night she had run came to her: of the boy's instructions, *look for the wagons*, the undertaker and his daughter. She remembered the woman, brown hair hanging loose around a face like a heart, pointed at the bottom. She remembered the woman stroking her arm, and then sleep had come, a blessed thing after the boy's screams, the unrelenting fear, the constant forward motion. And then suddenly Josephine had been awake in the dark. The woman and the man were arguing, the woman's voice so young and strong: *We cannot send her back. Would you have us send her back?* But the man had answered in anger: *She is with child, the risk is too great. We cannot help her.*

A fear had cut through Josephine as she heard those words, just as pain spooned deep within her belly. The two seemed linked, the understanding that these people would not help her and the twisting inside. Josephine waited, pretending still to sleep. She heard the man and the woman move farther into the barn, and then she crept away, out a side door, stepping through matted straw and then mud and then cool grass, back to Bell Creek. Where else was she to go? She kept off the road as best she could, cutting through grassy fields, corn rows, pastures with dry turned earth lying fallow and acre after acre of ripe, greening plants nearly ready for the harvest. As the pains came through her, she would stop and bend forward, the posture somehow easing the force of them. The sky boiled with black clouds shot through with brilliant lightning and claps that each time made Josephine start and move her legs faster, faster to arrive before the rains began to fall.

At dawn, as she neared Bell Creek, the storm finally descended and the rain soaked her cold and wet to the skin. She had stepped off the road and passed through an expanse of wild meadow and chickweed that brought her quicker to Bell Creek, but the wet grasses lashed at her ankles, the burrs and thorns tore at her feet. Finally the house rose into view, through the dim haze of the rain and the rising gray light, and she saw Bell Creek for the first time from a distance, the sight making her forget for a moment the twisting in her belly. She marveled at the house, at its size and solid square perimeters, how it took possession of that small hill upon which it was built. How could such a vast construction seem so confining within?

Josephine had come again to the front gate, latched closed as she had left it only hours before, but it seemed a lifetime ago, hers or another's. The realization that soon she would birth a child fell upon her with a raw terror. Her teeth shook in her head, her bare feet numb to the ankles, bloated and strange and disconnected from her body as she walked those last paces up the path. Through the front door she had tried to creep, up the stairs, but those slip-sliding feet would not do her bidding. Missus had heard.

"Josephine, what have you been doing?" Missus appeared at her bedroom door, fully dressed but her hair hung loose around her face, such a strange view because Missus never wore her hair down, only at night in bed would she allow Josephine to release it. "Where have you been?"

"Missus, I—" and Josephine had collapsed there on the landing, the weight of her body finally too great to bear, the floor rushing up to meet her and she had welcomed it.

Later, after Dr. Vickers had left the room and then Missus behind him, the silence stretched forward and around her, containing all that Josephine had never told and all that she now regretted. If she had run months before, when the undertaker would have helped her, where might she be now? Would she be holding a child, her child? Would she be a free woman in a free state? Josephine had wept atop that high bed, feeling as if she rested on the upper side of a cloud, and nothing could touch her because of what she had lost and her body seemed both empty and full of a terrible wisdom.

JOSEPHINE SHOOK HER HEAD TO clear away her memories. She had returned to the house now and stood just paces from the back door. There was no breeze and the wash hung limp on the line between the two oaks. Around her feet the chickens pecked and sauntered, their soft low murmurs sounding so much like comfort, like all the chickens sought to make one of their number see that this is a good life, the sun, the dirt, the cool dark of the coop; do not grieve for the way things are. Her hands were shaking, Josephine realized, with the force of her remembering. The drawers she had kept so carefully shut all these years were now flying open as though in deciding to run again she had let loose something rough and dangerous within herself as well.

With a sharp clap of her hands, she tried to scatter the chickens. "Go on," she said, and the words nearly did not come from her throat, which felt thick, closed tight, and she said it again, "Go on," hoarser and louder this time and the chickens flapped away.

Lina

S o, how are we doing?" Dan asked. Lina and Garrison were in his office for the first weekly meeting on the reparations claim. "Dresser will be here later, but let's get started. I may have to run out early." He checked his watch. "Who's first?"

Lina glanced over at Garrison, who was sitting at attention, his eyes pegged to Dan. Over the week, they'd spoken on the phone frequently but she'd barely seen him, each of them intent on their respective assignments, their digital clocks flashing through the billable minutes. Since Dan's refusal to send her to Richmond, Lina had focused her efforts on finding a plaintiff in New York. She had contacted people at the NAACP, the ABA, the National Bar Association, the Metropolitan Black Bar Association, the Black Women Lawyers' Association. On Wednesday night, she'd attended an ACLU cocktail reception where she wore a name tag, made polite conversation and described the reparations case, the search for a lead plaintiff, the requisite tie to an enslaved ancestor. On her desk sat a stack of jotted-down phone numbers and business cards passed to her by people interested in the case; Garrison had e-mailed his list of contacts. "I'll follow up in the next few days," Lina had told each one of them. But she hadn't made a single call. In Lina's office, the photo of Lu Anne and Josephine remained pinned to the corkboard behind her computer. And quietly, without billing her time, she had continued to research the Rounds family and the Underground Railroad. She had spent hours online and ordered some relevant books from various out-of-state libraries, but they had yet to arrive.

Lina wondered with a sinking dread how she would get through this meeting. After a week of research, she should have been able to identify at least a few names for Dan to consider, some stories for him to review. Garrison turned to her with eyebrows raised, and Lina nodded eagerly for him to go first.

"Dan," Garrison began, "let's talk about the problems with this case. We *have* to." Garrison paused, his face all intellectual torment. Dan did a slow blink and tilted his chin down with the slightest of nods.

"What about the whole idea that there is no loss?" Garrison said. "If you look at the numbers, the African American population of the U.S. is in a far better economic position today than if they'd stayed in Africa. You could easily argue that the transatlantic slave trade brought them to this country, which then gave their descendants the opportunity to take advantage of America's economic success. I mean, isn't any wrong done back then negated by the objectively *better* position we find ourselves in today, as compared to the people who *stayed* in Africa?"

"Mmm . . ." Dan leaned back in his chair. "Interesting point."

"And there's also the problem of defining the class," Lina jumped in, relieved that the discussion was taking them far afield from the lead plaintiff question. She wondered if Dan had asked this of them, to talk about the problems, and she had missed the e-mail. "I mean how can we pick and choose? Is anyone with a drop of black blood deserving of compensation? How could we possibly verify everyone?"

"Uh-huh, another good one."

Garrison launched in again and Lina, listening to him, realized three things: first, that Garrison had, in the past week, analyzed the case from all angles; second, that the problems were many and they were large; and third, that she hadn't missed the e-mail—this was Garrison's own meeting agenda.

Africans themselves kept slaves, Garrison said, it was part of the culture. Chieftains of one tribe gladly handed over prisoners from an enemy tribe to the European traders. And what about no retroactive application of law—did a more firmly rooted legal principle even exist? You couldn't penalize someone for doing something that was legal at the time they did it. That's arbitrariness at its worst. That's what *Stalin* did. And most of these antebellum companies had changed names, changed ownership at least once, maybe dozens of times, since the period when they were actually benefiting from slavery. Half the time there's no paper trail. How will we know with certainty that we're suing the bad guys?

Garrison was midsentence, onto something about calculating the correct amount of compensation now due, what interest rate should be used, when Dan brought his hand down on the desk, palm flat, fingers stretched. Lina jumped. Garrison stopped speaking.

"Listen." Dan's voice was loud and tight. "I don't want to hear about the problems. I know it's a tough one. I want to hear about how we are going to *win*. This isn't just any case. Don't you get that? This is the big one. Dresser is right, for all his eccentricities—and believe me, I know he's an eccentric bastard. But the guy is right." He slung his thumb at the bookcase behind him and Lina noticed for the first time the gold letters running up the spines: *United States Reports*. "I've got all the big Supreme Court cases in here, good and bad. The original printing. *Dred Scott, Roe v. Wade, Brown v. Board of Education, Marbury v. Madison,* the *Miranda* ruling. Don't you ever wonder—one hundred years from now, what will people look back on? What will they think are the important ones? The ones to keep, the ones to be ashamed of? This reparations case isn't some corporate big bucks, breach of contract, you-owe-me-money wah wah wah kind of bullshit. Haven't you ever wanted a case like this?" He gave a short, sarcastic laugh. "Jesus Christ, I have."

Dan closed his eyes. No one moved. Lina heard the creaking of the wind against Dan's windows.

When Dan resumed, the volume was lower than before but the words more clear. "I thought the two of you would *get* it. I thought you'd understand the bigger picture here. I mean, seriously, why did you even *go* to law school? This case is the ticket beyond all of this . . . bullshit. It's glory. It's immortality. Okay, maybe not quite, but almost. It's a whole shitload of money, sure, but it's the *idea*. I mean, this case is *history*."

Dan looked genuinely stricken, and Lina, recalling his enthusiasm as her partner mentor, recalling that on Wednesday he'd missed the twins' talent show (again, third year running), recalling his encouraging remarks about partner track, said: "Dan, you're right. This isn't like any other case. I'm with you."

"Thanks, Lina, I appreciate that," Dan said with a curt nod.

Lina looked to Garrison, who seemed to be studying his wingtips. Finally Garrison said, "Me too, Dan," in a small voice, and Lina felt a surge of relief. She didn't want Garrison to be taken off the case; she didn't want to be left alone on this one.

"I'm happy to hear that, Garrison," said Dan, giving him the same little nod. "And listen, I *know* there are obstacles in this case. But our attitude has got to be *win*. Understood?"

Dan's office door opened with a sudden jumble of hallway noise, and Mary, Dan's honey-voiced, silver-haired secretary, appeared in the doorway. Lina often wondered if Mary had once been like Sherri, and how Lina might help to effect a similar transformation. Mary's efficiency was legendary at Clifton; once, with Dan felled by food poisoning, Mary had drafted the cross-examination of a key witness in a fraud trial. Not a single issue left unexamined, Dan had raved afterward.

"Mr. Dresser is here for you," Mary said with a placid smile.

"Oh, great. Send him in." Dan looked at his watch again. "Shit, I'm due in court. Run through what you've done with Dresser," he instructed Lina and Garrison. "I don't need to be here."

Dan greeted Dresser at the door and gave his apologies. "Lina and Garrison will update you. So sorry, Ron, I've got to run. The judge on this case is killing me." Dan shrugged his shoulders and pulled out his aw-shucks, apple-pie grin.

"Dan, my friend, no worries." Dresser put a hand on Dan's shoulder. Today Dresser wore an expensive-looking gray pinstripe suit with a pink tie. His assistant, also in pinstripe, followed behind and quietly shut the door as Dan made his exit.

"Good morning," Dresser said and surveyed the room with his formidable, toffee-colored gaze, then ambled over to Dan's desk and sat behind it. The sight of Dresser in Dan's chair seemed to Lina strangely unsettling, as though Dresser's physicality had erased Dan entirely—not just for the period of his absence at the meeting, but permanently, forever. Dresser's eyes skated over the various personal items on Dan's desk—the deal toys, the photographs—and then he turned to the diplomas hanging on the wall. And somehow the weight of his gaze made everything seem cheap. The desk was solid mahogany, seven feet by four, and yet Dresser presided there as though it were plywood and he a king accustomed to grander surroundings. From behind her, Lina heard the assistant rustling papers. A pen clicked to ready.

"I'm glad we have this opportunity to speak, just the three of us," Dresser said. "Dan is a big presence in a room, wouldn't you agree?"

"Definitely," replied Garrison, with more eagerness than seemed appropriate. Lina looked at him sharply.

"Why don't you tell me the status of the case. Where we stand, what you've been doing."

Lina described the inquiries she had made to the NAACP, the ABA, the reception she'd attended, the books she'd consulted.

"The nature of the harm is so . . . vast," she concluded.

"That is true," Dresser said.

"I'm also following up a lead on an artist named Josephine Bell," Lina began with some caution, wondering if he would view the idea as Dan had: a waste of time and money. "There's been some press about her recently—maybe you've heard the story?"

Dresser nodded, leaned forward in his chair. "Yes, I saw the piece in the *Times*. Very compelling. Exactly the kind of angle I think we should be pursuing."

Conscious of Garrison watching her, Lina described the Bell paintings she'd seen, what Marie Calhoun had told her about the authorship controversy, her discussion with AfriFind and the need to conduct further research in Virginia.

"This sounds very promising, very. Let's send someone down to Richmond, see what we can find. Lina, keep up the good work."

Lina beamed.

"Garrison?" Dresser shifted his attention away from Lina, and she too turned to look at him. He sat in an uncharacteristic slouch, his long legs stretched before him, eyes trained on his toes, looking less like a corporate lawyer than a petulant teenager gearing up to challenge his curfew. Garrison inhaled and then said, "I'm going to ask Dan if he'll let me off this case, Mr. Dresser. I don't believe I'm the right person to be working on it."

Dresser raised his eyebrows. "And why is that?"

Garrison pushed himself out of his slouch, crossed right ankle over left knee, and looked squarely at Dresser. "I think it's an ill-conceived case. I think it will be laughed out of court. And, to be perfectly honest, it's not something I want to be associated with right now. The cause, I mean. The reparations idea. I think in the long term it will hurt my career."

Lina swallowed hard; he had never mentioned these reservations to her before.

"I appreciate your frankness, Garrison," Dresser said with a smile.

"It's always refreshing when a young person speaks his, or her, mind. I do hope you'll reconsider. It would be a shame to lose you at this stage. It would put us back."

"I'm sorry about that."

"And Garrison, I think you're wrong. I think you're just the person to be working on this case. You're—how old?" Dresser leaned back, settled himself into Dan's chair as though expecting to stay awhile.

"Twenty-five."

"And what do your parents do?"

"They're lawyers, both of them."

"Good education, good family. Such success so early in life. Now, just bear with me here for a minute." Dresser paused and smiled at Garrison, an easy smile, as if they sat together at the end of a meal and both their stomachs were full. "Let me ask you something else. You walk down the street here, outside this building, Midtown Manhattan, center of the world in many ways. People coming, going, important people, people with money, people with power. Now how many black people do you see?" He paused. Garrison did not answer. "How many black men driving cabs, selling hot dogs, hauling garbage or furniture or what have you? How many black women getting off the night shift, or pushing a stroller with a white woman's child inside? How many do you see? And then you step inside this building, how many black men and women do you see in *here*? How many are wearing suits? How many are giving the orders? How many are emptying the *garbage*? How many are dishing out the *macaroni*? Now multiply your little life by forty-one *million,* and is there a *need* for some acknowledgment that the deck is stacked? Of course there is. This case, the reparations *idea*, won't lift those men and women out of their disadvantage, but it will cause the whole rest of the world to take notice, to do some counting on their own. And not just the Caucasians, but you too, boys like you who have achieved success in this world easier than you thought you would.

Easier than your parents thought you would. We're talking about a conversation here, not a public whipping. It's just that money is the quickest way to get people's attention. You call it the legacy of slavery and nobody bats an eye. You call it six point two trillion dollars and it's a different story."

Dresser eyed Garrison levelly. Garrison did not meet his gaze; he swallowed, and his Adam's apple rose and fell like a cork on a rough ocean. On the other side of the door a photocopier started up and the office reverberated with its throbbing sound, the whoosh of paper slotting into plastic trays.

Abruptly Garrison began to speak, his words coming in a rush. "I mean, it's not like Dan is on board with any of this, not really. You know he's only doing this for the marketing. It's a PR thing, *diversity.*"

Lina watched Garrison's careful demeanor crumble. She glanced at Dresser, whose lips were pulled down in a grim frown. "Mr. Dresser," Lina interrupted, wanting only to rescue this rapidly deteriorating situation: if Garrison managed to lose a client as powerful as Ron Dresser, he wouldn't just be fired from Clifton—he would never find legal work in New York again. "What Garrison is trying to say is that . . . the firm values diversity, of course. But this case is so much more. Dan was just now, just before you arrived, telling us what sets the reparations suit apart. Why the legal issues are almost secondary here. This case will make history."

Dresser smiled. "Lina, don't worry. It does not surprise me that Daniel J. Oliphant the Third is not fully committed, body and soul, to the principle of reparations due and owing for the labor of our enslaved predecessors. I could care less what Dan *believes.* Dan is a businessman. *I* am a businessman. We understand each other, and we understand that I am calling the shots here." Dresser shifted his gaze from Lina to Garrison.

"If Dan was committed to this, personally committed, we'd be taking charity here, and that's not what I want. I don't want his charity. I want him to jump when I say. And he jumps pretty damn high. And someday you'll be talking to all sorts of baby Dans, and they'll ask *you* how high to jump. You see what I'm saying?"

Garrison nodded.

"So are you still asking to be removed from the case?"

"No." Garrison's voice was low. "No, I guess not."

"Good. Glad to hear it. You know, it's Lina who's got the harder road."

Garrison glanced toward her, happy, it seemed, for Dresser's focus to have shifted.

"She's a fish out of water, that one," Dresser said, as though she were unable to hear him.

"Um—" Lina stuttered, starting to laugh, to ask what he meant, but Dresser placed his palms on the desk and stood. From behind, Lina heard the assistant rise with a crack of knee.

"Well, I will leave you fine attorneys to it then," he said. "Thanks very much for the updates on your work. I'm glad we had this chance to discuss the issues. Discussion, always a good thing."

LINA SAT AT HER DESK, trying to study a list of prominent African Americans in New York City but really considering what Dresser had said. *The harder road.* Because she was a woman? Because she was short? Because her law school ranked top-ten but not top-five?

"Hey."

She looked up from her list. Garrison stood in the hall outside her office.

"Hi," Lina said uncertainly. Garrison had exited the meeting quickly, his head down. They had not spoken since.

"I just wanted to explain about all that earlier, with Dresser."

"Oh, no need." Lina waved her hand as though fanning away smoke. "I understood what you were saying. I was just worried Dresser might . . . you know, take it the wrong way."

"This case has been getting to me. And Dan, sometimes it's hard to take him seriously. But I shouldn't have asked to come off the case. Or said that about Dan. Dresser must think I'm an idiot."

"I'm sure he doesn't," Lina said, relieved to hear the old companionability in his voice. "Just make sure you impress him with the brilliance of your legal mind."

"If only it were that easy." Garrison gave a wide smile. "And I wanted to ask you about that artist angle. Dresser seemed really impressed with you."

"I wasn't sure I should mention the idea, actually. Dan's been against it from the beginning. He thinks it's a wild-goose chase. And a waste of money."

Garrison's gaze shifted to the corkboard behind Lina's computer where Lina had pinned a printout of *Lottie* next to the photograph of Lu Anne and Josephine on the porch at Bell Creek. Garrison moved into Lina's office and bent to examine the portrait. "Those eyes are so intense," he said. "Is that the artist?"

"No, that's her work, or some people think it is."

They both studied *Lottie* in silence and then Lina said, "Hey, do you want to go to the show? The exhibit opens tonight at a gallery downtown." The words were out of Lina's mouth before she had time to consider all the various ways Garrison might take such an invitation. They were just friends, weren't they? A sliver of doubt existed, and this uncertainty forced an unexpected rush of heat to Lina's cheeks as she waited for his reply.

"Sorry, Lina. I already have plans," Garrison said slowly, eyes still on *Lottie*. "Some other time, I promise."

LINA ARRIVED LATE AT THE *Art and Artifice* exhibit, just as Porter Scales was finishing his lecture. The gallery was packed, almost impassable, and with difficulty she nudged her way into an empty corner and stood on tiptoe to see Porter, who stood atop a small platform set up in the back gallery. Despite their numbers, the crowd was hushed, attentive. Porter spoke without amplification but his voice filled the space.

" . . . So, where does that leave Josephine Bell?" he was saying. "Based on my analysis of subject matter, brushstrokes, and materials, it is without doubt that the separate hands of *two* artists are represented in the Bell catalogue. In my opinion—and I stress that this is an *opinion* based on my experience as an art historian, academic, and critic—it seems most likely that Josephine Bell, the house girl, created the slave portraits, the Bell Creek landscapes, *Children No. 2,* and the other most accomplished, best-known works. I have come to the painful conclusion—and let me be frank, it has been a painful journey for me as one who has studied and loved Lu Anne Bell for many years. But the Bell works present *such* a departure from the formalistic plantation landscape of the time period that I believe only an artist who was removed, so to speak, from the confines of that world could have given us the realism and the sensitivity that make the Bell works such masterpieces today. Josephine Bell was an artistic outsider in every sense of the word. And it was only Josephine Bell who was beside Lu Anne Bell all day, every day during the relevant time period. It was only Josephine Bell who had the opportunity and the *reason* to create these pictures."

A ripple of heads turned toward neighbors, whispers and nods swept through the crowd.

"However," Porter resumed, "definitive proof is still needed before we can formally credit Josephine Bell with authorship. I would urge everyone who cares about this debate, who cares about setting the historical record straight, to support further research and analysis. I urge the Bell Center and the Stanmore Foundation to open up their archives and allow independent art historians to review the available materials." He paused, then smiled. "And I encourage everyone to enjoy the show tonight."

Porter stepped down and immediately the chatter of the crowd rose, loud and surprised. An elegantly dressed man next to Lina shook his head. "Jesus Christ," he said to a woman with long blond hair and bare shoulders standing beside him. "So what's my Bell *worth*?"

Lina slowly made her way into the main gallery where the portraits hung. The scene was chaotic—photographers and journalists everywhere, confused-looking critics, dazed and worried owners of Bell works—and progress was slow. Near the door, Lina stepped outside for some air.

Marie stood alone on the sidewalk, smoking a cigarette and adjusting the complicated shoulder straps of a long and tight burgundy dress.

"Marie," Lina said. "Congratulations on the show. You couldn't fit one more body in there."

"Ah, thank you." Marie lifted her eyebrows and exhaled a rolling column of smoke. "But did you hear? The Christie's guy refused to come tonight. The Stanmore Foundation says they want to sue me! Me!"

"But why?" Lina asked.

"Libel, they say. It is incredible," and she drew out the word, enunciating each syllable with her French throatiness: *in-cre-dee-ble*. "They say the Josephine theory is all political correctness, historical revision, no basis in fact, blah blah blah. But Porter is convinced, and he knows the Bell work inside out. And finally, *finally* the authenticators are starting to look at the canvases. X-raying and searching for fingerprints with these funny cameras they have. Handwriting samples. It will take some time to prove Josephine, that is all, but it is *killing* me." She sucked at the last bit of her cigarette and crushed it under a stiletto.

"How is Mr. South Virginia holding up?" Lina asked.

"Fine, but we can't sell a thing now, of course. Who knows what this will do to value? If nothing definitive comes out, the market for Bells will be flat, too much uncertainty. And if Josephine is proven, well, then they will go like little hotcakes."

Marie paused to reapply her lipstick, peering into a tiny silver compact she pulled from her slender purse, and Lina was seized by a sudden impulse, perhaps self-destructive, almost certainly unwise, but she followed it. "Marie," she asked, speaking quickly, "were you and my father ever involved? I mean, romantically?"

"Oh, my darling." Marie touched a finger to the corner of her lips and closed the compact with a sharp click. She sighed. "Yes. Yes, we were. Many, many years ago. You were just a baby."

With an immediate shattering sadness Lina thought of the photo of her parents, Grace's gaze fixed to Oscar's face, their hands clasped. "Did my mother know?" Lina's voice was faint.

"Ah." Marie shook her head and looked to the sidewalk, the crushed cigarette butts and stray plastic cups stained red with wine grit. She raised her green eyes, darkly shadowed with makeup, and looked directly at Lina. "I do not think so. But I could be wrong. It was a very . . . short affair. I knew your mother, of course. We were friends. It was not my . . . finest moment." Before Lina's eyes, Marie's glamor seemed to fade with this regret, her face turning pale, the makeup garish, and Lina wished, almost, that she had not asked the question. For a moment they remained motionless and silent on the sidewalk outside the gallery. Lina watched a yellow cab glide slowly past, looking for a fare. Confirmation of Oscar's lie had left her with a coldness in her limbs and a fluttery unease in her stomach, but she felt no antagonism toward Marie; Marie had told her the truth.

Lina reached out and squeezed Marie's shoulder. "Don't worry about it," Lina said. "Let's go back in."

"*Oui,* my tiny American," Marie said, with relief as bright as her lacquered fingernails, and together they reentered the gallery. Just inside the door, a tall man tentatively approached Marie.

"Ms. Calhoun?" he said and reached out his hand.

At that moment, Lina's attention was drawn toward the back of the gallery. She glimpsed an angular shoulder, a thin form, a flicker of familiar face. Was it—*Garrison?* Lina craned her neck but the figure melted away.

"And let me introduce Lina Sparrow, a lawyer here in New York." Lina turned back to Marie, who was making terse, efficient introductions. Lina took the man's outstretched hand and looked up: he had dark hair shaved close, large amber-brown eyes, the color of honey in a jar. Along the upper rims of his ears, where the cartilage curved with the delicacy of a seashell, jutted two studded rows of piercings.

The man tilted his chin down. "Nice to meet you." He seemed to Lina about her age, perhaps a bit older. Over a black T-shirt and green cargo pants he wore a tuxedo jacket that fit snug around his wide, wiry shoulders.

"Lina, this is Jasper Battle. He has some Bell pictures, so he believes, but he's uninterested in selling. I've told him that I'm in the business of *buying* art, I am not a freelance authenticator, but he has been very persistent." Marie flashed him a winning smile that undercut, somewhat, the irritation in her voice.

"I'm sorry I've bothered you. I just don't have the money for an authenticator." Jasper returned her smile, his genuine, a little sheepish.

Marie's gaze shifted, and she laughed and waved at a stout man in owlish glasses standing several paces away. "I'm afraid you must excuse me," Marie said, and flashed Lina a brief look of apology as she darted into the gallery.

"And she was the only one who even returned my e-mails," Jasper said, seemingly more to himself than to Lina, and rubbed a flat palm over his shaved head. Lina noticed slender tattoos that circled his wrists like bracelets or chains.

"So what makes you think you have some Bells?" Lina asked, unsure if she really wanted to hear the answer. Everything about Jasper Battle—from his piercings to Marie's obvious reluctance to speak with him—gave Lina reason to exit this conversation as quickly as possible. She skimmed the crowd, hoping for another sight of Garrison, a friend of her father's, anyone.

"Mine are so similar to these," and he waved a hand toward the wall of portraits. "But I have no idea who made them. They're family heirlooms, so my dad always said, but no signature."

"Family?" Lina settled her gaze firmly on Jasper's face. She noted the color of his skin: a burnished tan that could have passed for Persian, African, Latino, Caucasian. "So are you related to Lu Anne Bell?"

"I don't know. Either Lu Anne or Josephine, I guess, depending on who you believe." He shrugged his shoulders. "That's what I'm trying to figure out."

Suddenly the noise and bustle of the room fell away and Lina felt a sharpening of this little pocket of air and space where she and Jasper stood.

"Do you mind if we go someplace to talk?"

"Talk about . . . ?" A half-smile tweaked his mouth, though in flirtation or surprise Lina couldn't say and didn't care.

"About your family heirlooms."

"My dad died three months ago," Jasper said, picking at the label of his beer bottle. They were sitting atop high stools at a long mahogany bar strewn with bruised rose petals. After leaving the gallery they had wandered a few blocks south to a bar Jasper knew, a cavernous underground space lit by flickering torches affixed to the walls. The place smelled of woody incense and the salty heat of bodies and liquor.

"These drawings have been hanging in my parents' room for as long as I can remember," Jasper continued, not looking at Lina. "My dad always said that the artist was a distant relation. But that's all I know. He didn't talk much about his family. He was an only child. I never even met my paternal grandparents—they died before I was born."

Lina jotted notes as Jasper spoke. A tall cylinder of orange juice stood untouched on the bar in front of her. She sat with legs crossed tight, her back straight.

"When I saw that article in the paper about Lu Anne Bell, I recognized the style of the pictures they'd printed. I've got three that look just the same—one of a white woman sitting on a porch, one of an African American man, and the last of a man and a woman together, slaves or sharecroppers, at least that's what I always thought. Some real old-timers."

"I'd be interested in looking at them," Lina said, thinking of the Bell portraits she had seen—most were in oil. Were there any drawings? "I'd also like to do some genealogical research on your dad. Where was he from?"

"Arkansas. Real rural. I don't think he had the greatest childhood there." Jasper spoke slowly, his voice hard to hear. "He fought in Vietnam too, he lived through a lot. I wish I had asked him more." Jasper's elbows were propped on the bar, his back curved slightly. He had taken off his jacket and Lina could see the knobby bones of his spine through his thin T-shirt, and this sight struck her hard somewhere in the middle of her chest. She put her pen down.

"I'm sorry," Lina said. "About your father."

Jasper glanced at her and nodded once, an acknowledgment that gave away nothing of himself. "And why are you so interested in all this?" he asked, straightening on the stool and turning to face her. "You're a lawyer, Marie said?"

"Yes, with the corporate firm Clifton & Harp." She briefly described the reparations suit, her ongoing research, her search for a lead plaintiff. "We have some other candidates," Lina said, "but our client would like us to pursue the Josephine Bell angle. The artistic controversy will help with publicity for the case, and there's a strong . . . symbolism there." Lina took a long swallow of orange juice, ice cubes clattering in the glass. "But we need to find a descendant."

There was silence. Then a throat clearing. "I'm not really sure about any lawsuit," Jasper said. "I didn't realize that's what this was about."

"Well, it's not a *lawsuit* lawsuit. It's reparations, for slavery. It's historic." Lina heard Dan's voice echoing in her ears.

"But me? The *plaintiff*? I don't think . . . And my mom—she doesn't even know I'm looking into all this."

"I'd be happy to meet with her. This is a groundbreaking case, Jasper. Generations who just disappeared, who have never been memorialized. No one knows their names." Lina was leaning toward Jasper, their knees almost touching. She heard the earnestness in her voice, the utter absence of dignified remove, but she did not tone it down as she would have for Dan or Dresser or any of her clients. "This case will help tell their story."

"But, I'm not—I mean, I'm not even black. At least I don't *think* I am . . ." Jasper's voice trailed off. "I'm sorry, but I'm not interested in any lawsuit."

Lina realized she was losing him, and this—the looming possibility of failure—made it seem urgently and improbably true that here was Josephine Bell's descendant, discovered with a luck so pure Lina did not even question it, and she had only to persuade him to help her. Did the color of his skin matter? No, Lina decided, wouldn't his racial ambiguity be a strength? Wasn't this a history from which they had all emerged, every American, black and white and every shade in between? Porter Scales's essay came back to her: *Who is slave and who is free?* Jasper's uncertainty about his family roots would only serve to strengthen Dresser's point about the need to remember. She thought of *Children No. 2*, the closed eyes of that mysterious boy.

"Ready for another beer?" Lina said, smiling. "On the firm." She ordered one for herself as well and folded away the notebook. "So, tell me more about yourself."

Jasper hesitated and then he shrugged his shoulders and began to talk. He was a musician, he told her. His band, The Wisdom, played in and around New York City. All five of them were high school friends from Queens, the most underrated of the New York boroughs in Jasper's purely objective opinion. His parents had moved to Poughkeepsie after Jasper went away to college, but he still thought of Queens as home. Jasper was excited about the band's development; they were getting serious, getting better. They'd had some small successes, songs played on certain radio stations that Lina didn't know, gigs played at clubs to which Lina had never been.

They finished their beers and Jasper nodded at the tattooed blonde behind the bar. "This round's on me," Jasper said. Lina glanced at her watch, thinking she really should leave, but there seemed a tenuous connection between them now, their stools close, their heads bowed together over the bar. As people, they could not be more different, Lina decided, and this made it easier for her to focus. She wasn't looking to manipulate the situation, not exactly, but she knew what she needed to accomplish. Wasn't this part of her professional acumen, the ability to persuade, to convince the unconvinceable? The new beer arrived and Lina tilted back the bottle.

"So do you do this a lot, this reparations stuff?" Jasper asked.

"No. Usually I represent corporate clients. Contract disputes, that sort of thing."

Jasper's eyebrows lifted and fell. "You know, don't take this the wrong way, but you don't really seem like a lawyer."

"I don't?" Lina wasn't sure if she felt insulted or flattered. "Is that a good thing or a bad thing?"

"Depends on how you feel about being a lawyer, I guess," Jasper said.

"I've always wanted to be a lawyer," Lina answered quickly, disliking this shift of focus from Jasper to her. Reflexively she told him the story she always recited when asked why she had chosen the law, a story that Oscar often told too as part of their family lore. "When I was ten, I decided that I didn't need any more babysitters. I knew the subway, I had my can of mace. I didn't see why we needed to pay some teenager ten bucks an hour to read a magazine while I did my homework. So I convinced my father that I could take care of myself. And he agreed. He said, 'Lina, you'd make a great lawyer. You could argue the pants off any judge.' And I guess that just stuck in my head. It seemed to make sense for me. I could support myself, support my dad too if he needed it. It's a good, stable career, not too many surprises. You know, reliable. My dad's an artist, and I knew I didn't have what it took for that kind of life."

"How'd you know?" Jasper's gaze weighed heavily on Lina. She shifted on the stool and took a quick sip of her drink.

"Well, I was never very good at drawing or painting. Even photography, I don't have a good eye."

"So you didn't have what it took to be your *father's* kind of artist."

"If you mean successful, then yes, I guess so."

"No, I mean that anything can be art. Don't you think? If you do it well enough, if you love it."

Lina paused, trying to think of a suitable response, funny or sarcastic, but she felt unexpectedly stilled by him—his unabashed sincerity, this talk of love and art—and the feeling both terrified and thrilled her. That old story about her dad always elicited a smile from the listener, and for that reason Lina enjoyed telling it, but the anecdotal flipness now seemed ridiculous, dishonest.

"I do, I do . . . love it," Lina stammered. "Being a lawyer, I mean."

Lina remembered suddenly, vividly the immigration law clinic she had taken her last year at law school, a complete departure from the other, more practical classes in which she usually enrolled (Litigation Techniques, Trial Advocacy, Evidence). The professor, a harried, gray-haired mother of two, assigned Lina to represent an asylum seeker in Manhattan's immigration court. Lina's client was a young woman from the Sudan, and this woman—was she even twenty?—had looked at her hands and tapped one small, slippered foot as she told Lina her story.

Ange. Her client's name had been Ange.

But Lina did not tell Jasper this story. An abrupt, paralyzing shyness overcame her, a fear that speaking Ange's name would reveal something about herself that she was not ready to show.

"I'm sorry, it's late. I need to get home," Lina said, pulling some bills from her wallet and placing them on the bar. She stood and slipped into her suit jacket.

"Here's my card," she said. "I hope you'll reconsider about the reparations case."

"I'll . . . think about it." Jasper moved to stand beside her. "Carolina," he said, looking down at the card. "That's a pretty name."

"Um, thanks." Lina gazed at the floor and then up again at him, his eyes looking almost gold in the refracted light from the long glimmering row of liquor bottles. A spinning sensation overcame Lina then, perhaps from blood rushing to her head, or those two beers, or Jasper's smooth gaze, or the fractured feeling she'd had ever since reading those notes left by her mother. She felt herself tilt, the bar tending away from her, slanting toward the scuffed, dusty floor.

Jasper reached out and grabbed Lina's elbow. "Are you okay?"

"Yes. Fine. Head rush, I think." She steadied herself on his arm. "Long day." The tattoo around his right wrist, she saw now, was a bird.

JASPER PUT HER IN A cab, closing the door behind her, waving good-bye as the cab left the curb. Lina leaned back against the seat and closed her eyes. This evening had not gone as she had hoped— Jasper remained unconvinced, she had no definitive information about Josephine Bell. Even Porter Scales's lecture had been inconclusive as to authorship of the Bell works. And yet this tattooed, pierced stranger who played in a rock band, who had lectured her about *art*, offered the barest whisper of a chance in the reparations case. And Lina was unsure if it was this possibility or the memory of his arm steadying her, holding her up, that made her want to see him again.

Monday

Lina left the house early. Today she would again ask Dan to send her to Richmond. This time Lina was prepared, her arguments fleshed out, her reasons clear. Every press article dealing with the Bell exhibit was clipped and filed in a three-ring binder. A spreadsheet displayed the (shockingly minimal) cost of a one-to-two-day trip to Richmond. A bullet-point list described the reasons that Josephine's descendant would best represent the harm suffered by the class. They were nearing the deadline; Lina would work fast. Mr. Dresser fully supported the idea. And most important, she now had a lead: Jasper Battle, who might (or might not) possess some Bell works, who might (or might not) be a Bell descendant. This last she would not share with Dan, not yet. Too uncertain. But the information gave her an extra impetus, a little fire in her belly.

As she approached the office, Lina called good morning to Mary.

"He's in there with Garrison." Mary's tone was curt, as though this were information Lina should have known. "Is he expecting you?"

"Not really. But I can wait."

Mary tilted her chin down, her lips parted as if to speak again, and for a moment she looked at Lina with what seemed like pity. But Mary said nothing. She turned away from Lina and noisily retrieved a coffee mug from her top drawer, then disappeared in the direction of the break room. Lina watched her go, puzzled, and stood outside Dan's door, listening to the rise and fall of Garrison's voice. Animated, it seemed to Lina, as though he were arguing with Dan. The hallway was quiet; only a few of the secretaries and even fewer associates were in this early. Lina did not intend to eavesdrop but Garrison's voice rose, coming cleanly through the door.

"This case is just begging for some publicity, right? We need those cameras at the courthouse and the plaintiffs are an opportunity to hook them, early and fast. Am I right?" Garrison was saying.

Silence. Dan must have nodded, because Garrison continued.

"So, what if we found a plaintiff who already came with a bagful of built-in publicity. A story that's already being covered in the kinds of markets, read about by the kinds of people, who are—and might be in the future—clients of this firm. Josephine Bell is that story. I went to this amazing exhibit over the weekend, Dan. Amazing. I'm a big art fan. I love art. And this was something that grabbed me, from the moment I heard about it. An African American artist, never recognized in her time. I know it sounds silly, but looking at those pictures, I felt a kinship with her. I did. I felt her."

Lina knew she should pull away but was rooted in place by the elemental shock of hearing these words spoken by Garrison. She listened as he told the story of Lu Anne and Josephine, the white mistress, the black house girl, the canonization of Lu Anne by modern art circles, feminists, art historians. And now, behold, it had all been a lie.

Then Dan's voice: "I like it, I see where you're going with this. This sounds fantastic, a really great hook. Good work, Garrison." She could picture Dan, leaning forward in his chair, scratching his red wiry head, his cheeks flushed pink.

Lina knocked. She did not wait for an answer. She opened the door.

"Lina," Garrison said, turning around, surprise but no shame stamped on his face.

"Lina, good morning, you're in early," said Dan, good-natured and oblivious. "Come, join us. Garrison is just filling me in on this exhibit he saw over the weekend. This artist angle, it sounds like just the ticket."

Lina sat down. She did not look at Garrison.

"And I know, Lina, you mentioned something about this last week—and I know I said hold off. But now, hearing about it from Garrison, he's done all this extra research—the art exhibit, potential new client base. I think it's an exciting idea. There's a lot to recommend it. A lot." He turned to Garrison.

"So," Dan said. "Where are her relatives? When can I meet them?"

"Well, umm . . . we don't know yet." Now Garrison paused. Lina noted the return of the welcoming "we." She did not respond. Garrison cleared his throat. One breath. Two. Part of her wanted him to flounder. Hadn't she done enough to help the amiable Garrison Hall? But in Dan's face lived a chance that he would approve a trip to Richmond, that she could advance the search for Josephine. And Lina focused now on this prospect, on what she had come here to accomplish. Garrison, she decided, was peripheral.

Lina said, "Dan, as you can see, Garrison is excited about my idea to locate a Josephine Bell descendant to serve as lead plaintiff. But there's one hurdle—we still have to find one. There are resources out there that I just can't access from my desk. I need to go to Virginia."

Dan looked at her with eyebrows raised. Lina held his gaze.

"Okay, okay. Let's give this a try," Dan said. "But we are tight on time, team. *Tight*. So, who's going to Richmond tomorrow?" Dan tilted his head first toward Garrison, who shifted in his chair. Lina's cheeks stung as though she'd been slapped.

"Um, I really can't leave the city," Garrison said.

"Okay, then." Dan turned toward Lina. "Lina? How about it?"

"Of course I can go," she said steadily.

"Great. But listen—here's the deal. Fly coach, leave first thing tomorrow. Work one day, two max. Be back here Thursday at the latest. I'll ask Dresser for a few more days to work on the brief. He'll have a kitten but, hey, it is what it is. And keep expenses to a minimum, Lina. We're talking the Super 8, not the Four Seasons. Understood?"

Lina nodded and rose from her chair. She felt a sudden pressing need to be far from the company of Garrison Hall and Daniel Oliphant.

"Great work, team!" Dan called after her as she left the office. Lina turned down the hallway, toward the elevator bank, and heard the rustle of Garrison hurrying behind.

"Lina," Garrison said. She did not turn around. They arrived at the elevator together and she pushed the down button. Garrison eased up beside her.

"Lina, I know what you're thinking," he said quietly. "And you're wrong."

"What am I thinking?" Lina kept her eyes on the glowing arrow. "That you stole my idea to look good in front of Dan? How could you have done that?"

"I just thought it was a great idea, and that we should run with it, and I thought that maybe if he heard about it from someone else . . . I mean you already tried to explain it to him, didn't you?" Garrison's voice was level, reasonable, which served only to enrage Lina further. She felt something within her fly loose, the demise not only of her burgeoning friendship with Garrison but of something essential within herself as well, a vision of success here at Clifton and how she would undoubtedly achieve it.

"Garrison, I *trusted* you." Her voice rose too loud for the small space around them. A young paralegal waiting nearby glanced up and then quickly down when Lina met her eyes.

"And Dresser seemed so taken with the idea," Garrison continued in the same quiet tone. "I just wanted to redeem myself, show him and Dan that I'm committed to this case. But I should have talked to you first. I'm sorry."

The elevator opened with a cheerful electronic *ping*. Lina stepped inside. She turned and looked at Garrison, at his wide, intelligent eyes and articulate mouth as it opened to say something more, but his words were lost as the doors closed and Lina faced only a hazy image of herself reflected off the steel.

As the elevator descended, she began to cry with an angry frustration. She had let down her guard and forgotten the math: law firms presented a zero-sum game. How many associates would eventually make partner? Five percent? Two? Dan must have dangled the partner track promise in front of Garrison too. Every case mattered, every client meeting, every hour billed represented a chance for you to shine and your colleagues to stumble.

Lina dried her eyes on the sleeve of her button-down, straightened her back, and stepped forward to examine herself in the door's dim reflection. Lowering her chin, she wiped away the dark shadows of smudged mascara, tucked her hair behind each ear. She was going to Richmond, Virginia, where she would locate evidence of Josephine Bell's descendant. And this goal crystallized now within her in a new, harder way. Maybe she wasn't as cutthroat as Garrison, or as powerful as Dan, but she had what it took to excel here. Wasn't the law what she *did*? And she did it very, very well.

Josephine

The afternoon reached toward night and Mister did not return. As the sun burned low in an orange-blue sky, Missus wanted to walk and so Josephine took her down the front path to the gate, and back again to the house, and again, and again. Missus wore her everyday slippers; she did not ask again for the boots. Heavier with each pass, Missus leaned on Josephine's arm, but still she insisted they stay out. "I like to feel the sun on my face," Missus said. "Motion in my limbs." A trickle of sweat ran down the valley of Josephine's spine, where the cloth of her dress pulled away; she felt it like an insect on her skin.

As they walked, Missus gossiped about Melly, the spinster's shame, and remembered her own oldest sister in Mississippi, homely and bookish, and what ever became of her? Josephine listened and nodded and thought of Nathan and the road to the undertaker's. Could he tell her the route? She did not trust her memory to find her way again. This time the undertaker would not turn her away. Before, it had been her own fault, waiting so long to run, her belly low and heavy.

And Lottie? *Now is the time,* Josephine would say, *there will be no other. I have seen signs of the redemption.* The lump on Missus' neck growing wider by the day; the sparrow with its head like an arrow; the doctor's weeping skin, red and cracked, hidden beneath his suit. Did these not point to an escape? What would Lottie accept, what would she believe in?

Josephine prepared a simple supper for Missus Lu, bread and broth, steeped mint and a teaspoonful of brandy, and put her to bed. Still no sign of Mister. An ebbing line of orange hung on the horizon, the emergent night sky luminous and clear. The hours of darkness stretched before her and they seemed immense, immeasurable. How far might she go? How many miles to the city of Philadelphia?

Josephine walked down to the cabins. The night felt thicker here than up by the house. The cooking fires flickered along the row. Shadowy movement and sounds of the field hands preparing their suppers, a piece of meat left from the week's allotment, pig fat and beans, brown trout from the river, and the cooking smells mixed with the stench of the latrine. Otis worked by torchlight in the side garden where the field hands grew runner beans, carrots, collards, potatoes, squash. His back was bent, his hands in the earth. He looked up and nodded as Josephine passed.

Lottie and Winton sat outside their cabin. Josephine saw the silhouette of Winton's form on the front steps, and then Lottie as she stood and walked toward the fire, her gait rolling and slow, her shadow long and misshapen in the wavering light. She pulled a spoon from her apron pocket and poked it into the black pot that hung over the flame. Josephine stepped from the shadows into the circle of light thrown by the fire

"Evening, Lottie."

Lottie raised the spoon. "Oh, you gave me a fright. Don't go sneaking up on me like that."

"I'm sorry, Lottie, didn't mean nothing. Will you come inside?" Josephine tilted her head to the cabin. Lottie opened her mouth as if to speak but said nothing, just nodded and followed Josephine.

They sat on three-legged stools, the cabin lit only by the firelight that winked from a square window cut into the wall. In winter the window was covered with burlap, but now it was left open to the air and insects, smoke and light. Two sleeping pallets lay against the far wall, covered by Lottie's quilt. A small rough table sat beside the door and, upon it, a brown glass bottle held the bluebell stems that Lottie had picked that morning.

Lottie said, "Josephine, is it true the doctor came today for Missus? Calla seen him."

"Yes, the doctor came. He said Missus is dying. And Mister run off, I don't know where he went to. I am going, Lottie. I can't wait. Please come with me, won't you and Winton come?" Josephine heard the words come in a rush and they sounded simple and weak, not as she had hoped. She did not talk about signs of the redemption; there were no signs, just things that she saw without grand design or divine meaning, and she could not pretend now to Lottie that she believed otherwise. Fact was they all knew that a death meant sales. Who would be sold after Missus Lu was gone? Who would stay? Would Mister keep on at Bell Creek? They might all be sold, scattered to different parts.

Lottie shifted where she sat and looked away from Josephine, then back. "Oh child, how can we go? Winton's leg barely serves him now, Jackson keep saying he'll bring the whip down on account of it. And me, I'm too old for it."

Josephine took hold of Lottie's hand. "Please," she said. "Please, Lottie." She squeezed Lottie's fingers, hoping to convey the truth that she found herself now unable to speak: I do not want to go alone. "Please. Come with me." But Josephine saw no shift in Lottie's eyes, no change in the thin line of her mouth. Josephine released Lottie's hand; she knew what the answer would be.

"You go," Lottie said, her voice soft but certain. "Papa Bo always said he'd never sell Winton and me, we'd always stay together, right here. We'll stay. Jesus looking after me, don't you worry none. You go on."

"Lottie."

"You run fast and get yourself up north. I'll know how you're get-ting on. Jesus'll tell me, He will."

The moonlight glowed on Lottie's cheeks. "Good-bye," Josephine said.

She reached forward and hugged Lottie. There was nothing else to expect, Lottie would never leave. She knew how to get by, her quick fingers, her careful heart. Jesus coming for her, Lottie was waiting. But Josephine could not wait, not another day.

Josephine felt light-headed now, her skin stretched too tight across her face. She stepped out of the cabin into the night air.

Winton still sat on the step, and she stopped there, placed a hand on his shoulder. "Good night, good Winton. You take care now."

He nodded at her, winked. "Night, Josephine. We'll be seeing you."

Josephine walked past the fire and down the row of cabins, look-ing for where Nathan slept. It was not often that she came this way. She visited only with Lottie and Winton and whoever might be shar-ing their supper that night, but never with the others. Now there was only Jackson; Calla; young Otis; Therese; and Nathan, for a time, until his owner called him back. But the empty cabins echoed with the sounds of the others: Calla's children, Lottie's Hap, Jonas, Nora, Louis, Annie, Constance, May, the children Josephine had played with, James and Solomon and Harriet and Sue, all dead or sold, gone far off, who knew where. Apart from Lottie, Winton, and Louis, Josephine held no feeling for any of them. She had not known their fears or joys. Over the years she'd hear of a baby born, a broken leg; she'd hear of these things but took no part in them.

Lottie always said Missus looked to Josephine as a daughter of sorts, but Josephine didn't see it that way. She was just like the horse, the chicken or cow, something to be fed and housed, to do what it was born and raised to do. Josephine was not of one world or the other, neither the house nor the fields. This she could not explain to them, not even to Lottie or Winton, that she belonged nowhere.

Nathan stood outside a cabin, his mouth rolled in chewing though he held no plate in his hand and there was no cooking fire lit. Josephine approached him slowly across the hard-packed earth, but he gave no notice of her until she stood just before him. He shifted his eyes toward her, spat onto the ground, nodded his head.

"Evening," said Josephine.

"Evening."

"Can I sit with you a minute?"

He spat again, a wetness scudding across the dirt. "Come on," he said, and sat upon the cabin steps. There were no sounds from within; he slept here alone. A nervousness grabbed her then, a thought that if Jackson saw them together, he might suspect her plan. Josephine had no business speaking to Nathan—a house girl, a hired hand. But he was the only one who could help her. She would have to be quick.

Josephine sat beside Nathan on the steps and leaned forward, her elbows on her knees, her skirts falling onto the step below. With no fire she saw Nathan only by the ambient light from the row, the moon. His face seemed very dark, the whites of his eyes glowing against the skin, the pupils wide, his hair cut close and jagged. "Nathan, where did you go when you ran? Can you tell me?"

"Why you wanting to know? Are you really going to run?" His voice was hollow and unkind.

"Yes," Josephine answered firmly. "Tonight. I tried once for the undertaker's and I reckon I'll head there again, but I need to be sure of the route. I want to know where I'm headed."

"The undertaker?" Nathan gave a low chuckle and Josephine saw the yellow of his teeth and the black wad of tobacco as his lips pulled away. "I know the road." He stood and walked into the darkness behind the cabin. There was the rustling of underbrush, a snap, and he returned holding a stick of dead poplar. He took a grease lantern from a hook by the cabin door and lit the wick, and Josephine saw his face clearly now in its glow. His eyes were cold, set in deep sockets of shadow, as if he stared out from the bottom of a hole.

"Here. Look at this careful. Set it to heart." Nathan took the pointed end of the stick and began to trace a map in the dirt for Josephine. Bell Creek and the road that ran north-south. To the south, the Stanmores' place. And to the north, tending west, the road forked, then a second fork, two more farms, and then the undertaker's. "Here's where you're headed." He marked a big X in the earth. A simple farmhouse, Nathan said. Unpainted, a barn beside it, a low fence of stones, a hen house beside the barn. Seven or eight miles, maybe ten or twelve. This was the one area of uncertainty. "I never made it that far," Nathan said without emotion. "The undertaker, he'll take you from there, send you to Philadelphia, or up the Ohio banks."

Josephine studied the map, memorizing the turns of the road.

"Don't run, girl, you're a fool. You know what those patrollers do to a girl like you?" He laughed, a low chuckle that chilled Josephine's skin as though thunder were coming. "They eat you up, they won't even bother cutting your heels like they done me, they'll just tear you up when they catch you." He brought his face in closer to Josephine and she smelled the earth of the fields on him, the heat of that day's sun on his skin. His pupils stretched very wide now, only a sliver of white showing.

"Not a one makes it free. Not a one. We all get caught, one way or another, on the road, in town, someone say they help you, but lead you into a trick. Ain't no difference anyhow, up north and here, no freedom for the likes of us. You a fool to think it." He spat again and wiped his mouth with the back of his hand.

Nathan pulled himself up from the step, walked with his shuffling limp into the cabin. He did not say good night, just shut the door behind him. Josephine stood, smoothed her skirts with her hands, walked away from Nathan's cabin and up along the path. Her feet sank in the mud as she half-walked, half-ran back to the house.

Tonight. Now.

It did not shake her, what Nathan had said. Freedom was a curious thing. Were the chickens free, running their fool heads off in the yard? The horse, that still must fit the bit between its teeth? Was Missus free? But what else to dream for? There was no dream of Josephine's that did not contain a place where she might sit and look upon a field or a bird in flight or a person and ponder the lines of that thing, to capture them in pencil or charcoal or ink or pigment. Just to sit for a moment, herself, no one claiming her time or her thoughts or the product of her mind and hands. What other word to call that if not freedom? *Not a one is free,* Nathan had said, but Josephine did not believe that could be true.

She felt clearheaded, her steps sure. The night air, the chill moist ground, the sliver of moon filtering through streaky clouds, all was as it should be. An owl called and underneath all the night sounds was the hushing rush of the river's flow. Each step carried her away from the cabins, toward the house for the last time. Never again mount these back steps, open this door with rusty hinge and cracked doorknob, place her hand against this cutting table scarred with knife points and pig's blood, steady herself, feel her breath come too fast, calm herself. Never again this stone floor chilled and tough against the tough soles of her feet. Never again the enclosing air of this place, the dead air that clogged her throat and made her eyes weep, the still, dusty air that hung around the fine furnishings and the cracked china and seemed full of all those who had come before her, all those the house had sheltered and seen into the ground.

A mess from the supper she had prepared earlier for Missus Lu greeted Josephine in the kitchen, a pile of washing in a basket, the fire going cold. She walked past it all, then up the stairs.

As Josephine neared the attic steps, she heard a creak of floor from within the studio, a rustling. She turned and saw a light burning from beneath the closed door. Missus. Missus must have woken.

Josephine hesitated. The attic steps were close, her pack nearly ready. She could go now, leave Missus working alone, tread lightly and be out the door, down the road, fast and silent. But Missus might call for her and what then? If Josephine did not answer, would Missus go to the cabins? Would she ask Jackson for help? Or would she wait for Mister to return and then send him to track Josephine down? How much time would she have?

Josephine opened the studio door and a fog of heat hit her. The windows were closed, a fire burned in the grate. Missus stood in her nightdress before the easel, a canvas propped against it, and her hand held a brush dripping with red.

"Missus, it's late. This room is stifling. You need to keep your strength, the doctor said. Please let me get you to bed."

"But I was so cold in my bed, Josephine," Missus said with a child's petulance. She did not turn to face Josephine. "I needed to warm myself."

"Missus, I will fetch another blanket. Please now, come on with me." Josephine spoke too as though Missus were a child, with a tolerant calm.

"But look at this. I must finish it, look." Missus gestured toward the canvas before her: a still life, a scattering of potatoes and chestnuts, an apple and two pears grouped without symmetry or grace. "There are so many I have never finished. This one, I must finish just this one."

"Hush, there's time tomorrow, and the day after that."

Missus Lu turned away from the canvas, and her face appeared shadowy and bright in equal measure from the light thrown by the fire. "Josephine, I will be gone tomorrow. I can feel it. I can't keep my thoughts straight, I ache here, and here, and here." Missus touched her neck, her forehead, her breast. "There is something I must tell you, Josephine, and you will hate me for it. I am afraid you will hate me, and nothing I can do now will save me."

"Missus, salvation belongs to us all," Josephine said and her thoughts were of Lottie, the hope that such a belief was true.

"Does it? Does it, Josephine?" Missus laughed, her mood shifting, Josephine saw the flash of her eyes, the tears swallowed back. "You have no idea. You do not even have God, you never have. I hoped you'd read the Bible, that is why I taught you your letters. I wanted you to understand the natural order, that God wants us all to be true to our place in life. But you refused Him."

Missus dropped her brush to the floor. It fell with a soft *whoosh*, splattering red paint against her ankles, the floor, the wall.

"Shush now," Josephine said, frustration cornering its way into her voice. She could not stop the rising urge to run from this room, before Mister returned, before the night progressed too far toward dawn. "Missus Lu, come to bed."

"Yes, take me to bed, I must lay back now. I can't stand any longer. Josephine, there's something I must tell you. I must tell you."

They staggered from the studio, Missus leaning heavily on Josephine's shoulder, her feet dragging behind. Josephine led Missus to her bed and laid her down. Missus' chest rose and fell with her breathing, her hair was damp with sweat, her cheeks flushed pink. Josephine took a blanket from the chest at the foot of the bed and folded the bedclothes, the extra blanket, neatly under Missus Lu's chin. Neither spoke. Only creaks and groans as the house settled into night.

As Josephine stood to leave, Missus grabbed her hand. "Josephine, I must ask your forgiveness. I cannot leave this world without it. Please, please."

Josephine paused and sat down again upon the bed. A flush of power filled her, as it would in the studio when she stood with brush in hand, Missus hovering over her shoulder, watching every stroke, breathless. "Why, Missus? What cause would I have to provide forgiveness? You have offered me only kindness."

"Truly, Josephine? Is that truly how you feel? You know that all this, I have no part in it. I can't even bring a child into this world. I've only ever had you, and I know you're going to run. I know you'll leave me soon. I won't tell Robert. I won't tell a soul." Missus twisted her head sharply to the side, exposing the reddened lump to Josephine. "Just scratch it please, would you? It itches so, I cannot bear it."

Josephine remembered the boy in the field: a good deed for a dying boy. Josephine reached for Missus' hand and guided it to the spot. "See, Missus, you can reach. Here." And Missus' fingernails scrabbled at the raised hump, the skin pinking in thin strips beneath the pull.

"That is all, Josephine. Thank you. Good night, my dear. Go. You can go on now." Missus' eyes closed, her breaths lengthened.

As she watched Missus Lu settle into sleep, a pure rage gripped Josephine, at Missus' granting of permission, at her presumed powers of release. Would Missus deny her even the authority of her own escape? It was the sighted beggar stealing from the blind and Josephine felt a fracture open in her chest, a sliver of space that grew wider with each breath and a darkness spilled forth into the room. Missus' eyes danced behind the thin skin of her lids, and Josephine wondered what dreams dwelled there, memories of her suppers and her rich daddy, of Mister courting with flowers, of Papa Bo's sermons and his promise to them all, everyone who bowed to the Lord's will, of heavenly redemption. Josephine placed her hand above Missus' mouth and nose, the fingers hovering just above the skin so that Missus' heat was on her palm and the breath moist in the cupped hollow of her hand. To smother Missus would be an easy thing. She had no strength, there was no one to hear it done. The darkness flowed from Josephine, and for a moment she let herself be carried by its spirit of vengeance. Never had she felt this way before and wasn't it thrilling, wasn't it right, the power of her hate.

Josephine lowered her hand. It was Missus' face, stricken even in sleep, sallow even by lamplight, the scabbed gash like a bristling insect on her cheek, that stopped Josephine. Her face no longer young or beautiful, her wasted face. And it seemed Josephine's heart pulsed with the skittering movement of Missus' eyes, that the two of them lay prostrate together before the same cruel God. The two of them not so different after all, Josephine realized. All this time, these long, hungry years, each of them alone beside the other.

Lina

The run-in with Garrison earlier that day had left Lina feeling scoured clean, lighter, and somehow more self-assured. This, Lina thought, was what she needed, a blanket thrown off, a curtain lifted. Something truthful and necessary had happened that gave her this sense of simple resolve, clarified purpose, as she walked the Clifton halls, rode the Clifton elevators, made bland and proper chitchat with Meredith at the shared copy machine, told Sherri to book a hotel for her Richmond trip. The woman who performed these tasks seemed a simplified version of the old Lina. Lina improved, Lina redacted.

And it was this Lina who looked forward to tonight, the opening of Oscar's show, *Pictures of Grace*. Her fears and suspicions had receded, and she was left with a straightforward wish to see the pictures and be done with them. Oscar's lie about Marie, those random, contextless notes written by her mother, had muddled her thinking, confused and upset her. Oscar's pictures of Grace were nothing more than pigment, canvas, wood. That was all. No magic, no mystery. Her father was an artist, and he drew inspiration from his life, as all artists did. *I want to show you some things about your mother,* Oscar had said that first night in the studio, and now Lina felt ready to look, with calm reason, with dignified reserve. The visceral reaction she had experienced at home, when she saw the *Enough* portrait and those first raw images of Grace, would not happen again. Of this, Lina felt sure.

Outside Natalie's gallery, people crowded the sidewalk and leaned against the front windows. They held small paper plates loaded with cheese cubes and little salamis, glasses of wine, cigarettes. Festivities had been going for an hour already and the mood was celebratory, voices loud and off-key. Lina edged through the door, holding her bag sideways, and wove her way through the bodies. Everyone towered tall, outfitted in high heels and attitude.

The first picture Lina saw stopped her cold; she felt a flip in her belly, a stumble in her gait, a faltering of her new resolve. It was not a picture Oscar had shown her. It was Grace, naked from the waist up. Her breasts were beautiful, the nipples dark, hair falling to her shoulders, her mouth open. Lina looked away.

Her eyes fell next on a triptych, and in each panel Grace seemed a different woman. From this painting, Lina did not turn away. In the left-hand panel, Grace stared straight out, realistically rendered in a simple blue dress, the skirt just grazing her knees, her face flat and composed, hands hanging loose at her sides. The right panel portrayed the same woman, but her mouth was opened wide, wider than a mouth should open, her eyes looming large and wild as though she sought to devour everything before her. In the large central panel, Grace appeared in profile, and the side view filled the frame, just half a nose, a sliver of lip curled cruelly, one black eye staring out, trapped and enraged.

I'm trying to explore some things. Tell the truth, Oscar had said, and Lina wondered with a precarious detachment what truth was represented here. She thought of her own memories, Grace vague and smiling, a smell of pepper and sugar. That tune, hummed in moments of lazy quiet. The toy train in a dimpled hand. A feeling of contentment, soft and complete, a warmth that wrapped around Lina, swaddled her limbs, covered her toes.

But here, this angry woman, her wary gaze. Lina realized it was this woman (these women) who had written the notes Lina found in Oscar's studio:

What gives meaning? Who is free?

O does not understand, he cannot.

Nothing is as I see it.

A new image of her mother, different from the one in which Lina had always believed, was coming to her, and Lina did not shy away. She looked into the trapped woman's eyes, their whites veined with fine spidery red. How could a new mother find time to paint? How could Oscar Sparrow's wife carve a space for herself? What did Grace need?

Oscar's voice rose above the din and Lina saw him in a corner, his back to the wall, surrounded by a phalanx of admirers. He wore a sleek black suit jacket over a white T-shirt and dark blue jeans, his beard neatly trimmed, his hair glistening with some sort of product, and the entire effect was of urbane confidence and ease. Natalie stood to his right, her blond hair up, a few stray curls falling loose onto her shoulders. She wore a silver shift dress that sparkled and showed off her lean legs, and her eyes and face seemed to sparkle too, the result of some cosmetic wizardry. Natalie's hand rested lightly on Oscar's shoulder and he leaned into her and pressed his lips quickly, carelessly against the bare skin of her neck.

Lina caught Oscar's eye from across the room and in one fluid motion he stepped away from Natalie. He began moving toward Lina but was stopped at every step by well-wishers, friends, and finally a spectacled critic. For him, Oscar paused and began speaking earnestly, arms waving, with the occasional apologetic glance across to Lina. As she watched, Oscar's hand rose up and traced with a finger in the air the line of Grace's cheek drawn on the canvas, and the gesture was cold and analytical, having nothing to do with Grace, the woman he sought to memorialize, the woman he had loved.

Lina turned away and blindly stepped farther into the gallery, unsure of where she was going or what she had come here to see. She stopped and raised her eyes. On the wall before her hung a large, vividly colored oil painting, the shapes exaggerated and round. There was a woman viewed from the back, slim, long dark hair, her tight dress revealing soft curves: Grace's back. She stood upon an old-fashioned stage, a scrolled marquee above her, long dark-red curtains rippling at the outer edges of the painting. On either side of the woman, sharing the stage with her, sat two grotesquely rotund babies, each larger than the woman, each with a man's face—dark bushy eyebrows on one, a shadow of stubble on the other, both faces lined with fat and age—and these two overgrown babies screamed and reached for the woman, who remained oblivious to them both.

Was one of these babies Oscar? The shadowy beard, clear blue eyes saddled with flesh. He grabbed at Grace with selfish hunger, ravenous and greedy. And it was this horrible picture that finally toppled Lina's determination to approach the new Grace with rationality and control. Those shoots of anger Lina had carried when she was younger now returned with a furious blooming. All these years, why had Oscar kept Grace to himself? What had *happened*?

Her head down, Lina pushed her way through the crowd and out the door of the gallery, returning to the streets she had walked less than an hour before. The air smelled of cigarettes, garbage, and wine, and Lina's stomach clutched a tight knot of muscle that fought against her breath.

Two blocks from the subway, she thought she heard a voice calling her name, but she did not turn around, and then suddenly a hand was on her shoulder. "Carolina Sparrow?" She turned. It was the critic, Porter Scales, the one who years ago had given Oscar an achingly negative review, the one who had delivered the opening lecture at the *Art and Artifice* exhibit. Lina recognized his thick gray hair; a moneyed, year-round tan; the deep cleft marking his chin.

"Carolina Sparrow?" he said again. He was struggling to catch his breath, as though he had been running. "Are you Grace Sparrow's daughter?"

"Yes," answered Lina, surprised to be described this way. Always she was Oscar Sparrow's daughter.

"I thought so. You look just like her. My name is Porter, Porter Scales. I knew your mother well. I very much admired her art."

Lina took in his suit trousers, the impeccable white button-down open at the neck, the black cord around his throat from which hung a small, intricately carved piece of ivory or bone. "I know who you are," Lina said.

"Let me buy you a coffee," Porter said. "Or a drink if you'd prefer."

Lina hesitated. Her heart still pulsed with angry adrenaline but the rest of her felt wounded and raw, a condition that solitude, she sensed, would only aggravate. Her flight to Richmond left early the next morning but that was still hours away. Lina nodded. "A drink," she said.

She followed Porter into a small, high-ceilinged restaurant nearby, nearly empty and lit by flickering pillar candles placed on bare wood tables. They ordered cocktails—vodka gimlet for her, a dirty martini for him.

"So what did you think of the show?" Porter asked, expertly slipping an olive off its toothpick and into his mouth.

"I hated it," Lina said, surprising herself with the force in her voice. "What did you think?"

"Well, I'm afraid I generally don't talk about shows that I'm reviewing." Porter spoke quickly, as though to move the conversation along. "But I *can* tell you that those paintings made me remember your mother." He gazed at Lina with an intensity that made her shift her eyes away. "It was a shock to see you there, the image of Grace. I just wanted to tell you how much your mother meant to me. We were very good friends, and I missed her terribly for many years. I still do."

Lina remembered then the papers she had found in Oscar's studio, the sketch of a man she realized now was a much younger Porter, his hair darker and shaggier, his face leaner. *Porter, my anti-O,* Grace had written. And that painting: two overgrown babies clutching at one woman. An understanding came to Lina, fully formed and precisely drawn. Porter, Oscar, Grace. Shock weakened her for a moment and she looked away, aware that Porter was watching her. Perhaps he had assumed she already knew, but he was wrong; she knew nothing. Melted candle wax ran in a sudden spill onto the table and Lina watched it pool and begin to harden. That photograph of her parents at the restaurant—it was the only picture she had of the two of them together. She knew the photo so well it had ceased being an image and had become for her a memory: Grace's adoring gaze, her father's proud grin. Back then her parents had been so young, Lina reasoned, of course there had been others. Porter, Marie, who else? It felt childish to be so surprised, childish or prudish or something else she didn't want to be. And yet this final demise of her parents' perfect romance made her throat so stiff she feared she couldn't speak. Lina swallowed hard. She didn't think she could continue to sit here and maintain polite conversation with Porter, especially not with Porter. Lina almost walked out then, but she stopped herself. She had never known any of Grace's friends, at least no one who would speak with her about her mother, no one she felt comfortable asking. With a liberating clarity, Lina recognized the opportunity presented here.

"Where was my mother from?" Lina asked, and she gripped her drink, letting the cold glass push against her palm. Porter seemed surprised by the question and leaned forward in his chair.

"Your father hasn't told you much, has he?"

"No. I don't know anything about her," Lina said, straightforward, not inviting his pity; that was the last thing she wanted from him.

"Well. Oscar was devastated by her death, I can tell you that. And Grace was never very forthcoming about her past. She didn't talk about it, not much. She had a tough childhood and came to New York when she was young. To escape, I think. Originally she was from—Florida maybe? Someplace warm. I'm sorry, Carolina, I can't remember."

"Please, call me Lina. Everyone does. Everyone except my father, that is," she said, preserving this one small loyalty to Oscar.

They talked for 1.6 hours, and this is what Porter told Lina: Grace loved eggs Benedict; she loved Al Pacino; she cooked a mean chili con carne; her eyes were dark brown but in certain light, or as she smiled, they might reveal a deep mossy green; she listened to the Ramones, the Velvet Underground, all the cool New York bands of the seventies and also, unironically, to old country and western singers, Patsy Cline and Gene Autry, whose songs always made her cry. Grace knew how to knit and would make her own sweaters, things for baby Lina, a pair of pink booties, a soft fuzzy blanket. Grace loved Oscar, she did, but their relationship was fraught with worry and moods and jealousy. Grace did not have siblings, Porter believed. She never talked about her family or the place she was born. She was, of course, extraordinarily talented. She painted and drew in a hyperrealistic style, almost photographic, sometimes distorted as a lens might distort—fish-eye or wide angle. The small portraits that hung in Lina's room were intended as riffs on the nature of family connections: Can you create your own? What is blood and what is decision? Grace had been working on the project when she died, Porter said. She had invented an elaborate family tree stretching back generations, to the *Mayflower,* to imagined ancestral roots in Ireland, Mexico, Kenya.

"Do you know anything about the crash?" Lina asked finally, after two rounds of drinks. The restaurant was half-full; the volume around them had increased steadily for the past hour and now hummed within her, along with the vodka. She had been resisting her urge to ask about Grace's death—it sounded macabre, obsessive—but really this was the subject that nagged at her the most.

"Crash?" Porter said.

"That killed her. The car crash."

"Oh. I hadn't realized it was a car crash. I thought she had an aneurysm. A brain aneurysm, totally unexpected."

Lina felt a movement in her chest, something plunging heavily into her stomach, pushing her breath away. Porter looked at her with concern as she gulped her drink, a mistake that only made her cough. Finally her breath heaved into gear, and she coughed until her eyes smarted with tears.

"My dad always said it was a crash." Lina's voice was weak.

"Yes, I'm sure it was a crash," Porter said with meticulous care. "I can't even remember where I heard that about the aneurysm. I'm sure I'm wrong."

"Yes, you must be wrong."

"You know, your father wasn't really talking to anyone at that point. He wasn't returning phone calls, wouldn't see anyone. He didn't say a word about her death for—well, until this show really."

"Yes, I know." Lina shook the cubes at the bottom of her glass, watching them crack into jagged pieces. "Did you go to the funeral?" she asked at last, raising her gaze to Porter.

"I didn't," he said, and Lina heard the regret in his voice. "She and I lost touch in the six months or so before her death. She'd been at home a lot, not working. Looking after you, of course. And then she was just . . . gone. The funeral was private. I stopped by to see Oscar after I heard, but he just shook my hand on the doorstep. He didn't want any visitors, he said. It was only later, much later, that we came across each other professionally. He never forgave me, I think, for that first review, and we stopped speaking altogether."

Just gone. In those words Lina recognized her own experience, childhood confusion, a shapeless ache.

"Are you an artist too?" Porter asked.

"No. A lawyer."

"Ah." Porter smiled. "Wise woman."

"I'm working on a case about Josephine Bell, actually." Lina wanted to change the subject, to hide her disappointment that he could not tell her more about Grace's death, and to remove the sense of something not being right. A brain aneurysm? *She was just gone.*

"You're not representing the Stanmore Foundation, are you?" Porter's voice grew suddenly wary.

"No, no. A corporate client. Something completely unrelated to the authorship question."

"Well, that's a relief. You know, it *was* the house girl, I can tell you that much." He sounded now like the Porter she had heard speak at the Calhoun Gallery, self-assured and half-apologetic, the reluctant bearer of difficult truths.

"But why are the Stanmores threatening to sue Marie Calhoun?"

"It's about money, of course, and people's feelings getting hurt, but mainly about money. The Stanmores have made an industry out of Lu Anne Bell, and they're a powerful family—they donate a lot of money to the museums, and they buy a lot of art too. Nobody wants to piss them off. But they can't hold off the entire art world for very much longer. There's an army of authenticators waiting to get into the Stanmore archives. They'll figure it out. I did, just taking a critical look at the works, seeing the two styles, the different subject matters. They'll find something to conclusively tip it to Josephine. Handwriting, brushstroke. Or fingerprints. Sotheby's found a da Vinci fingerprint, did you hear that? A fingerprint from the sixteenth century, on some picture a guy bought at a yard sale." Porter shook his head in amazement, and Lina found that she had warmed to him—he had an innocence that belied the careful tan, the sparkling cuff links.

"I'm actually looking for Josephine Bell's descendants," she said. "Did Marie tell you about Jasper Battle?"

"Yes, he's e-mailed me too. Very persistent young man. Be careful, Lina. These kinds of people come out of the woodwork, really they do. As soon as it gets into the news, as soon as there's any money involved."

"You think he's lying?"

"I really don't know. I haven't seen what he's got. He says they're family heirlooms, but of course he's got no documentation. It'll be virtually impossible to establish provenance. There is no evidence anywhere of Josephine Bell having any relations, and believe me, people have looked."

Porter smiled at her, a tender, kind smile that seemed to contain an intimacy, and Lina welcomed it, off-balance as she was from the alcohol and talk of her mother, and she smiled back.

Outside the restaurant, Porter placed his hands on Lina's shoulders. "Good luck to you, Lina Sparrow," he said, and the glow from the restaurant's neon sign lit his face and he looked younger than he had before, and rueful, like a man who has behaved badly and now wishes only to be good. A beat passed between them, Lina felt the weight of his hands on her shoulders, and she moved forward to kiss him. The vodka brought an edge of recklessness, and this warm night, her father's horrendous show, and what Porter had told her about Grace, each fact a gift. In some deep recess too Lina wanted him because Grace had wanted him, or he had wanted Grace; the precise parameters of their relationship were still unclear, but the suggestion of a long-gone love thrilled her. Her mother had been loved by two men. More? Lina's image of Grace widened to include these other complexities, exciting and scandalous, and Lina longed suddenly for a sliver of what must have been her mother's allure, and talent, and passion, and willingness to embrace her own complicated life.

Porter was not tall, but Lina was shorter and she had to move forward and up to reach him. He did not step away as their lips touched and Lina began to press against him, but he pulled back, removed his hands from her shoulders.

"Lina, you are a wonderful young woman. I could think of nothing worse than having you hate me tomorrow morning," Porter said, and slowly he brought her close again and kissed her on the forehead. "Please, let's be friends. Call me anytime. Let me know how it goes with your case." And then he turned and walked away.

LINA ARRIVED HOME AND BEGAN immediately to pack for the trip to Richmond. Two trouser suits, two button-downs, a pair of jeans, pajamas, pens, her notebook, her laptop. She moved in a hurried, automatic haze that banished any thought of Porter or Oscar or Grace.

Lina grabbed her coat, her suitcase, and her handbag and left the house; she did not want to be home when Oscar returned fresh from the success and catharsis of his show. The dead bolt slid into place and she stepped down onto the sidewalk. Streetlights towered above her, their glare throwing wide circles of yellow into her path. She advanced through one and then into shadow again, light and shadow, light and shadow. It became almost a cinematic flickering as she walked faster, faster, faster, the suitcase on wheels bumping behind her over the uneven pavement.

It was twelve thirty on a Monday night. Her flight departed at seven A.M., giving her roughly five hours to fill before she had to leave for the airport. A couple strolled past Lina, holding hands. A man pulled at a small dog on a red leather lead. A woman spoke breathlessly into a cell phone cupped against her chin.

Lina paused at the intersection. She did not know where to go. She did not want to eat or drink or talk or smoke. She headed to the office.

LINA SWITCHED ON THE OVERHEAD light and her office flickered into view: her cluttered desk, hulking computer, the chair for visitors, the shelves filled with client files and old law school textbooks. For a moment it all looked one-dimensional, like a future museum exhibit of early twenty-first-century office life: Look at how those people lived! Why did they do it? Wasn't it funny, what they believed?

Perched in Lina's in-tray was a bulky package. She opened it to find some of the books she'd ordered last week for her research into the Underground Railroad and the Rounds family. She flipped through the titles and back-cover blurbs; most of the books were out of print, the product of academic scholarship from decades past. One cover caught Lina's eye: a black-and-white photo of a plain-faced white woman with kind eyes and a small smile, middle-aged, curly gray hair. *The Forgotten Feminist: A Biography of Kate Rounds Sterrett*, the title read. Kate was the older of the Rounds daughters, recipient of the letters Lina had found online last week. Lina had ordered the book thinking that perhaps Kate had written about the family's activities on the Underground Railroad. It was worth a shot; Lina's leads were few.

The back of the book read:

Kate Rounds Sterrett, the once-famous abolitionist, feminist, and writer, was committed to an insane asylum in 1855 after she threatened to divorce her husband. She divorced him anyway, managed to convince those who needed convincing of her sanity, and spent the rest of her life in determined agitation for the rights of women and African Americans. She was prominent in the earliest days of both the suffrage and abolitionist movements and saw the America into which she was born change profoundly over the course of her life. After decades of activism, Kate Rounds Sterrett died at the age of 102. Today, her name is largely forgotten. This biography seeks to restore her to the pantheon of America's earliest feminists alongside Elizabeth Cady Stanton and Susan B. Anthony.

Lina kicked off her shoes, opened the book, and skimmed through the first chapters on Kate's early life, looking for information on the Underground Railroad. Anything that told of individual fugitives who had been helped, or the onward routes they traveled, anything that might suggest Josephine.

But there was nothing.

Lina flipped through the chapters on Kate's later life in New York, the racism prevalent there, women's inability to vote or serve on juries, Kate's work as suffragette and abolitionist, the advances won, the setbacks suffered, why Kate's reputation should be restored, her writings studied once more.

At the back of the book was an appendix consisting of letters to Kate written by her younger sister, Dorothea. The introduction to the letters read:

In 1848, Kate left her family in Virginia to marry Gareth Sterrett, a clerk with the Bank of New York, and take up domestic life in New York City. Her younger sister, Dorothea, began a regular correspondence with Kate to keep her apprised of family and community news and, particularly, of the family's activities in the Underground Railroad. Sadly, Kate's letters to Dorothea have been lost to time but the flavor that Dorothea's missives impart—of life in a small Virginia town and of the family's commitment to the abolitionist cause—is worth examining. A detailed analysis lies beyond the scope of this book, but I include them here in their entirety as a fitting postscript to Kate Rounds Sterrett's life, a sideways view into the roots of her youthful idealism, the familial foundation of her later beliefs, and hints of the marital discord that later propelled her away from a traditional wifely role and toward the liberal causes and beliefs that are her enduring, though often overlooked, legacy.

Lina glanced at the first lines:

My Dearest Darling Kate,

> *The wedding flowers have only just begun to wilt & here I sit down to write. How I miss you already!*

With a jolt of recognition, Lina looked up from the book and her eyes settled on the photo of Lu Anne and Josephine on the porch at Bell Creek. Here was the full correspondence between Dorothea and Kate Rounds, Lina realized, the same letters she had read on the Virginia Historical Society's website, the same letters that were housed at the Society's center in Richmond. And here they were, in her hands, in New York.

Behind Lina's closed office door, the Clifton landscape stretched empty and still. The alcohol buzz had left her, though the memory of Porter beneath the neon light was still fresh. Why had she tried to kiss him? It now seemed a silly, impetuous thing to do. Porter was good-looking, true, in the way of an older man who is successful and just a touch vain, and kind. He had been very kind to her. But here, surrounded by sterility, the instinct that had led her to lean forward, to seek him out, seemed all but erased.

What remained from that encounter was Grace. The Grace described by Porter flitted in the far corners of Lina's vision like a shadow or hallucination or some sort of presence. A woman drawn in new particulars that Lina could understand: eggs Benedict, a hand-knitted scarf, Patsy Cline, a need for escape. With a curtain of dark hair, a quiet laugh, a smell of pepper and sugar. Lina felt closer to her mother now, in the silent gray lull of her office, than she ever had before.

Lina turned back to the book and began to read.

April 11, 1848
Dearest Kate,

I was so pleased to receive your letter this morning! I
opened it with trembling fingers & read it through in one
sitting. Mother & Father are both out—Father visiting again
with Pastor Shaw & Mother to the cobbler in town with
Samuel, as the poor boy's shoes were cracked & the seams
split. I am so glad that Gareth's work progresses well, although
his long hours spent at the bank can surely not be easy for
you. I trust that over time his load will lessen, once he has
proven to his employers that he is a clever & honorable clerk.
You have a lifetime together, do not forget it, my impatient
Kate!

I hesitate to start in on the sorry tale of our poor Samuel's
mother. The father's disappearance was not as blithely
innocent as it appeared. Sheriff Roy came here to examine the
woman's body, laid out in the barn by Father. She indeed did
not lie peacefully but it would appear was strangled around
the neck until dead. I shudder even to write such a thing, it is
so horrible. Poor Samuel did not hear the worst of it, I hurried
him out of the room once the Sheriff entered & kept him
busy upstairs playing with the toy steam engine—remember
that one, Kate?—as Sheriff Roy downstairs told of his sorry
conclusion.

It seems an impossibility—that a woman is so beloved by
a man, who together bore & raised a child, & yet that same
man would deliver upon that same woman such cruelty &
pain. Perhaps you think me naïve. But what God could allow
such a thing to transpire? The weight of the things I do not
understand would crush an ox.

I know Father hates me to question in any way his Faith, but ever since Percy's death I cannot abide by such childish fairy tales. The idea that all is ordained, that everything good shall come to the virtuous & only evil come for the wicked— this is no more true than the woodland fairy Mother had us chase in the forest when we were children. Do you remember that, Kate? How I did believe in her, that fairy with gossamer green wings & skin of palest blue. I believed that she watched over me on winter nights, when the wind howled round the eaves. With time I outgrew the woodland fairy & with Percy's dying I outgrew too those other fairy tales.

I remember so well Percy's small feet on the riverbank. He skipped after a dragonfly, I heard him call to me, his small voice breathless as he ran. I turned my head away but for an instant—Kate, an instant—& then the splash. In my dreams I am still searching in the dark water for him. My hands grasp only lily roots & swarms of tadpoles, their bloated bodies floating strange between my fingers. I am not to blame myself, you & Mother & Father have told me a thousand times if once. I hear the words, but at night, when I wake from those dreams, it is with a pain so deep I can scarcely breathe. The weight I feel, the sorrow. That I was not quick enough, that I left him in that cold place. I could not find him. It was I alone who could have saved him & I alone who did not. Where was God that day, I ask you, where was He?

Yours,
Dot

April 12, 1848
Dearest Kate,

　There is some news from town. Widow Price's field hand has not yet been caught, though it seems the whole county rides every night in pursuit, a whole cavalry of our landholders on the moonlit roads. They relish in the frolic of it, the shouting of glad voices came in through my open window last night & woke me. Perhaps the fugitive is long gone, perhaps he walks even along the streets of your city as I write this. In truth I hope that it is so. Widow Price grows graver by the week, her frown sinking deeper into the lines of her face as though fixed in stone, never to turn upwards again.

　Mother says that Widow Price has lost four slaves in the past month to flight, & isn't it perilous, a woman farming alone, her only son gone out west & never heard from again? But still, her pallor, the black robes she persists in wearing so long after her husband's passing, her eyes black as her skirts, her voice shrill & sharp at the children running after Sunday sermon—all this provokes in me a great unease. She seems one for whom mercy is a weakness, not a virtue, one for whom human suffering & pain are unremarkable & simply to be endured as they are, with no attempt to aid the afflicted. Would that all her field hands might flee.

Your most affectionate sister,
Dorothea

April 15, 1848
Dear Kate,

    So it is decided—Samuel shall stay now with us. It brings me great joy & I can see that it does too for Father & Mother. He will sleep downstairs in the spare room, & Father has made a low bed for him & a stool. He is a lovely boy, though solemn & thoughtful, not as whimsical & cheerful as our little Percy. O, I can hear your voice now—I must not compare the two. How could any child, any person for that matter, measure to our Percy? But at times when I am watching Samuel as he is quiet, after a meal or sitting in the morning as he awaits Father's summons to help in the barn or in the fields, I must turn my eyes away because his person is so much alike to Percy. The way he holds his boyish head, the straight line of his slender back as he sits. It nearly breaks my heart.

    Samuel I think is happy here, as happy as an orphaned boy can be. Mother tends to him morning & night & Father too has taken him under his tutelage, showing him the lathe & spinner & how to sand the wood in the direction of the grain. Neither Father nor Mother speak of it to me, but I can see a lightness now in their ways that has been missing these two long years since Percy's passing. I came upon Mother humming at her work in the kitchen yesterday—can you imagine! I wanted to hug her & clap my hands but I did not. I crept away & left her with her hands in flour & her tune echoing off the baking tins. Yes, Samuel has given new hope to us all, & for this I am very grateful.

    Jack Harper called today to speak with Father about some carpentry work. His mother is very poorly, Father said. Jack

nodded to me but Mother & I were busy with the early canning
& Mother bade me not tarry.

> *Your affectionate & dutiful sister,*
> *Dorothea*

～●✦●～

April 17, 1848
Dearest Kate,

    The heat is unbearable today, the air heavy to breathe.
It is early yet for such oppression, it bodes ill for the coming
summer. We buried Samuel's dear mother this morning, all of
us with tears of sweat on our faces as we stood grave-side. It
was a meager group, only ourselves, poor Samuel, & the Pastor.
Pastor Shaw spoke few words & his voice was low though his
face appeared troubled, he seemed occupied by some other
worry. Samuel remained brave, he did not weep. I held his
hand tightly throughout, & together we threw handfuls upon
her coffin. I do hate that sound, the dull thud of dirt falling
against the wood.
    Father has been busy in the barn all day & now even
as night has fallen I can see his lantern still burning in the
workshop window. He works too hard. His health remains good
but he works as though wishing to hasten along its decline.
Mother does not comment but she looks to the windows at
night as I do, hoping to see his form approaching the house,
ready to quit for the night, ready for rest. But he toils on. The
newly made coffins now seem almost to outnumber the living

of our congregation, as though Father were preparing for a great plague.

My eyes begin to close even as I write this. Sleep comes; good night, dear Kate.

Your sister,
Dot

❧

April 25, 1848
Dear Kate,

Our small chapel still echoes with the tones of Pastor Shaw's sermon delivered this Sunday last. It was a deeply affecting lecture, Kate, one that I continue to ponder even now three days gone. He spoke on the universal sanctity of life, how the taking of life regardless of the station of the person will always be viewed as a sin before God, that all men yearn for life & its natural corollary, freedom. His words flowed from him as I had never seen before. Jesus died for us all, the Pastor said, & it is not the privilege of men to pick & choose whose life may be considered sacred before the Lord.

Throughout the sermon I heard murmurs & coughs from the congregation, but the noise grew louder as the Pastor spoke on. And then suddenly Widow Price stood & departed from the church, even as Pastor Shaw still preached. I thought at first she suffered some sudden sickness, but her face bore a look of grim resolve & clear-eyed health. She very well stomped down the central aisle & slammed the church door behind her. Pastor Shaw continued without interruption but did not mingle with the congregation outside in his usual way.

Nor did we linger outside the church. Father hurried us
into the carriage & sped the horses onwards. Mother had a
queer look on her face, but shook me away when I questioned
her. Samuel & I sat close on the back bench, my arm around
his slender shoulders as we rode in silence towards home. And
I realized then that the pain of Percy's leaving, the weight of
my guilt, is lifting. Not always. Not every day. It is Samuel
that brings it on. Growing to know him &, yes, to love him,
not as I loved Percy, never like that, but a different sort of
love. It feels redemptive, if I may use a word from Pastor
Shaw's sermon. It feels like redemption. Like perhaps I will
not fall into the earth & be swallowed whole by my sorrow. It
feels like the dawn.

Your most loving & devoted sister,
Dorothea

❧

May 2, 1848
Dearest Kate,

There is some shocking news. Pastor Shaw is gone, run
out in the night. When first I heard, I could not help but
connect his departure to the last sermon he delivered with
such passion. Yesterday I questioned Father about it & he
seemed most discomfited. Father told me that three field hands
have been whipped to death in recent weeks, two by the Price
foreman & one by Mr. Stanmore himself, & it was these events
that had so aggrieved Pastor Shaw. Father believes the Pastor
spoke of equality of life as pertaining to slaves & that others in
the congregation saw this as blasphemous. It is a debasement

to a man's character to behave so brutally, Father said. Long have I known Father's views on the institution, but I had not heard him speak so openly before. Slavery breeds nothing but sloth & degradation among the landowners, he told me, & it is the greatest hypocrisy that extends it still within our national borders.

Father said that many of the slave holders amongst our neighbors had long believed the Pastor's views too liberal for our congregation, that he should have followed the Presbyterian New School to the North. Eventually Father broke off speaking & apologized, saying that such topics are outside a woman's sphere. But Kate, I wanted most desperately for him to continue. Such questions affect us all, do you not think?

Perhaps Pastor Shaw was asked to leave, perhaps he has moved on. But I fear for him. And are we too at risk of incurring our neighbors' approbation, given Father's friendship with the Pastor? Might it damage Father's business reputation & relations? Father continues on publicly as though nothing has happened. This morning in town he said loudly to Mr. Stanmore that he looks forward to the arrival of our new minister. Though when this will be, no one knows.

I hope that Pastor Shaw will soon send word. A simple note to assure us of his good health would put us all at ease.

Yours,
Dot

May 15, 1848
My dearest sister,

Something has happened but words fail me to explain. My
hand is shaking as I write these words, shaking still from what
I witnessed in the barn tonight, after our evening meal, after
Mother & I read to little Samuel & tucked him to bed. I will
try to tell the tale as I witnessed it, leaving nothing out.

To begin: Samuel was sleeping peacefully downstairs,
Father was working in the barn outside, Mother had retired
to her bed. I remained at the kitchen table, reading the new
Godey's when I heard a scream. I raised my head & heard
another. The sound was muffled but it seemed to come from
our very barn. I stepped outside & saw the light from Father's
lantern burning in the barn window. I hurried across the
yard and, as my feet sank into the soft mud of the garden, I
heard yet another scream. I shouted for Father and, receiving
no reply, swung open the door to the workshop. What met
my eyes shocked me to the very core. There stood our Father
with hammer in hand. A recently finished casket rested on
splints, the wood still yellow & raw. Its lid lay half askew,
the bottom half covered but the top half open to reveal a
man inside, a living man. His head & torso rose up from the
coffin & his mouth opened & emitted another scream, this
one directed at myself, as his eyes met mine, which I have
no doubt were wide with horror. Father turned then to see
me standing in the doorway. "You fool," he said to the man in
the casket. He spat the words with a tone of disappointment
& regret that I never before had heard from him. "Close the
door, Dot," he said to me. "Please, Dot, come in & close the
door."

I did as he told with shaking legs. The man in the casket remained silent but staring at me & truthfully dear Sister, I could not help but stare back at him unabashed. He was a Negro man, his skin black as the night, his hair shorn to his scalp, his torso covered with the most pitiful of rags. His eyes remained on me, suspicious & fearful, as I approached. "Who is this man?" I whispered to Father. He shook his head. "It is best if you return to the house. Forget what you have seen. And do not speak a word of this to your Mother." I did not answer. How could I forget this scene, forget the terror in this man's eyes, his arms that, now I stood closer to the casket, were marked with scars & scabbing? And our Father, was he this man's protector or his tormentor?

"Dorothea," Father said. "Go inside, go to bed." His voice soothed in the way that always calms me, when I am upset or missing you or cross with Mother. I do love him, & I looked at him then, at the worry darkening his eyes, his mouth pursed straight, the deep lines across his forehead. How could I disobey him? I returned to the house, climbed the steps & sit now in my nightclothes at the small desk you fashioned so long ago from the crate & stool, pen & ink before me, blotter to the side. I have just heard Father return to the house, the barn now is dark & silent. I know not what has become of that man, but I cannot shake his face from my mind. The line of his jaw, the set of his eyes. His was a face unaccustomed to kindness. What does Father do alone at night, with Mother, Samuel & I asleep, innocent & dreaming?

There is still no word from Pastor Shaw.

Yours,
Dorothea

May 17, 1848
Dearest Kate,

Last night I approached Father. I waited until Mother &
Samuel were sleeping contentedly. I did not wish one of them
to intrude for I knew not the matters that may be the subject
of our discourse. My stomach churned as I approached him,
sitting by the fire in his reading chair. (Father still reads his
Thoreau daily—I believe he feels closer to you by doing so.)
He raised his head & the light of the fire cast shadows upon
his face & made him look most fearful. I almost stopped then
& bade him good night, but I pushed my feet forward & knelt
before him, one hand on his knee just as I used to crouch
whilst a child listening to a story. I asked, "Please, Father, tell
me." Immediately he knew what I asked. He answered softly,
but his voice was solemn & firm. "Dorothea," he began, "what
I am about to say must stay between you & I alone. This is
of grave importance. Our livelihood & safety rests upon your
secrecy & discretion." I agreed of course, and my dear Kate, I
need not say that you too must breathe not a word of this to
anyone. I have sealed this letter with wax, & will do so from
this day forward.

And so: Father told me then of the Negro man in the barn,
that he was a runaway escaped from the Monroes some 30
miles to the south of us. Do you remember Miss Janet Monroe
whose lovely blond hair you so admired? It was on her father's
farm that the Negro had met the cruelest of treatment until
finally his suffering was so great that he chose the uncertainty
& risk of escape. Father acts, & has acted for many months

now, in the service of the Underground Railroad. Surely you have heard of such a thing, Kate? I had heard whispers of it, though in truth I had always believed it to be a story told by the abolitionists to lend some hint of success to their efforts. How wrong I was. The Railroad is real, it operates here in Charlotte County, Augusta, Franklin, & Bournemouth Counties too, stretching northward to Philadelphia, New York, & far Canada. It is like a flower with roots stretching beneath the surface of the earth, pushing its blooms up into the crisp northern air. Pastor Shaw too acted as a conductor on the Railroad, & it is Father's grave worry that he was discovered, & this prompted his hasty departure from Lynnhurst.

It is late now, Kate. I will write more tomorrow, I promise you. You might already guess at the method employed by Father to assist the escape of the runaways. It is quite ingenious & has so far proven universally successful. I will attempt to give you full particulars in my next letter.

Your faithful & adoring sister,
Dot

―⁙―

May 18, 1848
Darling Kate,

I sit tonight again with pen in hand & candle flickering to continue my tale. All day I have brooded on the stories Father told me, of the 34 Negro slaves he has assisted to date, all escaped from horrors that I can scarcely imagine, sent northwards towards freedom & kindness. I have wondered at the lives they are now living, the joys they may now experience.

*Father says there are hundreds of others, if not thousands,
acting as conductors along these routes. Most are free blacks
living north of the Ohio, themselves having escaped but who
now venture back to lead others northwards. They are assisted
by station houses such as ours, places of safety where the
fugitives might find food, clothing, a kind word and assistance
to pass further along the road. Father knows no names, only
codes & a few addresses of others like-minded, most small
farmers like himself.*

*It is quite amazing, Kate, the method that Father employs.
The reason he stood before that man with a hammer, the reason
the man seemed to rise like some apparition from the finished
casket, is that Father hides the runaways inside the casket
shipments he sends to northern buyers. The journey is three
days, first by wagon & then by train, & there is a man who
meets them at the station in Philadelphia & brings the delivery
to a place of safety where the caskets are unloaded & the
Negroes returned to the world. It is a daring ruse. And yet who
would suspect Father, he who already has been sending wares
to northern buyers for years? Mr. Taylor still ships dried beans
inside the caskets, but Father now fills an extra one or two with
the escaped runaways & the weight is scarcely distinguishable.*

*Father says that not one of his escapees has been
intercepted, as far as is known. He assisted even the fugitive
escaped from Widow Price! And to think of those search parties
passing by our door, & Father knowing all the while that the
Negro in question had already gone, safe within the confines of
his casket. And how do they survive those 3 days' passage? I can
hear your reasoned voice inquire. Father gives them a bit of
oatcake, but no more, & he drills small holes along the casket
sides to ensure proper ventilation. Can you imagine it, Kate,
a hammer nailing a wooden top across your face, insufficient
space even to turn from back to side? Darkness, stale air, no*

water, only the barest of provisions to keep your hunger at bay.
This the fugitives endure for a chance at freedom.

I wonder now about our neighbors, the Birches &
Stanmores especially, as to what transpires in their houses &
barns, out in their fields & meadows where the slaves crouch
dawn to nightfall. I have always shied away from political
talk—I suppose my interests have lain elsewhere, in childish
things. But now I feel the first stirring of political belief within
me. I know not where it will lead but it is a bit like waking
from a dream, or seeing the world through spectacles for the
first time. Everything is sharper, but unfamiliar. I am alert to
the details & complexities of this new world.

> Your most loving & affectionate sister,
> Dot

~∽⟡∽~

May 27, 1848
Dear Kate,

Pastor Shaw's body has been found dead, his eyes gouged
out. He lay in the woods near Juniper peak, found by Hiram
Birch who had gone hunting squirrels. Surely none of our
neighbors could be capable of such a vicious, blasphemous act?
To kill a man of God? The talk is that Pastor Shaw was once
a Quaker & Negro lover & that he had no place in Charlotte
County & it was God Himself who smote him down. This I
heard Liza Broadmoor whisper in town yesterday at Taylor's. A
whole gaggle of girls surrounded her. I could not bear to stay
long within their company & ran to find Mother again at the
counter. I did not tell her what I had heard.

Sheriff Roy spoke harshly of the act, & told the congregation that he would use all methods to ascertain what befell the Pastor. But in truth he seems little inclined to search out the truth. Father saw him yesterday exiting the tavern quite merrily, and not yet even 3 o'clock.

This cruel event makes me fear even more for Father's work & for our family's safety. Were Father to be discovered, what would become of us?

Yours as always,
Dorothea

    ❧❦❧

June 12, 1848
Dearest Kate,

Mrs. Broadmoor is unwell, & yesterday Mother & I brought her some cooked dinner & a jar of strawberries. Justin and the horrid Eliza were out, I am thankful to report. A house slave showed us in, a young man, the poor fellow was shackled about the ankles, he could scarcely walk. Mrs. Broadmoor saw our distaste, and explained that the boy Louis had attempted escape once and would henceforth be shackled and work in the house so that she might watch closely over him. Only when she was satisfied that all thoughts of escape were driven from his mind would she remove the chains— be it one week or ten years, she said, made no difference to her. Mother & I set about attending to Mrs. Broadmoor but my mind would not remain on the tasks at hand—again & again it strayed to the particulars of the life that boy must lead. What if it were I in such a position? To go about in iron shackles? And my studies, what would become of those? If I were not permitted to learn even the most basic of lessons, even to read, Kate, can you imagine how intolerable daily life would become? I longed to tell him that the means of escape were before his very eyes, that there exist good & honorable people in Charlotte County who might lead him to safety. But of course I held my tongue.

I bent my head to Mrs. Broadmoor & fed her soup as Louis moved about the room, sweeping and so forth. It was this sound that finally proved intolerable to me, the scratch scratch of the broom & deep, ugly clatter of his chains. I felt as though the walls moved towards me, that the room became smaller & the sound louder in that confined space. I leapt up just as Mrs. Broadmoor swallowed the last of the soup & I hastened from the room. Mother looked at me most strangely but she did not follow. I stood outside for a good while, gulping in deep breaths of air & walking along the riverbank until my heart calmed. Mother found me there, she had bid our good-byes to Mrs. Broadmoor alone & she said not a word of my fit as we walked the road towards home.

I am troubled greatly by what I see every day & feel a true abolitionist, yes Kate, is rising within me. Father is reluctant to involve me in his activities, but my heart & mind are increasingly committed. He thinks I am still a child & my fervor is a child's passion for something she cannot understand, but he misjudges me. I only seek to assist him, to further this most worthy of goals.

Your loving sister,
Dot

June 22, 1848
Dearest Kate,

 *Today brought the first sermon of our new Pastor Preston
Hoady. He preached on the Will of God & the Order of All
Things & it required no great effort to hear in his words a
reproof to that last oration delivered by Pastor Shaw. His voice
is strong & fiery & his person upon the pulpit inspires the
congregation. When I stole a look round at those assembled,
I saw faces transfixed. Scarcely a person moved or sneezed,
no babies cried, but all directed their full attention to Pastor
Hoady's swaying form. Even Samuel sat slack-jawed & quiet,
his heels miraculously ceased their knocking on the back
bench for the duration of the sermon. I believe I alone was not
so moved. True, there is something in the Pastor's manner that
invites inspection & I listened most attentively to the words he
spoke. I am troubled now as I write this, recalling the nodding
heads & Hallelujahs of our neighbors as his sermon rained
down. He seems to offer himself up as a sort of antidote to
Pastor Shaw, that we all are infected & now must be healed.*

 *Father continues to reject my offers of assistance. I fear now
that he sees how increased are the dangers, as Pastor Hoady
stokes our neighbors' sense of outrage & righteousness. I have
heard stories of abolitionists run out of towns even north of
the Ohio, of men tarred & feathered, whipped, hanged. Father
must feel sharply the weight of responsibility in the double life
he leads.*

Yours,
Dorothea

June 28, 1848
Dearest Kate,

At long last Father has allowed me to join him. Last night, I had already retired to bed but lay awake, as I so often do now, contemplating the days ahead & what they may hold. I heard muffled sounds, the front door closing softly, low voices, the screech of the barn door & an indignant moo from poor disturbed Molly. I pulled on my coat & boots & ran outside. All was still, the sky clouded & starless, the owls silent. A light blazed in Father's workshop window & I pulled open the door slowly, expecting to hear Father express anger at my disobedience. But he turned his head towards me with a look of calm acceptance. What a figure I must have made—hair askew, coat buttons open to the wind, boots muddied. "Dot," he said, "come in & close the door."

I stepped inside & noticed only then the poor figure who had come for his assistance, a man sitting amidst the sawdust & shavings of the workshop floor, his head resting back against the wall & his eyes closed as though his exhaustion was too great even to meet the light from my lamp. "Fetch a blanket from the house," Father said. "He will need better covering than what he's got now." I cannot tell you Kate how happy those words made me! He uttered them in barely a whisper but it shouted out to me all that I had hoped for.

I hurried to do as Father asked & truthfully Kate the remainder of the night passed as though I walked in a dream. We worked with few words, my eyes straining in the low light. We arranged the fugitive, a Mr. Alfred Joiner, who spoke few words to us but I came to understand had fled the Gilkeson place. He wore homespun pants, no shirt whatsoever, neither any shoes, and his feet were swollen near to bursting. Father sent me to a space behind the barn where most cleverly

*concealed within the stacked wood was a box and within it
all manner of clean clothing, blankets, and such. I collected
appropriate attire for Mr. Joiner which he accepted with a
glimmer of a smile. He had a wry manner, neither frightened
nor brave but seemingly accepting of all that might come to
pass, in a way that I suppose was indeed bravery of a type, or
wisdom at the least. "The world will do as it pleases," he said to
me. "I ride along best I can."*

*Just as dawn light grayed the workshop window, Father
fitted the coffin cover atop the man, who lay with eyes closed.
We had given him oatcake, & burlap sacks to cover & cushion
his person. The instructions to Mr. Joiner were simple: make
not a sound throughout the journey & collection will occur at
the Philadelphia station, from whence you will be transported
to a safe house & from there given advice as to travels further
north or other assistance as needs be. He clasped Father's hand
as we lowered him into the casket.*

*Kate, I sit now at my desk, dressed still in my nightclothes,
& write this in a sort of delirium. The man lies within the barn,
his casket alongside the others awaiting collection & transport
by the coach, due to arrive in a few hours' time. Father has
retired to his bed & I cannot say whether he is pleased or cross
at my participation in tonight's activities. He said scarcely a
word to me beyond the orders he gave, items to fetch. I can
only trust & hope that he is happy in the knowledge that his
daughter is so very happy & that we have together secured the
freedom of Mr. Joiner. May the world henceforth treat him well.*

*Yours,
Dorothea*

July 2, 1848
Dear Kate,

Jack Harper's mother has passed on. Jack came today to
the house & asked Father to ready a coffin & retrieve her
body for laying out. It was mid-morning & Samuel & I were
still engaged in lessons with Mother. She sent Samuel out to
fetch Father from his workshop & bade Jack come indoors to
wait, but he refused. He waited hat in hand outside the door
although the day already tended to hot. I brought him a glass of
the lemonade Mother makes to such perfection & he thanked
me warmly enough but his eyes barely met mine & he did not
engage in conversation. I wanted to ask after his brother Caleb.
Do you recall Caleb Harper, who went up to Philadelphia some
years back? It was quite a shock to his parents when the eldest
left the farm & there was some bitterness in the departure, as I
recall. I heard talk that he is studying modern medicine at the
college there, but that is all that is known of him.

Kate, perhaps you will think this improper but there is
something in Jack that held me & I admit that I did linger even
after he passed back the empty glass. Father finally arrived from
the workshop & shook Jack's hand. He murmured words of
condolence & the two walked off. My eyes followed them & Kate,
I felt such a stirring of sympathy for Jack—abandoned by his
brother, his Father not right in the head (so Mother says), & left
to arrange his dead Mother's interment. I am glad that Jack came
to Father, for he will lend a helping hand & a sympathetic ear.

Yours,
Dorothea

July 6, 1848
Dearest Kate,

Today we laid Jack Harper's good mother to rest. I
remember her scarcely at all, she was rarely in town & never
once called socially on Mother or for Father's services. But
no doubt she was a good, kind-hearted woman, I am sure
of it as Jack seems such a worthy person. All members of
the congregation were in attendance, save the poorly Mrs.
Broadmoor. Pastor Hoady spoke of Mrs. Harper's godliness
& thrift, her service as dutiful mother & wife, her striving to
fulfill God's will in all manners of daily life & toil. I could not
help but steal glances at Jack, who sat stony-faced beside his
Father. Nothing seemed to move him, no words from the Pastor
or well wishes from the neighbors who filed past following the
sermon. His Father too displayed no emotion apart from an
abject tiredness & he leaned upon Jack's shoulder as the well-
wishers filed past. Unlike the custom with Pastor Shaw, Pastor
Hoady did not invite the congregation to the parish house but
instead encouraged us all to retire to home & reflect in solitude
on the blessed journey of the departed.

Jack & his Father were fast into their carriage & away
but a group lingered, ourselves included. There was much
conversation outside the church, though I suspect less of the
sacred nature than Pastor Hoady would have wished. Mr.
Gilkeson was there, milling about with the other landowners,
speaking of the loss of his slave Alfred Joiner and where could
he have gone, he must have been aided by one among the
neighboring farms, and what he wouldn't do to any such
scoundrel caught harboring another man's property.

Mother, Samuel & I stood some distance apart from the
men but still I heard his words, he spoke them with such force.
Presently Father bade the group good-bye & came to join us &

*we made our way home under the noon-day sun. We rode in
silence, Father & Mother both with faces set and grim.*

Yours,
Dot

❦

July 21, 1848
Dearest Kate,

   I am sorry to be so long delayed in answering your last
letter. We have had much activity here recently, & my nights
have been full. I hesitate to describe the particulars of each
sorry case Father & I have seen appear at the barn door like
apparitions come from the darkness. There have been 5
since last I wrote, 4 men & 1 woman. Father seems now to
accept me as his helper, & we have arrived at a routine of
sorts. He hides the fugitive away in the barn & sets to work
on ascertaining the best means of escape while I prepare food
& drink & retrieve items of clothing or blankets, medicine,
or whatever else may be needed. I sit with the fugitive while
he eats & it is these times that have proven immensely
illuminating. Last night's fugitive was an elderly gentleman of
58 years, Langston Crockett was his name, born & raised on
a cotton plantation in Alabama, never traveled further than
the perimeters of that estate in his whole long life until setting
foot upon the path north, & now we find him, brought to
Father's barn by a neighboring conductor. On his right hand,
instead of a thumb he had only a stump of flesh, the result of
a punishment some 30 years prior for the sin of fainting dead
away in his pickers' row while ill with fever.

Father & I have arrived at a problem. We cannot send them all inside the caskets as Father's shipments are not so frequent as are the fugitives who appear at our door. Last night Father transported Mr. Crockett in the dead of night in the wagon, fitted now with a clever bottom panel such that the fugitives may lie beneath the floor of the wagon unseen by any who might examine it. Upon leaving, Father said that I was to bar the door, close & lock the shutters & remain inside until his return. The night was a long one. I scarcely closed my eyes, imagining our Father stopped by some patroller or the sheriff, but he returned unharmed, just as the sky showed dawn, with his task completed. But he cannot be ferrying large numbers in this manner. Such night-time activity will only rouse the suspicions of our neighbors and Father's exhaustion would soon leave us without a livelihood.

I plan soon to involve Samuel in our activities, to give him the satisfaction of participating in our family's good work. He has been quite taken with Pastor Hoady's sermons of late & indeed their effect is difficult to escape. The Pastor leads the congregation in chanting & at times a great emotional wave sweeps through the hall such that people cry out spontaneously, or fall to the ground with writhing. It is both horrible & intoxicating to witness & is most affecting to the younger members of the church. I believe Samuel suffers still from the sudden loss of his Mother & those lost hours during which he sat with her body alone, awaiting his murderous Father's return. With our parents' love and guidance, he will in time inure to the devious charms of men like Preston Hoady.

I have not yet spoken to Father about my intention, but I am confident he will agree with me as to Samuel's fitness for such work & indeed the need for another pair of helping hands.

Yours,
Dorothea

August 13, 1848
Dear Kate,

There has been a most distressing development. I have learned that the runaway from Mr. Gilkeson's plantation—do you recall my letter about him? The gentleman Alfred Joiner who came to our door these many weeks past?—has been recaptured & is now bound once again for Charlotte County. A slavecatcher discovered him in Richmond & I have no doubt, is happily awaiting the substantial reward offered by Mr. Gilkeson for Alfred's return. It pains me beyond measure to consider that this has been the outcome of his flight.

It was Jack Harper who told us the news. He came to call this afternoon, bringing Mother a basket of fine apples from their trees. He told us that his own dear Father had passed on, peaceably dead in his sleep, joining his own beloved wife in Heaven. Jack dug a simple grave himself, his Father having wished for no ceremony or fuss.

We sat, all 5 of us, to visit & express our condolences. Presently Jack relayed the story of poor Alfred & of Mr. Gilkeson's vow to whip him until he divulges the name of any & all who assisted him in his escape. Jack knows not where Alfred & the slavecatcher are now on their journey, but it seems certain they will arrive back in Lynnhurst within the week.

This is my worst fear realized—certainly we shall be revealed. And what then? Will Gilkeson take Alfred at his word? Shall we try to dissuade Gilkeson from believing in such a confession, that a whipped man is inclined to say any number of untrue things? Shall we leave town now,

even before the slavecatcher's return, forfeiting our home
& livelihood? Poor Jack throughout his visit knew not the
agitation his words provoked. I sat gripping the seat of my
chair as he spoke, & Father's face washed white as ash. Mr.
Gilkeson is adamant, Jack said, truly committed to discerning
the truth.

What will become of Mother & Samuel? Will our
neighbors believe that it was Father & I alone who acted
in defiance of the law? What will they do to Father? And
how might we continue to assist the fugitives? Think of the
numbers whom we might still help, think of the man or
woman who even now may be readying a pack, counting the
minutes until nightfall when escape will be at hand.

Yours,
Dorothea

❧❦❧

August 14, 1848
Dear Kate,

It is scarcely 24 hours since I posted my last letter & already
there is great change in our situation. Even as I wrote my
troubled lines to you yesterday, Alfred & the slavecatcher had
already returned to Gilkeson's farm & Alfred whipped to death.
He said not a word before his death but remained silent as
the grave, not even crying out in pain as the whip bore down.
Father heard the tale from Gilkeson's overseer, who himself
administered the lashes. We are not revealed, we can continue
unmolested in our efforts, that is the only solace here. The rest
is simple tragedy, pure & unrelieved. Surely Gilkeson does not

now believe that this example will weaken the Negroes' desire for freedom? The punishment meted out on poor Alfred will do nothing to dissuade others from fleeing. It will only strengthen their resolve. Men like Mr. Gilkeson or Mr. Stanmore cannot guess at the intensity of feeling to throw off the shackles & yoke. Perhaps it is that living as they do, Lords of their personal kingdoms with nary a voice to raise above theirs, they have no way of imagining a life bereft of autonomy. You & I can so imagine, can't we, Kate?

Today I have told Samuel of our work. I did not seek Father's permission beforehand & even now he does not know the extent of Samuel's understanding. Perhaps this was foolish of me, perhaps Father will scold me for it later, but we desperately need another to assist in our activities. Samuel can run ahead to the next safe lodging, he can fetch the supplies that the fugitives need for their journeys, he can perform any number of useful tasks that now have Father & I running to & fro all night long. He looked at me wide-eyed as I told him my tale—the man in the barn, Father with the hammer—and of the recent horrible events & our blessed release from suspicion. He asked me not a single question, only nodded his head gravely. Perhaps it was too much for him to take in at a single sitting & me in such a state today, weeping & so forth. Samuel is a good boy, I have great faith in him, that he will support Father & I. We must continue with even greater secrecy than before.

Your adoring sister,
Dot

August 28, 1848
Dearest Kate,

    What times these are for us, Kate. Last night a girl came to
the house. She was heavy with child, though she seemed not
to understand, she only wanted to flee. She would not tell us
from where she ran. It did not seem that she had come far, her
feet were hardened but did not bleed though she was nearly
delirious with exhaustion. I feared for her child & for herself,
she was not fully present in her mind. After much entreaty, she
told us that her name was Josephine.

Lina stopped reading. *Josephine. Heavy with child.* A descendant.
Lina looked to the photo of Lu Anne and Josephine on the porch
and smiled because of what this meant for the reparations case and
also for Josephine herself, for the girl running in the night, searching
for a barn, and at last it appears, a lantern perhaps lighting the path,
and Dorothea ready with some food, a blanket, an onward journey.

But what had happened? Lina checked the relevant dates: Dorothea's letter was dated August 1848, but the photo of Josephine and
Lu Anne at Bell Creek was taken in 1852. Why had Josephine gone
back? And where was her child?

Lina checked her watch. Only an hour remained before the cab
would take her to the airport. She resumed reading, faster now, her
pen poised over paper, jotting the important dates and facts: *Last*
night a girl came to the house.

    She had scarcely anything with her, no pack or parcel, just
an ear of corn in one pocket & a drawing of a woman in the
other, a drawing quite expertly made. I asked her who was the
artist but she did not answer, only looked to it with a certain
sadness. She was young, younger than myself, & Father & I

were both deeply moved by her. I sat with her quietly, stroking her head as Father fetched food from the larder & left the two of us to ourselves. Perhaps he thought that she & I would speak as girl friends might, or as sisters, but it was too difficult, our worlds were too far apart. She refused to speak of the events that had led her to our barn, despite my patient urgings. Instead she spoke of the colors of the sky & the mountains, chickens beset by a pox, children laughing & playing, a cow gone dry, sheets blowing on a dry wind. It was an odd story she told, not even quite a story but more a series of pictures she painted for me in the air.

When Father finally returned, she lay asleep across the floorboards, her head resting lightly against my leg. "We cannot send her," Father said. "She is not right in the head and her child could come at any time. She would never last the journey." Indeed I had considered the same, but what then were we to do? I thought it best for her to sleep, then we might give her a good meal, help her return to herself, & transport her in the wagon, on to another station in the Railroad, a less dangerous locale, where she might be safer. Father's reply surprised me. "We cannot risk her in the wagon. The space is close under the boards, she might scream or start to birth her child. The patrollers are more numerous since Alfred's capture & I cannot place us at risk."

I carefully shifted her head & stood so that I might look Father in the eye. "What then would you have us do? We cannot forsake this girl, she has come to us for help." He answered, "We cannot save them all. There are great risks for us, for Samuel & your Mother, were we to be discovered. Would you have us jeopardize all our efforts for this one?" We stood face to face as the girl slept on. I asked again what he would have us do. I have never spoken so coldly to Father before but anger & frustration rose up within me. Why this

girl? Why were the risks now too great? "Perhaps we might
bring her to the Sheriff with requests for mercy," Father said.
"I do not suggest we leave her on the road. We will arrive at a
solution."

Father spoke on but his solutions seemed impossible to
me, for they were merely different routes to the same end—
to return the girl to servitude & almost certainly to grave
punishment. And in our solution we were condemning her
unborn child as well. "I then will assist her. I will do it alone,"
I told Father, believing fully that I possessed the capability.
Who would suspect a girl such as myself? I would concoct a
story, load the wagon with supplies for the journey, carry the
small revolver that Mother keeps hidden away in the back
pantry.

But Kate, all of this was not to be. How I wish Father
& I had kept our voices low! For the girl Josephine awoke,
unnoticed by us. She must have lain as if asleep, listening to
our talk, to Father's reticence, to his plans of return. At some
point in our discourse—I know not if she ever heard of my
intention to act alone—she stole away from the barn & ran
into the cold night, storm clouds amassing overhead. I searched
for her, I called out as loud as I dared into the darkness but she
was gone.

Father said only, "I am sorry," but his face spoke what his
words did not. He saw a rift open up between us, & the rift
healed as the girl disappeared into the night.

But the rift is not healed. I cannot forget Father's
heartlessness towards the girl, surely the one most deserving—
of all the fugitives we have seen on our doorstep—of our help.
And it is this girl we failed to aid.

Yours,
Dorothea

September 1, 1848
Dear Kate,

I cannot look Father in the eye. Surely Mother has noticed, though she says not a word about it, she simply goes about her tasks as though nothing has changed. I feel almost a physical shift, as though the sky has changed its color or the air has thickened so that my breathing comes harder now. Samuel, in his quiet watchful way, has seen the change in me & stays close during the days. Yesterday he nary left my side from morning till night & finally I whispered to him the sorry story of the girl. It was long past Samuel's bedtime, he had crept up the stairs to slip under my blankets as he does after one of his nightmares.

At last we slept & I dreamt of her. She was running in my dream, but it was I who chased her, not the patroller or her master but I & she ran onwards, glancing behind her with eyes full of such fear as I struggled to keep up, breathless to explain myself. The girl's eyes were quite remarkable, did I tell you? They were green & blue, flecked with yellow, wide & clear even in her exhaustion.

This morning I sat in church & heard scarcely a word uttered by Pastor Hoady, my mind was worlds away. I gazed at the altar above the Pastor's head, the roughly carved cross that has darkened as the years progress until now it seems to gleam with a dark fire. Do you recall when the yellow grain still could be seen & each notch of the ax? When the wood was still new & green? I wondered at how the passage of time does not heal all wounds, how the hurt of Percy's passing still cuts me today as it did in those first moments on the riverbank, when

*Father heard my screams & finally pulled him from the water.
Time does not heal, Kate, but it does ease the hurt. My hurt
has eased. Already I feel as though it is my memory of that time
by the river that cuts me, rather than the hurt itself. Does that
sound foolish? And perhaps next year, it will be the memory
of the memory, & with each step I am further removed from
the true source of my sorrow. I do not know if this is better
or worse. I suppose it is necessary for me to live. I would not
survive myself to have always that grief so green & new. Will
time ease the weight I feel at failing this girl? Yes, I hear your
voice say & I do believe you. My pain will fade, but our error
still remains. The act cannot be undone & it is these acts by
which we are ultimately judged, by which we all must judge
ourselves.*

*All this passed through my mind, this morning in church.
I was thus lost until my attention was drawn away from the
cross to a lone figure turned backwards on the pew—his face
a flicker of pale against the sea of dark heads turned away, his
eyes on mine. Jack Harper. He seemed to care not if Pastor
Hoady saw his distraction. He smiled at me and I held his eyes
for a moment only & then could not bear it & turned my gaze
to my lap. When I raised my head again, his face was gone.
I saw only row after row of featureless heads, each so like the
next, but then easily I picked out Jack's: the glint of his dark
curls & the square set of his shoulders marked him for me as
though he stood alone.*

Yours,
Dot

September 10, 1848
Dearest Kate,

Someone has told. I know not who. Last night I awoke
to yelling & an ominous rushing sound, as though a
locomotive passed beside the house. There was the sound of
glass shattering, & Mother's voice high & hysterical. Father
yelled, "Stop there!" & I bounded out of bed & down the
stairs. A flickering lit the kitchen as I ran to the door & upon
throwing it open I saw our barn ablaze. Mother & Father
raced back & forth before it, their faces streaming black with
ash & tears, searching for a route inside to rescue our animals
whose cries rang horrible above even the rushing noise of
the fire. But the heat proved intolerable. There was no point
of entry. Father pointed towards the well & the three of us
began a hopeless rally of throwing bucket after bucket of
water towards the flames. Desperation drove us even as the
flames reached higher & the cries of those poor creatures fell
silent.

Finally we stopped & simply watched the conflagration. We
stood far enough away to breathe, though my lungs still burned
with every inhalation. The hair around my face is singed now,
my voice cracked & dry from yelling with fury into that awful
tempest. It raged all night & even as the sky lightened with
dawn the flames still licked at the last remaining corner beams
& through the gutted innards of the barn.

Samuel did not assist us at the well but stood apart
throughout the night & watched the mighty destruction from
atop the chicken coop. I was grateful he remained out of
harm's way. Upon morning I saw that he was black from head
to toe, his eyes red-rimmed & feverish. I took him in my arms
but he remained stiff against me, his body unwelcoming to
comfort & I let him go.

*The barn of course is no more, the animals dead, our
stores of grain & seeds for spring planting destroyed, Father's
workshop & all his tools gone. Father saw riders cantering
away from the barn in the earliest moments after he awoke.
Surely the fire had been deliberately set & we must leave with
first light tomorrow or else risk our lives as well.*

*Today we had but one visitor, although the smoke surely
gave notice to all our neighbors of our misfortune. It is telling
that none have offered help, do you not think, Kate?*

*And our single visitor, have you guessed? It was Jack,
our dear friend. He told us of the town's talk. He awoke this
morning to the smell of smoke & called first thing on Sheriff
Roy to report it, but the Sheriff displayed no surprise, expressed
no sympathy for the unknown victims, called on no team
to investigate. He instead directed Jack back towards home,
informing him that all matters had been concluded, that there
was nothing more to be done. Upon exiting the Sheriff's, Jack
saw on the road Gilkeson's man & two others who told him of
Father's betrayal, that Father harbored fugitives & would suffer
mightily for it. The men carried rifles, Jack said, & had been
drinking, a whiskey bottle sat in the dust between them. They
talked of Alfred & the other runaways from Charlotte County,
of Mr. Gilkeson's anger, of Widow Price's calm certainty that
we will receive our due reckoning.*

*Jack fears for us & urged Father to pack our things quickly
& leave forthwith. It brought me unexpected pain, to hear Jack
say these words, urging us to leave this place & thus leave his
good company. Will I never see Jack Harper again? Is this an
end to our renewed friendship? And where shall we go? Father
believes we should travel west, to the Oregon Territory where
they say land stretches unclaimed as far as the eye can see. We
can farm, Father can return to his carpentry, perhaps in time
again to undertaking. Mother wept as Father spoke of the long*

journey ahead, but then dried her eyes when she saw Samuel's stricken face. He has not spoken since the fire, despite my & Mother's attention to him. He seems to suffer some affliction, but I cannot say what to call it.

Your loving sister,
Dot

———⚬⚬⚬———

September 11, 1848
Dearest Kate,

 It is with shaking hand that I write this letter to you. It is Samuel who told, Samuel who brought the town's wrath upon us & broke our strictest confidence. I struggle to understand it. It was Pastor Hoady who informed us when he appeared at our house this morning. Our wagons stood half-packed, the ruined barn still smoked & smoldered. And truly like an apparition the Pastor appeared on the road from town, in black cape & astride his tall dark horse, seeming less like the man of God he professes to be, more like a rider out of Hades. Father, Mother & I all stood outside, busy in our preparations for the journey, but urgently Father waved us towards the house. "Inside," he said & the look in his eyes was fearful. Before Mother & I could enter, Samuel appeared at the doorway, his eyes round with fear but a fascination there too, his eyes never leaving the Pastor's & he stepped forward into the yard. It was then I knew.

 The Pastor looked down upon Samuel. He did not dismount. He said, "It is this fine boy who told me first of your betrayal," and he looked to Father. "I sensed when I first entered this parish that a certain evil pervaded it. I knew of

Mr. Shaw's heresy & I suspected he was not alone. It is the
hand of God that smote down your barn, have no doubt."
"Why have you come here?" Father asked. "We will be on our
way, you can see that we are readying to leave." "I am here
for Samuel," the Pastor said, & nodded towards our boy. "He
knows there is nothing but wickedness in your way. I am here
to take the boy."

"No." Mother, who had been silent all this time, Kate, who
had scarce said a word since the fire, save to comfort Samuel,
now spoke forth with such volume & strength, we all turned
to her. "No, you will not take him." She walked to Samuel &
wrapped an arm around him, bending her body as though to
shield him from the sun that shone brittle in the sky. Samuel
remained still as stone. He did not return Mother's embrace.

The Pastor smiled. "Do you understand what I have just
told you? It was Samuel who told me of the fugitives you
shelter here, of a pregnant girl you sent away. He came to me."
The Pastor's horse balked & fidgeted suddenly & he struggled
to stay astride. "Samuel?" The Pastor reached his hand towards
Samuel & beckoned him forwards. Mother bent now &
kneeled before him. She looked Samuel in the face, kissed him
again & again on the cheeks & whispered to him. I could not
hear the words. She embraced him & his childish arms went
round her neck, his face wet with tears. He shook his head at
the Pastor & took our Mother's hand.

"Go," Father said to the Pastor. "Samuel will remain with us."

"Samuel," the Pastor called as he steadied his horse, who
pranced with agitation. Mother & Samuel seemed not to hear
the Pastor's voice & they entered the house, Mother's head
bent low in soft murmuring. Samuel leaned against her skirts.
The door closed behind them. "Do not think I will be the last
to come out this way," the Pastor said then to Father, knowing
he had lost the boy, knowing that maternal forgiveness is

absolute. "Do not think you may remain here. Do not think you can be saved." And finally he let his horse loose & they galloped away.

"We must leave today," Father said to me. "Others will come for us, the Pastor speaks the truth in that at least."

The remainder of that morning we worked steadily without any talk. Father did not ask but he must have known it was I who told Samuel & thus my betrayal too that had led us to this sorry place. Various states of emotion swirled within me, Kate, all that long morning. Anger towards Samuel, guilt for my own transgression, sorrow at leaving, & fear at what would become of us. How were we to defend ourselves against the anger of those men? Against their rifles? If there had been no mercy for Pastor Shaw then neither would there be mercy for us. A great fear quickened my steps from the house to the wagon & back again, countless times. Mother & Samuel sat together on the settee, which we could not bring, it was too heavy for the wagon. Samuel lay asleep, his head in her lap. Mother's eyes too were closed but her face was tense with worry.

I write this with haste, I will post it at the first opportunity. We rest now for our last meal in our most beloved home. The sun sits low in the sky already but Father says we dare not spend another night here. We will not travel through town, we will first go south along the lesser-used roads. Father says we will ride all night & stop to sleep awhile in the early morning, off the road. Oh, I cannot bear to count the things that I will miss about this place. Apples fresh off our trees, sweets at Taylor's, trout from the river, my dear friends, & Jack Harper, whose face I will trace in my mind every day that we ride. It is his face I will trace in my mind for all the years of my life.

Your most loving sister,
Dot

September 12, 1848
Dearest Kate,

I am gone from our home, from our good Father & Mother.
I have departed upon a great adventure, just as you did so
many months ago, & it is with fear & happiness that I lay
pen to paper this night. Jack & I are married, Father himself
conducted the ceremony yesterday evening, in the waning
hours of that most horrible day as we readied to leave our home
(could it have been just yesterday? Already it seems like a
faraway dream).

Just as we packed the final things upon the wagon, Jack
appeared on his horse, the flanks flecked with foam from hard
riding. Jack dismounted, his face graver than ever I had seen it
before & he went at once to Father's side. I stood with Mother
near the horses, hitching them to the wagon, filling the feed
bag & could not hear what passed between Father & Jack,
though I strained to catch the words. In truth, my heart beat
against my chest at the very sight of Jack & a sadness gripped
me. I do love him, I first realized it then at that moment when
I believed we would be parted.

I did not dare imagine that Jack had come to ask for my
hand. But Father smiled & shook his hand & Jack turned then
to me, his look still grave but a relief & excitement in his eyes
& he walked to me & bent, there on the trodden-down dirt &
black ash, onto his knee and took my hand. I nearly swooned.
The fear & rush of the last days, the fire, the swirl of emotions
at leaving our good home, all that has transpired with Samuel,
& now my greatest joy realized. But I did not swoon, I clasped
his hand in mine & nodded yes. There was not a moment's

hesitation in my heart & Jack rose & circled his arms around me. Mother came to our side, tears on her face & I hugged her, myself crying now too & Father, stoic & stern as ever, kissing both my cheeks & grasping my shoulders.

Because time was so short, Father quickly determined that he should conduct a ceremony of sorts that very evening, & the marriage blessed by our parents, by darling Percy in heaven, & by Samuel, Mother's changeling boy. He has begun again to speak, at least there is that. Mother stays so close to him, a hand always on his shoulder, his hand in hers. She has lost one boy, she will not lose another.

Jack & I bade them good-bye, the three sitting close upon the bench, Samuel between Mother & Father, his small dark head still so much like Percy's, but now I realize all that is different about him. Their wagon rolled into the harsh rays of a low-hanging sun. The sky was clear enough for stars to guide their way. I struggled to smile as they left, to remain cheerful & hopeful for all that would come, but tears marked my cheeks & wet my lips & it is that salt I taste still as I write this. I fear they may be apprehended on the road. I fear that something in Samuel is not right, that again he will do them harm in some unknowable way. I fear common thieves, wolves, the Indians who they say prey upon the settlers to avenge the loss of their western frontier. Every moment it seems another danger flashes through my head & it is upon them, in my imagination, & I am helpless to assist.

Still, there is true hope within me. I grasped Jack's hand this morning, the two of us together at his table. He will sell his family farm & we will find another with more land, better land. A few cows, chickens, we will grow wheat, some vegetables for our meals. It is not much that I need for happiness, this I realize now. It is not in the grand sermons of our churches, or the political affairs of state. I will strive in my own way for the abolitionist cause. I will assist others as I can on the Railroad. And this is really all that I ask, to be a good wife to Jack, to work alongside him, to find comfort where I may, to give comfort to others as I am able. Is it too much to wish for such a life? Is it too little?

I wish you & Gareth all the happiness the world can bring. Someday I will see you in your great City, some day we will embrace again, my sister Kate.

Always,
Dorothea

Lina closed the biography. For a moment, Dorothea was present with her in the office, layered in skirts and petticoats, with her convictions and resolve, talking to Lina. *Is it too much to wish for such a life? Is it too little?* Lina laughed with tears in her eyes because the words written 150 years ago by a young woman she would never meet seemed truer than anything she'd read in her textbooks, anything she'd been told by her law professors or by Dan. *Law is the bastion of reason. There is no place for feeling. We reason, we observe, we analyze. This isn't about emotion or any kind of absolute justice.*

Justice.

Lina's eyes roamed again to the photo of Josephine and Lu Anne. Josephine's eyes were restless, searching for the road ahead.

A girl heavy with child . . . A drawing quite expertly made . . . She said her name was Josephine . . .

That night, Josephine had been pregnant and distressed, and Horace Rounds had refused to help her. By 1852, the year when Lu Anne Bell died and Josephine disappeared, the Rounds family was gone from Lynnhurst, Virginia, run out by their slaveholding neighbors. Josephine could not have used the Underground Railroad to escape in 1852. There were no other stations within a reasonable distance of Bell Creek; Lina had checked. Perhaps Josephine ran again without help from the Railroad? Or was she sold after Lu Anne's death? Or did she die, and the death go unrecorded, forgotten?

But of course it was no longer Josephine Bell who Lina needed to trace; it was the child. This new understanding hit Lina with the force of a slap.

What had the woman at AfriFind told her? Lina quickly reviewed her research notes. Slave owners themselves often kept records of their holdings, the woman said. The Bell Center contained the largest holdings of papers relating to Lu Anne Bell, Bell Creek, and Charlotte County. Lina looked at her watch. Her flight to Richmond left in ninety minutes, but would the records at the Virginia Historical Society tell her anything? It seemed unlikely. Maybe there was information that Lina had not yet uncovered—an Underground Railroad station in Charlotte County that was still operational in 1852, property or estate records that might show Josephine's transfer to a buyer or Bell family member. Yes, she would go to Richmond as planned, Lina decided, slipping the biography of Kate Rounds Sterrett into her suitcase. She would begin at the Historical Society, but then she would take an unscheduled detour. She needed to go to the small town of Lynnhurst, Virgina. She needed to go to Bell Creek.

Josephine

The paper roll, secured with twine. Josephine's lesson book, the margins marked with shaky letters, alongside the firm examples in Missus' hand. A small wooden horse carved by Winton that she had played with as a child. A tallow candle wrapped in paper. The food. Josephine gathered these things inside a green wool shawl Missus had given her last winter and pulled two corners over tightly, then the opposite two, gathering the four ends into a single square knot. She lifted the bundle off the bed, testing the weight of it. The dirt map that Nathan had drawn glowed red when she closed her eyes, the route burned there to guide her.

Josephine bent to slip her feet into Missus' boots and at that moment heard the sound of horse's hooves. She stopped, cocked her head to listen for more. The back door opened and closed. Uneven knocks of booted feet, the clatter of dishes.

Mister had returned.

Josephine froze. She heard him walking unevenly through the downstairs, pausing and then resuming, seemingly without direction or purpose. Surely he must be drunk. Josephine remained unmoving, silent, not wanting to risk a creak of wood or a footfall's thud to remind Mister of her presence upstairs. There was silence for a long spell, and Josephine thought perhaps he had fallen asleep in a chair, on the floor, his wanderings finished for the night. Slowly she bent again to the boots and the floorboards creaked with her shifting weight, the sound high and thin, nothing to notice on a busy day, but now it shook through her and she stopped, the fear stilling her muscles and breath, only her heart thumping loud in her chest, in her ears. Nothing. Silence from below.

And then Mister's voice rough and deep, dragging her name through gravel: *"Josephine."*

She remained rooted to her place, not knowing where to go, how to hide. She must go to him, there was no way to escape if he climbed the narrow attic steps. Her window was too small and high up for her to reach, and she lifted her head and looked at it now, unblinking, until her eyes burned and the window seemed to swallow the whole wall and the attic opened up to the night sky.

Her bundle lay on the bed, ready; the boots waited beside her bare feet.

Mister called again, "Josephine!" his voice louder now. He was at the bottom of the stairs calling up, Josephine knew that's where he stood. She opened the door and started down the steps.

"Mister, I'm here."

"Why, I been calling and calling for you, girl. I thought you was asleep, I'd have to come up there and wake you up."

His words ran one into the next, and his head swayed as he spoke as though his neck lacked the strength to hold it up. Josephine descended the steps halfway and stopped, one hand on the banister.

"Mister, what do you want?"

"I'm hungry, Josephine, make me some supper, would you."

Josephine stepped to the bottom of the stairs, walked carefully around him, and made her way to the kitchen. Mister followed heavily behind her, his breath ragged. From the side cupboard she pulled salted pork, bread, pickled cucumbers, and set to fixing a plate for Mister. She heard his steps wander away again through the house and then reenter the kitchen. Josephine turned and he stood in the doorway, leaning against the frame, his eyes tired and unfocused, the lids half-fallen.

"I am much aggrieved by this news of your Missus."

Josephine bent her head to the plate, spreading butter on the bread, hopeful that he might eat his supper and retire to bed. There was still time for her to reach the undertaker's house if she ran, if she kept to the shadows, where the moonlight did not reach.

She placed the finished plate on the kitchen table, but Mister remained in the doorway.

"I am much aggrieved, Josephine, much aggrieved."

"Mister, I must retire now to check on Missus. May I pass?" She managed to say this with a cool detachment, as though today were just like any other day. But these strangled minutes in the dark kitchen felt like no others that had come before: Mister drinking again, Josephine with the blood sounding loud in her ears, a cold sweat rising on her palms and the tight places of her dress as she stood before him, his thick form blocking the door. There was the smell of bodies in the air, her own and Mister's, ranker and mixed with whiskey. "Mister, may I pass?" Josephine asked again.

He lunged at her then, a movement fast and fluid, she would not have thought him capable of it. His hands grabbed her shoulders, his breath was heavy and foul. She saw how the hairs of his beard left his face, the root buried in the skin like a pin in a cushion.

"Josephine, I am so sorry. You do not know how sorry I am." He crushed her to him, and she smelled smoke in his clothes, and mud and horse.

Josephine pushed her palms against Mister's shoulders but could find no purchase on the floor. Her heels scrabbled against the stone, she felt herself off-balance, her arms powerless against the weight of him. He crushed her back against the wall and the plaster was cool beneath the thin cloth of her dress. There was a slipperiness on her neck, a wetness from his mouth or perhaps his tears.

Josephine said, "Mister, Mister. I hear Missus calling. I hear her calling me."

Josephine heard nothing, only the jagged sound of Mister's breath and her own pounding heart, but Mister stopped, straightened his back, relaxed his grip, enough for Josephine to right herself, half-step away. They both remained silent, listening. And then:

"Josephine, Josephine. I need you." Missus' voice, like a thread spooling down the stairs, the faintest gossamer twisting in the still air of the kitchen.

Mister turned his head toward the door as though Missus Lu herself stood there and watched him with her eyes tired from sickness, from the years of striving alongside him.

"Go," said Mister, his voice a whisper, a sudden place of stillness in the struggle between them. And he released her. He collapsed onto the floor. His back heaved, though in sobs or sickness Josephine could not say.

Josephine ran from the kitchen, up the stairs, to Missus' room. Missus sat upright in bed, her hands kneading the sheets, clasping and unclasping, her knuckles raw, her eyes open wide in the low light of the room, disks of ghostly white staring as Josephine stood in the doorway.

Josephine tried to calm her breath, relax her shoulders, disguise her fear. "Missus, what is it?"

"I dreamt the most horrible dream. I am afraid, Josephine."

Josephine moved into the room and sat on the bed. She removed Missus' hands from the bedclothes, placed one atop the other and took them in her own, stroking the tops, smoothing them as if smoothing away the wrinkles from a sheet.

"Do not be afraid," said Josephine, and she wondered if Mister would come to the room and wait for Missus to return to sleep, wait for Josephine to emerge.

"I have never told you," Missus said. "And I fear it is my damnation. I know my time is short now, I have no illusions." Missus' bones relaxed into the bed as Josephine's hand stroked, stroked, sliding over the knuckles, down the long slender fingers to their tips. Missus' head fell back against the pillow, and moonlight from the window struck the planes of her face, hiding the cut in shadow. On the side of Missus' neck the tumor throbbed, the redness creeping now toward the front.

"What have you never told me, Missus?" Josephine asked, her voice faint, but as Missus Lu's eyes began to close she asked again, louder this time: "What have you never told me?"

"Oh Josephine, look away. I cannot bear your eyes on me."

Josephine turned her head toward the window and recalled the kitchen knife she had thrown that morning; she thought how the bone handle must reflect the moon, that surely it could be found in the long grass now, easier perhaps than if she had searched in the day.

"Josephine, there was one baby who lived. One."

Josephine noticed a trickle of blood, dried to dark, on the windowsill. Missus' blood that Josephine had not seen to wipe away.

"Yours, Josephine. Your baby lived. You were so young, you did not understand. I was able to ease your pain throughout, Dr. Vickers assisted me. You remember it as a dream, don't you, Josephine? That is how I wanted it. I did not want you to remember. I wanted you to think it had died. Like all of mine."

Josephine did not look at Missus. She stopped her stroking and took her hands away and put them in her lap. The air passed through her lungs, thicker with each breath, and the room seemed suddenly adrift, disconnected from the house and earth, tipping, rocking. It seemed to Josephine that she and Missus rode a boat sailing toward some distant, terrible shore. She tried to stand from the bed but her legs felt unsteady; she tried again and, though her legs still trembled, she made her way to the door.

"Was it a girl?" Josephine asked, turning back to face Missus, and she heard her own voice as though it had traveled through a long, deep tunnel.

"A boy," Missus said. "You had a boy."

"And where is he?"

"I took him to the Stanmores. What's one more nigger head, I thought. They have so many."

Josephine paused in the doorway and looked down at Missus Lu lying there in the bed, blankets pulled up on this hot night, her face flushed, damp with sweat, her eyes dark and not there in her own head. The tumor just visible from where Josephine stood. Josephine remembered again the morning she had returned to Bell Creek and yes, it had been this bed, her mistress's tall bed, where she had lain down and given birth. The relentless pain, the sound of rain slapping, the crow at the window, Dr. Vickers's rough hands, her emptiness. A complicated elation flooded Josephine now, knowing that her child had not died, no, her child had breathed and cried and lived, stronger than Missus' own babies, stronger than the pull of their spirit selves, the cold spirit fingers that must have clutched at his new warm body. But the elation was a selfish one, and this she understood, because where was that boy now? And what did he know of his mother?

The moments of silence widened like the sea between Josephine at the door and Missus Lu in the bed. There was no movement from below or above. Only the sound of the wind came to Josephine, insistent and strong through the willows by the river, rousing the flowers in the beds skirting the house, the latch on the front gate rattling with its force.

"Do you forgive me? Josephine, I ask your forgiveness. You were so young. It was all that could be done." Missus' voice trembled.

Josephine said nothing, she made no movement of her head to indicate yes or no. She stepped into the hall and softly closed the door behind her; this was the only act of kindness she could perform. A no, and Missus would not be at peace, she would go to her grave dirty with this sin, burning with it; but a yes would be a lie, and Josephine wanted no more of lies, not for herself or for Missus. In the hall, she listened for Mister but it was Missus' voice that came to her, higher pitched now and muffled: "Do you forgive me? Josephine, do you forgive me?"

Josephine climbed the back stairs to the attic and crouched, easing into Missus' boots, fastening the buttons snug tight against her ankles. She took her bundle from the bed and walked down again, careless now with the creaks and stomping. Past the studio door, Missus' bedroom, down the grand staircase, past the kitchen where Mister's body lay quiet on the stones, his knees drawn up to his chest, his head turned away.

She made her slow way out the wide front door, down the porch steps, the rockers silent now, still as the dead and gone. There was the moon, just a slice thin as her smallest fingernail, just enough to see by.

As she had imagined, the knife's bone handle shone white against the dark grass, and she grabbed it and pulled. She stood for a moment in the yard and cleaned the dirt from the blade against her skirts, then pushed the blade into the bundle. She walked down the path, through the front gate, and paused in the dust of the road.

To the south lay the Stanmores', the great lurking house and the rows of slave cabins and acres of fields. To the north lay the undertaker's and, beyond that, town, and roads leading farther along, to the wide Ohio River and its verdant, free northern bank. Philadelphia, Louis had said. She would meet Louis there one day, the Broadmoors' locks would not contain him.

Josephine paused in the dust of the road. Missus' boots pointed in neither direction. A look behind her: no movement, no sound.

She did not pause for long. It was only later, with Caleb, that she returned to this moment outside the gate and thought of the choice she had made, the way the road toward the Stanmores' dipped down a little and then rose sharply up and the hill breached in a straight hard line and beyond it she could see nothing.

Josephine did not pause for long because the choice did not seem a difficult one. She would leave him there, yes, she would leave her son behind. The pull that had been within her all her days, every hour at Bell Creek, poised against a newness she did not yet understand. How could she not run? How could she not? A cloud passed over the moon and darkness fell around her, the shadows winked out and she thought with a sudden fierce joy: *All the time in the world, there is all the time in the world. A life is long and it can be good.*

The moon returned and Josephine turned left toward the undertaker's, keeping close to the long night shadows thrown by the old sycamores that lined this part of the road. She felt no fear. The willows of Bell Creek whispered to her their good-byes.

PART THREE

Lina

Caleb

Josephine

Lina

At dawn Lina set off from her Richmond hotel, gray clouds rolling overhead. For forty-five minutes she drove through a wet landscape, the sky racing dark above her, past dripping telephone wires and fields painted bright green and yellow. The tires splashed along the rural roads with their ruts and dips, but she was following the rain, not in it, and at last, just before she reached the town of Lynnhurst, the clouds parted and the sun appeared glistening and ripe, hanging low in the sky. The last stretch of the journey took Lina along an old carriageway, paved now but only just, the road rutted with potholes and surging root hills, and she drove slowly. Rows of sycamores towered beside the road and cast flickering shadows across the cracked pavement. Lina squinted her eyes against the sun's glare. The windshield, the trees, the landscape, all seemed to glitter with suspended drops.

Bell Creek was now the Bell Center for Women and Art, a museum-gallery-school that granted residencies to qualified female artists. The women were given a small bedroom, use of a communal kitchen, studio space in which to work, mentoring from visiting faculty members, and a weekly stipend. The residencies were generously funded by the Stanmore Foundation, Lina had read, and were highly competitive. Since the Bell Center's inception in 1971, rural Lynnhurst had been transformed into a destination for arts-minded tourists.

Lina saw the sign, *The Bell Center* in curling script, and pulled into the empty visitor parking lot, a soggy stretch of trodden-down gravel and mud. The air smelled of wet earth and far-off manure as Lina made her way along the paved path toward the main house. She looked up and felt herself cocooned by the Blue Ridge Mountains visible in all directions, a series of soft sloping hills tinted gray and hazy with morning mist. They did not feel enclosing but rather protective and somehow feminine, a landscape of many limbs folded, arm over arm, soft curves and rounded tips.

Lina turned a corner in the path and there it was, Bell Creek. The house stood up on a slight slope, surrounded by landscaped plots of exuberantly blooming flowers, the names of which Lina was sure she didn't know, and the air turned suddenly to their fragrance. The lawn stretched wide and green away from the house and the flower beds, down to a fresh white picket fence with a waist-high gate that fronted the road.

Lina felt for a moment displaced. The still heat of the morning, the sweat beginning already to dampen the nape of her neck, under her arms, and the familiarity of this house, the gray-scale photo she had studied so many times now suddenly made full-color real.

It was 8:20 A.M.; the museum opened at 9:00. There seemed to be no one else around, only the twitter of birds, a crow's call, the occasional drone of a passing car. Sticking to the gravel paths, Lina circled west toward the rear of the house. The backyard was carefully clipped and verdant green with a plotted vegetable garden, a pretty little old-fashioned well painted a bright white, and some artfully arranged old farming implements—a rusty plow, a red tractor with weeds sprouting up through the engine box. Lina heard the dull rush of water flowing but she could not see the river. The back lawn stretched fifty feet or so until dense vegetation and a row of trees—some willows and others, older and taller—blocked the view.

A twisting gravel path led to the tumbled remains of various outbuildings, and Lina followed it, stopping to read the plastic plaques, warped and buckled by weather, that identified each site. *Here stood the old curing barn, destroyed by fire in 1851. The meat house, used for smoking and storing dried meats. The dairy, where milk, cheese, and butter were made and stored. These iron pots were used to launder clothes.*

Completing her circle around the house, Lina again found herself standing before the porch. She now noticed the two wooden rockers placed there, angled together, and she wondered if these were the same chairs—had Lu Anne and Josephine posed here, so long ago, for the photographer?

And Lina realized then that nowhere did she see evidence of the cabins that must have housed the slaves of Bell Creek, or any signs at all referencing the others who had once lived here side by side with Lu Anne and Robert Bell, plowing the fields, reaping the harvest, grinding the wheat, cleaning the clothes, picking the blooms. The Bell Center documented these tasks now only in the passive voice: Clothing was laundered. Cheese was made. Meat was smoked.

Just then a youngish woman wearing a red dress exited the house and propped open the front door.

"Morning," Lina called to her. "I'm looking for the Bell family archives."

The woman looked at her watch. "Nora should just be opening the doors now," she said and directed Lina away from the main house, along another path that led east toward the parking lot.

"It's a five-minute walk," the woman said. "I'm sure our archivist, Nora Lewis, will be able to help you. Nora knows everything there is to know about the Bells."

Lina followed the path the woman had indicated back toward the parking lot and then up a steep hill. At its crest, she stopped and saw below her a one-story, largely windowless rectangular building. It had the look of a modern prison or hastily constructed temporary classroom at a community college, though the paint was the same bucolic shade of white as the main house. The building seemed to float atop the lawn, no person visible inside or out, but the front door was propped open and Lina thought she could see a light inside. THE BELL CENTER HISTORICAL ARCHIVES, a sign read.

Lina made her way down the hill and entered cautiously. An electronic bell pinged.

"Hello?" she called.

An expanse of dark, dirt-concealing carpet stretched before her. A few chairs, a full bookshelf, and a round table stacked neatly with art books and paper pamphlets were to Lina's left; PUBLIC REFERENCE AREA read a sign on the wall. In front of Lina stood a long chest-high counter constructed of an old, honey-colored wood that seemed lifted from another building completely. From behind this artifact now popped a woman, her eyes a pale blue, her gray-blond hair fastened in a long braid that fell over one shoulder like a pet python.

"Why, good morning!" she said with significant cheer. She was stout, but not fat, with an ample bosom and an armful of bracelets that chimed faintly as she moved. The woman's voice lilted with an accent Lina had not heard before—it was not TV southern, more soft roll, less twang.

"Good morning," Lina said. "Nora Lewis?"

"Guilty as charged." A loose, sleeveless maroon top flowed from her shoulders and gold-colored disks hung from her ears. Nora Lewis was the closest thing to a hippie that Lina had seen since entering the state of Virginia.

"My name is Carolina Sparrow. I was hoping you could help me. I'm a lawyer involved in a class action lawsuit," Lina began, wincing at the practiced formality of her own voice. "I'm looking for information about Josephine Bell, specifically if she had any children. I'm working under a tight deadline and was hoping I might consult some of your documents."

"Oh dear, are you with the Stanmore Foundation? They've already come by for all the relevant materials."

"No, I'm not. I'm with a law firm in New York City, Clifton & Harp."

Lina fished out a business card from her purse and held out the creamy tab of heavyweight card embossed in royal blue to Nora Lewis, who glanced at it with disinterest.

"And have you tried the Historical Society, in Richmond?" Nora said without taking the card. "They have just reams of information about Charlotte County. You might find something there about Josephine Bell."

Lina got the distinct impression that Nora Lewis was trying to put her off.

"Yes, I've already been there," Lina replied. "I'm afraid I didn't find anything helpful. They actually directed me here. To you." Lina's hand, still holding the business card, hovered over the counter. With a deep sigh, Nora Lewis reached out and took it. At first she read the card with narrowed eyes and a scrunched-up look of physical pain but then her features relaxed, her eyebrows lifted.

"*Sparrow*," she said in a different voice altogether, something almost approaching congeniality. "Now *that's* an unusual name. You're not related to Oscar Sparrow, the artist, are you?"

"Well, he's my father, actually," Lina said weakly. Oscar's fame still surprised her and invariably made her uncomfortable, as though to admit his paternity was an act of arrogance on her part. But she saw now an openness on the face of Nora Lewis that had been lacking just a moment before. Lina smiled. "He'll be thrilled to hear he has a fan in Lynnhurst."

"Oh, how wonderful! I do enjoy his work." A pause, and Nora

Lewis looked again at Lina's card, studying it with a concentration that seemed directed at something more than Lina's credentials. She was deciding, Lina realized, how best to exercise her small but determinative power. "Well, we do have a procedure for use of the archives—an advance written request is usually required. We've been *very* strict recently, what with all this authorship brouhaha." Nora Lewis rolled her eyes. "But most everything relating to Lu Anne was taken away last week by the Foundation, so I can't imagine what the harm would be . . . May I ask what specifically you're looking for?" Nora Lewis held Lina's eyes, and she was sweet and steely at the same time.

Lina hesitated before answering. Should she tell her about the slavery reparations case? This was the South after all, a region as unfamiliar and exotic to Lina as a foreign country. Literature, history, and politics had prepared her for a certain kind of lush landscape peopled with hard-bitten men and carefully demure women, but Nora Lewis, with her braid and bracelets, had already fallen well outside these expectations. For the briefest moment Lina considered concocting a story, but it seemed certain that Nora's unflinching gaze would see through any attempt at fabrication. And so Lina told her the truth. She explained about the reparations case, the premise that a descendant of Josephine's might serve as lead plaintiff, Dorothea's letters, Lina's hope and belief that Josephine had given birth to a child at Bell Creek, that her bloodline had continued. But the crucial next step was discovering what had happened to Josephine's child.

Lina stopped. Her hands had been in motion as she spoke and she let them drop now to her sides. Nora was seated behind the counter, looking up at Lina.

"My. How interesting," Nora said. "That is certainly a new one. The Stanmore folks, they're interested in *losing* Josephine Bell, not in finding her, if you catch my drift." She smiled grimly. "I may be able to help you," she said. "There are some documents related to the farm and the slave holdings that might be of interest. If you come back in an hour or two, I'll pull some materials together for you."

"Thank you, Ms. Lewis. I appreciate it immensely," Lina said. She felt the sweet rush of success.

"Call me Nora. Everybody does." She gave a little shake of her head and the earrings sparkled.

AT ELEVEN THIRTY LINA RETURNED to the Bell Center, which now bustled with visitors, the parking lot nearly full with tourist buses and vans, the paths dotted with women walking slowly, pausing to read a plaque, smell a flower. Only the archives building remained empty, the light dim, the air conditioner steadily humming. Nora was seated before a large black electric typewriter, typing as a hen pecks its feed, slow but efficient.

"Oh hello, dear," Nora said. Bracelets jangling, she emerged from behind the counter. Nora wore open-toed strappy sandals, her toenails painted a brilliant blue. "Follow me," she said.

Lina trooped behind Nora, down a narrow passageway cut between tall shelving units, each stocked with rectangular boxes, typewritten labels affixed to the ends. At the far end of the building, Nora pulled open a heavy door. Fluorescent strips flickered overhead and they stood in a gray room that reminded Lina of the large internal conference rooms at Clifton & Harp, bleakly vast and devoid of any decoration. The room was empty save for a rectangular table surrounded by metal chairs and, on top of the table, an open cardboard box. Beside the box sat a thick leather-bound book that looked fragile and ancient.

With a grating scrape, Lina pulled out a chair and sat. Her hands were shaking. She felt heat in her belly, and then cold, the feeling she always got just as a plane took off: the rush of acceleration, the anticipation of liftoff and then the sinking sensation as the nose tipped up and, in that exact instant, you were airborne.

Nora gestured toward the book. "That there is Robert Bell's farm book. It's got most everything to do with any of the slaves, including Josephine. I've picked out some other things for you too, papers to do with the farm mostly." Nora patted the top of the box. "I sincerely hope you find something for your case. I don't suppose that would be a popular position around here, but I wish you the best of luck with it."

"Thank you, Nora."

"And there's one last thing. Remember to wear these when you're handling the materials." She handed Lina a pair of thin white cotton gloves. "Your fingers are like little death rays when it comes to these old papers. Oily and dirty, even if they don't look it."

"I understand," Lina said solemnly as she slipped on the cotton gloves.

With a wink, Nora left the room.

Lina pulled the first pages from the box and began to read.

Lists: lists of kitchen utensils; furniture; types of fabric and what each covered (blue chintz—curtains, brown damask—settee); flowers; foodstuffs; first names (Clara, Charlotte); colors (indigo, red); birds and their calls; insects; vegetables; book titles and their authors. Tables of figures, sums added. Household expenses, the price of tobacco, number of bushels picked and by whom.

Receipts: for sale of thirteen head of cattle; chickens; a plow; ten cords of wood; sugar, tea, and salt; Otis, a mulatto slave of good physique.

The pages, it seemed, had belonged to a number of different people; Lina noticed several varied handwritings. One was heavy, hard to read, the ink often blurring across the page as though the author had not waited for it to dry before placing the page into a desk drawer or folding it in half. Another was distinctly feminine, the letters angled far to the left so they appeared to lie down across the page, the ink fine and pale. And a third hand, or perhaps more, it was difficult to tell. A hand that was at times childish, uncertain, but other times confident and bold: the list of books and authors looked as though written hastily, but the vegetable list seemed labored, each letter formed slowly, blotches running darkly across the paper where the ink had pooled.

Lina turned next to the leather-covered book, the top swollen, the edges of the thick pages uneven and frayed. The inside front cover read, *The Farm Book of Bell Creek, Virginia, 1830—Mr. Robert Bell, Proprietor.* The first pages catalogued the number of acres, acres planted and with what (tobacco, corn, wheat), planting dates, harvest dates, livestock owned. Following was a section titled "Slaves." A list of first names, with a date listed beside them. Was this the date of birth? Date of purchase? Lina could not be sure. The names: Therese, Winton, Lottie, Rebecca, Josephine, Hap, Otis, Josiah, Jonas, Nora, Louis, Annie, Constance, David, Henry, Jackson, Nellie, Calla, May, James, Solomon, Harriet, Sue, Nathan. Each had an additional notation by the name, a date alone or a date plus a dollar amount: death or sale, Lina realized.

Lina flipped the page and there was another list, this one without names or title. Only: Boy, Girl, x, Boy, Boy, x, x, Girl, x, Girl, x, x, x, Boy, Boy, Girl, x. And beside each listing, the same date written twice, separated by a dash. Birth and death. The same day. A span of thirteen years was represented here, and Lina counted the children born without a name to Lu Anne Bell: seventeen. Seventeen miscarriages and stillbirths. Seventeen pregnancies. And then, the last listing, "Boy, August 28, 1848–" with no date listed for death.

Lina looked again at the notation. It must have been Robert Bell's writing; all entries in this book were in the same hand, the heavy pen strokes. It was well documented that the Bells had had no children who'd lived more than a few moments past birth. Had Robert Bell simply forgotten to write the date of death? Had he been too distraught? That child had come when Lu Anne was thirty-nine years old, two years after the previous notation, probably an unexpected, surprise pregnancy. Perhaps they had thought, hoped that this last one, with so many behind them, would survive. That a Bell child would be born.

Or maybe the child was not Lu Anne's?

Turning to the slave pages of the book, Lina looked again for any slave child with the same date of birth. No, each child born to one of the Bell slaves was listed by name under a separate heading titled "Increase" with the birth date written beside it. Each child's name was also noted beside the name of its mother, with additional relevant notations. "Lottie, 1813. . . . Hap, born 1839, died (stung) 1851." The last child born at Bell Creek was in 1842, to Calla, and died the same year. Beside the listing for Josephine, no child's name appeared.

Lina checked the notes she had taken on the Dorothea Rounds letters. What was the date of the letter that referenced Josephine? *Last night a girl came to the house. Heavy with child.* When did the girl come?

Dorothea wrote to her sister Kate on August 28, 1848, the same day the Bell baby was born. Lina felt a warmth, a quickening of her pulse.

A heavily pregnant Josephine came to the Rounds barn and left in the night. The next day, a baby was born at Bell Creek. Lina refused to believe in coincidence, in luck; she knew with a swift certainty, here was evidence that Josephine's child had been born at Bell Creek and that Robert Bell had recorded its birth.

Lina checked again the other pages: there was no record of the child's death or sale. What had happened to the boy?

After Lu Anne died, Lina had read, Robert Bell did not stay long at Bell Creek. He promptly married the local schoolteacher, declared bankruptcy, left the state of Virginia, and settled in Louisiana. But what happened to the people who had lived with him at Bell Creek?

Lina looked for the last notation in the farm book. *House, goods, slaves, and all other chattel sold to Mr. Justice Stanmore of Stanmore Hill, on this day the 10th of November, 1852.*

And today it was the Stanmore family who retained control of the Bell Center, the Bell estate, the Bell art, the legacy of all that Robert Bell had sold away.

With care, Lina flipped through the book's remaining pages, all of them blank. At the very end, folded against the back cover as if someone had placed it there for safekeeping, nestled a loose paper folded once. Cautiously Lina pried it loose, the paper coming away stiffly with a tearing sound, but the page itself, she saw with relief, remained intact. The book's back cover showed a yellow-edged rectangle where the paper had rested. *How long has this been hidden here?* Lina thought. She unfolded the paper, her fingers seeming thick and unwieldy. She saw first the word REWARD in large thick black type, the ink so heavy it seemed almost fresh. Underneath in smaller type, the poster read:

Runaway, my Black Woman JOSEPHINE, gone since Sept. 24, 1852. Seventeen years of age, well grown, tawny skin, eyes of unusual color, a valued house girl and nurse. She took with her one pair of leather boots, one blue and white dress, one green shawl. REWARD of $100 upon return to me ROB'T BELL, near LYNNHURST, Charlotte County, Virg. or secured in jail wherever taken.

The paper felt gritty and rough through the thin fabric of her gloves, and with an inexplicable urgency Lina refolded the page and replaced it within the farm book. She pulled off the gloves and wiped her fingers against the wool of her trousers as if this final page had somehow dirtied them.

Josephine, gone since Sept. 24, 1852.

So Josephine *had* run again. Once in 1848 and then again in 1852. And the second time, she did not return to Bell Creek. Lina grinned in the cool, airless room as an image came to her, of Josephine on the road, heading north, away from the Bells and her intolerable life there. But in that image, Josephine was alone; she did not escape with her son. Lina's grin faded. Josephine must have left her son behind, and this realization unexpectedly clouded Lina's sight and she closed her eyes. Maybe she was wrong. Could she be wrong? No. If Josephine had run with a child, surely Robert Bell would have stated as much in the reward poster. A fugitive slave traveling with a child would have been easy to spot; she would have been easy to catch.

A knock at the door startled Lina. She raised her head and felt momentarily disoriented here, back in the Bell archives, the digital clock flashing red on the wall, Nora hovering in the doorway with eyebrows raised, her long gray braid and cotton skirt, her rubber-soled sandals and noisy bracelets. The physical qualities of the room, the faintly flickering light, the smell of dust and mildew, the cool metal table intruded on the past and brought Lina back to herself.

"So, did you find anything?" Nora asked.

Lina gave a tentative nod. "I think that I did. But I may need some more information. I'm interested in the sale of slaves from Robert Bell to Justice Stanmore on November 10, 1852. What exactly did Justice Stanmore buy? He must have noted more details about the purchase than Robert Bell did about the sale."

"Mr. Stanmore had a farm book, similar to the Bells'. I'm sure that kind of information would be included." Nora brushed a stray hair from her face. "But I'm afraid all the materials relating to the Stanmore family are held over at the Stanmore Foundation. It's just across town, but they are very strict about their viewing policy. Academics only." She gave a sly smile. "I could request that they send it over here, though. Can you come back tomorrow?"

BACK IN HER BUDGET HOTEL room, its walls painted a withering shade of yellow, Lina opened her laptop and searched online for information relating to the Stanmore family. A daguerreotype of Justice Stanmore appeared: a potbellied, fair-haired dandy, his lips too fleshy, his eyes too pale. He looked as though he burned easily in the sun and did not look favorably on work. The Stanmore plantation was now on the historical register of protected sites in Virginia, Lina read. In the spring and autumn months, tour groups trooped through its gardens, down to the tobacco fields, the old dairy house, the blacksmith shed and meat house, into the curing barn where the bundles of bright leaf were still hung to dry and darken.

She followed a link to the Stanmore Foundation's official website, a glossy affair with rousing background music, fade-in historical photographs alongside modern shots of smiling schoolchildren on field trip visits and straight-backed men, black and white, amid the green of the tobacco fields. Over $12 million in grant money had been awarded last year in the foundation's focus areas of cultural enrichment, community development, social justice, and race relations. Every year, the Justice K. Stanmore Award provided an outstanding individual with $50,000 for his or her work in promoting racial harmony in the state of Virginia.

Nothing on the foundation website mentioned Lu Anne Bell, Josephine Bell, or the artwork controversy.

Lina's fingers hovered over the keyboard, and her thoughts turned to Jasper Battle and his family heirlooms. *Coming out of the woodwork,* Porter had said. *Be careful, Lina.* But Porter's suspicions seemed at odds with the Jasper Lina had met, his clear eyes and how he spoke about his father. *Jasper Battle,* Lina typed into a search engine. Up popped several dozen hits: links to a middle-aged tax attorney in Pensacola, Florida, to a gaming website where hordes of locusts fought for supremacy in the Battle of Jasper, to a high school student in Duluth who enjoyed lacrosse and partying with his homies. Finally, toward the end of the list, a website for the rock band The Wisdom appeared. Lina opened the link. A photo flashed onto the screen of four indie-rock-looking men, all in their twenties, all tattooed to some degree, with varying heights and skin tones, and there he was, staring out with a frank, direct gaze, identified as

"Jasper Battle: Bass." As Lina explored the site, a few simple pages popped up, of gig dates and performance photos. One showed Jasper as a dark silhouette on a backlit stage, his arms blurry with motion across a bass guitar, legs spread wide, head down.

Lina dialed the number Jasper had given her last week. He picked up on the first ring.

"I'm sorry," he said.

Jasper's tone was so contrite, so genuine that Lina wanted immediately to reassure him, but of course the apology wasn't intended for her. "Jasper . . . this is Lina Sparrow, from the law firm?"

"*Lina.*" Now he sounded embarrassed, but half-laughing. "I thought you were someone else."

"So I gathered." She wanted to ask what he was sorry for, who the someone else was, but she stopped herself.

"Sorry—" he said and then paused. "I mean, I'm sorry I . . . said that."

Now it was Lina's turn to laugh. "Don't worry. Don't be sorry. How are you?" She held the phone to her face, enjoying the novelty of speaking to someone other than Dan (two calls, to check in) or Garrison (three messages, all contrite) or her dad (one bland message, one bland conversation, one hang-up).

"I'm good. Nice of you to ask. So what can I do for you, counselor?"

Lina liked his teasing tone but it threw her off-balance. She didn't know how to match it and so she found herself veering into formality, her words coming out stiff. "I've found evidence that Josephine Bell had a son," she said. "Tomorrow I'm hoping to get some information that will help me track her descendants further."

Jasper seemed not to notice her awkwardness. "That's great news. Even if it's not me, you know. It's still pretty amazing that you found something." His tone was admiring as much as congratulatory, which succeeded only in deepening Lina's unease. Maybe he thought she had been fishing for a compliment, or bragging? But she hadn't been, and Jasper was right. It was amazing: Josephine Bell had a son.

"Yes, it *is* great, isn't it?" Now Lina allowed herself to be excited too and to let Jasper hear it. "And I don't think anybody else knows about it. I mean, just the two of us."

"Your secret is safe with me." Jasper was mock-serious, again teasing her, but this time she laughed, then asked, "Listen, could you tell me your dad's full name? And date of birth? It would be helpful, if I get that far down the road."

"March 16, 1947. Christopher Caleb Battle." He enunciated each word carefully as Lina wrote the name in her notebook. She thought she heard his voice shake just the tiniest bit. Then he added gently, "But you know, I'm still not interested in being your plaintiff."

"I know, but if I'm searching for Josephine Bell's descendants, I might as well search for your father. You're my biggest lead right now, Jasper. Do you have any cousins?"

"One, actually. Though I don't think you'd like him very much."

Lina smiled against the phone. "Jasper, I'd really like to see your Bell pictures. I think we can help each other on this. But first I need to see what you've got. I'll be back in New York tomorrow."

The band had a show tomorrow night, Jasper told her, at a place on the Lower East Side. "You should come," he offered. "I could show you one of the pictures afterward—I don't live far from the club."

"I'll be there," Lina said without hesitation, and she registered a prickle along her spine, a fizz of excitement that seemed almost foreign, a sensation she had nearly forgotten herself capable of. But she didn't allow herself time to consider it fully. Jasper Battle was her potential plaintiff, that was all. They said their good-byes and Lina took out her BlackBerry to e-mail Dan with her news about Josephine Bell. The image of Jasper remained open on the screen of her laptop: his head down, his face hidden.

•   •   •

Thursday

At nine A.M., Lina drove back to the Bell Archives. Already the day was bathwater warm, the sky a washed-out blue studded with small puffball clouds. The air smelled of damp and flowers. Nora greeted her at the door, today wearing a loose yellow cotton dress, another row of bracelets, another braid. But her cheer had vanished.

"Those Stanmore people," Nora began. "They are so full of themselves. I swear, they don't even care about the art. They act like this is all about them. The Stanmore *reputation*. What a bunch of phonies. Josephine Bell lived here too! It's not like Lynnhurst'll just fall into the ground if she made those pictures. There's still so much to be proud of." Nora exhaled loudly and fanned her face with an outstretched hand.

"My sincerest apologies, Lina," she continued. "I don't normally get so upset, but it's been a trying time, these last few weeks. And I was just over there at the Foundation, trying to get the Stanmore farm book for you, which is just *sitting* there. But they would only let me copy out some pages." From her bag Nora pulled a messy stack of papers. "Old Mr. Stanmore did not keep very good records so I just had to guess at what to copy. I hope there's *something* in here that'll be of use."

"Oh, I'm sure there will be." Lina felt a downward tug of disappointment as the papers spilled from Nora's hands into an untidy heap on her desk. She summoned a smile. "Thank you for taking the time. I'm sorry it's caused so much trouble."

"Oh, no trouble at all. To be honest, it's good for me to go over there, speak my mind a bit. They all think I'm batty." Nora lifted her eyebrows and widened her eyes. "Oooh!" she said, and gave a little flap of her outstretched hands. *"Please."* And she lowered her hands, pursed her lips. "If they want batty, I will *show* them batty one of these days."

• • •

NORA LEFT LINA IN THE archives reading room with the copied pages, sixty-eight in total, full of cramped handwriting and columns of figures.

Like Robert Bell, Justice Stanmore had kept a farm book to record information relating to crops, acreage, livestock, yields, as well as the purchase of new slaves, their births and deaths. Unlike the Bell book, Stanmore's did not list the slaves by name—just gender, age, and a basic description ("mulatto," "dark," "R thumb missing"). The name of the seller was usually written, or the auction house, but many purchases were dated only with the year or left undated entirely.

Lina began to read. Her progress was slow. Pages were out of order, dates difficult to decipher, and Justice Stanmore's writing was barely legible, cramped and slanted so severely that Lina thought he must have turned the paper on its long side to write.

Finally, on page forty-two, Lina found a notation for a purchase from Robert Bell. The date listed was only "1852." Stanmore paid $5,522 for the sixty-three acres of Bell Creek, all its furnishings, farm equipment, livestock, outbuildings and their contents, and six adult slaves, three women, three men.

No children.

Lina flipped the pages, looked to the margins, searching for any evidence of a child; she read the same lines again and again with increasing disappointment and a frantic speed. She was so sure that Josephine's child had been born at Bell Creek, that it must have been sold to the Stanmores after Lu Anne died.

Justice Stanmore was sloppy and inexact but he would not have missed a child, not one he had paid money for. No.

Lina looked away from the papers and rubbed her eyes. The boy must have died. Or perhaps he'd been sold at birth, taken away immediately, far from Bell Creek, and Lina would never find him; she would never find Josephine. She checked her watch: 1:36 P.M. She had been hunched over Justice Stanmore's pages in this gray, airless room for 4.1 billable hours without food or drink; she hadn't touched the plastic cup of water that Nora had tiptoed in with hours ago.

Lina thought of Lottie's portrait, the dark eyes, the unearthly, glowing flowers. The distant landscape behind the cabin so much like the sea, a great shifting expanse. Lottie's bottomless eyes. Waiting. What had she been waiting for?

With a mounting sense of defeat, Lina returned to the Stanmore papers and scanned the remaining few pages. Her right foot, crossed over her left leg, had fallen asleep and she massaged it awake, the flesh tingling with the rush of blood. Those business cards still waited on her desk in New York. She hadn't called a single person, but tomorrow, back in her office, she would have to. She would find another plaintiff. There was nothing Lina could do about the tragedy of Josephine Bell, another nameless, faceless woman lost to history.

The last page of the Stanmore papers was headed *Negro Sales*. The transactions here occurred well after Robert Bell's sale to Justice Stanmore, and the notations seemed to cover only sales Stanmore had made, not slaves he had purchased. Lina scanned the columns of the last page, Justice Stanmore's cramped handwriting with the oddly shaped *y*'s and *j*'s. She was rushing now to finish, her thoughts jumping ahead to the return trip to New York, Dan and Dresser, and the fast-approaching deadline. And then Lina's eye caught.

One figure was boldly underlined: $2,250. A date, *February 10, 1853*. And a name beside it: *Joseph, age 4*. Lina shivered. $2,250 was an astronomical sum to pay for an able-bodied male slave, let alone a child. She would have thought the price was an error. But the underline: look at this, look at what I have done.

Lina stared at the figure, imagining Justice Stanmore's pale fleshy hand writing the number so many years ago, the hand that accepted the wrinkled bank notes, the dully flashing coins. The boy from Robert Bell's farm book; that child had been born on August 28, 1848. He would have been four years old. *Joseph, age 4*.

Lina looked to the column of names, the list of buyers. Who had delivered such a sum?

Sale to Mr. Caleb Harper, no fixed address, Stanmore had written.

LINA EMERGED FROM THE ARCHIVES reading room and made her way to the front of the building, blinking in the sunlight that filtered through the dusty air of the stacks. Nora sat behind the wood counter, her back to Lina, with a pile of index cards and bottle of Wite-Out.

"Nora—" Lina called, enthusiasm making her voice louder than she had intended.

Nora started and swiftly turned in her chair. "Oh, goodness, you gave me a fright!" she said.

"I'm sorry. I just wanted to thank you for copying the Stanmore papers." Lina grinned.

"Oh, you're very welcome. So I take it they helped?"

"Yes. I think so. Do you know anything about the Harper family? A man named Caleb Harper?"

Nora's lips parted slightly. "Harper?" she said. For a moment her eyes lost focus and she seemed to recede inward, as though she were considering a grave problem that no one could help her solve.

"It seems a man by the name of Caleb Harper purchased a young boy from Justice Stanmore, a boy named Joseph. He paid an astronomical sum. I'm just interested in why. Why would he do that?"

"Why indeed."

Nora fell silent, her face tense.

"Nora?" Lina ventured. "Is everything all right?"

"Yes, yes. Everything's fine." Now her tone was brusque and resolved. "No, I've never heard of a Caleb Harper." Nora half-turned in her chair, looking toward the wall where a framed reproduction of *Lottie* hung. She turned back to Lina with a bright, brittle smile. "Is there anything else I can help you with?"

"No, nothing, thank you." Lina realized she had done something to upset Nora, but she could not guess what it was. "Then I'll just head back to my hotel . . . my flight leaves in a few hours." Lina paused, waiting for a word of explanation, but Nora offered only that same stiff smile. "Well, thank you for all your help, Nora. Good-bye."

Nora turned back to the index cards. "Good-bye," she called over a shoulder.

LINA PACKED UP THE RENTAL car and refilled the tank. If she made good time to Richmond, she'd have an hour or so at the Virginia Historical Archives to research Caleb Harper before heading to the airport. On her way out of Lynnhurst, she idled for a moment at the sole stop sign on Main Street. The town lulled in repose, lush and sleepy on this summer afternoon, sunlight slanting low across the grass and through the arching branches of a row of magnolia trees, the flowers open, their cupped petals like small pink hands. Along the sidewalk ambled knots of tourists, mostly women, clutching their guidebooks and the map of Lu Anne Bell's Historic Lynnhurst, a copy of which Lina had picked up earlier at the tourist information booth. The map rested on the car's passenger seat, and it fluttered to the floor as Lina accelerated past the stop sign and out of town.

Lina left Lynnhurst, driving slowly through rolling farmland, then speeding up as she hit a wider, newer road. Past a McDonald's, a strip shopping mall, a gas station, and Lina closed her windows to shut out the humid breeze and turned up the air conditioner. *Caleb Harper,* she thought. *Who are you?*

Just after Lina turned onto the freeway, her phone rang. She slowed and carefully pulled to the shoulder.

"Lina, have you left yet?" It was Nora, breathless.

"I'm on my way to Richmond right now. Is everything okay?" Lina winced as a car rushed past with shuddering speed.

"Lina, I have something to give you. Can you stop by the archives on your way? Just for a minute?"

Lina looked at her watch. She didn't really have time to go back, but she heard an urgency in Nora's request that seemed the very opposite of her cool dismissal earlier that day. "Did I leave something behind?" Lina asked, though she knew she hadn't.

"No, nothing like that. I wasn't sure what to do before, when you asked me about Caleb Harper. I just froze. I apologize, dear. I'll explain when you get here."

Indignation and curiosity rose up in Lina in equal measure. "Oh. Nora," she said as curiosity prevailed, "I'll be there soon."

Lina hung up the phone and scanned the five lanes of traffic. Just up ahead she saw a police turnaround, highly illegal for civilian use but extremely helpful for someone looking to change directions fast. Lina waited for a break in the traffic, then accelerated hard and angled the car neatly across the five lanes and into the turnaround. She spun the wheel. The speed of the revolution left Lina with a flash of dizziness, a moment when the clear Virginia sky and the wide verdant fields bordering the road seemed to twist and meld together, a disjointed landscape of vivid blues and grays and greens, but as the car pointed southward, Lina's head returned to level and she accelerated along the straight road back to Lynnhurst.

LINA PARKED THE CAR AND hurried down the hill toward the archives building. Nora was sitting on the front steps, partially hidden in afternoon shadow. "Lina, I'm so glad you've come," she said. She stood and turned toward the door and Lina saw that her hair was unbraided, beautiful, flowing across her shoulders in silvery cascades of gray streaked a yellowish white, the effect almost ghostly. A colorful embroidered cloth bag was slung across Nora's body on a thick black strap.

Together they entered the building and Nora turned and flipped the dead bolt, locking them inside. "Last thing I want is a surprise visitor," she said.

They stopped in front of the wood counter, a few paces apart.

Nora started toward the stacks but then changed course, her hair drifting wavelike behind her, and then stopped again, looking to Lina with wide eyes. Nora seemed lost. She took a deep breath. "Let's just sit on down. We're alone in here." She turned in to the public reference area, and Lina sat across from her at a tidy round table. As Nora removed her bag and placed it on the table, Lina saw that her thin fingers were shaking.

"Well," she said, and drew from the bag a large white envelope. "I want to give this to you. This will, I think, help you in finding Josephine Bell's family. It's a document written by Caleb Harper. A sort of story, or letter, though I don't believe it ever reached its intended recipient. I found it sealed among some papers that came to us from the estate of the Stones, who many years ago bought the farm where Jack Harper and his wife, Dorothea Rounds Harper, once lived. I filed them away in the archives as documents of a general sort of county interest. But this document here"—she patted the envelope—"caught my eye. You'll see why. It's a very sad tale, a very sad letter. But I did not connect it directly to Lu Anne Bell until this artistic . . . scandal came up. And when I realized its significance, well, I took the letter. I took it home." Pride and some degree of fear wavered on Nora's face.

"I knew it wasn't the right thing to do, but I couldn't bear it. I didn't want the Stanmore lawyers to get hold of it. Lord knows what they would do with it. The shenanigans that have gone on, I can't tell you. I love Lu Anne, really I do, but I can't be part of a lie. Josephine made those paintings, not Lu Anne. There's nothing I or the Stanmores or anybody else can do about that, no matter how hard they try."

Lina reached out and took the envelope.

"What shenanigans, Nora?"

"Oh Lina, it's not my place to say. But there's been a lot of . . . dishonesty around here. There are so many people upset about this, about losing Lu Anne. Or not losing *her,* but, oh, it's hard to put into words. Losing the idea of her. Do you know what I mean? It's just heartbreaking."

"I do know what you mean," Lina said, her voice low. A curtain of dark hair. A sense of contentment.

"And Lina, I'm sorry I didn't give this to you sooner. I . . . wasn't sure I could trust you. And taking something like this, out of the archives, keeping it away from the Stanmore lawyers. Well, I'll lose my job." Nora's voice was thin, and then she said, with more force: "But it's *time,* I think. Don't you?"

Lina nodded.

Nora pushed up from her chair. "Well, I don't want you to miss your flight. Thank you for stopping back here."

"Thank you, Nora." Lina stood and hugged her, their two bodies roughly the same height, each yielding and tough in opposite spots.

Nora stepped back first. "My goodness, I almost forgot to remind you," she said. "You must be careful with this document! It's very old, very fragile." Her tone was all business. "Don't forget—*always* handle these pages with cotton gloves. People don't realize, the acid on their fingers. It's such a *struggle* to keep all these documents from falling into the dust. A struggle." Nora sighed and winked at Lina, and Lina winked back.

THE FLIGHT TO NEW YORK traveled through a dark sky; there was no view to occupy Lina, only a blurred reflection of the lighted compartment and a dark shadow of herself in the glass. It was with considerable effort that she did not tear open the envelope that Nora had given her, but Nora's last admonishing words still rang in her ears—cotton gloves! Cotton gloves! Caleb Harper would have to wait.

Instead Lina unfolded the *New York Times* she had bought at the airport. Porter's review of Oscar's show was due to print today and there it was, spread across the front page of the Arts section, a photo of Oscar wearing paint-splattered jeans and a forced smile beside the *Enough* portrait of Grace. Lina stared at the grainy photo of her father, his carefully trimmed beard, close-cropped hair, a pair of sunglasses (*sunglasses?*) propped on his brow. His face presented no emotion, no hint as to why he had created these pictures, what he had been hoping to convey when he painted Grace, his dead wife, in the ways that he did. Lina almost folded the paper away again but she paused. Curiosity, of the kind associated with car crashes and natural disasters, seized her and she began to read:

ART REVIEW: OSCAR SPARROW'S
EVERLASTING GRACE

By Porter Scales

Natalie Mason Gallery
West 26th Street, Chelsea
Through August 21

Oscar Sparrow's new show, *Pictures of Grace,* offers up searingly intimate, oversize portraits of his wife, Grace Janney Sparrow, an artist who died nearly 20 years ago at the age of 28. Having known Grace myself, I approached his new work with some trepidation. Oscar Sparrow is well known for his artistic riddles; indeed, the intellectual subterfuge he brings to a canvas is part of his appeal, but it can also diminish the emotional experience of his art and, for some, the ultimate heft of his work. Does he merely dizzy us with his layers and clues? Is Sparrow selling us smoke and mirrors? After viewing a Sparrow, I am often left wondering whether the riddle's answer is worth the exhausting task of the looking. I knew Grace Sparrow as a loyal friend and talented artist with an insightful and inspiring mind. I did not want to see her subjected to myth-spinning contortions. I did not want her torn apart and stitched back together, misshapen and deformed, on canvas.

My fears, however, were unwarranted.

Every person is many people: wife, mother, artist, daughter, friend, lover, rich, poor, peaceful, tormented. Sparrow's portraits—a series of 18, all of Grace, all multimedia—capture his wife's complexity with an examination of both gorgeous minutiae and broad, step-back scope. One, a study of the parting of her hair, shines, each strand etched with silver leaf, woven through with brilliant crimson paint. It is heart-stoppingly lovely. Another, a triptych of three Graces (even if her name had been otherwise, the piece still earns the title), depicts her as a featureless housewife; a ravenous, screaming harpy; and, most chillingly, in the central panel, a woman trapped within the strict lines of the frame, her one visible eye stretching large and carrying within it a desperation and claustrophobia that lend deeper, more troubling significance to the flanking images.

We see in Grace a young woman at the height of her beauty, in the prime of her life—a young bride, a new mother, an up-and-coming artist—and yet the overarching sense is of turmoil and dismay, a thwarted energy, a wasted talent. Grace Janney Sparrow died before she was able to fully explore and develop her prodigious gifts. We know that she dedicated the last years of her life to her husband and young daughter; she showed no work during this time. During this period, she removed herself from the downtown artistic community of which she had been such a vibrant part, while her husband, Oscar, continued to show and to lay the foundations for his much-lauded breakthrough show of 2000.

In this way, Oscar Sparrow has achieved what may prove surprising to his legions of fans: he has created a feminist examination of a lost woman. He has, in effect, painted Grace with such love and truth that underlying his work is an attack on the domestic life that he, in fact, pushed upon her. Did he intend this self-critique? Are these paintings offered up to us, the viewers and critics and historians of art, as a sort of apology?

The riddles in these pictures are riddles of the heart, and, un-like Sparrow's earlier work, they offer up no easy solutions, no a-ha moments of epiphany. Instead, from their examination of a single woman, we are left with a resounding sense of wonder and of loss. These images of Grace Janney Sparrow are tantalizing, evocative hints of our own deprivation. We are richer for these paintings but so much the poorer for the loss of their inspiration.

With great care, as though the newspaper were a fragile thing, Lina refolded the Arts section and placed it on her lap. A long knit-ted scarf. Patsy Cline. Isolation. Motherhood. A thwarted energy. A wasted talent.

I want to explain some things, Oscar had said. *Tell the truth.* Lina closed her eyes and placed her forehead flush against the cool glass of the plane's window. *Can't work, can't think, can't breathe,* Grace had written. *She is the loveliest thing I have ever seen.* And Lina felt a sudden penetrating sadness for the young woman who had been her mother, for the young child who had been herself. Had it all been too much, or not enough? Had Grace stopped painting? Only twenty-four years old, with a husband, a child, a house. Lina did not know what motherhood required, or being a wife, but Oscar was an artist, and Lina understood what that meant: obsession and uncer-tainty, dedication and toil and frustration, time and focus. Perhaps Porter was right, perhaps the paintings were an apology. But the apology was not to the historians of art, or to the viewers and collec-tors of art. The paintings were an apology to Grace. *I always loved her,* Oscar had said, and Lina knew without question that this was true.

LINA ENTERED A GLOOMY HOUSE, the curtains drawn; a single lit floor lamp cast dusty shadows around the living room. She had just under an hour to shower and change before heading to Jasper Battle's show. Lina moved with care, certain that Oscar was sleeping. After an opening, Oscar became a bear in hibernation, a great hump under the blankets, appearing only for bagels and beer.

But Lina heard voices and the chime of silverware hitting a plate, and smelled cooking, something warm and rich, like a roast chicken or ham. Lina left her suitcase in the hall and wandered into the kitchen. Oscar and Natalie were seated at the table, the remains of an elaborate dinner spread before them, half-full wineglasses and yes, the small carcass of a chicken or—Lina stared first at her father, who was midsentence in conversation with Natalie, and then at the frayed, half-eaten bird.

"Guinea hen!" her father said, laughing. "It's a guinea hen! How's that for culinary skill?"

Natalie turned around in her chair and looked at Lina with a smile. "He's a very good cook, you know. He's been working hard at it." Her cheeks were flushed from the heat of the kitchen and the wine—Lina saw one empty bottle and another open on the table. Two lit candles burned between plates strewn with small, sucked-on bones. Lina felt a moment of dislocation, as though she had wandered into a house strikingly similar to her own but different in its fundamentals. Her father, a gourmet chef? Natalie, relaxed and casual, at their kitchen table? The difference between how Lina saw the world and how it truly was seemed suddenly vast and breathtaking, and Lina felt again as if she were four years old, mystified by a loss she could not control and events she did not understand.

Oscar stood and gave Lina a wide, firm hug, and kissed her on the top of her head. "I didn't think you'd be back for another day or so. How was Richmond?" He stepped away and glanced at Natalie, who rose stiffly from her chair and came to stand beside Oscar, her hair mussed and golden in the candlelight.

"You know Natalie, of course," Oscar said to Lina, muscling through the awkwardness with a bemused grin and brisk scratch of his beard. "We've been . . . spending time together lately."

Natalie conjured her own brilliant get-through-this smile and said, "Oscar, you're making this harder than it has to be. Of course Lina *knows* me," and she stepped forward and gave Lina a quick hug, which surprised Lina enough that she instinctively returned it.

"I'm sorry you left the show so quickly the other night," Oscar said. "I tried to follow you but you walk so goddamn fast, Carolina."

Her father's cheeks were rosy, his eyes clear and happy, and Lina considered for the briefest moment leaving him here with Natalie to finish their dinner, drink their wine. But she felt still the echo of the plane's forward thrust and she didn't want to lose that sense of momentum, she didn't want to waste it. She felt too a need to reclaim this space and her father. A possessiveness grabbed her, an impulse to stake herself here and say what she felt. "I read Porter's review," Lina said. "Is he right? Is the show an apology?"

Oscar's smile vanished and he leaned back against the countertop. "Well. Yes. Maybe. I don't know, Carolina. I think Porter's review was . . . more on target than some of his others."

"Did she want to be married to you? Did she want to be a mother? Why did she stop painting?" The questions came fast, and it was not a desire to hear the answers that propelled Lina; she was aware only of the fact that she had to ask.

"Oh, Carolina. Don't do this. Not now."

"You say you want the pictures to show me something but I don't understand them, Dad. I don't know what you're trying to say."

Oscar looked to the ceiling. He pulled at his sleeves, fidgeting like a little boy. "Grace and I had a bad marriage," he said. "Toward the end. She was very angry at me. It was no one's fault. It just happened. I wasn't a good husband, I wasn't. I had an affair with Marie—I didn't want to tell you that day at the gallery. I didn't want you to be angry with me, or to think you couldn't ask Marie for help with your case. But your mother was unhappy well before Marie. And she fell in love with someone else, I think."

"Porter Scales? Was it him?"

Oscar exhaled, his arms folded against his chest, and Lina knew she was right. "How do you know that?" Oscar's voice was suddenly sharp, an old anger stirred. "Did he talk to you?"

"He did talk to me, but no, he didn't tell me. He only told me that he'd been her friend and admired her art." Lina remembered that night, Porter's rueful gaze, her gratitude to him for those small, wonderful facts. And with the remembering, Lina's disquiet returned. *She was just gone.*

"Dad, how did she die?" Lina's voice was soft but purposeful. Steadily she watched her father.

Oscar paused. "A car crash," he said. "You know that." But she saw the strain on his face, the downward tic of his mouth.

"Oscar, you've got to tell her. She's an adult." It was Natalie, and the sound of her voice surprised Lina. She had almost forgotten Natalie was there. Lina turned to look at her, leaning against the counter, such a strange sight in their kitchen—a space intimate only to Oscar and Lina—and yet Natalie spoke with authority, as though she were the one who belonged here and knew them best.

Lina turned back to Oscar. "Tell me what, Dad?" Of course there was something to tell. Hadn't Lina known this all along? And for the first time in her life she felt ready to hear it.

Oscar shook his head, tilted his neck, left, then right, and Lina heard the crack of his spine. He exhaled. "Nothing. There's nothing to tell," he said.

A fierce disappointment flooded Lina and she looked away from her father. In the silence that followed, Lina struggled, wanting not only to slap him but also to stop wanting it, to release her curiosity and anger into the warm air of the kitchen, where they would dissipate and fade. Because did it really matter what had happened? Did it matter if she knew?

Lina studied the brief stretch of old black-and-white linoleum that Oscar said every year he would replace, but never did. Maybe someday he would; maybe Natalie would help him. And Lina saw with prescient clarity the two of them, Natalie and Oscar, on hands and knees, ripping up the tiles, sanding down the old wood under-neath, wiping dusty hands on old jeans, and Lina, a visitor, standing in the doorway, commending them on their work. "It looks amazing," she would say. "I'm so glad you finally did it. Why did you wait so long?"

And in those moments, Lina arrived at a decision. It emerged as a giant air bubble, trapped so long beneath the surface and now ris-ing finally into the open air where it emerged with a pop.

"There's something I need to tell you," Lina said. "I've decided to move out. I think it's for the best. I think it's time I lived on my own."

How easily these words flew into the space between them, and wasn't this what she should have said months ago, years ago? The house encircled her, comfortable, known and knowable, burdened with memories and wishes, but it was just plaster and bricks. Lina would carry her memories with her, they transcended these walls, this old kitchen; they transcended even Oscar's pictures, his memo-ries of Grace that Lina did not recognize and did not want to face. She would continue to believe in that curtain of dark hair, that pep-per and sugar smell, that sense of contentment. Who could tell her those things were untrue? Truth was multilayered, shifting; it was different for everyone, each personal history carved unique from the same weighty block of time and flesh.

Oscar looked startled but he nodded once, a single downward beat, curt and unhesitant, as though he'd been expecting this mo-ment and his surprise was due only to the fact that it had taken so long to come. "Carolina, if that's what you want. Whatever you de-cide will be for the best." He smiled, the corners of his mouth giving the smallest of lifts, a smile in name only. Lina saw something cloud his blue eyes, tears or fear or guilt.

Lina turned and passed through the arched kitchen doorway, along the dim hall, into the living room, where she stopped. The half-light, the messiness, Natalie's coat thrown across the couch, Lina's suitcase in the doorway, and she again experienced a sensation of strangeness amid the familiar. In that moment the room faded away to become the living room from her early childhood, a smaller couch, a study of a row of spoons hanging where Lina's portrait hung now, a rocking chair in the corner, its yellow paint chipped and worn. And a woman who was her mother, perhaps, or perhaps not, sat on the floor and played with her. They had blocks, wooden blocks painted in bright primary colors, and a small train with black wheels that the woman (the mother?) rolled atop the blocks as though they were a track. *Puff puff puff, up the hill,* the woman sang. Was this woman's hair black as jet, falling halfway down her back like a curtain, like a black screen? Or was this not a woman but a girl, a high school student, earning some extra money, counting down the minutes until she might leave? Or was it a man who sat with her? A father all the time, who scratched his beard with both hands and laughed as Lina soared her train up into the air?

IT WAS JUST PAST TEN o'clock when Lina arrived at Jasper's show. A short line threaded out the club's unmarked door and it was crowded inside, a hundred or so people, both younger and older than Lina, all races, men and women, fashionable and staid. Lina wore jeans and a top she'd bought last summer for a planned vacation that never happened, and she stood alone at the bar, holding a plastic cup of beer and waiting for the show, comfortably invisible amid the chatter and changing contours of the crowd.

She heard someone calling Jasper's name and "Good luck, man" and then Jasper was standing beside her at the bar.

"Lina, you came," he said, his voice full of surprise.

"Of course I did," she said, matter-of-fact, and returned his smile.

"How was Virginia?" Jasper leaned down as he spoke and Lina angled her head toward him, struggling to hear over the noise from the bar.

"Very interesting. I'll tell you about it." She spoke into his ear, the studs a glittering row of silver and anthracite.

Jasper motioned toward the stage. "We're up soon. Let's talk after the show." Then he took hold of her wrist, a gesture that might have been awkward or strange, but his fingers felt warm against her skin as he squeezed gently. "I'm glad you came," he said, and she felt again that tension along her spine, and a pleasant falling away, a dimming of the crowd and noise from the bar.

As Lina finished her drink, the lights went dark and there was the scuffling sound of bodies taking the stage, guitars lifted, microphones adjusted, and then a spotlight illuminated the lead singer—not Jasper but another man, short, skinny, and pale, with a nerd-chic haircut and thick black glasses, a guitar slung across his chest. The first song was all strumming guitar, hushed soulful singing, and the crowd became restless, heads turned away from the stage, conversations resumed. Lina felt a pang of worry, as though her stake in this performance was greater than that of mere observer, as though it fell to her that these four young men should achieve some measure of success tonight.

The song ended to a spatter of applause, a few hoots, and then the band started up again. This time the drums began first, a loud knocking that Lina felt deep in the center of her chest like a mechanical heart, and then Jasper on bass, a steady electric strumming, and then the guitars, and the crowd surged into life with a collective rush. This was what they had been waiting for.

Lina kept her eyes on Jasper. Fascinated, she watched and realized that he no longer looked like the Jasper she had met that night at the Bell show, or even the one she had just spoken to at the bar. Onstage, he appeared cold, removed, with a complete sense of self-containment that she would have envied if it had not looked so lonely. She recognized the look—it was the same go-away posture her father took on in the studio. Right now Jasper was his own separate universe, oblivious to everything and everyone apart from the instrument strapped around his shoulders. He didn't play to the crowd. He didn't preen or pose. The lead singer chatted to the front row in between songs, scanned the audience, sang out, tried to connect. But Jasper, for the most part, kept his eyes closed. He hung back from the edge of the stage and let his head hang, swaying like a hyped-up pendulum in time to the low tones of his bass. He might as well have been alone in the room. In fact, Lina, watching him, got the distinct impression that this was what he would have preferred—to be playing these songs alone.

Song followed song and Lina did not think of her father or Natalie or Grace; she thought of nothing at all, only the music and the people drifting sweaty and hot around her, the sensation of being buoyed by all these diverse bodies, hard and soft in their various joints and joinings. Jasper's bass was a percussive, deep vibration, and a trembling began at the bottom of her stomach, and the beat there swelled beyond herself, into the floor and the walls and the exuberant movement of the crowd. Lina felt herself moving with the music, with everyone, and then suddenly Jasper looked down at her—was he looking at her?—and she closed her eyes and became just another joyful body there on the floor.

After the show, Jasper found her, his T-shirt and scalp dark with sweat.

"Come with me," he said.

"Where?"

"This bar we go to after shows. It's not fancy. It's pretty grungy, to be honest, but we can talk and play cards, if you want."

"Cards?"

"Gin rummy. I'm a little obsessed."

"But what about the Bell pictures?"

"I can show you later. After a game or two."

The lead singer suddenly appeared at Jasper's elbow. He had a white towel around his neck and pulled from his back pocket a dog-eared pack of cards, which he waved slowly back and forth in front of Jasper like a matador with his red cloth.

Jasper turned to Lina. "See what I mean? Obsessed. So are you coming?"

With the feel of the show still inside her, a phantom reverberation, Lina nodded yes.

THE BAR WAS INDEED GRUNGY. Low lights, a pool table, some pinball machines, a thick-fingered blond woman behind the bar who laughed once to reveal a mouthful of silver and black. Jasper and his bandmates Callum and Mike settled at a table, and Lina played hand after hand of gin rummy with them. At first, Lina won—as a preteen, she had played with Oscar nightly, betting chocolate chips and pieces of gum—but first Mike and then Jasper beat her again and again, and she insisted they keep going. They were drinking gin, in honor of the game, and the liquor warmed her at first, then dulled her, made her sloppy.

They left latish, Lina wasn't sure what time. She stumbled on the curb and leaned against Jasper, who took her elbow and steered her along the sidewalk, helping her up a flight of stairs, into a crowded apartment where everyone seemed to be talking and laughing, someone playing guitar and a woman with outsize earrings and red lips singing the most beautiful song.

"This is our place," Jasper said. "Me and Mike. We always come here after the shows."

Lina left Jasper and wandered into the mix. Candles burned on low tables, a person-sized lava lamp glowed in a corner, and talking wove through the room, up and down, highs and lows, a cacophony but one with some sort of rhythm. She talked to a personal assistant for a semifamous actor, a waitress/dancer, a waiter/actor, a publishing intern, another dancer, an actor, a musician, another musician, a student of philosophy, a student of art history, and in these discussions—random, odd topics, everyone happy and drunk or stoned, expertly holding all personal sorrow at bay—Lina remembered herself as a child standing in footed pajamas at the top of the stairs, listening to Oscar's parties below. Sometimes she would steal down and mingle among the crowd for a spell, before Oscar caught her and carried her giggling back up to bed. Those nights felt like this now: a creative energy, a limitless enthusiasm, a faith that talent and will and work would ultimately prevail, and a fatalistic wryness about the whole spectacle too—*of course* we are all creative and interesting, *of course* everyone will know our names, but tomorrow and the next day and the next we must go to our low-paying jobs where we sit on stools or take orders for food or clean up messes that no one else wants to clean; at least tonight we can say we are artists.

Very late, after Lina switched to drinking water, after she helped the singing woman find a lost earring, she happened upon Jasper in a hallway. He was alone, smoking a cigarette, and it felt suddenly to Lina (Was it the gin? The thrill of new people?) as though they were lifelong friends, separated by some tragic mishap, and here they were, at last, united again. Lina grinned at him.

"So do you want to see the Bell picture?" Jasper asked, crushing out his cigarette in an ashtray he held in his hand.

"Yes. I'd love to see it."

"I have one. The other two are at my mom's in Poughkeepsie. Come on."

Lina followed him down a short dark hallway, pressing against bodies as she went, excusing herself and sidestepping to avoid collisions and spills, and into a small room. Jasper closed the door behind them and the noise from the party immediately became muffled and accented with the thumping bass line of an unrecognizable song.

The bedroom was small, so narrow that Lina could have touched both walls with her arms outstretched, and neatly organized. A tall many-drawered chest stood beside a twin bed pushed against the far wall, a guitar case leaned upright in a corner. A reading lamp by the bed lit the room, harshly illuminating a narrow cone of space but leaving the rest in shadow. On the walls hung several shelves, an unframed poster of Miles Davis, and one framed picture. Gingerly, Jasper removed it from the wall and handed it to Lina.

Lina sat on the bed and put the picture under the light, angling away the glare. It was a charcoal drawing of an African American man, young, probably about the same age as Jasper. He stood in a field, sloping hills behind him, his hands at his sides, not working at that moment but alert, his body ready for motion. He looked directly at the viewer as though the two shared a secret. There was an intimacy in his gaze and in the way he stood, an ease and self-possession, the way you would stand before a lover. It was not a large drawing, and not particularly detailed, the fields barely suggested, the sky unfinished, but still it was something.

Lina exhaled. "Josephine Bell made this picture."

Jasper sat beside her on the bed. "How can you be sure?"

"I don't know. But it feels the same, it looks the same. Wait—do you mind if I take it out of the frame?"

"Sure. But be careful."

Lina turned the frame over. A dozen or so small rusty nails held a cardboard backing in place, and she eased the nails out of the wood, each releasing with a creak and shower of fine red dust. Beneath the backing was page after page of old, yellowed newspaper, the type irregular and old-fashioned, the paper nearly disintegrating in Lina's hands. Finally Lina reached the painting itself, and, yes, as she had suspected, written in a neat, careful script, the same handwriting she had seen on the pages at the Bell Center, was a name: *Louis*.

They sat together on the bed, Lina and Jasper, and looked at the faint but unmistakable letters.

"This is what Josephine Bell did with all her portraits," Lina said. "She wrote the name of the sitter on the back. According to Porter, this is one of the things they'll use to prove Josephine was the artist. Handwriting. And maybe some fingerprints, if they're still detectable."

Jasper took the picture carefully between flattened palms and turned it face up. "Louis," he said.

"You should take this to an authentication expert. Once the authorship question has been put to rest—I mean, once Josephine is fully recognized as the artist of the Bell works—if you *are* a descendant of Josephine Bell, you could have a legal claim to all of them, I think." Lina was talking quickly, her thoughts moving from one idea to the next, and she stood up to pace the small room. "And I know you're not interested in cashing in, but think about it—right now virtually all the art is owned by the Stanmore family. It doesn't seem right that they should be controlling Josephine's work. I think the Stanmores are more interested in protecting their investment in the Lu Anne Bell enterprise than they are in figuring out the truth."

Lina stopped pacing and stood before him. "Porter thinks you're lying, you know. About any connection to Josephine Bell." She watched him carefully.

"And what do you think?" he asked levelly, meeting her gaze.

"I don't think you're lying. I think there are so many uncertainties." She resumed her pacing. "Did Josephine make the picture? How did your dad get it? Can we actually prove that you're related to Josephine?"

"Are you always like this? I mean, so determined?" Jasper asked with a teasing smile.

Lina cocked her head, taking the question seriously. "It's my lawyer mode. Sometimes, with my dad for example, I'm not determined at all." Those moments in the kitchen with Oscar and Natalie returned: Should she have pushed him? Should she have demanded that he tell her the truth?

Jasper's eyes went then to his bedside table, and Lina's gaze followed his, to a photograph, this one in a simple metal frame propped upright. Lina bent to examine it: a color snapshot of a middle-aged man caught pre-laugh, that moment just before the lips curl and part, when the smile is held only by the eyes. The man was handsome; he looked like Jasper, the same tawny eyes, dark hair, full lips.

"Is this your father?" Lina asked. She did not pick up the photo; she did not want to overstep.

"Yes. That's him. This was his fiftieth birthday party. My mom surprised him." Jasper's voice was even but soft, hard to hear, and Lina leaned toward him to catch the words.

"Come on," Jasper said, louder now, standing from the bed. "Ready for some more gin rummy?"

He opened the door of the bedroom, and Lina was sorry for the intrusion of noise and smoky air.

"Okay," she said. "One more game."

FRIDAY

A door slammed somewhere perilously close to Lina's head and her eyes flew open. She lay on the floor, on her left side, and her hip ached, her head ached. Her gaze dimly registered a thin blue rug and, among its wrinkles, discarded tops of beer bottles, a crushed cigarette, a few strands of dark hair. She sat up. Beside her, the two of them sandwiched between a battered couch and a coffee table laden with empty bottles and full ashtrays, was Jasper. Both of them wore their clothes from the night before. Jasper was asleep, silent, his face serene.

Lina stood, careful not to disturb him, and wandered to find the bathroom. It was a small apartment, but the number of sleeping bodies seemed sufficient to populate a small village. Draped over chairs, lying in corners, underneath the kitchen table, in jeans and jackets and shoes. The apartment smelled of stale beer, cigarettes, sweat, and the lingering sweetness of marijuana. Outside a garbage truck clanged, a horn beeped. Lina rubbed her head. She wondered what time it was. If she had enough money for a cab. Where was her BlackBerry?

"Lina?" She heard Jasper softly calling her name.

"I'm here." Lina turned a corner and walked right into him, her nose colliding with his chest, their hands touching, and she laughed. "Careful!"

"Good morning," Jasper said, and stepped back, rubbed his face. "That was a good party for a weekday."

"Oh my God." Lina looked at her watch: 8:45. "I have got to get to work. Hey, can I borrow your jacket?" She was eyeing his tuxedo jacket, hanging over the back of a chair.

Jasper smiled. "Sure," he said.

She picked it up, sniffed a lapel, and slid her arms through the sleeves. "Not too bad," she said, rolling up the cuffs.

Just then Jasper bent down and kissed her. Without thinking, she leaned into the tall length of him and returned his kiss, testing the pressure of someone new, his taste and warmth. And then as abruptly as the kiss began, it ended, both of them stepping back.

Jasper said, "Well," and rubbed a flat palm across his head. As his arm raised, Lina saw the flash of his tattoo. A strip of taut skin appeared above his waistband as his T-shirt rode up. Curry and beer smells permeated the kitchen, a digital clock on the table blinked a red 12:00, 12:00, 12:00, waiting to be reset, and with a crippling rush Lina felt awkward and out of place, nervous and shy. "I . . . I . . . really can't be doing this," she stammered, regretting her words even as she said them. "I could get into trouble. At work. I mean, our connection is professional."

"You know, nothing happened last night." Jasper's hand came down, his voice was quick and guarded.

"I know," Lina said. "I know it didn't."

"I didn't realize that . . . last night, it was all business. I don't want to get you into trouble. With work, I mean."

"Don't worry about it. Really, it's my fault. I'm sorry," she said. These last twenty-four hours had happened to her with a spinning suddenness, and this was the only way she could think of to slow the pace, calm her heartbeat, regain control. "I'll call you later, Jasper. About the case."

"About the case. Okay." He nodded stiffly and unlocked his front door.

— 293 —

With a small apologetic wave, Lina descended the empty echoing stairwell, down four narrow flights, the walls tagged in black and red spray paint, the floors painted a dingy blue. She emerged onto a sunny street, the corner of Essex and Rivington, spicy smells of Mexican food from a tortilla place on the corner, the beeping of a truck as it reversed down a narrow alley, and stopped. She turned and looked at Jasper's building, and almost headed back inside. Why couldn't she do this, kiss someone new, be late for work? Somehow everything from this morning and the night before seemed parts of a whole, Jasper's show and the confrontation with her father, her decision to move out, the kiss, this buzzing of her senses and the faint musky smell of Jasper on the jacket she wore, all of it strange and exhilarating.

Just then Lina felt her BlackBerry vibrate in her back pocket, and she pulled it out. *Meeting with Dan—9:00 A.M.*, popped onto the screen. Already it was 9:01 and she saw Dan checking his watch, rolling his eyes at Garrison as they waited for Lina to arrive. And with this image, she seized up. She turned away from Jasper's building, thinking already of an excuse for her lateness—subway trouble? Lina raised her arm for a cab.

AT 9:18 A.M. LINA SLIPPED into Dan's office and hovered for a moment by the door to survey the scene, gauge the mood. Today she was meeting with Dan, Garrison, and Dresser to discuss the reparations case and, more specifically, developments in her search for Josephine Bell's descendant.

The mood, Lina quickly ascertained, was not good. Dan sat behind his desk, looking annoyed. Garrison perched in his chair, looking annoyed. Dresser's voice boomed from the speaker phone, definitely annoyed. "Let's get this show on the road, people. There's a critical mass behind this case now. I can't tell you how many folks I've spoken to recently, they're all behind us. We've got a movement here. And we need to move."

"We hear you, Ron," Dan said. "We're very close to finalizing the brief for your review. Very close."

"We better be. I've been talking to Dave"—Lina knew that there was only one Dave at Clifton & Harp, Dave Whitehead, the firm's managing partner, head of all thirty-seven worldwide offices and more than two thousand lawyers, known to the associates as El Gran Jefe—"and he's right behind me on this. I told him I'm waiting, I'm waiting, I'm still waiting on you, Dan. And today you're telling me I've got to wait some more? I want this to be the last call we have, Dan, the last call where I hear the word *wait*."

"I hear you, Ron. Loud and clear." Dan raised his gaze from the phone and his eyes fell on Lina. He waved her over with a tired flap of his hand. Pouches of purplish skin hung beneath his eyes, saggy as used-up tea bags. Lina approached the desk and settled into her usual chair, the too-low backrest familiar, comfortable (almost) if she stayed perfectly upright, if she did not attempt any type of relaxation.

"Here's Lina," Dan said. "She's just back from her trip to Richmond. She's ready to update us on her findings. Lina?" And he pushed the phone in her direction.

Lina shifted, unbuttoned the tuxedo jacket, which she realized now smelled distinctly of smoke, and wished with a passion rarely attributed to beverages that she had stopped for coffee.

"It was a very useful trip," she began, feeling her hangover recede as she spoke. "I found some extremely helpful documents at the Bell Center archives. These documents appear to establish that Josephine Bell had a child in 1848, and that child was sold to a Mr. Caleb Harper."

"Cut to the chase, Lina," Dresser barked from the speaker phone. "Do we have a plaintiff? Do we have any names?" Lina felt Dan's unblinking gaze heavy on her, and she met his stare head-on. She was aware of Garrison in the chair beside her, watching.

"Well, yes," Lina said. "I do have a name. Battle. Jasper Battle. He's a musician. He's in New York."

Dan's mouth fell open, his eyebrows shot up. "Fantastic!"

"Excellent work," Dresser said, his voice fainter now, as if he had stepped away from the phone. There was the rustle of other people entering the room, soft footsteps on thick carpet. "Lina, what do you think of his backstory? Is he verifiable as a Bell descendant?"

"Yes, I think so. There's still some work to be done in that regard." Her voice wavered and she cleared her throat. "But on the face of it he seems . . . legitimate." Lina felt heat in her cheeks and wondered with a rising panic how she would prove that Jasper was Josephine's descendant. Would he ever talk to her again? Why had she not taken hold of his face, why had she left his apartment?

"Well, I look forward to meeting him," Dresser said.

Dan thrust his head toward the phone and said, with a conviction bordering on maniacal: "Ron, you have my word—give us a few more days. *My word,* we will have this brief for you by Tuesday. At the *latest.*"

Garrison tapped Lina's arm and she turned toward him. *Tuesday?* he silently mouthed with great exaggeration and implied outrage. Today was Friday. Tuesday was soon. Four days for them, Garrison and Lina, to draft and edit the brief on a legally complex, highly contentious, potentially historic claim that other (presumably) talented lawyers had previously argued and, in all instances, lost.

"Great, I look forward to reading it," Dresser said. "I've got to run now, people. Dan, thanks for the call."

The line switched to a painfully loud dial tone, all three of them jolting in their chairs with the sudden awful noise. Dan groped for the off button, the phone went dead, and for a moment it seemed they might all have suffered some irreversible damage to the ear or head. Lina felt the cruel return of her hangover.

"Well, I'm happy to hear the trip paid off, Lina," Dan said and scratched his scalp vigorously, red curls thrown into frenzied motion. "Let's get this Battle person in here *asap.* Tuesday, team. You heard me. You're working through the weekend, obviously. We've got four more days."

. . .

BACK AT HER DESK, HER office door closed, the enormity of Lina's lie fell upon her with a sudden suffocating weight. She could not yet prove that Jasper was descended from Josephine Bell and, perhaps even more important, he had made clear his complete disinterest in becoming involved in the lawsuit. What had happened that morning—her hasty departure, the collapsed look on Jasper's face—did not bear contemplating. Not now. She had to focus or this case would fall apart. Without a lead plaintiff, there would be no reparations lawsuit.

Lina picked up the phone and dialed Jasper's number.

AFTER SOME AWKWARD PLEASANTRIES AND a beseeching "please" from Lina, Jasper had agreed to meet her at NYU's main library, a tall tower of red stone known for its soaring open-air atrium and the highly literate and pornographic graffiti found in the third-floor bathrooms. Lina almost didn't recognize him as he walked toward her across the wide marble-floored expanse. Gone was his musician's swagger and all-black ensemble. Now he wore khakis, a white button-down shirt, the cuffs nearly covering his tattoos; he carried a canvas briefcase. Lina waited by the circulation desk as his steps echoed against the stone.

Jasper stopped in front of her and leaned his head toward the glass revolving doors. "Let's sit outside." As they moved away from the desk, he unpinned a plastic name tag from his shirt and waved to a dark-haired woman who was shelving books.

Lina watched the exchange. "Wait—do you *work* here?" she asked.

"Yeah. I'm a part-time reference librarian. I was in a Ph.D. program, music history, but I'm taking a break. Not sure I want to finish it. Seven years is a long time."

"Will they let you back in after your break?"

"Maybe. Not sure."

"That would make me crazy. The not knowing." They were walking briskly now, moving against the flow of sidewalk traffic. Lina maneuvered through the lunchtime crowds, not looking at Jasper.

"Not knowing what?" he asked.

"Where I was going, what I was doing. You know, the uncertainty."

"It's okay," he said. "And who says I'm not *going* somewhere?" Abruptly Jasper stopped. "You think I'm some kind of loser, don't you?" he asked, and Lina stopped too, half a pace ahead, and turned to face him.

"No, of course I don't." Lina was taken aback by the defensiveness on his face, the hurt in his voice. She felt painted into her own little corner, and she had put herself there. She stepped toward Jasper, into the path of a man in a blue suit, who swerved and cursed and continued on his way.

"Jasper, that's the last thing I think," Lina said. "I think you're . . . brave." She remembered how, onstage, each stroke of his bass had echoed with a deep, exquisite tremor.

The flow of strangers continued around them. Jasper's face softened. "Let's go to the park," he said. He resumed walking and Lina fell into step beside him.

They crossed the street to Washington Square Park, the buzz of skateboarders and teenagers swirling across the pavement. A man with dreadlocks and a limp ambled past, eating a strawberry ice cream cone. The chess tables were full. Lina and Jasper sat on a stretch of green-slatted bench.

"I need to talk to you again about the reparations case," Lina said, and inhaled as though she were diving into a pool. "I did a stupid thing. I told the partner and the client on this case that I had verified a Josephine Bell descendant and that he had agreed to be our lead plaintiff. And that the descendant is you."

The silence that followed seemed impossibly complete for such a crowded, public space. Lina heard the creak of the bench beneath her as she shifted in place, waiting for Jasper's response.

"That is kind of stupid," Jasper said at last, though he did not appear alarmed. His left eyebrow rose in a smooth arched curve.

"Wait, how do you do that?" Lina asked. "The one eyebrow?"

The eyebrow flattened. "It's weird, I know. It happens when I'm curious. I'm curious as to what you're going to do now. You've got a lot of ground to cover." Jasper was matter-of-fact, but not unkind.

"I know," Lina said weakly. The same swirling she'd felt that night at the bar with Jasper and outside his building, of events flying beyond her control, came over her again. Her right foot began to rapidly tap the concrete. Calmly, Jasper studied her.

"Can I ask you a question, Lina? Why do you do this? I mean, this job? Doesn't it make you crazy?"

"This job? Well . . . ." She met his eyes and then looked away, to where the pigeons scurried at their feet, swallowing bread crumbs with great backward curls of their oily necks. That old story—Oscar's comment, the pants off any judge—suddenly seemed ridiculous. Why did Lina do this job?

"I really loved law school," she began. "Right and wrong, resolution, justice. The rule of law. All that stuff. I worked on an asylum case for an immigration law clinic I did my third year. My client was a woman from Sudan. Ange was her name—the last client I had with a name that didn't end in Corp. or LLP. She was young and afraid, her story was atrocious in every way, there was nowhere for her to go, and somehow she found her way here, to New York. She looked at me as though I had the answer to every question. But I thought she was amazing, just the fact of her being here, alive, after all she had seen and endured. That's why I do this job, or why I *thought* I did it."

"Did you win the case? Did she get asylum?" Jasper's eyebrow flew up again into a neat arch.

"Yes. She lives in Flatbush now." Lina remembered the night she went to Ange's apartment for dinner, a few weeks after the asylum decision, and Ange had cooked a spicy stew with beef and cinnamon and shown her a faded, cracked photograph of her mother, who was pretty and smiling, her head draped with an orange scarf.

Lina looked up. Jasper was watching her with his honey-colored eyes. "I've been thinking about it," he said. "I talked it over with my mom. I'll be your plaintiff, Lina. If you want me to be. I mean, if I *am* related to Josephine Bell."

Lina did not know immediately what to say. She was not accustomed to asking for help, she did not know how to respond when it was offered. "Thank you" was all she could summon.

"You're welcome," Jasper said with a mock-serious smile, and stood. "Okay, I've got to get back."

Lina rose and moved to hug him. He did a funny dance, half moving away, but then gently he kissed her on the cheek.

"Good luck, Lina," he whispered into her ear.

AT HOME, IN THE MIDDLE of a workday! Lina couldn't believe her nerve. The house was quiet, no sign of Oscar, and lit up with sun in a way that seemed oddly vivid, as though light fell more urgently on weekdays.

She ran up the stairs. Nora's document, which lay inside the white envelope, which sat inside her handbag, which rested on the floor of her bedroom, remained unread. This was why Lina had come home on a Friday afternoon. Tomorrow she was meeting Garrison at six A.M. at the office to begin drafting the brief.

But first: cotton gloves. Cotton gloves? Lina rifled through her boxes of winter things, her underwear drawer, her sock drawer. No gloves, but she found a clean pair of thin cotton socks that she slipped onto her hands. Nora would approve, Lina felt sure.

With cumbersome socked hands, Lina opened the envelope and slipped out the pages. There were twenty at least, a thick packet of crinkly paper, covered in neat, even handwriting. They smelled dry and faintly sweet, almost like burnt sugar. Sitting cross-legged on her bed, Lina began to read.

The moon hangs low and lights this page. I have put
away the candle for it is a full moon, a harvest moon my
father would have called it, beaming down brighter almost
than a midday sun. Tonight is the last I will spend under
my brother's roof with you asleep in the room beside. I have
not said my good-byes, though this, I think, is for the best.
Forgiveness is not easily earned, not for me, and I have
no wish to trouble Jack further with my presence here.
It is hard for him to bear, I can see it in the set of his jaw,
the way he turns his face away from me. He is busy with
preparations for your journey west, to the Oregon territory
and a new life there, and I distract and remind him of
what he seeks to forget. Perhaps you have sensed already
that I will not travel with you. I suspect so. Children know
more than we adults care to fathom, and you I feel are wise
already.

I know well that the circumstances of a child's birth
and raising, the hopes and frustrations of his parents, their
fears and desires, shape in ways great and small the kind of
man that child in time becomes. I do not want you always to
wonder how you came to Jack, about the events that set your
life in forward motion, away from your mother and the place
where you were born. You should know all that I know, and
it is this aim that guides my pen tonight.

In such an exercise, there are limitations, and of these
I am manifestly aware. I am not practiced in the narrative
arts and what I set down here may turn rough or discursive.
There are things you will read about myself, about Jack and
Dorothea, about Josephine and Mr. and Mrs. Bell that may
cause you some distress. Once you have finished with these

pages, you may think of me in a new light, a harsher light. You may wish that my conduct had been different, better, braver than it was. When you are older, you will, I hope, learn something of the world and understand that each man carries with him imperfection and regret, and day by day he strives to make right the wrongs he has committed, to repair what he has broken. This is what I have struggled to do, in ways human and flawed.

It is difficult for me to consider my past and not be consumed by a great and abiding sadness, a sense that nothing I have touched will stand for good. That no amount of amends I perform will account for the wrongs already done. I hope that wherever else I have failed, whatever harm I have caused to strangers and friends, that you may speak for me. Not before a pulpit or upon a stage. Not with words great or loud. But only to be, to persist, to live a life with pride and worth. In twenty years' time, thirty, or forty, I hope that you may sit upon the porch of your home, look out upon a greening field that you have tilled, see your children surrounding you with love, and think for a moment upon me. That is all now that I truly wish for. To be for a moment in your thoughts, when I have long passed from this earth, and perhaps in that way I may find my redemption, an earthly redemption, not everlasting, but sacred nonetheless.

Here then is the story, Josephine's story, your story, and mine.

The day I first saw Josephine is etched clear and bright in my mind. It was a late summer morning in the year 1852. I had slept scarcely an hour when Little Sullivan, one of Mr. Rust's boys, called round for me. He knocked so hard on the guesthouse door that I awoke thinking there was a fire or flood or some other manifestation of God's wrath bearing down on me. I looked out the window and saw Little below, motioning up at me. We need you, Doc, Little called. Down at the barn.

Little was not a man known for patience or good humor. I gathered my things with haste. My head ached from the previous night's drink and my knees seemed partial to giving way as I stepped slowly down the stairs and onto the porch. The stale taste of whiskey still filled my mouth and I spat into the dry grass. That September had seen summer stretch further than it ought, and the haze on the horizon, the cloudless sky, indicated another humid and close day. But the morning had not yet turned to hot and I thanked the God that still remained to me for the air cool on my face. I nodded at Little as he brought my horse round and before mounting I shook my head to clear the haze that hung there too.

I followed Little to a field about three miles east outside of town, to a place I had come to know well. There had once been a farm here but not in my lifetime and all that remained now of that failed venture was a falling-down pile of rotting timber where the house had once stood and a gray leaning barn, its walls and roof slanting towards the earth at such an angle that the lessons of physics surely could not explain why it still stood.

The sun was right and truly risen when we reached the barn and I narrowed my eyes against it as I looked at what the patroller Josiah had brought. This was when I saw her first, the girl, Josephine. She was hitched to the back of Josiah's old mare, a sorry sway-backed animal that twitched its ears in mad frustration as the wind hit them. Her dress seemed the dress of a house girl, not homespun, but it was stained with sweat and blood, and the hem was frayed and torn. She wore fine boots, and Josiah pulled them off her as I watched and stuffed them inside his pack.

There were three runaways that morning, Josephine and two men, one who'd been beat within an inch of his life and the other named Bo. The men were sat on the ground beside the barn, their backs against the gray slatted wall, the first either asleep or unconscious, I couldn't say which.

I could tell right away that Josephine was poorly. Her right eye was crusted over shut, yellow pus seeping from the corners, and she seemed only half-aware, something vital gone from her face and the good eye that rolled upwards as she stood and swayed beside the mare. Josiah let her loose and brought her to the edge of the barn where I waited next to a three-legged stool left out by Mr. Rust for these occasions. She sat, shaking as her knees bent to shift her weight.

Watch this one, Josiah said and pointed his chin towards the girl. She came on us with a knife.

I examined her in the methodical way I'd been taught at the medical college, working from head to toe and left to right. She seemed to notice me no more than you would a bird passing overhead or a beetle crawling beside your toe. Part of her had already departed this world and her head swung from side to side like a doll's as I looked in one ear then the other. She moaned once, I remember, a deep throaty sound that reminded me of heaven and hell, of the preacher's moans when his eyes rolled up after sermoning on sinning and its consequences.

As I conducted my examinations, Josiah stood to the side awaiting his payment and working his hat in his hands. He was a small man, stoop-shouldered and bony, like his horse. I heard Mr. Rust tell once that Josiah was burdened by a wife who would not stop bearing children, nine at the last count, and a dry farm that barely yielded enough for two hungry stomachs. He had come to patrolling out of need, not design, and I felt a degree of sympathy for him. This was not a job for a family man, nor for any man with a heart and sense of justice.

Once I'd finished, Mr. Rust inquired with eyebrows raised as to the value of the goods on offer. I nodded towards the girl and Bo, but not the other. The risk with him was too high, the Lord's breath was in his face already or it'd take him so long to recover from his beating that any profit would be spent on feeding and housing him in the meantime. I wasn't sure what made me choose Josephine, she could have been the same as the other, too much risk. Maybe something in that moan, a spirit sound from deep down, or maybe the way she kicked her legs when I tapped the kneecaps, like she was still running, showed me she was mostly alive in there.

I cannot say that it was then, that morning, I began to love her. Such thoughts were the furthest from my mind. I saw only limbs, a head, a body requiring repair, and I the one charged to do it.

I should explain something about my position, how I came to be there with Josephine and the others at the barn on that wind-riven day. We were thieves, of a sort, though the kind sanctioned by the federal legislature. Since passage of the Fugitive Slave Act, all manner of men had turned their hand to slave catching, the sole requirement for the subject of their attentions being simply a Negro face. It made no difference the true status of the man, woman, or child—be they rightfully free, or another man's property, or indeed a slave escaped from any manner of indignities that no creature should be made to bear. On the sugar fields and great cotton plantations of Mississippi, Louisiana, South Carolina, Florida, the need for slaves was great, the sums paid beyond imagining. Five, six, sometimes ten times the prices in Virginia could be fetched at market in New Orleans. It was a simple calculus for the men engaged in such larceny.

I was employed by one of their number, a slavecatcher by the name of Benjamin Rust. He stood tall and bony, a beady-eyed man with a long dark mustache, droopy at the ends, that traveled up and down as he spoke. He had no God and never spoke a kind word if it wouldn't serve his own benefit but for all his wanderings and deals, his ambitions were not great. The accumulation of wealth and the things it purchased were his only cares. Most days I could barely stand to look at him, but I worked beside him, I did as he bade me, I took the notes he paid.

A long cloud has drifted across the moon and tempers its rays so I have lit a candle to continue. The flame is weak and flickering but it will serve until the clouds recede again.

As I look at the black, hard center of the flame, it is clear to me that I must go back, I must redraw this narrative and begin long before the day I first saw Josephine. Long before even the day I met Mr. Rust.

Certain events begat others, and these then followed on to more, a cascading flow of places and people, sorrow and guilt, a river that led me to you, and you to Jack, in ways that perhaps lend a purpose to the unspeakable tragedy that befell us. The tragedy that my hand delivered.

This is not a digression that I begin here, but a prelude of necessity to what came after. After I departed my brother's house in disgrace, after I left respectable employ and became a spectacle of ridicule and contempt, after Mr. Rust found me shoeless and sick outside a tavern, after I tended to the fugitive Josephine.

But, before. Before.

Before, I had worked alongside a good and kind man, Dr. John Coggins.

Dr. Coggins was my professor at the medical college in Philadelphia. He instructed us in anatomy, medicinal herbs, and medicinal topography, his specialty. He was white-haired and whiskery, with sharp green eyes and a face lined like the body of a tortoise. Though he stood short of stature, his deep, grave voice and the very presence of him always seemed to me much larger than his physical size. In my memories he is always towering above, looking down at me as if from a great height.

I looked to him as I imagine a young man might look to a father. I do not think he ever regarded me in quite the same familial way, but he did take a shine to me. While a student, I often met him on weekends for walks along the banks of the Delaware and paths of Port Richmond Township. We would collect herbs and flowers and later press them between heavy gray sheets of paper bound with twine. This plant, he would tell me, is for bettering the spleen when mixed with arrowroot, or the bark of that tree helps ease a woman's pain when birthing. I committed all his lessons to memory.

During my final year at the medical college, Dr. Coggins invited me to join him in bringing medicine to the rural folk throughout the small towns in southern Virginia. His plan was to establish a clinic in Randolph Township in Charlotte County. This was a place I knew well. My childhood had been spent in neighboring Lynnhurst, a town I had left at the age of 15, vowing never to return. Although eager to accept Dr. Coggins's proposition, I was loath to return to that familiar region, full of failing tobacco fields, ruined mansions, the poorest folk in all the South, and the bitter memories I still held of my upbringing there. You see, my parents never developed a true fondness for me or my younger brother Jack, it being difficult for them to feed and clothe us adequately. I would not describe my early years as aggrieved, seeing as all my base physical needs were met, but I had no desire to extend the period of my youth any longer than was necessary. As soon as I could ride a day's distance on horseback and knew how to fire a pistol, I set my departure.

I urged my brother Jack to accompany me. Although as distinct as potatoes and peas, we were as close as I believe two brothers could be. I saw no future for him if he stayed on our father's meager farm. But Jack declined. He was but 13 when I left, and slight in size, his height had not yet taken. He looked still like a child, and it seemed the child in him could not foresee a life outside our parents' house, no matter how oppressive that life might continue to be.

During my years away from home, working first in Philadelphia as a physician's assistant and then later attending the medical college, I rarely thought of my parents. I wrote but once. My letter notified them of my place at the college and my intention to remain in Philadelphia until I earned my degree, perhaps longer.

My thoughts, however, turned often to Jack. I hoped he studied the books I had left. I hoped my father's beatings had lessened in frequency and degree. I wondered when he might leave that place. But still, year after year, I did not write to him. I knew not the words to use.

It was Jack finally who sent word to me. In the spring of 1849 I received a letter informing me of my father's death. Jack asked that I return home to pay respects to both my father and my already dead mother whose grave I had never seen. He explained that he had sold the family farm in Lynnhurst, purchased another in the neighboring town of Stanton, and recently married a woman whom we had known in childhood, Dorothea Rounds. It was Dorothea's father, the undertaker, who had helped him with the burial of our mother and it was over our mother's funeral rites that Jack had again met Dorothea.

Dorothea and Jack welcomed me to their marital home, he wrote. And so I came.

That summer I slept under the attic eaves of Jack's house and listened to the swallows clatter on the tin roof in the evenings and to the rooster's solitary *kaw-kaw* in the mornings. I would rise with the sun to find Dorothea and Jack already busy with the morning chores. My memories of that time are always of Jack in motion, a speeding burst of activity, hands busy, shoulders lifting or hauling or pushing, and his Dorothea beside him, a calm presence, dark haired, lovely, an angel.

Jack was the same serious, upright boy I remembered from our youth. Two years younger but now two inches taller than me, lanky and lean, with a mop of dark curly hair and eyes the color of rich earth. He had few neighbors, and the nearest town was 12 miles of hard riding. The isolation suited them well, Jack told me. He and Dorothea had grown weary of the folk in Lynnhurst and had sought a new beginning, away from the familiar scenes.

As the summer wore on, Dorothea's waist thickened and her belly pushed out the front of her dress until I could not help but remark that she appeared to be with child. Why yes, she answered, isn't it wonderful? Dorothea and I were in the kitchen alone when I said this—I had thought such a matter might embarrass my brother if discussed openly. I smiled and congratulated her, and then later that day in the field, I clapped a hand on my brother's shoulder and smiled my congratulations to him. He understood my gesture and looked abashed at the ground, only the barely upturned corners of his mouth showing me that he smiled as well.

That summer with my brother, my thirst relented. I did not drink spirits, or rather I drank rarely and only with Jack beside me on the creaking wooden chairs of his front porch. There was a physical tiredness in me from the farm work that seemed to slake what had propelled me previously to the bottle. I could not explain it any further then, and cannot now, only that those three months were the driest I had known since leaving home.

I returned to Philadelphia in September and began preparations for my final exams. Back in the city, surrounded by friends and associates, my thirst returned and I fell back into the desultory life of a student. I heard nothing from Jack for many months. That winter, I wrote to inform him of my position with Dr. Coggins and the planned establishment of our clinic within Charlotte County. In truth, the clinic's proximity to my brother's farm had induced me at last to accept the post. I had enjoyed my time with Jack and Dorothea far more than I had imagined possible and I fancied a return, to family and familiar sights. I felt my childhood bitterness begin to lift, the memories that I held—barely worth remembering—reshaping into ones that I might tolerate and perhaps even embrace. The agent of this change was Jack. He had not suffered as I had in my parents' home; he remembered moments and events that seemed drawn from a different childhood altogether, different parents, a different home. While I listened, he told Dorothea of a pie our mother would bake with peaches and cinnamon; a toy train our father made from an old tobacco tin, its track fashioned from wood scraps fit together and sanded thin and smooth; the winter night our father brought me, delirious with fever, to the doctor's in town. Why did I recall none of this? Did he imagine his stories? Did he invent them for my benefit, or for his own? I cannot answer. But whatever words Jack speaks to you of that time, the stories he tells of our childhood in Lynnhurst, our parents and the lives they led, he speaks the truth.

I wrote to Jack a second, and a third time. I inquired as to conditions on the farm, his first harvest, Dorothea's health and the coming arrival of their child. Still I heard nothing from him. Perhaps he sent a letter that was lost in the rural post. Perhaps he had been too busy to write. Perhaps, I thought only later, there was an element of retribution in his conduct, a kind of rebuke to me, to my disappearance from our parents' farm, to all the years he labored alone beside our father. Now the borders of that small warm circle he had made with Dorothea would not part so easily to accommodate me, the prodigal brother, no matter how great my regret or true my love for him. And for this I could not reproach him.

Dr. Coggins and I were occupied throughout the closing weeks of the year 1849 with preparations for the future operations of our clinic. We opened the storefront in Randolph on the second day of January, 1850. In the morning hours we saw patients at the clinic, with the afternoons and evenings reserved for house visits and the like. The weeks passed quickly and I did not dwell on my unanswered letters to Jack. In his own time, I believed, Jack would contact me and we would persist on the course we began that previous summer to become brothers once more.

A month after our clinic's inauguration, I finally received word from Jack. It came in the form of Langston Knowles, one of Jack's neighbors, a man whom I had met the summer before. He was unmarried, tall with a long dark beard that he would stroke as he spoke, and the ends of it seemed threadbare and sparse from the handling.

Langston arrived late one night at the clinic door.
Finding no one, he called then at the sheriff's to determine
my or Dr. Coggins's home address. A doctor was needed
urgently, Langston said, to attend a medical emergency at
Jack's farm. The sheriff directed Langston to my apartment
on the second floor of a boardinghouse in town, and
Langston knocked loudly until the owner, Mrs. Bursy, awoke
and opened the door.

I did not hear Langston's knocks because at the time I
was sitting stupefied at the end of my bed, my gaze directed
at my own pale reflection staring back at me from the glass
of the darkened window opposite. I do not know for how long
I had remained in this position before Mrs. Bursy entered
my room, only that I had drunk nearly all of a bottle of not
very good whiskey since arriving home from the tavern,
where I doubtless had already consumed my fair share of
drink. Having been awakened so urgently by Langston,
and not hearing any reply from her at first polite and then
louder taps on my door, Mrs. Bursy opened it to find me in
this state. She shook me on the shoulder and explained that a
grave medical emergency involving my brother required my
immediate attention and would I come downstairs quickly?

I had only ever treated my patients in a state of strict
sobriety. On that day, the day that Langston called, the
practice of medicine was everything to me. It was an arena
sacrosanct in my mind, pure and precise, shimmering with
all the advances that science had provided, all that she
would provide in future and I thanked God every day for
bringing me within her careful orbit.

An urgent medical emergency, Mrs. Bursy said. There
at the foot of the bed I sat and looked into her rheumy eyes,
weeping at the corners just enough to wet her upper cheeks.
I had regained sufficient sobriety to know that the effect of

drink still remained within me, and a great terror gripped me. Not a terror for my beloved brother or his wife. No, I feared only for myself. I feared the coming together of my two selves—the nighttime wanderer and drunk, the dedicated daytime physician. Would this bring a debasement beyond repair? For the good Dr. Caleb Harper to look himself in the eye, to truly look and recognize the darkness within, would this render the entire construction unsustainable? Yes. The construction of my self would come crumbling down.

Perhaps Mrs. Bursy recognized my terror. I do not know. I never saw her again after that night. I remember her blinking rapidly, wringing her hands in great agitation. She repeated the words. *A medical emergency.*

The situation did not allow for hesitation. I knew that had Dr. Coggins been called, he would have acted swiftly, and I strove to do the same, asking to speak at once to Mr. Knowles. I pulled up my suspenders (I still wore my clothes from that day) and followed Mrs. Bursy downstairs to where Langston waited, standing outside on the porch before the still-open front door.

My good doctor, Langston said, please come quickly. It is your brother's child, it is coming now and something is not right with Jack's Dorothea, she has been laboring too long. Please come, I have brought a horse.

Tied to the porch rail were two horses, their breath clouding the cold night air. I steadied myself against the door frame and turned to fetch my black leather medical bag, a recent gift from Dr. Coggins. The contents of the bag—glass vials of liquid held upright by steel casters, white paper sachets of powders, rubber-tipped hammers, gleaming scalpels—were still mostly unknown to me. Here is your future, Dr. Coggins had said when he passed the bag to me. Guard it well.

I took down the medical bag from the shelf in my closet, pulled on a jacket and my riding boots, and joined Langston outside where he waited, already astride his horse. We rode through the dark streets of Randolph and westward towards my brother's farm. We did not stop and slowed only once, as the horses started from the sudden sound of coyotes, their howls low and insistent in the starless night.

Langston and I arrived at Jack's farm and despite the dark, I could see it was much changed from my time there just 6 months previous. The small gray house now had a mended roof and yellow curtains; the front door was painted a cheerful red and festooned with branches of holly heavy with berries. The barn, the chicken coop, the outbuildings, all bore signs of Jack's handiwork and Dorothea's craft, patches and fixes and simple homey touches. The fields stretched beyond the house in darkened shadow, the full smell of turned earth lying fallow for winter.

The ride had done much to rid me of drink, the cool wind and night air seeming to purify my blood and clear my head. This is the truth. I willed myself to sobriety and felt my faculties return.

I dismounted and hitched my horse to the post. There was no sound, not an owl's hoot or dog's bark, only the jangle of the horses as they shifted in place and my own labored breath coming fast from the hard ride. I blinked sharply to clear my vision. Light burned in nearly all the windows of the farmhouse, making it look at first to my wind-scoured eyes like the house was aflame. Jack, having heard the noise of our arrival, rushed outside to meet us.

She is bad, he said, and his eyes were wide and white. Dried blood smeared his forehead and I could see it on his hands. The midwife has come and gone, he told me. She said there was nothing to be done.

I gripped firmly the curved leather handle of my bag and
followed Jack inside. I heard Langston depart again in a full
gallop but I knew not where he went.

Dorothea was upstairs, spread on the marital bed in a
nightdress whose color was now obscured by her sweat and
blood. Her eyes were closed, her breath raspy and distinct,
and her bulging stomach bloomed like a rose from the bed.

You were right to call for me, I said to Jack. The fear that
had gripped me at the guesthouse was far from me now. My
eyes saw with a grim clarity the danger to Dorothea and her
unborn child. My head was clear, as though I had slept a full
night, as though no drop of alcohol had ever passed my lips.

I examined Dorothea in the methodical way I had been
taught at the medical college, from top to bottom and left to
right. Jack stood anxiously at my elbow, his breath loud in
my ear.

She stopped pushing, Jack said. She screamed at the last
and stopped pushing, I don't know why.

I put my hands on Dorothea's stomach and felt for the
outline of the baby inside. When I could determine nothing, I
pushed down on her stomach harder, then reached between
Dorothea's legs. She turned her head and moaned faintly as
I probed.

I realized then that the position was such that Dorothea
could not deliver the child, no matter how great her strength.
The baby lay head to toe across her stomach, perpendicular
to the point of exit, transverse and lodged against her rib
cage, perhaps dying, perhaps dead already. This knowledge
came to me plainly, as though printed before me in a
medical textbook set on the bed, and I knew there was
nothing I nor any doctor could do now to improve upon the
prognosis. Dorothea, having labored so long and hard, was
doomed from the very first contraction, likely had been

doomed some months before, when the fetus first turned its head away from her heart, stretched its legs long across her abdomen, and pointed its stomach down towards the earth that it would never meet.

I looked at Jack, who studied my face, and I did not say a word but he read my thoughts in the thin line of my lips and a rapid blink that had overcome me, now unable to meet his gaze.

Can you save them? he asked. Please. Please save them.

Dorothea's chest still rose and her eyes twitched beneath their lids, rapid skittering movements. There were few options available to me but as I gazed at Dorothea, at her face so beloved, a single path opened before me that offered an outcome most satisfying, most fortunate. *Save them,* Jack had said. Dorothea was alive, but

There was a loud knock at the door and Lina lifted her head. She heard the creak of floorboards, the shifting of feet.

"Carolina, it's me," Oscar said.

Lina did not respond. She knew that eventually they would talk, about her move, about Natalie, perhaps even someday about Grace, but not now.

"Carolina, please."

But something in his voice, an edge of resolve, made Lina put aside the page she was reading, pull the socks from her hands, stand, walk to the door, open it. Her father stood in the hallway holding a tall stack of books and papers; *Women in Love,* Lina read along one of the spines. Oscar peered out from above the pile, and she stepped aside to let him in.

Carefully Oscar placed his cargo on a small space of clear floor. "I brought you some stuff. Some of Grace's things," he said. "I should have given them to you a long time ago, but I didn't want to . . . upset you. I didn't want to upset *myself*. But it's high time you had them."

Lina nodded. She was still standing by the door and she sat now, back onto her bed, where Caleb's pages were divided into two neat piles: read, unread.

"There's something I have to tell you, Carolina." Oscar's face seemed cast in metal, the darkness of the folds and lines, the gray pallor. He was not wearing his glasses, and his eyes were watery and an angry red.

"Dad, you've got to wear your glasses more. You're really straining your eyes."

Oscar smiled. "You're always trying to take care of me," he said. "I'm glad you still are. But it's okay. I'll be okay, you know. And Natalie, she's a good egg. You'll like her if you give her half a chance."

Lina shrugged her shoulders and then hoped the gesture did not seem dismissive; she would tolerate Natalie, she would give her half a chance.

"Listen, I don't know how to do this, Carolina. I have told this lie for so long it almost feels like the truth, and for a long time I thought it could be." Oscar's voice was hard to hear. His face lost its usual joviality and became suddenly the face of an old man, tired and fearful. Lina straightened her back, her heartbeat slowed, the muscles of her face relaxed. She nodded for her father to continue.

"Your mother, Grace, she really wasn't well, Carolina. She didn't want to be a wife, or a mother. I don't know what she wanted. She loved you, she did, so much, but she worried all the time that she wasn't a good mother. She hated me, she hated our marriage, and I was so caught up in my own things, I didn't really see what was happening to her. Or I didn't understand it. I should have tried harder, I know that." Oscar stopped talking and it seemed he was struggling. His hands were tight in his pockets. "Carolina, your mother didn't die," he said, and his voice was low, but the words were clear. "Grace didn't die. She left us."

"*What?*" Lina said, but Oscar did not repeat himself. He looked at her straight-on, he did not shy away. She sat perfectly still, and at first she returned her father's gaze but then she did not want to look at his face, so she studied instead his knees, baggy in his old blue jeans, the fabric ripped there, a few white-blue threads hanging down. What he had told her seemed like words, only that, as when someone speaks to you in a language you do not understand. You guess at the meaning, and Lina insulated herself in this way. She listened to the sound of his words and she tried not to truly understand.

"I don't believe you," Lina said, though she did, of course she did. Oscar shook his head and lowered himself to sit beside her on the bed. He placed an arm around her shoulders in a hug of sorts but Lina did not turn toward him. She pulled her knees up near her chin, wrapped her arms around her legs, drawing herself into a tighter and tighter self-contained unit, something she remembered having done as a child, trying to reduce herself. To see if she could make herself disappear.

I cannot bear to leave her. I cannot bear to stay, Grace had written all those years ago.

Oscar continued, less afraid, it seemed, now that the secret itself was out, the most important words spoken. "Three years ago, she sent me a letter, just a few lines, just to let me know she was okay. That's what she wrote, 'I'm okay.' You were in law school, you were in class when I got the mail, and it just seemed so . . . unreal. It seemed amazing, and horrible. She said that she would contact you. I waited for her, every day I thought I'd hear a knock and it would be her. And I couldn't write back, she didn't give an address. I couldn't ask her what was going on. After that letter, I thought about her all the time. I started remembering her, before she left, before you were born, when she was young, and thinking about why she left, what I had done, what had happened between us. So I made the Grace pictures. Those were my answer to her. And to you, Carolina. That's why I made them."

Enough. The woman drowning in a blank expanse of blue. The woman trapped within a frame. Lina shook her head and began abruptly to cry, silently but with a great volume of tears. She swiped at her eyes, scratching herself, and the pain sparked in her a brief, futile anger directed not only at her father, but at Marie Calhoun, who had betrayed her mother, and Porter Scales, who had loved her, and the books her mother had read, the pictures her mother had made; and anger at Grace herself, for leaving. And Lina realized why she and Oscar had stayed, all these years, just the two of them, in a house Oscar couldn't afford, a house that was too big: he had been *waiting* for Grace to come back. He had been waiting.

Lina released her legs and stood up, looking down at her father. "All this time—you lied to me. Why did you lie?" Her voice was wobbly and rough from the tears and she saw him wince as she spoke.

"Grace didn't want you to grow up thinking that she had abandoned you," Oscar said, speaking quickly. "She asked me to tell you, to tell everyone, that she had died. She thought it would be better for you. *I* thought it would be better. And it was all I could do for her. She made it clear that she wanted nothing else from me." Oscar stopped speaking then and his face was pained, desperate for Lina to accept that he had had no other choice. "Carolina, I am so sorry."

He said these words in a voice Lina had never heard before, and their effect was sudden and profound. She felt her anger spin away, but in its place was a new crushing confusion. Lina recalled those sketches she'd seen of herself as a baby. *Daughter. Daughter. Daughter. Daughter,* Grace had written.

"But why did she disappear? People get divorced, they split up. Why did she have to leave *me*?" Lina's mind clenched tight around this question and would not release.

Oscar looked at his hands. "I don't know, Carolina. She wanted . . . something else. To make art, to live alone. I don't know."

This answer left Lina hollow, but instinctively she knew it was all Oscar could tell her. How many times must he have asked himself these same questions? Those interminable months after Grace left, and it wasn't purely grief that had kept him inside and alone, it had been guilt as well. Grace had left them both behind: Lina, a motherless child; Oscar, forced to sustain this lie. Lina turned away from Oscar and dropped where she stood, kneeling on the hard floor. All at once she stopped crying and wiped her eyes on the back of her hands.

Oscar spoke carefully then, as though he had been preparing these words and wanted to say them well. "I want you to know that being your father is the best thing that ever happened to me. The most inspiring, the most creative. I've been so angry at Grace for leaving us, and angry at myself for not being able to help her. But really, too, I'm grateful to her. Because I got the chance to be your father in a way I wouldn't have if she'd stayed. She's missed so much, Carolina, and I've been so lucky."

Lina's throat ached with Oscar's words, but she did not cry again. She felt his presence behind her, anxious, exhausted by all of this, waiting for her to do something, to yell or weep or embrace him, but she stayed where she was on the floor of her room. Silently the minutes marched forward and Lina's feet began to prickle, her knees to ache, and she stood and walked to the window. She stared at the branches of the linden tree she had climbed as a child, at the blank window across the street where her third-grade best friend had lived, at the metal fire escape where once she had seen a small monkey, calm and watchful, chewing an orange. As the shadows lengthened and the air cooled into evening, a calm descended on the room and on Lina. Oscar remained on the bed. She felt empty and clean, like a stretch of damp new sand left by a retreating sea.

"Do you know where she is now?" Lina asked at last, and her voice was small but steady.

"No. No, I don't."

"Has she contacted you again?"

Oscar hesitated. "Yes," he said with purpose, as though he had anticipated the question and only now had decided how to answer.

Lina turned sharply from the window.

"When? What did she say?"

"After Porter's review was in the paper. Grace read it, and she called me. She wants to talk to you, she said. She left a number. When you're ready." Oscar pulled from his back pocket a scrap of paper with a scribbled string of digits. He came to stand beside Lina at the window.

As Lina took the paper, she looked directly at her father. Everyone always said she looked like her mother, but Oscar's eyes were her eyes, she realized now: different in color, but identical in shape and the way they fractured the light, the way they inadvertently showed emotion, Lina and Oscar both powerless to hide behind them. His showed relief and regret and love.

"Call her when you're ready." Oscar hugged her then, and Lina did not relax fully into his embrace but still she allowed herself to fall against him, to rest her head on his shoulder and smell the Brooklyn air and turpentine and oil and cigarette smoke, the closed-in house dust, and, yes, the sweet perfume from Natalie, all the elements that composed his scent.

Oscar released her from the hug, squeezed her hand, hugged her again, as though worried that the disparate pieces that fit together as Lina were now at risk of clattering broken to the floor.

"I'm okay, Dad. We're okay." She said these words and knew they were true. It would be easy to blame Oscar for where she was now, alone and unsure about so many things, but it wasn't his fault. It wasn't even her mother's fault. Lina could not blame a stranger. Her life was her own, and a life could be a good one, or it could be one of an empty wishing for more, for something different.

Oscar hugged her one last time and then silently left the room. Lina remained standing at her bedroom window. She watched the streetlights flicker on, the building go dark and then illuminate again in patches as people moved into rooms, their bodies quick and colorful; she heard the front door slam as Oscar went out and she watched him walk east along Sixth Street, his head down, hands in pockets, then turn the corner toward the subway and disappear.

Finally Lina turned away from the window. She looked toward the door, then to her bag, her BlackBerry. Should she call her mother now? Was she ready? There was a sudden restless energy in her, and the idea of going for a run—just gliding through the park, around the loop again and again and again—seemed delicious, but it was too dark, and physical exhaustion would not erase this peculiar discomfort, this staggering new reality.

Looking back at the bed, Lina's eyes fell to Caleb's letter and her pulse settled, her energy found a place of focus. She needed to finish the letter, and her urgency derived as much from her desire to see the story's end as to escape, just briefly, from all that would undoubtedly follow tomorrow, next week, next month. *Grace did not die. Grace did not die.* Every time she repeated her father's words, she felt a small, terrible, glorious shock. But now, at this moment alone in her darkening childhood bedroom, Lina fixed her thoughts on Dorothea and on Josephine.

Save them, Jack had said. Dorothea was alive, but weakened from loss of blood. The baby, I could not rightly say. I recalled a lecture at the medical college, given not by Dr. Coggins but a colleague of his, a specialist in obstetrics, about the surgical procedure of opening up the woman's abdominal cavity so that the fetus might be removed, sometimes with the effect of saving mother and child, sometimes of saving one, and other times with loss of both. It was possible. I had the tools to operate; my sharp knives waited within my bag, and Jack could fetch what else I needed. But life was ebbing away from Dorothea, I could see the blood seeped deep into the mattress on which she lay, her face pale under the light of the gas lamp glowing on the bedside table. *Save them.* I knew that I must act quickly. And so I did.

You must know already the end of this sorry episode. I do not want to fix in your mind the images that will remain forever in mine so I will end here with no further particulars.

Dorothea did not survive, her blood loss was too great, nor the baby boy that we pulled from her, purple and still. Jack held the infant to him with one arm as he sat beside Dorothea on the bed, clutching her still-warm hand in his. As I watched him, I felt a coldness in my limbs as though I stood at the center of a frigid storm, myself alone at its dead calm center. I could not move, I could only bear mute witness to the enormity of Jack's grief. By and by I went to the bed and sat with him. I do not recall if any words were spoken or embraces exchanged, only that we sat together, mourning, and that was the last Jack and I have ever been so long and so peaceful in each other's company.

After a time, we heard the sound of horses arriving. The dawn had now broken, and a pale pink light streaked across the floor of the room where the two of us huddled by the bed and the lamp as though it were still night. I looked outside and saw Langston dismount and Dr. Coggins rushing towards the house with his black doctor's bag, the mirror image of mine. I heard his heavy steps on the stairs. I stood before the door as he entered the room.

What has happened here? Dr. Coggins asked me, his eyes casting quickly over the scene of Jack and Dorothea and the little one. Jack remained perched on the bedside and did not acknowledge the new arrivals.

I began to recount the night's events but Dr. Coggins held up a hand to stop my narrative and stepped closer to me, putting his face directly in front of mine, so close that I could count the stubbed gray whiskers on his chin.

Have you been drinking? he said. I smell it on you, on your breath.

Langston stood some distance behind Dr. Coggins, his head turning from the trio on the bed to me as Dr. Coggins uttered his accusation. It was the set of Langston's jaw, solid and sure, and the slight nodding of his head that told me he had informed the doctor of my state when he had come to collect me from Mrs. Bursy's.

I did not reply to Dr. Coggins. There was nothing I could say. Cold were my fingers, my feet numb, the distance between myself and these others—their cheeks warm and red from riding, so sure in themselves and their rightness—stretched boundless before me. Dr. Coggins walked to the bed, to the ruined body of Dorothea, gazing all the while at the blood, the blood everywhere in the room that in the darkness had not seemed so blackish red as it did now in the dawn light.

You are a disgrace, he said. At the words, Jack lifted his head away from his sorrow, staring at me, the horror reflected in his eyes. Nothing that I do, no wounds I suture or fevers I chill, will ever erase that image from my mind.

Still I said nothing. I backed away from Dr. Coggins, from Jack's gaze and Langston, still nodding, and left the room. What was I to say? I have returned again and again to that night, to the knock on Mrs. Bursy's door, the curve of the baby's spine under Dorothea's tight skin, the movement of her eyes, the first cut of the scalpel as I began the procedure, each step that led to Dr. Coggins's accusation, my departure.

Please save them, Jack had said. In the years since that night I have asked myself, what should I have done differently? Would a better man, a more sober man, a more sober doctor, have chosen a different course?

The answer I have come to again and again is no.

After the death of Dorothea and the little one, named Michael Abel before his burial, I left Randolph Township and the company of Dr. Coggins and all others I knew there. I made no efforts to clear my name or salvage my professional reputation; they would have been in vain, I am certain, and I lacked the wherewithal to try. A great despondency descended upon me.

I traveled south. In Jackson, I renewed my acquaintance with the bottle and sought out temporary work where no one would care what my past held so long as I could mix powders and poultices, stitch a wound, bleed a fever, pull a tooth. I worked there for a spell, and then moved on, and then again I moved. I became a sort of wandering country doctor, roaming from one town to the next, finding cheap lodging, seeking out my patients wherever I might find them. In the main I treated poor farmers, whites and free blacks, rural folk who lived far from towns or any manner of apothecary. Burns, broken limbs, chilblains, cuts. Cholera, malaria, smallpox, typhus, other maladies the likes of which I had never seen nor knew the first bit of how to cure.

In the spring of the year 1851, my wanderings brought me again to the state of Virginia. I wish now that I could say that some noble purpose prompted my return. A desire, perhaps, to attempt reconciliation with Jack, to atone in some way for the death of Dorothea. In fact no such thoughts entered my mind. I traveled without purpose or design, from one accommodating tavern to the next, from one paying patient to another, and in this way I came again to Virginia.

My faith in the things I had once held true and dear, the medical sciences, and indeed the Lord above, had all but left me. There was no place for me, I believed, no profession, no family, no home.

And that is when Mr. Rust found me, lying on the ground one cold and damp morning outside a tavern that I had begun to frequent. He knew I was a doctor. He had noticed me ministering to the sickly and infirm of the surrounding area, so he said, and wanted to offer me a professional position at a decent wage. I listened to him, not there that morning but later the next day when we met as planned at the same tavern. He bought a bottle and poured me the first glass, the liquid fracturing the light from the late-afternoon sun that filtered through the tavern's open door, looking to my eyes like the light that had burned out the open windows of Jack's house that night. I drank it back and held out my glass for another.

My assignment was simple. Fugitives, both real and supposed, were delivered regularly to Mr. Rust. Generally, he conducted his own medical examinations on the offered goods but was never certain what he might be looking at. He often suffered losses on account of deaths, or damage so severe the fugitives weren't fit for any useful purpose. I was to be an improvement upon his methods—an insurance policy, of sorts. I would examine each fugitive before a sale was concluded and say yea or nay to each, so that Mr. Rust could be certain that what he was buying, even if it looked broken beyond repair, could be mended and sold on. But the mending I did would be of the most minimal sort. My instructions were to disguise, to treat ills only as far as they would impede a sale, with remedy appearing only as an occasional and incidental result. This is the scheme to

which I agreed. That day in the tavern, I drank with the
slavecatcher Mr. Rust, and I shook his hand.

Why did I make company with a man like Benjamin
Rust? It is a question I know you are bound to ask and I
have no simple answer. I have never been a political man. I
reckon the workings of government and the law are best left
to philosophical, intellectual, considered men, among whose
number I have never counted myself. That is why his offer
did not strike me as either right or wrong in its particulars; it
simply was, just as the institution of slavery, that I have lived
my whole life in close approximation to, simply is. Fugitive
slaves in the possession of men like Mr. Rust are likely to
be needing medical attention of one sort or another, and I
reckoned that I was as good or bad a candidate to supply it as
any other.

Even this is no explanation, I realize. Mine was a choice
made of the basest kind of weakness. It was not even so
much a choice as a simple surrender. My funds were all but
exhausted, my health was poor, a cough racked my chest at
night, and my clothes hung as though I were a strawman
intended to frighten away the birds. My life was devoid of
any purpose or meaning, any person to watch over me or
give me care, any person for whom I felt the barest stirring
of emotion. In this state of near death—and it was a sort of
death, I know that now—I had existed those long months
since Dorothea's passing. Every day I drew breath, I drank
my whiskey, my heart pumped nothing more than blood. I
was empty of all but the barest markings of a man–legs to
walk, a mouth to drink, a head to nod as Mr. Rust instructed
me to meet him the next day at the abandoned barn. I shook
his hand. Yes, I said. Yes.

•   •   •

The next day I arrived at the assigned place, at the hour instructed, and the first delivery came, shackled behind a gray mule led by a patroller whom Mr. Rust greeted by name. Hiram, he said. How fine to see you. Many of the patrollers who sold to Mr. Rust were lawfully required to return any fugitives back to their rightful owners, but Rust paid sums far greater than the rewards offered for return. And so they came instead to him, in secret, many of them shamefully. The patrollers had some base code amongst them, despite the nature of their work, but for most avarice was a more powerful urge and it was this instinct to which Mr. Rust appealed.

I remember well that first morning. I remember the mule's braying loud and hoarse as a foghorn throughout the hours as I examined the fugitives on offer. I remember a girl, her clothes nearly torn from her back, her legs bloodied. I remember an elderly Negro man, and the shaking of his head. I bought my freedom, he said to me as I probed his ribs. I'm a free man. A free man. A free man. A free man. A free man. He said it again and again, and sometimes his voice was drowned by the god-awful braying of that mule, and sometimes it seemed he whispered into my ear, even long after he was sold, long after I left that place and went directly to the tavern, not even stopping to wash the smell of sweat and blood from my person.

Once I commenced working for Mr. Rust, my days took on a routine more or less, with all my work accomplished by midafternoon and my nights free for the tavern. This was the purgatory to which I was condemned, and it seemed like God's hand. Retribution for what I had done.

So it went, month after month, the dark faces and cracked bleeding feet of my patients blending one into the other just as my days and nights blurred into one long blinding twilight.

So it went, until the morning I saw Josephine.

The day after I first examined Josephine at the barn, I rode to Mr. Rust's farm to check again on the status of her injuries. I would often administer further care in cases like hers where the wounds were severe or unsightly and might, if not healed properly, affect the price to be fetched later at sale.

I loosed my horse in Mr. Rust's side field and walked through the long grass to the wooden shed he had erected on his property for the purpose of sheltering slaves before they were sold on. His was a neglected, aging farmhouse with sloped roof and graying shingles, the land overgrown with tall grasses and chickweed. There had once been cattle, I think, and some horses—the barn is still there, the doors sagging on their hinges. It was next to the barn that he had built the shed, just a thin-walled box of a place with cracks in the timber and a tar-paper roof that in a heavy rain dripped down onto those souls locked inside. Inside were six low cots, three on either wall, and a table set at one end with two three-legged stools pushed beneath it. There were no windows, and a large padlock secured the door.

I released the padlock and the door swung open silently. Bo was directly to my left, on his side with his back to the door, and he breathed steadily in sleep. Josephine was laid out on the cot farthest from the door, beyond the circle of light that fell from the open doorway. Someone had covered her with a blanket, and that, and the darkness of the room, had the effect of shrouding her body. Her head was turned towards the wall, and all I saw of her was a knot of dark hair cast across the pillow. She was still and I worried that she had died in the night, that I had been wrong to think there was something inside her that would persevere.

I stepped forward to check her pulse, and she turned her head towards me, and for a moment I froze there, looking down at her across the expanse of empty cots. Her good eye—the left—was toffee-colored, lighter than I would have expected, shot through with green or blue, some color that seemed not to belong there. The light struck that eye and the contours of her face and I could see her studying me, examining.

I advanced into the room, pulled a stool to her bedside and sat; all the while her eye remained on me. Carefully I unwrapped the dressing on her bad eye to reveal a lid tightly closed, the skin swollen a dark purplish black. Josiah had said he didn't touch her, that he'd found her with an eye like that, and I did believe him. But someone must have struck her across the face, and looking down at that good eye, exposed and alive, I felt a bristling, a sense that something was wrong with a world that permitted, indeed encouraged, the infliction of pain without reason or consequence. During my medical training I had been taught to characterize symptoms and measure the markings of disease, to remove emotion from all our scientific inquiries and attempts at remedy. It was a course that had always come easy to me, which is perhaps why I had remained in the profession, even after Dorothea's passing. I could focus my mind on the patient as a combination of numbers, colors, symptoms, and facts.

But Josephine's one-eyed gaze troubled me more than I could say. I saw her not as a doctor, but as a man of faith who had lost himself. Why had her left eye survived? Why had the other closed so firmly with perhaps, as I then feared, a permanent loss of sight? Was it kindness that had spared the left and brutality that had closed the right? In the case of sickness and accident, it was God's will or fate or luck that struck a person down. But here it was a man's fist, a man playing at God. A merciless God. And myself playing at it too, in my work for Mr. Rust. I looked at her face and saw no healing there. Just an angry man with heavy fists, a wasted life, a stinking mouthful of drink and shame.

I was shaken and turned away from her gaze. I completed my examination quickly. I applied dressing to her wound, the fresh gauze white and fine as new clouds, and then I left, pushing my horse to a full gallop on the road to town so that he was covered in a frothy sweat and my breath was coming hard and fast when finally we arrived.

The next day, the sky pale and cloudless, I went again to examine Josephine.

I could not wait for the Lord to release us, she said to me. She commenced talking the moment I laid my hand on her face to unwrap the gauze. It came away cleanly and I prodded gently the purple eyelid. The others believed it was God's will to be enslaved, she said, and only some divine intervention or unmistakable sign of redemption would cause them to break away. She believed different, that is what she told me, and the words were uttered harsh and pure, rousing the rattle in her chest. I had ceased worrying about the eye, it seemed to be healing well, but it was the cough that now gave me pause, as consumption afflicted a great many in the region. Her spasm lasted 30 seconds, perhaps 45 but no more than a minute, and she reached a hand from below the blankets to wipe her wet mouth. When she laid it back against the cover, I saw no blood, which gave me some comfort.

Don't send me back, she whispered to me then. Don't. The good eye stared up at me again, those threads of greenish blue blazing. The cabin was stifling, and sweat pricked my brow. Outside I heard the whistle of a meadowlark.

That was when I first began to think of freedom. I believe that was the moment, if I had to pinpoint the exact time, which I want to do now, to remember it all and fix it here for you. That was the moment. The weight of her eye on my face so heavy it was like a hand, the closeness of that small shack, and the bird's distant call. I thought of freedom for her and for myself.

I didn't speak. Don't send me back, she said again, and those words charged the distance between us, the space seeming to wave and pulse, waiting for my answer.

I finished my examination and applied a poultice, some medicinal herbs in petroleum jelly that gave off a strong smell of licorice and left her bruised lid heavy with shine. Still I said nothing. I felt afraid and I did not know why.

Josephine's left hand lay atop the blankets and I picked it up. She did not fight me though for a fraction of an instant I felt her body tense and it seemed that she might snatch her hand away or even raise it to strike me. But she didn't, she allowed me to pull down the covers and place her hand gently onto her chest and then pull the covers up around her chin.

I will bring you something more for your eye, I said. I will be back later today to check on you again.

She nodded, her good eye on me. I met her gaze then and I think she saw that I was afraid because she looked slightly puzzled, her eyebrows drawing together and down as she studied me.

As before, Bo seemed asleep. I heard his breathing steady and strong and presumed he did not need my attentions.

I turned and left the room, fixing the padlock as I closed the door. I sat down hard on the front steps of the shack and looked back across the unkempt green field towards Mr. Rust's farmhouse, some 20 yards away. Mr. Rust just then opened the front door and stepped squinting into the morning sunlight, rubbing his shiny forehead and holding a leather hat in one hand. He placed it on his bony head and directed his gaze, now shaded, towards the shack and me.

I did not wave or acknowledge him as he came wading through the field towards me, slapping at the tall grass and wayward corn stalks left from when a farmer lived there. He stood before me, his belt just level with my eyes, and I did not raise them to his face.

So how are our runaways doing? he asked. I've a mind to just sell them on straightaway, not wait for them to heal up. Too many niggers to catch.

He laughed and told me then of a trap he'd orchestrated at the old Rounds farm, once a station on the Underground Railroad but deserted now for some time. Fugitives still went that way and Mr. Rust paid the overseers throughout the region to perpetuate the illusion that safety might be found there. Patrollers waited nightly to catch unsuspecting runaways and the success of the endeavor had well exceeded Mr. Rust's expectations. He told me this with apparent pride in his own cleverness as he slapped his palm against his thigh with quick, jerky movements.

Well, I answered slow, my mind working. The female is healing well though her one eye is still swollen shut and the boy Bo is strong and healthy as an ox.

Good, he said and looked back towards his farmhouse and the dirt path snaking from the front door towards the road as though he were expecting a visitor. I think we may have a buyer soon, he said, his head still turned towards the road. Customer from down south, New Orleans–ways. Sugar. There was a pause. He turned back to face me.

I need to fetch some iodine for the girl's eye, I left my bag back in town, I told him. I stood from the steps and Mr. Rust fell into the shadow I cast.

Go do it, he said with disinterest, but be back before nightfall, the buyer'll be here then. He'll be wanting to hear your warranty, he's a suspicious fella.

I nodded, and cut across the field back to my horse and the path out to the road.

At that moment, I did not know what I would do.

I rode back to town, to the guesthouse where I had been staying, to the black medical bag that Dr. Coggins had given me so long ago. I concentrated on maneuvering the horse through the pitted street, past the saloon where Mr. Rust first found me, past the general store where ladies bought their hats and fine cloth sent from Paris, past the buggies and the people of the town who crowded the street on that sunny September morning.

I hitched the horse before the guesthouse and took the steps two at a time to my room, which smelled of whiskey and smoke and sunshine. I retrieved the iodine bottle and some cotton from the medical bag and stood for a moment with the top open, staring down into its divided compartments at the stoppered bottles and gleaming steel instruments. I wondered if these were as marvelous as once I had thought them, all of these cures to aid the sick and dying. At least half were unopened, untried, and the contents of my bag—so carefully collected, so jealously guarded— seemed worthless to me suddenly, a collection of shiny toys.

I left the bag behind, taking with me only the iodine, cotton, and a thick roll of bills I retrieved from beneath a loose board in the floor, all my earnings from my time with Mr. Rust.

It was nearly noon when I rode back to Mr. Rust's farm. I knew that he would be in the saloon at this time, drinking his midday meal alone at a table, or with one or two others with whom I often saw him, chewing and spitting their tobacco and talking of money.

Sure enough, Mr. Rust's horse was gone and there was a stillness about the place. I walked purposefully to the shack with iodine bottle in hand and fitted the key into the padlock. The door creaked open and now Bo was awake and Josephine asleep. Bo sat half-upright on his cot, his bare torso supported on his elbows, and looked at me without expectation. A long, thin scar cut across his chest and stomach, a raised band of flesh colored a dirty pink that seemed not yet fully healed. He lay back down, eyes open to the ceiling, and I walked past him to Josephine's cot. I touched her shoulder and immediately her good eye flew open and she started, her hand rising up to shield her face.

I have the medicine for your eye, I said. I must administer it outside, I need the light. Can you walk? Josephine peered up at me, lowered her arm, and she seemed to decide something then, and I was glad that I did not have to say more.

I helped her up. She leaned on my arm and we walked awkwardly past Bo, who turned his head away from the ceiling to watch us. His scalp was shiny with sweat and the whites of his eyes lined with red, and I quickly looked away and led Josephine out the door. As we stepped into the hot, breezy air, I heard a growl from inside, a sound an animal would make. As I closed the padlock on the door, the well-oiled mechanism clicking evenly shut, Bo said: Take me too, doctor. It was not a scream but a cry of naked desperation and I shook my head to rid my ears of the sound.

Take me too, he said again, louder this time. I heard a pounding on the back of the door, a furious frenzied noise as Josephine and I walked down the steps, along the dirt path towards my horse.

Josephine looked back, and then up at me. I threw the iodine away into the tall grass and she didn't say a word but hurried her steps to keep apace with mine.

Then suddenly, as we neared the hitching post, she darted away to the door of Mr. Rust's house and disappeared inside. I hesitated, unsure if I should follow, unsure if she understood the urgency of our circumstances. I heard noises from within, clanging and items falling to the floor, and just as quickly as she had disappeared, she emerged again, holding a bone-handled knife in her hand. This is mine, she said, and tucked it into the waistband of her dress.

Can you ride? I asked as I untied the horse's reins. She shook her head no. Well, just hold on then, I said and I mounted and pulled her up behind me. Her arms circled round my waist and, as I spurred the horse on to a gallop, tightened so that I felt the thinness of her forearms and hard pressure of her fingertips against my stomach.

Why did I not take Bo? Why did I not leave the lock open so that he too could run? Was Josephine more deserving than he? Did I believe it might hinder myself and Josephine in our escape were I to let Bo free?

Because of what came later, I have asked myself these questions many times. I have searched for a complexity of purpose, a reason or intention within me; but in truth nothing of the sort existed. The answer is simply that I did not think of Bo. It did not enter my mind to release him. Something in Josephine moved me. Her youth, her voice, her eyes that seemed a reflection of the sea and the sky together. I cannot say what it was exactly that moved me but she did, and Bo did not.

I did not even think of him as a man, which is the sorry shameful truth of it.

• • •

Where were Josephine and I to go? I had brought nothing with me; I had not packed a bag or loaded provisions onto the horse. All I possessed was the blanket strapped across my horse's back, the clothes I wore, and, stuffed in the top of my right boot, the thick pile of bills. It was by no means a fortune, but I expected it would get us far enough.

As we rode, first over open, grassy country to skirt the town to the east and then back towards the road heading north, I fixed on our destination: Philadelphia. Although I had never moved within abolitionist circles, I knew that my connections at the medical college would prove helpful, at least in providing an introduction to those who might aid a fugitive slave. With the Fugitive Slave Act, Josephine would be truly free only once past the Canadian border. Finding her passage along the Underground Railroad, its conductors expert already in the Canadian routes, would surely be safer and faster than my own northward wanderings.

I slowed the horse and half-turned in the saddle to tell her of my intention. She nodded in agreement and smiled, the first time I saw her do it, just a slight upturn of her lips but it was indeed the sun that shone forth from her face, and I felt her whole person relax onto the horse as though only then did she truly accept my assistance, more than a need but a choice she herself was making, the two of us riding together, northwards, to the city of Philadelphia.

For 10 days, we traveled on seldom-used roads that threw dust into my face and meandered us past dry used-up farms, for a time along the cracked bed of a far-gone stream, through the odd small town, on up all the way to Philadelphia. The unseasonable heat continued, both a bane and a blessing for us. We camped away from the road, lighting only small fires; the warm nights required nothing more. But the days riding were hard, the sun bearing down on us, and Josephine without a hat. I fashioned one for her from a scrap of waxed tarp and some rope, and it seemed to ease her discomfort. Once, heavy into our third day, the sky blackened suddenly, and a temple of rain opened upon us. We rode through it, grateful for the cool, and we both lifted our heads and opened our mouths to let the water slide down our throats.

The spectre of Mr. Rust rarely left my mind. Perhaps I was extreme in my caution, paranoid even, choosing such a circuitous route, never hiring us proper lodging. But I had once seen him track down a fugitive, a boy no more than 13 or 14. Mr. Rust had been unrelenting in his search, sparing no amount of time or expense to bring the sorry boy back. I could not say what he'd do to catch the pair of us, but I imagined my involvement would only further harden his resolve to have Josephine returned to him.

As we traveled, the night fires were sheltering, the warm sky was close. In those rare moments when I forgot our pursuer, forgot the circumstances of our coming together, it seemed like we were not running but rather existing in a sawed-off separate place where the days were ordered by constant forward motion and the sun, the nights by firelight and the sound of Josephine's voice.

At night Josephine talked. Not much at first but more and more as the days passed. I have heard tell of the deep oil reserves in the far West, emerging at first as a trickle and then a moment comes when the powers of the earth unrestrained push the oil up with a great and sudden rush and there is no stopping it. This was how Josephine's talking came on, and I the prospector there to catch it.

The people of her early life, perhaps you have heard their names already from Jack. Mr. and Mrs. Bell, her owners at

Bell Creek. Lottie, the closest she had to a mother. Louis, the boy who cared for her, who was sold away. Great hardship was delivered on Josephine there, though in many ways her lot was better than that of the field hands. Her physical needs, she said, were met. Food, clothing, and the like. She spoke well of the lessons she received from her Missus, an invalid for whom she cared. And her painting, a subject on which she spoke most passionately. She carried with her some pictures of her own creation, on the back of each she put the name of her subject, and they are indeed marvels. There seemed a tenderness in Josephine towards her Missus for these kindnesses, and it was indeed rare I think for a house girl to be given rein to pursue such activities. But Josephine held a deep anger too. The details she conveyed were spare. I did not press her to explain.

Josephine's determination never to return again to Bell Creek was steadfast. She had run once before, some years previous, and circumstances had required her to turn back. She wished never to repeat that journey, and her conviction on this point left no room for doubt. I knew she would find her way to freedom, with or without my assistance. I remember her face alive in the weak flicker of our low fire. It was some days still before we would reach Philadelphia when she told me of the morning she had returned to Bell Creek after her first attempt at escape. She described a sudden storm, crows circling overhead as though expecting a death, and her despair. Her face became a flame itself then as she talked, melting half into darkness, half into the brightest light.

Those 10 days and nights with Josephine were a salve to me, the cool night air on my skin and my mind clear, free of drink. I do not know if she sensed my feelings for her, that I had begun to love her. It seems strange to write that word, yet I can think of no other.

The experience of love, for me, was new. There was an element of protection in what I felt—she was only just beyond girlhood, 17 she believed was her age, and her injuries as I have already described were grave. Her cough did not relent as we traveled but grew worse with the hardships of our journey, the constant exposure to open air and sun and dust. I did my best to keep her cool in the days and warm and dry at night, but I feared such efforts were paltry gatekeepers against the illness at the door.

I wished to protect her, yes, but there was more. How to describe it? A purity, a release, a calm. I wanted nothing from her, only to hear the timbre of her voice as my feet rested on the dirt and my eyes leaned heavy in their sockets. Only to watch her face as she spoke. I told her of my parents, my upbringing, the medical college and my work as a country doctor. I did not tell her of Dorothea or that night at my brother's farm. In truth I was ashamed, I did not want to disturb the peace of those nights, and her image of me. She saw me, I believe, as a good man who had wandered astray and had acted, as I pulled her up onto my horse, to return to myself. I did not wish to dissuade her of this view. If she believed it, perhaps it might be true, and I found great hope in this. There was that, too, in my love for her. Hope, for a different way, for a life where she and I might sit and talk for hours, undisturbed, where my past did not matter, nor the color of my skin nor hers. Hope for myself, that in saving her I might too save myself, and save in a way the lost Dorothea. It may seem strange but I saw in Josephine much of Dorothea. The same spirit and tenderness and a quickness, too, in her eyes, that behind them lay vast imaginings and journeys and struggles, a world unto herself, and I wished only that she might allow me residence there for it seemed a place of many marvels.

During the days, as we rode, my thoughts raced along, past Philadelphia, up farther north, to a new life for us together. I wanted to believe in it and I suppose for a spell I did: I pictured us dressed in clean cottons and walking beside a river under towering maples, or oaks, continuing until the river widens and spills out into a vast harbor and then the sea. I treated a man once who had been to Boston and he told me about the cool spray of salt on your face and the deep calls of the ship's foghorns as they left the safe harbor, the smart horse carriages traversing the roads and the spiny red lobsters, their meat the sweetest you might ever taste. It seems the city is built up against the sea, and the river Charles leads you along until you are there, directly before it, with nothing to see but white surf and a disappearing dark horizon until the great cities of Europe.

It was a dream of my own imagining. I did not tell Josephine. I never said a word of love, nor did she. The city of Philadelphia was our destination, and there I would ensure her safe passage to Canada, and we would part ways. We did not speak of continuing farther on together and I do not know if the thought ever crossed her mind. I wish now that I had said more. Now, I revisit those nights and I think how events might have changed had I said to her, *Come with me, let us both escape.*

If there is one lesson I wish to bestow upon you, one shred of wisdom I have gained from my living, dying days, it is this: let your heart lead you, do not be afraid, for there will be much to regret if reason and sense and fear are your only markers.

Finally we neared our destination. I set up camp in a small clearing by a winding creek, just outside the city limits. Alone, I went farther along the city road with the aim of finding Josephine some proper clothes, for her ragged attire marked her as a fugitive. Recently the city had seen rain, and the water falling upon the dry dust of many weeks had turned the road into a veritable river of red mud that slowed my passage and clumped heavily around my horse's hooves.

At the city's southern periphery, I found a suitable shop. The woman at the counter was not keen to serve me, rough and unshaven as I was from the days and nights we'd been riding, but she saw that my money was as green as the next man's and so she obliged me. I walked out into the sunshine with a simple ready-made blue dress and shoes with long leather lashes, a razor, and some soap for myself, and I rode back to where I'd left Josephine at our camp.

It's nice, she said when she saw the dress, and touched its clean blue length. She washed in the creek while I waited and she returned a different-seeming woman, with the dress fitting close to her shoulders and waist, her hair smoothed back and her high clear forehead, and the bad eye open, the skin nearly healed. I do not know much of beauty but Josephine then in that new dress is the picture I hold in my mind of the word.

We rode first through the smaller southern townships, Kingsessing and Oxford, and then eastwards, towards the Delaware and the city proper, which seemed much changed from my time there three years before. The streets rattled with an unholy clamor of carriages and surging crowds and reeked with the stench of horse and steam and rubbish. After our time of travel through empty grassland, it was an assault to the senses, both exhilarating and nauseating. Josephine said not a word as we rode through the streets, but I felt her body tense behind me in the saddle and twist and turn as she looked at all that we passed.

I directed us first towards the university district, the area with which I was most familiar. As we rode along the wide and busy Market Street, I saw a notice affixed to a post: REWARD written in thick black letters. Such advertisements were common enough, Philadelphia being a center for abolitionist activity and consequently a frequent destination for fugitives. This poster was similar to others I had seen but, as we passed it, I leaned forward to read the full notice and there, I saw her name, Josephine. I felt Josephine stiffen behind me: she too had read the poster, the description of herself there for all to see, the $100 reward offered by Robert Bell for her return.

I spurred the horse onwards. Immediately I navigated us away from the university, as far as I could think to go, away from that poster and any who might have read it. I turned towards the navy yard, close to the river, a district largely unfamiliar to me but one I knew to be more accommodating to people of all walks and stations, a place where someone desiring of privacy might easily find it.

I hired us a pair of rooms over a simple tavern with a washtub between them. The man who handed me the key looked at Josephine from head to toe and after refused to meet my eyes.

Josephine's room was small and bare: a thin mattress on a metal frame, a small table set beside it and a picture of white frothy flowers tacked above. On the far wall was a single window dressed with a long pale curtain through which filtered weak, streaky sunlight. The air within was hot and used and reminded me that countless others had passed time here, slept here, breathed and coughed and washed here.

Josephine went immediately to the window and pulled the curtain back. I closed the door behind me and stood just inside the room with my hat in my hand like a visitor.

Thank you for bringing me away from there, she said. Her shoulders were a square of dark against the rectangle of light in the window. She turned to me and the gratitude shone on her face and I stepped farther into the room. I stood beside her at the window and watched the figures on the street below: a man with muddy boots leading his horse, two finely dressed gentlemen deep in discussion, a hatless woman struggling to keep hold of two small children as they turned their heads, distracted by all that the big city had to show.

When I placed one hand on her shoulder, it was not to reassure her or suggest an intimacy we had not shared. I meant only to reassure myself, to feel that her living breathing person stood beside me, that we had come safely from Charlotte County, Virginia, to this place, this sun-streaked room in the city. She did not seem to mind my hand, and we stood like that at the window, looking down at the ordinary people passing on the road, the seconds seeming paused for us, as though the movement below bore no relation to the stillness above. After a spell I let my hand fall back at my side and told her that I must venture out. I had an idea of where to go to find those more knowledgeable than I in the practice of freeing slaves. There was a Vigilance Committee there in Philadelphia, with funds and connections, well known for its abolitionist efforts.

I paused in the doorway as Josephine moved to sit upon the bed. I didn't know what I'd find beyond the gate at Bell Creek, she said in a wondering, quiet way.

She looked at me, the softest I had seen her face in all our time together. And what have you found? I asked.

It took some time for her to answer. Finally she said, The first time I ran, I was afraid, and I found no help and so I turned back. The second time, I was ready, I felt strong. But the men at the undertaker's were waiting for me. It made no difference, what I'd done and what I'd tried to do. I thought then that Lottie was right. There was no hope for me, no hope for any of us because it was not the time. There was no use in trying if redemption was not upon us. But you have shown me different. She paused. I found you, she said.

I could only repeat her words. I found you.

At that moment I saw the exhaustion in her. Her cough remained very bad. She had tried in vain to hide from me the blood that spotted her hands after a spell passed through her and I could see the disease gaining strength as it progressed through her weakened form. Rest now, I told her, and she nodded. She raised her hand and waved good-bye to me and smiled as I closed the door.

I had an address for the Vigilance Committee, but it was not a street with which I was familiar. On foot, I walked north, away from the river, in the direction I believed the Committee offices to be located. For over an hour, it seemed, I roamed. I was directed first this way by a passerby and then that way by another. Having no map, I relied on these directions from kindly strangers, but the results were often inconsistent and I soon found myself in knots, going around the same perimeter of blocks located still within that low district where we had found lodging.

It was on one such pass that something in the mud of the road caught my eye. A gem or nugget of gold, I thought at first, some prospector's treasure dropped here from a pocket or saddle bag, but when I bent to pick it up I saw it was merely a simple stone, no bigger than a plum, but cut through with brilliant colors that seemed to capture the very essence of Josephine's eyes. I wiped the mud from the stone and slipped it into my pocket with the idea of giving it to her, a small token of our time together.

I lifted my gaze and it was then I saw Bo. He was unmistakable: tall, strong, his head a striking smooth and shiny convex of the darkest brown. He was standing beside a shop window, staring straight at me as I paused in the mud, my hand still within my pocket, gripping the hard round shape of the stone. The hatred and bitterness on his face were very strong. Beside Bo, his back to me, was the figure of the patroller Josiah. I knew that where Bo and Josiah were, certainly Mr. Rust would not be far off. Surely they had brought Bo to assist in the capture of Josephine.

I held Bo's burning gaze and, for a fleeting moment, I wondered if he might not hold his tongue. Josiah himself had not seen me, so perhaps I might evade detection. But I recalled the sounds Bo had made as he beat upon the locked door of Mr. Rust's shack. I recalled the smooth steel of the padlock as I slipped it closed. Bo would show me no pity, nor any to Josephine. I had assured that outcome as surely as if I had stood on that street corner and called to Josiah myself.

I turned and fled.

As I hastened back to the tavern, the red mud of the road sucked at my boots such that every step required great effort. I heard shouts from behind and turned to see the figures of Bo and Josiah pushing through the crowds, following me. I increased my speed, seeking to lead them away from our tavern where Josephine waited, but my sense of disorientation was extreme and I found myself passing the tavern door once, and then again as I struggled to find my way. The streets teemed with commerce, navy men and gamblers, the crowd spilling at one point from an open saloon door, and it was only the great commotion of this afternoon brawl that allowed me, at last, to evade my pursuers.

Finally, certain that Josiah and Bo had wandered far afield of our accommodation, I crossed the tavern threshold.

My boots now were caked with earth from my flight, their weight nearly double what it had been at the outset of my journey. I left red weeping footprints as I mounted the steps to Josephine's room and cursed my slow heavy motions. We must leave at once. I felt the greatest urgency.

I knocked upon Josephine's door but heard no movement from within. I called her name, softly at first but then louder and louder. Again and again I knocked and then tried the knob but it would not give way. Finding myself with no alternative, I threw my shoulder against the door. The weight of my body forced the cheap lock and, with only the barest of groans, the door swung open.

Inside, the room was empty and calm. The curtain blew lazily before the open window and a chair was pulled to the sill, as if recently someone had been gazing out. I wondered what Josephine had seen from this view, if she had witnessed Bo and Josiah's relentless pursuit, if she had feared I was leading them here to her. Once before she had walked into a slavecatcher's trap. Had she imagined another one?

A great unease came over me. I considered then that perhaps Josephine believed me akin to Mr. Rust, that she had fled from my company and now wandered the streets alone. I moved to the window and looked down to the street below, my feelings now so far removed from the peace of those moments I had lingered there with Josephine. Frantically I searched the street for Josephine's form, for Bo, Josiah, and Mr. Rust. But I saw only the passing faces of strangers.

I turned from the window, thinking I must go out to find her, but I saw then her shoes, the ones I had purchased just that day, set neatly beside the bed. For a moment I stood in the center of the room in a state of confusion and despair. Where had she gone? It was only then I remembered the washroom adjacent. A narrow door on the far side of the room allowed admittance and this door was closed. I walked to it and knocked once, then twice with no response. I held my ear to the wood and heard at first silence but then a gentle lapping of water. Josephine? I said and my voice, hoarse from my previous calling, rang rough and hollow in the room's still air. There was no reply. I did not want to impose upon her modesty, but I longed to explain myself and the need to leave this district, perhaps even the city, at once. And so I opened the door.

She was there, in the tub, the water full against the edge. The red of her blood colored the water a dark crimson close to her arms and across her chest but flowed into a lighter red and then pink as it traveled down her legs and feet and into the open end of the bath. Her bone-handled knife rested on the tiled floor, its blade shining as though afterwards she had rinsed it clean. Her eyes flickered open as I entered and she turned to look at me and smile. It was like the smile of gratitude she had given me earlier that day, but fuller: full of exhaustion and forgiveness and escape. I thought of the open window and the unmistakable figures of Bo and Josiah, the pistols that hung at their belts, their loud angry calls as they chased me through the streets. The reward poster with her name and description. Josephine had believed we were found. And her illness, the blood in her cupped palm: she could run no further. Her resolve never to return to Bell Creek had been absolute, and this I understood.

I kneeled against the cold tiles and took one hand from the bath; it was cool and wet and slippery from the blood that still coursed from her opened wrist. I held her fingers gently as though they were the greatest of treasures. I held her hand until it went slack.

In that tavern room Josephine left for me a request. A note on the bed. She had written:

Stanmore plantation, Charlotte County, Virginia, a mulatto boy of four years old, my son. Deliver him from that place.

There is a certain kind of man who is forever searching. He wanders from place to place, he looks hard into the eyes of women and men in every town, maybe he scratches the earth or wields a gun, remedies illness or writes books, and there is always a vague emptiness within him. It is the emptiness that drives him and he does not know even how to name the thing that might fill it. No idea of home or love or peace comes to him. He does not know, so he cannot stop. On and on he moves. And the emptiness blinds him and pulls at him and he is like a newborn baby searching for the teat, knowing it is there, but where?

And sometimes such a man is handed a gift. A gift of direction. A path that is marked for him and there, yes, this will ease your suffering, it is sure. This will cure you, it will fill you up, at least for a time. There will be a home, and love, there will no longer be the sorrow when you look at a cold night sky, the sorrow as the sun rises and the mist burns away. This is what Josephine gave to me. The love I felt for her found its purpose in you.

I traveled to Charlotte County. I saw the deserted Bell Creek, the place she had left. It was empty save for squirrels fat from the unused seed. No one could tell me where Robert Bell had gone, only that his wife was buried there, in a poplar grove beside the mounds of her dead children.

I saw the fence, the river, the slave shacks where Josephine began her life. Only God above knows what became of the ones left after Mrs. Bell's death, Lottie, Winton, and the others Josephine described to me, their names already gone from my memory.

I queried those I met as to the location of the Stanmore place. They pointed me there and, finally, I found you.

You have your mother's eyes, the turn of her lips and long graceful arch of her neck, and the instant I laid eyes upon you I knew you were her son. Mr. Justice Stanmore was a wealthy man, a very fat, very pale man whose eyes seemed to grow in size and sheen as he realized the extent of my interest in you.

At the Stanmore place they called you Joseph, they said it was the name you came with, and so this reminder of your mother Josephine you keep every day.

With this letter I enclose your mother's pictures of the boy Louis, Lottie and Winton, and Josephine's mistress, Lu Anne Bell. The stone that reflects the colors of Josephine's eyes, I have kept for myself and trust that you will forgive me this small liberty.

I know that I can never be so deserving as to call you son. My sins pile up around me, voices of those men and women sold back into enslavement by my hand call to me at night, and I know that peace is beyond me now. The happiest days I have known were the ones with your mother and the summer spent with my brother and his Dorothea. That is why I leave you here with Jack. I know that he will be the best of fathers to you, that you will thrive in the new western lands. I know that your mother watches over you. I know that you will lead a good and happy life and grow to be a far better man than ever I could be.

Yours most faithfully,
Caleb T. Harper

Lina sat unmoving in her twilit room. She had not thought to light a lamp as she read and now she sat with the pages close to her face, resting against the tops of her legs, her knees drawn up, her back against a pillow on the bed. She had forgotten she wore socks on her hands, she had become so adept at turning the pages with them, but now the scratchy feel of the thin cotton surprised her when she reached up to wipe her eyes. Outside the street seemed hushed, as though the modern world had, for the moment, gracefully retreated.

Caleb wrote about Josephine's pictures, the ones that Jasper now held: Louis, Lottie and Winton, Lu Anne Bell. But Nora had said that Caleb's letter was sealed when it came to her. Did Joseph ever know the truth about his mother? Was this why the meaning of those drawings had been lost to time?

Lina removed the tidy, frail pages of Caleb's letter from her lap and replaced them into the envelope Nora had given her. She needed nothing more. The path ahead was easy. The 1870 Oregon census, Jack Harper, Joseph Harper, marriages recorded, births announced, deaths noted. Lina could now trace from Josephine's son to the next generation and the next and the next; now she would know Josephine's descendants, their names, where they lived, their occupations, when they died, who they married, who they left behind.

It was silly to think of this as a loss but Lina felt it nonetheless. She had known that Josephine was dead, of course she had, but for Lina, Josephine had breathed and planned and run. She had run away to someplace better, but she hadn't found it, and Lina felt this as an aimless sort of grief, the kind she had felt in her father's studio, looking at the pictures of a Grace she didn't want to see. She felt cheated of a possible past that had never been. Lina wanted to write a different history and, for a time, she thought that she had.

TUESDAY

Gray-faced, rumpled, and staring, Lina and Garrison slouched in their usual chairs in Dan's office. Neither had slept more than three straight hours of the previous seventy-two. The reparations brief, all 112 pages of it, sat on Dan's desk.

Dan and Dresser walked in, the two of them chuckling as though one had just finished telling a discreetly clever joke. Dresser wore uncharacteristically casual clothes—a pale pink button-down shirt tucked into stiff dark-blue jeans, and the look made him seem smaller, somehow less authoritative. Dan walked to his desk, and Dresser folded himself into the chair beside Lina. Dresser's assistant, also in jeans, entered last, closed the door, and perched on the edge of a chair by the window. Lina still had never heard the man's name.

"I'm afraid Jasper has been delayed," Lina said. "Jasper Battle, the plaintiff. He just called me and said he got stuck underground, some problems with the subway, but he's only a few blocks away now."

"No problem," Dan said. "Gives me a chance to say to the two of you, well done." He patted the brief as though it were a small dog. "I know you worked hard on this and it shows. Excellent work."

"Yes, I must agree," Dresser said.

Movement outside drew Lina's attention away from Dresser. On the other side of the windows, a cleaner edged into view, pulling his platform of gray aluminum farther into Dan's hard-earned Manhattan view. The cleaner floated: wiper, hard hat, sky.

"I'm particularly pleased that we managed to find Josephine Bell's descendant," Dan continued. "I was just reading about her in the *Times*—Ron, did you see that piece? I understand the Stanmore Foundation is issuing a claim against the gallery. It's all great publicity for us. Josephine Bell will be the most famous slave since . . . since . . . Well, she'll be famous! Regardless of where this whole authorship question ends up. It's a fantastic controversy. Fantastic."

As Dan spoke, Dresser shifted in his chair and momentously cleared his throat. His lips parted in preparation for speech.

Just then the door opened and Mary's head popped through. "Sorry to interrupt. Jasper Battle is here."

Jasper had worn a suit, though Lina hadn't asked him to, and it was just a touch too short in the sleeves and ankles, making him seem boyish and, to Lina, charming. He was pink-cheeked and damp around the temples from his crosstown dash to make the meeting. Hovering in the doorway, he bobbed his head in a general way toward the assembled group and smiled awkwardly, his eyes scanning for Lina, and then he saw her and the smile broadened. He stepped fully into the room.

"Jasper, come in," Lina said and rose to greet him. The others stood as he entered and there was the rustle of trouser legs straightening, the crack of knee joints bending, the squeak of chairs releasing their occupants, and then complete silence.

"This is Jasper Battle, Josephine Bell's great-great-great-great-grandson," Lina said. No one spoke. Garrison, Dan, and Dresser all stared at Jasper, who smiled back at them with some confusion.

"Nice to meet you all," Jasper said.

Lina glanced at Dan. His face was grim, the face of a man who suspects that his perfect win record may soon be coming to an end.

"Mr. Battle," Dan said, reaching out his hand. "A pleasure to meet you. Thanks for coming down, but we'll have to do some thinking on this one." He glanced at Dresser. "I'm not sure you're quite what we need for the lawsuit."

"He's Josephine Bell's direct descendant," Lina said. "I've fully verified him with public records."

"Mr. Battle—" Dan began.

"Please, call me Jasper."

"Jasper. You're too white. What else can I say? We can't have a white guy leading a lawsuit seeking reparations for the descendants of African American slaves! I don't care who you're related to!" Lina could almost see Dan's blood pressure rising beneath his blue shirt, his enlarged heart pumping furiously. "And the earrings? And I see you've got some *tattoos*? No, this isn't going to fly."

Jasper's face, open until that point, now hardened. "I—" he began, but Garrison interrupted him.

"I agree with Dan. You're not black enough." Garrison's hands were in his pockets, and his chin was angled down. "It just won't work," he said and slowly shook his head.

"Friends, friends—" Dresser held up a hand, palm outward in the universal symbol for *Stop*. Lina realized she had been wrong about the jeans; wardrobe notwithstanding, Dresser presided over a room with supreme authority. "Please, let's all sit down. Regardless of Mr. Battle's skin tone and whether it is the appropriate shade for our purposes, I'm afraid I must call a temporary end to our work on the reparations lawsuit."

"What?" Dan lowered himself heavily into his chair.

"Unfortunately, I can't go into the specifics. I'm afraid certain high-ranking government officials, on both sides of the political and racial divide, have expressed some . . . concern about Dresser Tech being associated with a lawsuit of this type. I understand that the federal apology for slavery will *not* be forthcoming. Not anytime soon. That will leave us without any sort of pressure against the corporate defendants, and with no graceful exit from the federal suit. And *that* will leave Dresser Tech high and dry. I can't sue my biggest customer, now can I? I'm sorry, but that's all I can say. I thought that we had an opening, some leverage where we needed it, but I was . . . overly optimistic."

Lina glanced at Dan, who was watching Dresser with a look of dismay.

"We need to wait," Dresser continued. "Bide our time. We'll come back to it when the circumstances in Washington are more amenable to the idea of *repair*. When my personal business interests won't be so negatively impacted. I won't let this case disappear, I promise you that, but I can't say when we'll be back. It may take some time."

Dan's door slammed shut, and Lina realized that Jasper had left the room. She ran to the hall and saw his tall back receding. "Jasper," she called. He stopped and turned and they faced each other down the gray carpeted passage, empty but full of the muffled *pat-pat* sound of typing, the incessant electronic beeping of an unattended phone. The space between them stretched long under the cold light and then a side door opened, a meeting spilled out, suits and khakis and cardigans, and when they cleared away, Jasper was gone.

Lina slipped back into Dan's office, into her chair, her feet pressed firmly to the floor, her arms gripping the side rests.

Dresser's assistant whispered loudly, "Ron," raised his eyebrows and tapped his watch.

"Now," Dresser said, glancing at the assistant, "I need to catch a flight but I wanted to come in personally and give my thanks for your hard work. This is a cause close to my heart. I'm grateful to you all for your dedication. Dan, we'll be talking again soon, no doubt."

Dresser and the assistant rose. Dan and Garrison jumped up to see them out, but it was Lina whom Dresser approached. She remained seated and he gazed down at her. "Lina, it was a pleasure to have worked with you. If you ever find yourself in need of employment, please give me a call." He handed her a card. "I need people with commitment to a cause. People who believe in what they're doing. It's a rarity in this world."

Without comment, Lina accepted the card. From the corner of her eye she saw Garrison, his features adrift with the effort of hiding his envy.

Dan ushered Dresser out of the room and then returned, falling into his cushioned desk chair with a soft whoosh of expelled air.

"I'm sorry to see this case go," he said, turning toward his antique law books. His face softened and, for a fleeting, hallucinatory moment, Lina saw a younger Dan gazing fixedly at the spines of the *United States Reports*. Under-eye shadows softened; the furrows beside his mouth relaxed; his hair became less obvious, more sincerely the characteristic of a man who didn't care what he looked like, who thought about justice and injustice, the workings of history, the cases to celebrate, the cases to be ashamed of. Then Dan turned his chair around and pulled himself flush against the desk, his face falling straight under the glare of a strip light and again he was Daniel J. Oliphant the Third, partner, Clifton & Harp LLP: tired, rushed, and annoyed.

"But it is what it is," Dan said. "And I've got a shitload of derivatives work coming in. A shitload. And to be frank, this reparations case has been a tough sell for the partnership. Dave doesn't think we need something like this right now. Easier ways to make the diversity point—it looks like we're making up Joe this year."

"Joe Klein, in M & A?" asked Garrison. Lina didn't know Joe Klein, besides knowing the fact that he was black.

"Yeah, Joe Klein." Dan nodded. "I probably shouldn't have mentioned it, it still has to go to final vote, but he's been working like a dog. The guy has no life. This isn't affirmative action, believe me. He's earned partnership. He'll slide by. So that will make three black partners, which is one of the better numbers in the city, trust me on that." Dan was speaking quickly, scanning through some papers on his desk, not looking at Lina or Garrison. Lina knew he shouldn't be telling them this kind of information, but something seemed to have come loose in Dan.

"And Garrison, your name is being bounced around for a white-collar matter. Something with Dave."

"Dave, Managing Partner Dave?" Garrison asked with a quick eagerness.

"The one and only. Be on your best behavior. If you impress him, you'll go far. Now get back to your office. I'm sure his secretary will be calling you soon."

Garrison left, casting a half-smile and raised eyebrows at Lina; he looked self-satisfied but dazed too, like a man who has just been given the thing he'd been asking for but is now unsure if it is in fact the thing he wants.

Lina knew she should leave too. There was no reason to stay. But was this really where the case would end, with the too-sweet smell of Dresser's cologne still hanging in the air and that photo of Dan's ageless, grinning twins staring at her?

The window washer hung suspended behind Dan's desk. His arms were in constant motion: circle, circle, pull, circle, circle, pull. He seemed perfectly at ease, more at ease than any of them, more sure of himself and the rightness of his task, the utility of it. Suspended thirty-four stories above a hard concrete planet.

"Did you read what I found?" Lina asked. "Did you see?"

"Yeah, good work, Lina. Probably a bit more detail than we need for the initial brief, but a good first draft. You'd make a great private investigator. I'll remember that about you. You're like a dog with a bone."

On another day, Lina would have said thank you. Or laughed. But now she said nothing.

She thought of Dan sitting in this office, looking out over Midtown, Bryant Park and the library, and, if he leaned his cheek against the glass and kept his gaze level, he would see the rising expanse of Lower Manhattan, Wall Street, and, long ago, the Twin Towers. The best of New York there from these windows. Dan spent his days and nights behind this expanse of glass, his wife and children behind glass, his antique books behind glass. Everything there for him to see, but he didn't know what any of it really felt like.

The harder road to walk, Dresser had said to her. And now, finally, Lina got it. Her road was not here. She didn't know where it might be, but it was not at Clifton & Harp LLP.

Lina stood up to leave. Dan had his head down, shuffling pages. A blue vein on his neck pulsed faintly. He said nothing as she walked out.

Back at her desk, Lina closed her door and opened the reparations brief to page thirty-four. She reread what she had written there:

As established by historical records, Josephine Bell gave birth to a boy, Joseph, on August 28, 1848, at Bell Creek in Lynnhurst, Virginia. Joseph lived until the age of four at the nearby plantation of Justice Stanmore, the largest antebellum tobacco grower in Charlotte County, Virginia. In 1852, Josephine Bell escaped from Bell Creek and died shortly thereafter in Philadelphia, PA.

Mr. Caleb Harper, an acquaintance of Ms. Bell's, purchased Joseph in early 1853 from Mr. Stanmore. Caleb Harper then transferred Joseph to his younger brother, Jack Harper of Stanton, Virginia, a widower with no children. In March 1853, Jack and Joseph Harper moved from Virginia to the new Oregon Territory, where they settled in what is now Hood River, Oregon, and raised cattle and wheat on a 110-acre farm.

Although he was born and raised in Virginia, military records indicate that Caleb Harper fought for the Union Army during the Civil War. He died in 1862 at the Battle of Antietam.

In 1866, Jack Harper formally adopted Joseph as his son.

Joseph Harper married Marietta Simpson in 1876. Marietta gave birth to two children, a daughter, Dorothea (1880), and a son, Caleb (1883). Jack Harper never remarried; he died in 1903, survived by Joseph and his two grandchildren.

Joseph Harper remained on the family farm until his death in 1921.

Dorothea Harper married Edward Shipley in 1900 and had five children. They remained in Oregon on the Harper family farm, increasing its size and diversifying its output to include flax and apples. The Shipleys became well known as pioneers in the use of grafted fruit tree production and Shipley Growers remains today one of the largest apple orchards in Oregon.

Caleb Harper married Amanda McCray in 1904 and had three children. The family relocated to New York, NY, where Caleb became a train operator and lived until his death in 1947.

From 1900 census data, it appears that Dorothea Harper

Shipley self-identified as African American and Caleb Harper self-identified as Caucasian. The family split along racial lines at this time and it appears that the Shipley and Harper branches did not maintain contact.

Between them, Dorothea Shipley, née Harper, and Caleb Harper were survived by six children, who had children, and they in turn had children who today reside in five different states and two foreign countries.

Although Josephine Bell died in 1852 at the age of seventeen, her descendants live on today. Her great-great-great-great-grandson, Jasper Battle, a musician, currently resides in New York City.

Mr. Battle is the lead plaintiff in this class action lawsuit seeking reparations for the historic harm of institutional slavery in the United States of America.

Lina flipped the cover of the brief closed. She walked out of her office, past Sherri's cubicle, past all those associate offices with half-closed doors, past the elevator, and up six flights of stairs until she reached Dan's office.

Outside, Lina paused to catch her breath. Then she pushed open the door.

"Dan, I need to talk to you."

Dan looked up slowly from the papers on his desk. "Lina. Yes?"

"I quit," she said and felt an uncomplicated, lovely thrill.

"What?"

"I quit. I'm leaving." Again, that rush.

"Hmm . . ." Dan frowned. "Why?"

Although Lina had anticipated this question, she still wasn't sure how precisely to answer it. "I—I—I can't do this job anymore. I don't *want* to do it. Clifton isn't for me." The words flew across Dan's expansive carpet and landed on the polished surface of his desk, weightier than any brief, truer than any law.

"Ha. I used to think the same thing." Dan tilted his head back. His eyes roamed the ceiling and then he lowered his gaze. "All right then, go." He shooed his hand at her. "And make sure you release all your time. We've decided to bill Dresser by the hour for all the reparations work. None of this contingency bullshit."

"Okay," Lina said. "Will do." She had been expecting some kind of drama, raised voices or persuasive argument, or at least a hug, but Dan remained firmly rooted behind his mammoth desk and Lina did not move toward him. "Bye, Dan," she said.

Dan smiled a tired smile; his climate-controlled bookshelves shifted off with what sounded like a sigh. "Good-bye, Lina."

LINA RETURNED TO HER OFFICE. Sherri was standing just outside her cubicle. "I heard you quit!" she said, giddy with the gossip.

"*Already?* But it just happened."

"Yeah, well. Mary." Sherri shrugged her shoulders, her neck disappearing for a moment within the muddle of her curls. "But listen, what do you need? The security guards will be here soon so—quick, how can I help?" Lina had never seen Sherri so eager to assist.

"Security guards?"

"Clifton doesn't like people hanging around. No long good-byes. Too much opportunity for sabotage." The last word Sherri said with a drawn-out drama as though this were a Bond film and Lina the turncoat.

Lina handed Sherri her copy of the brief with its numbered exhibits and the additional documents she'd uncovered in her search for Josephine Bell. "I need three copies of this. In three separate envelopes," she said.

"No problem." Sherri winked at Lina. "You know, I never pegged you for a Clifton lawyer anyhow."

Lina scanned the hallway for approaching security guards, but saw what could only have been a stray law school student attempting without success to send a fax. She heard the young woman curse faintly. Lina closed her office door, picked up her phone, and dialed the number for the Bell Center archives.

"Nora," she said. "It's Lina Sparrow. I was hoping we could talk about the Stanmore Foundation."

SHERRI RETURNED WITH THE COPIED documents and helped Lina pack up her things. There wasn't much—Oscar's small painting, the snow globe, the photo of her parents, an extra pair of pantyhose. The statuesque Meredith passed Lina's open office door and stopped, wide-eyed.

"You're *leaving*?" she exclaimed, and hugged Lina good-bye with a sincerity that made Lina wonder if, all this time, she had misjudged Meredith. Perhaps they could have been friends after all, and Lina felt a shallow stab of regret.

"We'll miss you, Lisa," Meredith said, and Lina only smiled and grabbed her cardboard box, which was small enough to fit under one arm. She marched steadily down the long hallway toward the elevator bank, pausing only at the office of a corporate partner who liked to play high-volume reggae music on his Bose system. Steel drums and *Stir it up, little darling* drifted from his half-cracked door. Lina listened for a moment, catching a glimpse of a bald, bobbing head, and then kept walking.

In the elevator, Lina exhaled as she sank away from the canned office air and light, down to the gleaming lobby of black marble and chrome, out onto the sidewalk, people and sunshine and smog, honking cars, a bus wheezing to a stop at the corner and Lina quickened her pace to catch it.

THIRTY-SIX MINUTES LATER, LINA STOOD in a different sort of office building, this one ivy-covered and loud with rushing students, walls cluttered with posters announcing end-of-year exam dates, review sessions, books for sale. After wandering through a maze of narrow, cluttered corridors, Lina finally found the right

door: PORTER R. SCALES, STERLING J. HAWKES PROFESSOR OF ART HIS-
TORY. According to the website for "Modern American Painting," the
class he was teaching this semester at Columbia, Porter was currently holding open office hours. Lina knocked.

"Just a moment," Porter's voice called, and she heard the rustling
of papers, a cough, and Porter opened the door.

"Lina! How nice to see you. I thought it was odd, someone
knocking on my door. No one comes to office hours. I mean, not a
single student. Am I so brazenly clear in my lectures? Or do they
just not care?"

"Brazenly clear, I'm sure," Lina said.

"Please come in," Porter said and Lina stepped into his office,
which was small and jumbled but with a lovely view over the Columbia quad, emerald-green trapezoids bordered with straight-edged
paths, the students moving along them with the purpose and steady
pace of worker ants.

"I can't stay long," Lina said. "I just wanted to give you this." She
handed over the packet of copied documents. "This is everything
I've uncovered in my research into Josephine Bell. Josephine was the
artist, not Lu Anne. These documents prove it."

Lina paused. Her heart was beating very fast.

"And I've written down the phone number of Nora Lewis, the
archivist at the Bell Center. She's agreed to speak with you. The
Stanmore Foundation isn't playing fair. Their lawyers are destroying
evidence. Nora will give you the details."

Porter took the papers from Lina and looked at them with confusion.

"But why are you giving all of this to me?"

"I've quit my job. And the reparations case has been suspended,"
Lina said quickly, not pausing to explain any further. "But Porter, I
want you to write about Josephine Bell. I want you to tell her story. I
want her to get credit for what she did. Please. She can't just disappear."

Porter said nothing. And then a smile spread wide across his face, of understanding and of gratitude. "Of course. Of course I'll tell her story. This is huge, Lina."

"I hope so."

"You know, I've been wanting to write about her. Since this whole thing blew up. A book, maybe. It's been a while since I wrote a book. I want to call it *The Forgotten Slave* or maybe *Genius Denied*. Something like that." Porter narrowed his eyes and tilted his chin in contemplation.

For a moment, Lina did not respond. She gazed around Porter's office, at the framed Bell reproductions on the walls, *Lottie, Bell Creek at Dawn*, and then she saw another familiar picture, a pencil drawing no larger than an apple, of a young Porter, shaggy and smiling, and etched in the corner, a name: *Grace Janney Sparrow*. "What about calling it *The Artist: Josephine Bell*?" Lina said.

"Ah, yes." Porter nodded vigorously. "You're right, of course. Much better."

At the door, Porter paused, looking away from her, hands in pockets, and Lina remembered the last time they had seen each other, beneath the neon sign. The attraction she had felt for him that night had vanished, and Lina stepped forward and hugged him with a deep, genuine, platonic affection.

"Thank you, Porter," she said. "I'm so glad we can be friends."

As she crossed the Columbia quad, Lina called Jasper, a number she now knew by heart.

After an interminable number of rings, he picked up, his voice flat. "Hello, Lina."

"Jasper, don't hang up!"

"What do you want?"

"I want to apologize."

"Why did you set me up like that? I felt like an idiot. Too white. Jesus Christ."

"Listen, I've quit my job."

"You're kidding. Over this?"

"Yes and no," she said. "I'll tell you about it. Where are you now?"

Jasper did not answer immediately. A hot button of panic began to pulse within her. What if he wanted nothing more to do with her? "I'm sorry, Jasper," she said. "I really want to see you again. I don't want this to be the end."

There was a pause of rampant possibility, and Lina let her mind and heart be still for just this one small moment to wait for Jasper's response.

"I don't either," he said.

Lina stopped walking, and a part of her went quiet. The urgency of the morning, the thrill of quitting, all of it dropped noiselessly away. "Can I meet you somewhere?" she asked.

Jasper hesitated. "I want to, Lina, but I'm not sure I have time." He was on his way to Grand Central, he told her, heading to his mom's for a couple of days to talk about Josephine Bell and his father. "There's a lot we need to think about," he said.

"But I have some documents to give you," Lina responded, gratified that finally she was in a position to help him. "It's everything from the reparations case. You'll want to see these—they'll help you make any claims on the Bell work." She also felt a strong need to finish what she had started just hours ago in Dan's office; it was like an itch, almost an ache.

"Lina, why is it so hard to say no to you?" Jasper laughed. They agreed to meet at the clock in twenty minutes, ten if Lina could find a cab and traffic was moving.

Lina hung up the phone. Backpacked students swerved around her on the path, their bodies bent under the weight of their loads, but she didn't move. She stood and breathed in the smell of spring. Here the quad's lush lawn seemed to produce a different quality of air, better than sidewalks or subways or corporate law firms. Her attention was drawn across the grassy expanse and Lina watched in awe as a young man flung himself into the air with expert grace and precision and caught, behind his right calf, a yellow Frisbee.

LINA ARRIVED AT GRAND CENTRAL first and sat on the ground beside the tall, four-sided clock, her back against the kiosk wall. The stone floor chilled her and she pulled her cardigan tight around her shoulders. To Lina, Grand Central Station had always seemed the absolute center of the universe, and the arched ceiling—painted that otherworldly blue with planets and stars within their careful orbits, marking out stories in the sky—seemed to confirm her theory, and the shared faith that, yes, this was where paths crossed in a dance of fate and luck and science, this was where new constellations formed. Here, if your patience held, you might see every person, not every person on the planet but everyone who mattered to you, past and future, and you might lock eyes or you might pass each other by and never know that chance had brought you once before in such proximity, close enough to touch. Lina loved that sense of possibility. The opening up of humanity, so many faces presented here in states of departing and arriving, each a perfectly contained, self-directed presence and yet vulnerable too to the greater forces of timetables and weather, accidental looks, brushed hands, stumbles, the lost and found. Perhaps the man she would marry was in this hall right now. Perhaps her new roommate. Or whoever had bought Oscar's *Enough* portrait of Grace, someone who now looked every day at a picture of her mother. Perhaps Dan's wife and children, hurrying to their weekend home. Or her father with Natalie. Or even Grace herself, continuing a journey that began long before Lina was born, that had nothing and everything to do with Lina. Maybe a shiver traveled down Grace's back and she looked behind her, just as that dark-haired woman did now, paces from where Lina sat, the woman's face pale and blank, her arms crossed against her chest, her body set in a posture of waiting.

Lina saw Jasper before he saw her. He was walking down the incline that led from Forty-second Street, through the public art room and down into the hall. He was backlit, his face and body mere silhouette, but Lina recognized the square of his shoulders, the long legs, the smooth head. He wore his librarian clothes and carried a duffel bag in one hand. She squinted into the light and waved. He waved back and before Lina could stand, he was at the kiosk, placing his bag on the ground, sitting beside her on the cold stone.

"Hi," she said.

"Hi."

"I wanted to give you the documents. You may need some of this, if you do try to assert rights over all the Bell pictures." She handed a packet to Jasper, the librarian–rock star, the white-black man, the near-stranger who was not a stranger to her.

"I still don't know what we're going to do. I'll talk it over with my mom. But thanks." He slid the packet into his bag. "So, no more lawyer." He turned to look at her. "What are you thinking now?"

There were many ways to take this question and many ways to answer it. Right now Lina was thinking about Josephine Bell, and Jasper, and how improbable it was that the one had led her to the other. How improbable and wonderful that Jasper was here at all, sitting beside her on the cool stone. She looked at him, at the eyebrow arching plumb true over his left eye, at his eyes gleaming gold as the rim of the clock over their heads. He was waiting for an answer. Lina, what are you thinking now?

"I'm not sure," she answered. "Maybe immigration law. Or maybe I'll go work for Mr. Dresser, or leave the law altogether. I need to think about it for a while." Just a few weeks ago, the idea that she did not have a plan, that no chart outlined her future career goals, would have been unthinkable. But something had released in her, expectation and desire had altered. She did not want six-minute increments and clients' whims to dictate how she spent her waking hours; she did not want to live a life ruled by reason.

Lina looked up at the celestial ceiling and she thought of her mother, the woman who hummed a wordless tune, who smelled of pepper and sugar, the woman in Oscar's paintings, the woman Porter had loved, the woman who drew those portraits, who invented a family tree, the woman who could not bear to leave her daughter but could not bear to stay.

And Lina remembered the scrap of paper, the number that, for the past three days, she had carried deep in her pocket. "My dad gave me something," she said. "A phone number to call." She wriggled down to pull it out. She flattened out the wrinkles on her thigh, smoothing the paper with her palm.

"Whose is it?"

"My mother's. I haven't seen her or spoken to her in twenty years. Since I was four. I thought she was dead. But she's not."

A confluence of arriving trains spilled people onto the concourse, and Lina felt herself and Jasper suddenly cocooned by the shuffling feet and knobby knees of passengers in transit. She heard snatches of conversation, caught a whiff of floral perfume that followed a woman with a pink suitcase gliding silently behind her on rollers.

Jasper sat up straight and turned to Lina. "Twenty years. That's a long time," he said. Just that, and as the rush of passengers trickled away, Lina felt an intense gratitude that she did not have to explain, she did not have to answer any questions. Yes, it had been a long time. And in those years lived an ocean of sadness and of love, she and her father, moments over meals, together in silence and in play, Oscar's laugh and paint-stained fingers, the small straight line that appeared between his eyebrows when he focused hard, the line that Lina saw furrow deeper every year, elaborate birthday hats and tidy grocery charts, and her childhood self posing for that portrait with the frog, and Lina suddenly and vividly remembered the frog, with a smell like moss, shimmering eyes, and its skin had not felt slimy, only damp and clean in her own small hands.

Lina handed Jasper the phone number.

"Will you dial?" she asked.

Jasper pushed the numbers and Lina took back the phone and listened to the empty distant ringing. Jasper's hand slid into hers, the fingers strong and warm, and she felt a little heart pulsing there in her palm where her skin met his, and she waited for a voice to answer.

Josephine

Josephine walks along the edge of the road, the dry dirt making the smallest of sounds beneath the weight of her boots. At first she is cautious and she starts at every noise, stopping in the bushes at the hoot of an owl, the far-off bark of a farmer's dog, but then she is bolder and she edges away from the shadows, toward the unrutted center of the road. She walks steadily, with purpose. The road lies straight ahead and straight behind and it is clear of people and animals. The wheat fields to her left and right ripple in a soft breeze, and it is silver that she thinks of, not yellow. It was yellow she always saw at Bell Creek when she'd look out over the distant fields, yellow as Missus painted them, but these fields are silver now as the stalks bend in the moonlight, a luminous and reflective silver that seems not of this world or any she has ever imagined.

Missus Lu did not bury my baby, Josephine thinks. It would have been an easy thing, another small body laid down among the others. Did she hold that little boy and look into his eyes, hear his cry and only then decide to spare him? Or had she determined all along to show mercy? Josephine thinks of the seventeen small mounds, and the one long one for Papa Bo, and Missus Lu will soon lie there too, and then Mister beside her, and who next? Who will be left? Who have they loved? Who has loved them? She feels a sharp pity for Mister and Missus Lu, the people who have owned her, and then the feeling is gone.

She thinks of Rebecca, her mother, and the slave cemetery situated just east of the Bell family plots, just beyond a rigid row of poplars. Mister liked to say the trees grew that way by nature's design but Josephine always believed it was some person who planted them, some human hand that made that division, for nothing in nature is ever so straight and clear. On the north side of that line of trees, Rebecca lay buried, and Hap, Calla's children, and perhaps Lottie and Winton too someday. Josephine hopes they will lie there together, that the end of their days will see Lottie and Winton side by side.

Josephine hears the night crickets singing, and the sound seems suddenly loud and raucous, as though they have just noticed her passing on the road and are singing to her for comfort, for joy.

Again she looks to the wheat, and beyond to the dark sleeping mountains, brooding against the deep blue-black of the sky, and the fields appear silver, they do, not yellow at all. It is silver, a pure shining silver that glows heavenly in the moonlight and she does not question it, she knows it is silver she sees, for she is an artist with the untethered eye of an artist and everywhere beauty lies down at her feet.

Acknowledgments

I n researching the antebellum South and the Underground Railroad, a number of sources proved invaluable to me. *Bound for Canaan: The Underground Railroad and the War for the Soul of America* by Fergus M. Bordewich, *The Hemingses of Monticello: An American Family* by Annette Gordon-Reed, and *The Known World* by Edward P. Jones all helped me immeasurably to better understand the complexities of the time period and the diversity of individual experience. I also returned again and again to two websites: *Born in Slavery: Slave Narratives from the Federal Writers' Project, 1936–1938,* contained on the Library of Congress website (http://memory.loc.gov/ammem/snhtml/snhome.html), and a site maintained by the University of Virginia, *The Valley of the Shadow: Two Communities in the American Civil War* (http://valley.lib.virginia.edu). I would encourage anyone interested in the time period to make use of these valuable resources. For information on slavery reparations claims, I found the work of Deadria Farmer-Paellmann and the Restitution Study Group most helpful. It goes without saying, of course, that any errors of history, fact, or law contained in *The House Girl* are mine alone.

This novel would have remained in the depths of my computer files had it not been for the encouragement, friendship, and support of a great many people. Thank you to all the family and friends who provided such constructive commentary on the various drafts and voices of *The House Girl* and offered your support in innumerable other ways: Cheryl Contee, Elissa Steglich, Mari Hinojosa, Jay Conklin, Christina Conklin, Laura Conklin, Riisa Conklin, Drew Dresman, Kate Conklin, Nicola O'Hara Cregan, Beth McFadden, Art Chung, Jessica Silverthorne, Karen McHegg, Carol Vogt, Adrienne Spangler Connolly, Beth Shepherd, Ruth Whippman, and Shannon Huffman Polson. Thanks to Peter Mountford and his Hugo House class for helping me finish my book and to Karen Kennedy and Will Rieley for guidance on historic Virginia. I owe an enormous debt to Michelle Brower for picking me out of the slush pile, and to Katherine Nintzel and Lorissa Sengara for making the manuscript sing. Most important, to my children, Freya, Luke, and Rhys Maddock, for putting up with a mother who spends a lot of time in front of her laptop, and to my husband, Nicholas Maddock, for always saying *when,* never *if.*

About the book

Read on

About the author

Insights,
Interviews
& More . . .

Reading Group Guide

1. As a servant in the Bells' home, Josephine is literally "The House Girl." But how does this title also apply to Lina's character? What is the significance of Lina's leaving her father's house at the close of the story?

2. Separated by more than two centuries, the characters of Lina and Josephine never meet, but Conklin tells this story through each of their perspectives. What similarities do you find between these two women? What would each be able to teach the other?

3. On an empty page in her favorite book, Grace Sparrow writes "who is free?" We know that Josephine, Lottie, and the others at the Bell plantation are literally enslaved. But who else experiences a lack of freedom in this story? Do you think these characters achieve freedom by the close of the novel?

4. Lu Anne Bell's relationship to Josephine is complex. She shares the most intimate moments of vulnerability with her, allows Josephine freedoms that others enslaved at Bell Creek do not enjoy, and yet she does nothing to protect Josephine from Mister's violence. How do you explain these contradictions? And how does Josephine feel toward Lu Anne? How does she perceive her role in Lu Anne's life?

5. The definition of "family" is unclear in this story: Lina's mother is absent for all of her life; Josephine's son is fathered by her married master. As Lina reflects on her mother's artwork she wonders whether you can create family connections: "What is blood and what is decision?" What is your response?

6. Taking us back and forth between Josephine's and Lina's worlds, Conklin gives us an intimate look into the lives of both women. But Caleb Harper and Dorothea Rounds also act as narrators, speaking through their letters. What did their narrations add to the story? How did they change your understanding of Josephine and others living and working in the Bells' community?

7. At the close of the story Lina quits her job and announces to Oscar that she will move out of his home. Where does she find the resolve to make these two significant decisions? So little time has passed since she told Jasper that "not knowing" what her future held "would make [her] crazy." What has changed that Lina now feels bold enough to take such action?

8. Josephine "keeps" her memories in Mr. Jefferson's chest of drawers. How is this similar to Oscar's paintings of Grace? And how does Lina deal with her own memories of Grace? In both Lina's and Josephine's worlds, how do these characters confront the loss and pain they've experienced? How do they hide things away?

9. Jasper is humiliated when Dan and Garrison tell him that he is too white to be the lead plaintiff in the reparations case, and Lina is shocked to see him sent away. What does race mean to the men at Clifton & Harp? What does it mean to Lina and Jasper?

10. Josephine is shocked to learn that the son she gave birth to at age fourteen has survived and lives on a nearby farm. But even with this knowledge she decides to run alone. What do you make of this decision? Did she make this choice out of selfishness, a mother's love, or something else entirely?

11. Mr. Dresser says that the reparations lawsuit is worth $6.2 trillion, but is the money the most important thing to him? What does the reparations case mean for Dan? What does it mean for Lina?

12. Many of the characters are trying to atone for acts committed in the past—Caleb for his work with the slave catcher, Dorothea for her brother Percy's death, Oscar for not being a "good husband" to Grace. Do you think they are successful?

13. What is the role of religion in Josephine's world? How does religious belief both help and hinder Lottie?

14. Lina and Dorothea are both women seeking to excel in areas dominated by men—Lina, at a corporate law firm; Dorothea, in the abolitionist movement, what her father calls "not work for women." How do their experiences differ? How are they the same? ▶

15. In the final pages of the novel, Lina decides to call her mother, asking Jasper to dial the phone number. Why does Lina not dial the number herself? And what do you think Lina will say to Grace? Is she ready to build a relationship? Has she forgiven her mother for leaving?

The Story Behind
the Book

I was born on St. Croix in the US Virgin
Islands, a place known for rum and perfect
weather, and grew up in Stockbridge
Massachusetts, an old New England town
where houses have dirt basements and you
have to watch out for icicles falling off the
eaves in wintertime. These places could
not be more different, and yet my parents—
my mother an English teacher, my dad a
social worker—chose them both as home.
I don't remember much about St. Croix,
but I remember the stories my parents told
of their work at a local school, of the midwife
who raised me up to the sky when I was born,
and of their reasons for leaving: the threat
of violence so strong it thickened the air, the
group of high school students who routinely
broke into their house and, right before my
parents moved off the island, killed one of
their two kittens—the black one they left
alive, the white one they strangled. Now, this
is a metaphor I would not put in any story:
too obvious, too unbelievable. But this is
what slavery had done to that beautiful place,
my dad would say, the hurt was still raw.

In Stockbridge, some of those dirt
basements were said to have harbored
fugitive slaves on the Underground Railroad.
As a child I often imagined the people who
perhaps had hidden under our floors, fled
through our back gate. In third grade, we
studied the case of Elizabeth Mumbet
Freeman and walked to the Stockbridge
cemetery to make rubbings of her mossy
tombstone. She was born a slave but sued
for her freedom in a Massachusetts court
and won, and I remember being surprised
later—much later, in college—that no one
else had ever heard her name. Mumbet,
I remember saying. How could anyone
forget the story of Mumbet? ▶

The Story Behind the Book *(continued)*

I did not set out to write a novel about race or Virginia or slavery. In truth, I did not set out to write a novel at all. I have always written stories, but it was something I did for myself, and my stories always stayed safely within the confines of my notebooks and computer. About five years ago, I was working (relatively happily) as a corporate lawyer when I read a biography that used the term *slave doctor*. And for reasons I still cannot explain, an image came to me of a character, who I know now is Caleb Harper, riding a horse. Caleb holds out his hand to a young woman, a slave, and pulls her up onto his horse. That was it, the words *slave doctor* and that image. From there, I wrote the story of Dr. Caleb Harper and the slave whom he tries to help, Josephine Bell, and the woman he cannot forget, Dorothea Rounds.

After I finished the first draft, I put the story away, as I had done with all the others I'd written over the years. It seems a little dramatic to say that I then became obsessed with Josephine Bell, but I can't think of a more suitable word. I couldn't stop wondering about her world, how she lived, who she loved, what she wanted for her life. Over the next few months, I started to write Josephine's story, working early in the morning and late at night when I wasn't at the office, when my kids were asleep. As I wrote, I read: slave narratives, histories, novels, primary documents I found online. Two sources in particular were enormously enlightening and showed antebellum history in a way that, for me, was entirely new: a nonfiction book, *The Hemingses of Monticello*, by Annette Gordon-Reed and a novel, *The Known World*, by Edward P. Jones. Each book showed the complexity of relationships during the antebellum period and the vast range of individual experience, enslaved and free, black and white.

Those books surprised me. A few other things that arose in my research surprised me as well: that today there is no national museum dedicated to slavery, no national monument memorializing American slaves, no easy way to track African American ancestry in the same way it's possible to track relatives coming through, say, Ellis Island or other ports of entry for European immigrants. Indeed, very few historic plantation houses maintain the slave quarters or any evidence at all of the slaves who once lived there. Perhaps these things should not have surprised me, but they did.

At a certain point, I stopped reading. My research had become more paralyzing than helpful. The history of slavery in America is of course completely overwhelming. The mind can't stretch around the numbers or the horror, the massive waste of life. I kept returning to Josephine, this one woman, and her story. How did she run? Who helped her? What was she looking for? How did she survive? What did she think of the people who enslaved her?

I wrote a first draft of Josephine Bell's story and a series of letters written by Dorothea Rounds, a young woman active on the Underground Railroad. Dorothea's letters tell of her family's involvement in the Railroad and the night that Josephine appears at their door. In writing about Dorothea, I was indulging my old childhood fascination with the Underground Railroad, but I also had come to see her story as a necessary counterpart to Josephine's: two young women similar in so many ways yet separated irrevocably by the single most defining element of their time—race.

I now had three distinct but related narratives, those of Caleb Harper, Josephine Bell, and Dorothea Rounds. But I also had a full-time job and two small children. Once again I put the stories aside and turned my attention to family and profession. It was about this time that I realized a couple of things: first, that I was no longer happy in my law career; and second, that if I did not try to finish this book, I would always regret it.

So I quit my job. For what seemed like a very long time, I stared at my draft stories and wondered how to fit them together. Now, finally, I began to envision a novel. This is when the character of Lina Sparrow and the idea of a reparations lawsuit came into view. In my legal career, I'd always been interested in how the law has been used to make sense out of large-scale atrocities and injustice—through criminal prosecutions, payment of money, restitution of property, formal truth-telling or amnesty. I wanted to explore this idea in the context of American slavery, but not in literal terms—that is, I didn't want to focus on the legal issues (which would not make for a very compelling novel) but the ideas more generally of repair, identity, and personal justice. How does one repair the hurt done by a lost past? Who do you blame? How does an individual—not a society, not a "class," but an individual person—find some kind of peace, some kind of justice?

Lina is an organizer, levelheaded and driven. She's a better lawyer than I ever was, and her character helped give the book its structure and narrative arc. I wrote and rewrote Lina's section; I put all the stories together and took them apart again and again and again. Over the course of about nine months editing, cutting, restructuring, and rethinking, I arrived at *The House Girl* as it now (more or less) exists. Although the four main characters are as distinct as, say, St. Croix and Stockbridge, each is searching, I think, for the same things: personal meaning, a sense of home, and a sense of freedom. ∾

Q&A with Tara Conklin

New York Times bestselling author Maria Semple (*Where'd You Go, Bernadette*) sat down to chat with Tara about discovering Josephine's voice and how her upbringing in both St. Croix and Massachusetts inspired her writing.

This interview originally appeared on the blog Book Club Girl.

Maria Semple: *Tara, huge congratulations on* The House Girl. *How did this novel come into being?*

Tara Conklin: Thanks, Maria. The novel began as a short story that I wrote about six years ago. I came across the term "slave doctor" in a book I was reading, and the words made me stop. I became curious as to why a person dedicated to healing would take on such a role. From that initial spark of curiosity, I wrote a short story about a slave doctor, Caleb Harper, and two women appeared in his story. I say "appeared" because that's really how it seemed to happen—Josephine and Dorothea just showed up and demanded my attention. I couldn't stop wondering about these two characters, so I started writing separate stories about them, and I just kept writing.

MS: *Josephine, a house slave in 1852 Virginia, became one of your narrators. The other, Lina, is a lawyer in present-day New York. You practiced law before you became a novelist. Did Lina's voice come easily by comparison?*

TC: No, I actually found Lina's sections tougher to get right. I think because Lina's external world is more similar to mine, it was more difficult to imagine her—I kept bumping up against my own experience.

MS: *That's so surprising, that Josephine was the easier voice to get right.*

TC: Josephine came to me very organically—I felt that I knew who she was and what she wanted early on in the writing. Her character was inspired by two people: one was an African American artist named Mary Bell and the other was a former slave, Elizabeth Mumbet Freeman, who lived in my hometown during the eighteenth century. Mumbet said that if she could have one minute of freedom, only to die afterwards, she would make the trade. That strength of purpose helped me understand Josephine.

MS: *While she's not a narrator, the character of Lu Anne Bell looms large over the story. She's quite mysterious and wonderful. I'm curious if she, too, is partly based on a real person.*

TC: No, she is entirely fictional, but I'm glad that you thought otherwise! I wrote quite a bit of backstory for Lu Anne that never made its way into the novel: her childhood in Mississippi, how she met Mister, why they fell in love. I see Lu Anne as an essentially tragic figure—I think she wants to break out of the world she's been born into, but she can't quite transcend it.

MS: *You were born in St. Croix and grew up in Stockbridge, Massachusetts. Did growing up in these two vastly different environments influence you as a writer?*

TC: Both places are steeped in history, so they've given me an appreciation for and curiosity about the past and how it helps shape the present. Both places also have substantial ties to slavery. I don't remember much about St. Croix, but I grew up with my parents' stories of the island's racial tension, the horrible legacy of the sugarcane fields. When I was in elementary school in Stockbridge, I learned about the Underground Railroad and Mumbet (mentioned above), a slave who sued for her freedom in a Massachusetts court and won. These stories really stayed with me over the years.

MS: *What are you reading now?*

TC: I always have several novels on the go at once. Right now I'm reading *Zone One* by Colson Whitehead and *Wolf Hall* by Hilary Mantel, and I'm rereading *A Thousand Acres* by Jane Smiley, one of my all-time favorites. ∾

History Behind the Story*

THE UNDERGROUND RAILROAD occupies a near-mythical place in the American imagination. As a child, I remember envisioning actual iron-and-wood railroad tracks buried deep below the earth, basement-to-basement connections that ferried fugitive slaves from Southern plantations to freedom in the North. Of course, the "railroad" was not wood and iron, it was flesh and blood: farmers, merchants, doctors, pastors, teachers, lawyers, laborers, Southern and Northern, women and men, black and white. "Conductors," often former slaves themselves, would guide fugitives to safe houses, called "stations," where the "stationmaster" would provide them with food, clothing, shelter, and directions to the next station. The first organized efforts to transport fugitive slaves to safety began in the 1810s within the Quaker community, but it wasn't until the late 1840s that the term "underground railroad" became common and efforts involving people of all religions and colors spread from Florida to Canada. Before 1850, aiding a fugitive slave was illegal, but conflicting state laws allowed abolitionists to operate relatively openly in free states. Threatened by the movement's successes, Southern congressmen pushed for stricter controls. The Fugitive Slave Act of 1850 imposed harsh federal penalties for aiding fugitives and made free states responsible for returning escaped slaves to their owners. This law exacerbated the already high tensions between slave and free states and is often cited as a prime contributor to the Civil War.

I think it's difficult for us today to imagine the strength of feeling on both sides of the

---

* Facts and figures taken from *Bound for Canaan: The Epic Story of the Underground Railroad, America's First Civil Right Movement* by Fergus M. Bordewich (Amistad, 2006).

abolitionist debate, a political question that encompassed morality, religion, and what we now think of as basic human rights. Participants in the Underground Railroad were our earliest civil rights activists; they risked and sometimes lost their lives to help further the abolitionist cause person by person, house to house, mile by mile along the road to a better America. It is perhaps this dedication to freedom, that most American of ideals, that still manages to capture our imagination today.

The railroad's dramatic scope tends to eclipse the details of who, what, and where. The secrecy with which railroad participants were forced to act has made it difficult for historians to compile accurate statistics. Between 1800 and 1863, an estimated 100,000 enslaved Americans were helped in some way by the railroad. The number of people who participated in the railroad remains almost impossible to estimate; the historian Fergus M. Bordewich puts the figure at anywhere from 9,000 to 12,000 individuals. As familiar as the idea of the Underground Railroad is today, the names of its leaders and participants remain largely unknown. Perhaps you have heard the name Harriet Tubman, the most famous of conductors, but what about Levi Coffin, William Lloyd Garrison, David Ruggles, John Rankin, William Still, Lucretia Mott, Jermain Loguen, Josiah Henson, William Lambert, or George DeBaptiste? Their stories are waiting for a wider audience, and I urge you to seek them out.

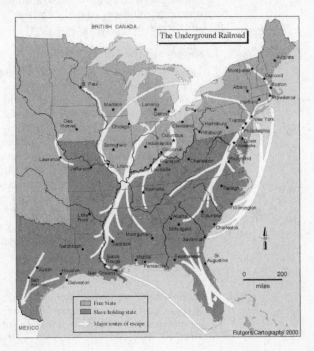

Recommended Reading List

I CONSULTED a variety of sources while researching and writing *The House Girl*. A few of these I note in my acknowledgments section, and I will expand on that list here. First off, let me say that I don't offer up these titles as an exhaustive or authoritative collection of source material for the antebellum period, issues relating to slavery reparations, or African American art—all of which have been the subject of many insightful books, articles, websites, and more. Any dedicated online search will undoubtedly yield a wealth of valuable work. What follows is a very personal, somewhat random, and definitely eccentric compilation of works of history, academic scholarship, and fiction that I recommend to anyone who remains interested in the history and themes of *The House Girl*.

Slavery and the Antebellum South

Throughout the eighteenth and nineteenth centuries, approximately 150 first-person accounts of slavery were published in the United States as books or pamphlets. Today these slave narratives are available in any number of general and specialist anthologies; many are also printed as stand-alone texts with their own introductions and commentaries. I used an anthology printed by Chicago Review Press, *I Was Born a Slave: An Anthology of Classic Slave Narratives,* volumes 1 and 2 (The Library of Black America Series), Yuval Taylor, ed., and foreword by Charles Johnson (Chicago Review Press, 1999).

Six Women's Slave Narratives (Oxford University Press, 1989). Only a fraction of published slave narratives were written by or about women. These six narratives offer perspectives from a variety of women with diverse backgrounds who discuss their lives while enslaved and the challenges they faced after escape.

Incidents in the Life of a Slave Girl by Harriet Jacobs (Dover Publications, reprint edition, 2001). Jacobs's story appears in some anthologies, but I wanted to highlight it here, too. After fleeing her abusive master, Harriet Ann Jacobs spent nearly seven years hidden in the attic crawl space of her grandmother's house. The situation evokes Anne Frank's annex hideaway, but Jacobs's story is far less well known. Jacobs offers a detailed account of the particular suffering that women endured under slavery: routine sexual abuse at the hands of white slave owners, mistreatment by white mistresses, separation from children and partners.

The Hemingses of Monticello: An American Family by Annette Gordon-Reed (W.W. Norton, 2008). Awarded the Pulitzer Prize for history in 2009, this book details the relationship between Thomas Jefferson and Sally Hemings, as well as their children and extended family. I found it fascinating, both for the complexity of the relationships described and Gordon-Reed's ability to interpret historical events and documents with fresh eyes. She also discusses Hemings family members who "passed" as white and their reasons for doing so, which provided inspiration for Jasper Battle's personal history.

Bound for Canaan: The Epic Story of the Underground Railroad, America's First Civil Rights Movement by Fergus M. Bordewich (Amistad, 2006). This was, for me, the most illuminating and readable account of the Underground Railroad. Bordewich recounts the birth and development of the railroad with novelistic flair while also examining its role in the larger context of the abolitionist movement and the run-up to the Civil War.

Celia, A Slave by Melton A. McLaurin (Avon, 1999). This book tells the story of Celia, an enslaved woman who killed her master in self-defense after years of rape and abuse. In 1850 she was tried in a Missouri court for murder, a trial that took place against a backdrop of the roiling national debate over slavery. Her story is one that should be read.

Slaves in the Family by Edward Ball (Ballantine Books, 1998). This is a fascinating account of a white Southerner's efforts to trace the slaveholders in his family and learn more about the people they had once enslaved.

A Free Woman on God's Earth: The True Story of Elizabeth Mumbet Freeman, The Slave Who Won Her Freedom by Jana Laiz and Ann-Elizabeth Barnes (Crow Flies Press, 2009). This biography for young adults tells the story of Mumbet, an enslaved woman who sued for her freedom in a Massachusetts court and won. The decision eventually led to the abolition of slavery throughout Massachusetts. Mumbet was one of my inspirations for the character of Josephine Bell. You can learn more about this amazing woman at http://mumbet.com.

Fugitive Justice: Runaways, Rescuers, and Slavery on Trial by Steven Lubet (Belknap Press of Harvard University Press, 2010). This book focuses on the operation of the Fugitive Slave Act of 1850, a law that allowed people ▶

like Benjamin Rust in *The House Girl* to operate with impunity. Focusing
on three seminal court cases, this may be of greatest interest to lawyers
and law geeks (like me), but the stories behind the cases are riveting and
show how the Underground Railroad's operations increased tensions
between North and South.

Carry Me Back: The Domestic Slave Trade in American Life by Steven
Deyle (Oxford University Press, 2006).

Women's Rights and Transatlantic Antislavery in the Era of Emancipation,
edited by Kathryn Kish Sklar and James Brewer Stewart (Yale University
Press, 2007). This book includes diverse and fascinating essays by a variety
of contributors that examine the close ties between the early women's rights
and antislavery movements in the US and abroad.

Been in the Storm So Long: The Aftermath of Slavery by Leon Litwack
(Vintage, 1980). This is a classic, revelatory book about the challenges faced
by African Americans in the years after emancipation and the ways that
the legacy of slavery influenced, and continues to influence, black-white
relations.

Art and Literature

Landscape of Slavery: The Plantation in American Art, edited by Angela D.
Mack and Stephen G. Hoffius (University of South Carolina Press, 2008).

The Planter's Prospect: Privilege and Slavery in Plantation Paintings by
John Michael Vlach (University of North Carolina Press, 2002).

Six Black Masters of American Art by Romare Bearden and Harry
Henderson (Zenith Books, 1972). The first chapters of this book focus on
two black antebellum painters, Joshua Johnston and Robert S. Duncanson.
Johnston worked as a portrait painter in Baltimore in the late eighteenth
and early nineteenth centuries, but his work remained largely unknown
until the 1930s, when an amateur art historian uncovered striking
similarities in a series of unsigned family portraits and began searching for
the artist's identity. This book recounts the fascinating search to identify
Johnston and authenticate his large and remarkable body of work, some
of which now hangs in the National Gallery of Art. Although I learned of
Johnston's work only after writing *The House Girl*, his story contains many
similarities to Lina's and Porter's efforts to authenticate Josephine's
paintings.

"The Mysterious Portraitist Joshua Johnson" by Jennifer Bryan and
Robert Torchia, *Archives of American Art Journal*, vol. 36, no. 2 (1996),
pp. 2–7, published by the Smithsonian Institution. This article (available
on JSTOR) expands on the history of Joshua Johnson/Johnston.

*The Emergence of the African-American Artist: Robert S. Duncanson,
1821–1872* by Joseph D. Ketner (University of Missouri Press, 1993).
The son of freed slaves, Duncanson worked as a landscape painter and

portraitist in Michigan and lived for many years in Canada, where his work drew widespread acclaim.

Phillis Wheatley, Complete Writings, edited and with an introduction by Vincent Carretta (Penguin Classics, 2001). The poet Phillis Wheatley was famous throughout America and Europe during her lifetime. Seized in Senegal/Gambia and brought to America in 1761 at the age of eight, she was bought by the Wheatleys, a prominent Boston family, who taught her to read and write. She began writing poetry at age thirteen and was the first African American woman to publish a book, first in the UK and later in the United States. Despite Wheatley's early fame, she died in poverty.

The Bondwoman's Narrative by Hannah Crafts, edited by Henry Louis Gates, Jr. (Warner Books, 2003). Dating from the 1850s, this novel is believed to be the first written by an African American woman and the only novel credited to an escaped slave. The introduction by Henry Louis Gates, Jr., describes his discovery of the unpublished manuscript and the ensuing efforts to authenticate the text and identify its author. The novel itself tells the autobiographical story of a young woman's escape from a North Carolina plantation via the Underground Railroad and her eventual resettlement in New Jersey. Both Gates's account and Crafts's story are fascinating.

In Search of Hannah Crafts: Critical Essays on the Bondwoman's Narrative, by Henry Louis Gates, Jr., and Hollis Robbins (Basic Civitas Books, 2004) These essays examine issues surrounding *The Bondwoman's Narrative*, including authenticity, art, literature and slavery. Of particular interest is the debate over the true author of the novel. Was Hannah Crafts really a former slave? Or a white woman?

Fiction

These novels share similarities in theme and time period with *The House Girl*. I highly recommend them.

The Known World by Edward P. Jones (Amistad, 2004).
All Souls' Rising: A Novel of Haiti by Madison Smartt Bell (Vintage, 2004).
Cane River by Lalita Tademy (Warner Books, 2005).
Beloved and *A Mercy* by Toni Morrison (Vintage, 2004 and 2009).
Wash by Margaret Wrinkle (Atlantic Monthly Press, 2013).

Slave Reparations

My Face Is Black Is True: Callie House and the Struggle for Ex-Slave Reparations by Mary Frances Berry (Vintage, 2006). This book tells the astonishing story of Callie House, a former slave, washerwoman, and mother of five who fought for government pensions for newly freed slaves in the years following the Civil War. As leader of the National ▶

Recommended Reading List *(continued)*

Ex-Slave Mutual Relief, Bounty and Pension Association, Callie House organized, lobbied, and advocated locally and nationally for the payment of pensions, based on those granted to Union soldiers, to former slaves. The association's efforts were met with hostility from politicians and former slave owners. Eventually convicted of mail fraud by an all-male, all-white jury, Callie House spent time in prison and her organization folded. The book includes information about the modern-day reparations movement.

The Debt: What America Owes to Blacks by Randall Robinson (Plume, 2001). Robinson has written a passionate, controversial book in support of slavery reparations. I wasn't able to find a book that offered a counterargument to Robinson, but many articles and online materials take a contrary position. Most famous perhaps is Henry Louis Gates's op-ed "Ending the Slavery Blame-Game" published in the *New York Times* in 2010 (http://philosophy.wisc.edu/hausman/341/Gates-Reparations.htm).

Lawyer Deadria Farmer-Paellmann and the Restitution Study Group (RSG) brought a number of slavery reparations lawsuits in the early 2000s that used an inventive approach: They claimed that corporations with historic involvement in the slave trade were guilty of fraud if such involvement was not disclosed to consumers. The success of these litigations has led to slavery era disclosure laws in six states, with more pending. The RSG website include links to primary documents submitted in the various litigations: www.rsgincorp.com.

The National Coalition of Blacks for Reparations in America (NCOBRA) was founded in 1987. Its website (ncobra.org) contains links to other reparations-related information.

Internet Resources

Born in Slavery: Slave Narratives from the Federal Writers' Project, 1936–1938, http://memory.loc.gov/ammem/snhtml/snhome.html. More than 2,000 slave testimonies are compiled here, some as short as a page, others much longer. The site offers PDFs of the original pages typed up by the interviewer, which (for me at least) give them an immediacy and intimacy that I find generally lacking with online source material. The interviewers tended to spell words phonetically so as to preserve the speakers' specific dialects, which at times makes the transcripts difficult to understand. The content, however, is worth any extra effort. The names compiled by Lina for her "nature of the harm" chart are all taken from these narratives.

The Valley of the Shadow: Two Communities in the American Civil War, http://valley.lib.virginia.edu. The University of Virginia maintains this wonderful website containing primary documents—letters, journal entries, military records, newspaper clippings, census records, and more—dating from 1859 to 1870 of two counties, one free, one slave, located on either side of the Ohio River. The document transcripts include an original version and one with modern spelling and word usage. The personal letters I found here helped me greatly in capturing the voice of Dorothea Rounds.

The Trans-Atlantic Slave Trade Database, http://slavevoyages.org/tast/index.faces. An incredible resource that contains information on more than 35,000 slave voyages between the sixteenth and nineteenth centuries. ⌒

Meet Tara Conklin

Mary Grace Long Photography

TARA CONKLIN has worked as a litigator in the New York and London offices of a corporate law firm but now devotes her time to writing fiction. She received a BA in history from Yale University, a JD from New York University School of Law, and a master of arts in law and diplomacy from the Fletcher School at Tufts University. Born in St. Croix, she grew up in Massachusetts and now lives with her family in Seattle, Washington. *The House Girl* is her first novel. ∽

Don't miss the next book by your favorite author. Sign up now for AuthorTracker by visiting www.AuthorTracker.com.

7 Hawth Powell's Used $5.50
House Girl

9780062316080
Conklin, Tara   106   9/20/2018
LIT-C